Jericho's Heart

Jericho Series Book 2

James Bonk

Storming Strongholds LLC

Dedication

This book is dedicated to those who see things differently, and still don't give up.

"Ninety-nine percent of who you are is invisible and untouchable"

–

Buckminster Fuller

Books By James Bonk

Jericho Series

1. The Tower's Shadow

2. Jericho's Heart

3. Jericho's Legacy

Light of the Ark Series

1. Light of the Ark

2. Shadows of the Ark

3. Light of the World

- Isaiah and the Sea of Darkness (standalone prequel)

More Fiction

- Christian's Look Back at Life

Stay up to date on new releases and email exclusive content:

https://hello.jamesbonk.com/signup/

Contents

1. Chapter 1 1
2. Chapter 2 8
3. Chapter 3 15
4. Chapter 4 20
5. Chapter 5 23
6. Chapter 6 28
7. Chapter 7 34
8. Chapter 8 37
9. Chapter 9 41
10. Chapter 10 47
11. Chapter 11 53
12. Chapter 12 58
13. Chapter 13 61
14. Chapter 14 65
15. Chapter 15 75
16. Chapter 16 82

17. Chapter 17 86
18. Chapter 18 94
19. Chapter 19 97
20. Chapter 20 108
21. Chapter 21 113
22. Chapter 22 120
23. Chapter 23 130
24. Chapter 24 133
25. Chapter 25 142
26. Chapter 26 150
27. Chapter 27 152
28. Chapter 28 158
29. Chapter 29 164
30. Chapter 30 169
31. Chapter 31 185
32. Chapter 32 191
33. Chapter 33 196
34. Chapter 34 204
35. Chapter 35 209
36. Chapter 36 214
37. Chapter 37 221
38. Chapter 38 229
39. Chapter 39 247

40. Chapter 40 256
41. Chapter 41 264
42. Chapter 42 281
43. Chapter 43 284
44. Chapter 44 289
45. Chapter 45 292
46. Chapter 46 296
47. Chapter 47 300
Fullpage image 309
Chapter 1 310
Chapter 2 319
Thank You! 332
The Author 333

Chapter 1

"Tell me, Darren, what made you smile this week?" his mother asked as they rounded the corner of the supermarket aisle.

The five-year-old Darren hesitated, distracted by the colorful images and characters on the boxes all around him. The supermarket always seemed like such a joyful place to the young boy. There were boring aisles, of course, but the cereal and snack aisles were like a toy store. He couldn't wait to see all his favorites, smiling at him from the front cover.

"Answer your mother, boy," his father said sternly as he tapped the boy's shoulder. The nudge pulled Darren out of his imagination, where Cap'n Crunch sailed the seas, always with a full bowl of deliciousness and a jolly smile.

"What, Ma?" young Darren asked.

"What made you smile this week, sweetheart?" she asked.

"Oh," he said, then paused as he thought. "Lunch was great!" he finally erupted. "Matt had Oreos and he was eating ONLY the inside!"

"No way," his mother said.

"He started stacking the cookie parts," he said, motioning with his hands as if he were building a tower. "But then Jimmy kept knocking the tower down!" He laughed as he spoke.

"Jimmy is sneaky, huh," she said.

"And then we'd all steal a piece before Matt could rebuild," the boy said in a whisper.

"Oh, you're all being sneaky, aren't you?" his mother said with a smile as she poked Darren's ribs, pulling out a giggle. "Was Matt okay with all that?" she asked.

"Yeah, he doesn't like the cookie part," Darren said, an ear-to-ear grin covering his face.

"I always knew that kid was off," Darren's father said matter-of-factly.

"Oh, hush." His mother batted at the man's arms.

"Why does he get Oreos in his lunch if he doesn't like the cookie?" the father inquired.

"Because he LOVES the middle part!" Darren burst out.

"That's nice, sweetheart," his mother said.

"Sounds like a waste to me," his father muttered under his breath. An elbow shot out from the mother and the man winced as it caught his side.

"DunkAroos! Mom, can we, please, please?" Darren jumped forward and grabbed a box off the shelf.

"Speaking of waste," the father said.

The young boy heard and his body sank over like a wilting flower.

"Always no," the boy whimpered as he put the box back on the shelf.

"Because it's garbage food," the father snapped.

The boy's mother stared daggers at him.

"Sweetheart, we're making No Bake Cookies. That's our treat this week," the boy's mother interjected with a sympathetic touch to the side of young Darren's head.

"More sug—" the father tried to say, but she sent another elbow at him, this one more forceful instead of playful.

"I think we should grab some berries. Hun, can you go grab some? Whatever looks in season and only organic," she said, and Darren perked up a bit.

"You're making cookies but have to buy organic?" the father replied.

"Only organic, hun."

"No, the regular kind is fine," he protested.

"Would you spray weed killer on your salad before eating it?" she replied.

"I don't eat salad."

"Hun, organic only," she said, her expression inching closer and closer to more stern.

He took the hint and stepped back but couldn't stop the objection welling up inside of him.

"I pay for private school so he can learn to steal Oreos, his feelings get a boo-boo because he can't have garbage food, and now you want me to pay twice as much for the same fruit? I mean, what are we doing here?" the father ranted. "Have you seen prices lately? My pay ain't keeping up with it!"

Darren's eyes went to the floor, avoiding his father's gaze as the man's stern look engulfed the boy like a spotlight in a dark room. Eventually, the look shifted to the boy's mother, who retorted with the raised eyebrows that only a disappointed wife can give to her husband. A thousand words, each sharper than daggers, impressed back on the man from her stare.

With an exhale of disgust, he slowly did an about-face and then left the aisle, but Darren still eyed the floor.

"No DunkAroos, sweetheart," she said sympathetically. "But I'd love your help making the No Bakes later."

"Okay," Darren said, his face rising to uncover a frown.

"I'd consider a peanut butter version too. What do you think?" the mother asked.

"Yes!" The boy's face lit up.

They moved down the aisle and soon turned down the next. As they walked around a football- and BBQ-themed endcap, the mother caught a concerned expression on the boy.

"Darren, what's wrong?"

"School wasn't all good this week," he sheepishly admitted.

"Tell me more, sweetheart."

"Stephen..." he said softly as if speaking it would give the memory life.

"Recess again?" she asked.

The boy nodded.

"The teacher?"

"She loves him, and never believes us."

"I'm sorry to hear that, sweetheart. That must be tough."

Young Darren exhaled, looking up and down the otherwise empty aisle. "Yeah..." he agreed, and his shoulders dropped and rose again as he finally allowed himself to breathe.

"What do you think you should do about it?" she asked.

"Can you call the teacher?" he pleaded.

"I could, but help me learn more. What's an action you could take?"

"Punch him in the face," Darren said through gritted teeth.

"Ehhh..."

"But, Mom, he hits us and makes fun of us. It's awful!"

"I'm sorry you have to deal with him, sweetheart. Sometimes difficult people and situations come into our life."

"Why would God allow people like Stephen?" he asked.

The mother pulled back in surprise.

"Sweetheart, remember, God made him too. And it's hard to hear, but God loves even the bad guys. I'm betting Stephen is scared or anxious or something, and he doesn't know how to act properly. Whatever it is, God loves him too."

"Yeah..." the boy dismissed.

"I think ignoring him will help. It's not good to be around bad people."

"But he's in my class, and he finds me every time."

"I love you, sweetheart. That's hard. Let's think about this more and talk later, okay?" She touched the side of his head.

"Okay, Mom."

They walked another aisle and passed by other shoppers. One woman was trying her best to ignore her young toddler screaming for their sippy cup. The child's binky fell and bounced in front of Darren and his mother. He instinctively picked it up and held it out for the exhausted mother. Her dazed look took a second to recognize the favor, but she snapped back from her sleep deprivation and thanked Darren.

"That was nice of you," Darren's mother said to him as they moved down the next aisle. She grabbed an item here and there, slowly filling their cart.

Once again, she noticed the concerned look on her son's face.

"You still thinking about Stephen?" she asked.

"Kind of," he said.

She gave an understanding nod and then turned to check their shopping list.

"Mom?" He interrupted her train of thought. "Stephen reminds me of Dad. Why are you nice and Dad is mean?"

Her hand shot up and covered her mouth.

"Sweetheart, your dad loves you," she said.

Darren looked down and kicked at the floor.

"Can I not be around him? You said not to be around mean people," he said.

"Why do you think he's mean?"

"He's always telling me what to do, and I never do it right, so then he gets mad and tells me more things to do that I can't do!"

"I don't agree with everything your father says and does, but remember, he loves you."

"I don't see it," he said under his breath.

"Don't talk like that," she snapped, but caught herself and squatted to meet her son at his level. "He has his own way of showing it."

"Can you just tell him to not yell at me or spank me?"

Her eyes watered as she looked at her son.

"Darren." She gently touched his chin and pulled up his face to make eye contact. "Your father and I are different. I'm more sensitive than him, and at your age, it's easier for me to cuddle you like crazy." She broke a smile that infected the boy, but soon the sadness returned. "But your father goes out and works hard to provide for us. I'm sorry he's rough around the edges. We've been through a lot together, and before God gave us you, your father's rough edges got us through some VERY rough times."

"I found his pictures," the boy admitted.

Her eyes widened. "From the desert?"

"Why were there all those bodies? They were cut apart."

She hugged the boy. "Sweetheart, your dad was in war. It was called Desert Storm and there were very bad people that your dad and his friends were trying to protect others from."

"He killed all those people. He's going to hell."

"Sweetheart, I want you to remember two things. First, that your father loves you, no matter what. I'm sorry he can act mean, but I'll talk with him about his words. And second," she pulled back his face as the boy tried to look away, "if there are bad guys, and there are, then good guys must kill the bad guys; otherwise, there aren't really any good guys."

Darren gulped as he looked into his mother's watery eyes. His father came around the corner, holding a stack of plastic containers. They were all organic berries.

Chapter 2

The four stood in the living room of the apartment, the excitement and confusion of each waking from the life-like dream of Empyrean.

"She killed us," Kirk said.

"She killed our future selves," Chris added.

"That's not me, that's some Enak guy, who might I add is more angry day-to-day than I've ever been in my life. That's just not me," Kirk responded.

The brothers looked at each other, waves of confusion still flowing over them. Meanwhile, Darren finally let his eye catch Kelly's. She'd been watching him, sensing something the brothers didn't know.

"You've been back and forth before, haven't you?" Kelly asked as Darren met her eyes.

He nodded yes.

"What?" Chris exclaimed. "And you?" he looked at Kelly.

"No, well, in a dream, but it's hard to explain. Not like this, not putting on the glasses and being there."

"Glasses?" Kirk shouted, then he darted into Darren's room, quickly finding and grabbing the glasses before Darren could stop him. "So we have nightmares, but these things are your virtual reality?" he said.

"More than that," Darren exhaled. "Guys, you know I went to an eye doctor recently, right? Well, he put the photo-play thing over my–

"It's a phoropter," Kelly interrupted.

"Yeah, that. Anyway, he put it on and, boom, I was there. It was like I was that person Kaden, but every time I died there, I woke up here."

"And how'd you get back?" Chris asked.

"I'd check on Kelly, who was always still peaceful, and I'd put my glasses back on and, boom, again, right back to being Kaden," Darren said.

Kirk held up the purple glasses toward Kelly with a questioning expression.

"Yup, but this is the first time I died, or well, Kira died," she said.

"Well, I don't love having nightmares of those charcoal demons and some Beth-whatever lady putting me down like a suffering animal. Screw that place," Kirk said, tossing the glasses on the table. Darren and Kelly lurched as if pieces of priceless art work were being carelessly handled.

"What happens if you put back on the glasses?" Chris asked.

"I think we go back," Kelly said, watching Darren's face grow stern.

"No way!" Kirk shouted. "Hallucinations!" he cried as he grabbed the black-framed glasses and moved them toward his face.

"No!" Darren and Kelly shouted, but they were too late, Kirk already had them on. He stood frozen like a statue, his eyes bulging and staring at Darren.

"His body didn't go limp like yours did," Darren said as he and Kelly slowly crept toward the statue-like Kirk.

"Guys... What's going on?" Chris asked.

"He might be back in Empy—"

"Gotcha!" Kirk jumped and threw out his hands like a magician showing off the grand reveal.

"Ugh," Darren exclaimed. "I forgot our glasses only worked on each of us."

"Yours didn't work on me," Kelly reiterated.

"So what if you each put yours back on?" Chris asked, nodding to his brother. Kirk reluctantly gave them each their pair.

Darren looked down at them, thoughts of the Elites and Beth-ell waiting for him. "You can end this," Beth-ell's words echoed in his mind. Why would she say that before killing him?

"Do you go back to when you died?" Kelly asked, pulling Darren from his thoughts.

"I... Well, not precisely. Remember when you dragged me from the Outer Ring back to our apartment?"

"I sure do, ya heavy bastard," Kirk blurted out before catching himself. "I mean, Enak does... Not me."

"We could wake up right in front of the Elites," Darren said.

Kelly shook her head.

"I don't like those things," Chris added.

"I think only Thornhill does," Darren remarked.

The group looked at him curiously.

"Who's Thornhill?" Kelly finally asked.

"Oh, he's Pinnacle," Darren said.

"Ummmm," Kelly said as the three looked at each other, then back at Darren.

"The most powerful and evil person, if he's even a person, in all of Empyrean is here too?" Chris asked.

Darren thought a moment, trying to come up with the right words and wishing he could share the visions Jericho shared with him. Eventually, his head bobbed as he spoke.

"He's a businessman. I met him at the eye doctor's. He was friends and partners with Dr. Abrams," Darren said.

"And who's Dr. Abrams? The same guy who put the photo-bomb on you and gave you these glasses?" Chris asked.

Darren and Kelly both shook their heads yes.

"I get the sense he's not just an eye doctor," Chris said.

"Nope, he's... He's Jericho," Darren said.

"Oh great, we have the worst dictator of all time award winner in Pinnacle and the man, the myth, the legend himself crossing worlds with us. This all sounds lovely. Just a couple of jolly businessmen running an eye care shop here in Georgia. Why not?" Kirk said.

"You know those dreams were weird, and both of us having it, and matching theirs? Just try to listen and learn—" Chris said before Kirk snapped, cutting him off.

"No, you listen and learn. Those dreams were freakin' wack–a-doo, and those demon things, scary. Yeah, I'll admit it, they were freakin' scary. I was scared and I don't want to go back there. So throw the dang glasses out and give the eye doctor hut a 1-star review. Done with all this," Kirk ranted.

"I'm sorry, bro. Once you see, you can't unsee," Chris said.

"What does that mean? Of course you can 'unsee' anything. I saw Grandpa getting off the toilet when we were kids. I had to unsee that," Kirk said.

"I don't think you can unsee that," Chris said.

"Oh, shut up, you didn't see it," Kirk fired back.

"Guys, GUYS!" Kelly screamed. "You two don't have glasses, and regardless of what you think..." She eyed Kirk. "Regardless, we've all been to Empyrean. In our dreams or through these glasses, we've been there. Now we decide if we go back," Kelly said.

The brothers remained quiet, looking back and forth between themselves and Kelly. She met their eyes and reassured them with a confident look, then she turned to Darren.

"Hun, you've been a bit too quiet. What's on your mind?" she asked.

He took in a deep breath, his eyes on the floor, then he raised his eyes to meet theirs as he let the breath out.

"She said, 'You can end this' before we died. 'You can end this. When you die, go end this before it begins.' Why would she say that?" Darren said.

"Beth-ell is Pinnacle's next in command," Kelly said.

"You sure you heard it right?" Chris asked.

Darren nodded.

"I heard it too," Kirk said.

"Jericho showed me things when I was there. He showed me the history between him and Thornhill. I think Beth-ell wants me to kill him," Darren said.

"Kill Jericho? That's nuts," Kelly said.

"Hey, that's a pretty brutal world. One man for many?" Kirk said.

"No, I mean kill Thornhill. I think Beth-ell wants to end it all before it begins," he said.

"You can't do that," Kirk said.

"What happened to 'one man for many?'" Chris asked.

"Why we killing anybody here?" Kirk said. "You want life in prison because you knocked off an eye doctor? I'm sure the judge will understand that he was a really bad guy in a future dream world," Kirk said.

"We can't just kill people," Kelly said, touching Darren's arm.

"I know, but what if we could stop the whole thing?" Darren asked.

"What if it is inevitable?" Kelly asked back.

"What would Jericho do?" Chris said and brought the room to silence.

Darren shrugged. “I don’t know. He’s the only person more powerful than Pinnacle. I’d ask why we’d let all this happen in the first place. He could have stopped him but didn’t.”

“And didn’t Pinnacle just rip his heart out? I’d say Jericho is a distant second to that guy in the power race,” Kirk said.

“Look, I’m not saying I’m going to; I’m just saying...” Darren paused.

“What are you saying?” Kirk asked.

“I need time to sort this out. My head is spinning,” Darren said, turning and walking back to his room. Kelly took a seat on the couch while Chris moved back to his room.

“Okay, that solves a lot,” Kirk said, throwing his hands up and slamming them down against his jeans.

“Just chill, bro. Take a power nap,” Chris hollered from his room.

Kirk mouthed a mocking response then went back to his room. He looked at his closet door, wanting to see if the object he woke up with was still there or if he was hallucinating like his dreams. Moving to the door, he slowly opened it. There on the top shelf, right where he hastily tossed it when he woke up and found it clutched in his hands, was the worn black leather Moleskine journal. Kirk took it out and held it to his chest.

“Darren, you okay?” he heard Kelly call out. Kirk jumped and hid the journal back on the top shelf, now pushing it behind other items.

Meanwhile, Kelly walked into Darren’s room and closed the door. She stood in front of the walk-in closet, rapping her knuckle on the door. “You okay, hun? Let’s take a nap and talk more after some rest.”

“I think I need some fresh air,” Darren said from behind the closed door, thinking he couldn’t let her know his thoughts or next actions. It’d be by far better if she didn’t know.

He took out the hand gun stored in the small gun safe in the back of his closet where a watch his grandfather gave him and the American flag his dad used to hang outside their house rested. Sliding the gun in the back of his belt, he opened the door and was met with Kelly's eyes. The auburn haze of her hair, perfect curves of her lips, and her hazel eyes urged him to stay. He longed to kiss her and lie down, getting much needed rest, but the cold of the gun's handle pressed against his lower back.

"Get some rest. I'll be back soon," he told her.

"I'll come with you. Want to walk around the lake?" she asked.

"No, I'll be bad company. Let me just... go for a drive. I need to shake off some cobwebs in the fresh air," he said.

"Okay, I'll wait in here..." she said reluctantly, feeling passed off.

He didn't kiss her good-bye as he left the room, determined to find and kill Dr. Thomas Thornhill.

Chapter 3

He left without seeing Chris or Kirk. As he started his truck, Kelly's face sat in his mind as if seared into his eyes from staring at the sun, but again, the cold steel of the gun reminded him of his purpose.

"Okay, you showed me hell and now I'm supposed to kill the devil," he said aloud as he looked into his own eyes in the rearview mirror. He held the shifter but paused, realizing the practical part of his rash plan had a gigantic hole. "But where...?"

The side door of his truck opened, jolting him from his thoughts. Before he could object, Kelly jumped into the seat.

"What are you—" he tried to say.

"He runs Pinnacle VC; it's in the city," she said, grabbing his phone and punching in the code to unlock it.

"Hey, I have to do this a—"

"Alone? No, you don't. Jericho talked to me too, ya know? You aren't the only one seeing the future through magic eye glasses, so don't assume you're the only one who can do something about it," she said.

"Kelly, you don't need to be implicated in what I have to do," he said, reaching out and grabbing her forearm as she punched in the address to his maps app.

"I know you, Darren. You had the same look on your face just now as you did when you agreed to speak at your grandfather's funeral. I know that look; it's a look of dread, but it's a look of duty," she said, putting her hand on his.

"I have something with me, from my safe." He stared at her, using every ounce of will to not say the quiet part out loud.

"Yeah, I checked your safe. You left it open... Look, I don't agree with you, but we're in this together," she said, and she pulled a small box of bullets out of her pocket. "I grabbed something from the safe as well. Just in case we need more than one clip."

"I love you," he said.

She paused as they looked into each other's eyes, but she pulled away without returning the phrase.

"An accomplice to murder is lovely. Regular ol' Bonnie and Clyde." She turned and looked out the window. "What are you doing, Kelly?" she said, shaking her head.

"I don't like it either, but why else would he show us that future and then allow us to come back, if not to do something about it now?" Darren said. "The only problem is, I have no idea where to find Thornhill. I've only seen him at Abrams' office, but that's closed."

"Pinnacle VC," she said as she pressed a button on his phone. The computerized female voice came on, telling him the first step of the drive. "I did a quick search after I saw you took your gun." She held up her phone and showed a stylish web page with the title "Pinnacle VC." Various messages of human health advancement and business value were expertly crafted and pleasing to the eye.

"Think he'll be there?" he asked.

"I'll search for more on the way, but it's our best shot," she said. "The first news article said there's a board meeting today."

Forty-five minutes later, they were parked on the side of a one-way downtown road, in view of the beautiful, glass-encased lobby of the towering office building. “Pinnacle VC” in gigantic letters glowed from the side of the building high above them, in between numerous other office buildings.

A light rain began falling, pattering the roof of his truck and turning their view of the glowing sign into a smeared light.

“This might be a waste of time,” Darren said as they waited. “You want coffee or food?”

“I’m good. Come on, let's imagine we’re on a stakeout,” Kelly added.

“We are on a stakeout, Nancy Drew,” Darren said, a smile cracking over his lips as their eyes met. “And they always have coffee and donuts in those old-school stakeouts.”

“Darren.” Her smile turned to a frown. “You really want to carry through with this?”

“No. I really *don’t* want to,” he said.

“But changing the future by killing someone in our present? I mean, I feel like this is a case where people see us on the front of a newspaper and we’re clearly murderers. That’s not us,” she said.

“If we believe in the world we saw, then I think it’s not about what I or anybody else wants. More than ninety-nine percent of people die in the coming wars, and this man accelerates all of it. He’s at the helm of the Hope Drug; it’s inside all of us by then. The New Breed, The Tower, the Elites...” He shook his head and leaned forward, squinting at a man jogging past Pinnacle VC’s entrance but resolving it wasn’t Thornhill. “We go from a populated globe to one city left. I don’t want death as much as you, but if we could really stop that, we have to.”

“I don’t think that’s true,” she said.

“You don’t think we should try to stop a global catas—”

"No, not that. I mean, only one city left. I don't think it's true there's only one city left," she said.

"What do you mean?"

"I told you I found a book in the tunnels. It's a journal, and I think Jericho put it there. It talks about the Lighthouse, and what really happened."

"The Tower teaches Agents that Jericho died when Elites raided the Lighthouse. That he became a nuisance to Empyrean, giving false hopes and spreading lies," Darren said.

"We've seen Jericho, so clearly, that's not all true," she said. "The book says that Jericho built Empyrean, then left to build more and Pinnacle took it over. It turned to hell once Jericho left."

"He was out there building and Pinnacle never killed him at the lighthouse battle?"

"I'm not even sure it was a fight. From what I read, Jericho could flick his wrist and even Elites would fall at his feet."

"But that can't be right; we just saw him die. Pinnacle wins in the future. Jericho is dead and the Lighthouse Remnant is wiped out."

"Not totally wiped out. There are twelve of us, including you," she said. "If we ever get to go back, you need to find and read that book. I stashed it away before they brought me to The Tower," she said.

"Where'd you hide it?"

"Right where I found it." She shrugged.

They sat in silence while the rain played on the roof. Beads of water holding on to the windshield and then falling, grabbing more beads and growing as it rolled off the glass.

"I am getting cold. What were you saying about coffee?" she said, but Darren didn't respond. He was leaning forward and looking out the windshield, staring at a figure that ran out of the glass-enclosed lobby and toward the connected parking garage.

"I don't believe it," Darren whispered. "That's him."

Before Kelly could get a look at the figure, Darren was out of the truck and darting through traffic. He disappeared into the parking garage.

Chapter 4

Entry #1

The bloodwork tells a story my mind struggles to accept, yet my heart has known from the beginning. When I first saw the results, I dismissed them as contamination or equipment error. But after the seventh replication, I can no longer deny what's happening within my cells.

The cancer should have killed me years ago. Instead, I'm watching my body heal itself at a cellular level that defies modern medicine. It's not just remission – it's regeneration. Something in my blood carries a signature unlike anything we've documented before. The mitochondrial activity alone should be impossible, yet here I am, documenting the impossible. Arthur C. Clarke wrote that 'Any sufficiently advanced technology is indistinguishable from magic,' and now I'm seeing that play out before my eyes and within my body.

Thomas is ecstatic, of course. He sees dollar signs where I see divinity. He talks about patents and trials while I sit in my office, watching the sunrise and wondering why me? Why now? The world stands at a precipice – cancer rates increasing, fertility dropping, climate talk paired with pending nuclear wars, and all stacked on a convoluted healthcare system. Perhaps that's why this gift has been given. Not to create another overpriced drug, but to show another way.

Sarah says I'm different. Not just healthier, but changed in ways she can't explain. The children sense it too. Last night, Emma asked why my eyes "sparkle like stars" now. I caught a glimpse of what she meant in the mirror – there is a light there I can't explain. They're becoming a brilliant gray, almost white light. The same light I've seen in my dreams.

The dreams... They come every night now. Visions of a tower rising into darkness, and a lighthouse standing against the storm. I see faces I don't yet know, but know I love them as I would my own family. I see choices that will echo through centuries. Most of all, I see my role in what's coming, and it terrifies me.

I've spent my life putting my faith in science, in what can be measured and proven. Now I find myself stepping into mystery. The blood samples show cellular regeneration, yes, but they also show something our instruments can't quantify – a fundamental restructuring of reality at the quantum level. My cells don't just heal, they resonate with a frequency that I can't explain or find other examples of in our universe.

Is this what the prophets felt? This terrible and wonderful knowing? This weight of purpose?

My comprehension of the world and time is changing. I record these notes knowing they will be found someday, when they're needed most. I see the faces of every reader in the shadows behind my eyelids. And to you, reader – know that what happened to me was no accident. It was not a random mutation or lucky coincidence. It was a gift, given not for my sake, but for what's coming.

The healing in my blood is real. The power growing in me is real. But they are only signs pointing to a greater truth – an incredible darkness is coming, but light still shines in darkness, and the darkness will not overcome it.

Thomas wants to mass produce this, to "optimize" it, to control it. He cannot see that this gift was never meant to be controlled. It was meant to be given freely, like grace itself.

I am still a doctor. I will still heal those I can. But now I understand that physical healing was only ever a shadow of true wholeness. Science has shown me the what, but faith is showing me the why. Helping people see has taken on an entirely new meaning.

I close this first entry with words I never thought I'd write in a medical journal: There are mysteries greater than medicine, and some truths can only be measured by faith.

The light is coming. God help us all be ready for what it reveals.

Chapter 5

Darren ran into the parking garage after the tall figure. The towering, muscular frame of the man was unmistakable, even with the rainy conditions. Darren slowed as he got into the garage and out of the rain. Water dripped from his shaggy brown hair.

The man he was chasing was approaching a luxury sedan, a Mercedes Benz S-Class that sparkled in the overhead lights of the garage. He saw Darren and stopped, a smile creeping onto his face.

"I remember you," Dr. Thomas Thornhill said.

"I'd expect someone like you would have a driver," Darren said.

"Sometimes you need to take matters into your own hands." He shrugged. His chiseled jawline and tall frame cast a long shadow as he stepped away from his vehicle and toward Darren. "You look different, not the same *boy* waiting for his turn."

"I've seen things, horrible things. And you make them happen."

"Yeah? You're not one of those 'profit is evil' kind of people, are you?"

"No," Darren said, his hand twitching as his mind thought of the handgun tucked in his waistband. "I'm an evil is evil kind of person."

"You're finally taking control of your life. That's good to hear, but sounds like you're misguided, my boy."

"I'm not a boy."

Thornhill raised his eyes in mock surprise. His three-piece suit was a tailored fit. It slimmed as it went down his torso, giving his already broad shoulders a wider appearance.

"I cared only for myself and did foolish things. I spoke as a child, understood as a child, and thought as a child. But now I'm a man who puts away childish things and has a duty for the lives of others that you will destroy."

"I *will* destroy?" Thornhill said, stepping closer.

"Your Hope Drug cannot go to the public. It will create a chain reaction that will seed horrible cellular conditions in the population."

Thornhill stopped his steps, his perfectly manicured short blonde hair glistening with the bits of water from the rain. His jaw clenched and the muscles on the side of his mouth flared. But then, he smiled and a laugh came out. The laughter grew and he bent over, his hands on his knees as he slapped his legs.

"Funny, boy," he said through his laughter.

Darren pulled the handgun from his lower back and pointed it at Thornhill.

"It's not funny. I've seen it," he said, and to his surprise, the gun didn't tremble. He might be able to do this.

"Whoa whoa," Thornhill said, putting his hands up. Yet his smile remained as a laugh escaped.

"I'm sorry for this, but you cannot take the path ahead of you," Darren said.

"You mean the path of pending war, or the path of infertility, or the path of cancer? Let's not even talk about the known carcinogens that the population has been warned about, yet still consumes, or the faulty monetary system and the printing of money." Thornhill's face grew serious. "No. You focus on my work. While it seems to me that my companies are working on solutions for these things while you're here with a gun threatening me, *BOY*. Abrams sent you, eh? He had such potential." Thornhill shook his head. "His work twists the mind, makes people feel too righteous for their own good, but at least they are peaceful–outside of you. Most are calm enough to just shut up and stay out of the real fights. Fights that I wage on your precious doctor's behalf. The *real* work to be done."

"You're twisting the situ—"

"Am I?" he interrupted. "I am dealing with geopolitical conditions that impact nations. I'm helping to give hope to the hopeless. Why do you think it's called the Hope Drug? You know, I liked you. For some reason, Abrams took a liking to you and that got me curious. But now I see you're a *boy* who can't see the facts in front of you. This is beyond you, so sit down and watch daddy work, boy!" he shouted as the veins in his forehead bulged and his dark eyes flickered with a perfect salt and pepper gray coloring.

"I can't let you leave here and create the Hope Drug," Darren said, the tip of the gun wavering as his hand subtly began trembling as he thought of pulling the trigger.

"It's already created." Thornhill leaned back and shrugged. "I'm not sure what you think you'll solve, except get yourself thrown in jail, or... Worse," he said and he stared at Darren like a cruel child who used the sun's rays and a magnifying glass on an ant. He was enraged, yet he enjoyed it.

"No," Darren said, shaking his head.

"Did you come here alone?" Dr. Thornhill asked.

Darren didn't respond, but his eyes darted to the side, giving his answer away.

"Oh." Thornhill looked out the entryway of the garage, squinting at Darren's truck. "I think I see a woman in there. Oh, you dog you, you are taking more control. Good for you."

"Stop it," Darren said, and Thornhill took a step forward.

"Pity, I would have liked to meet her," Thornhill said. "Too bad about that car accident. Hit and runs are terrible, ya know?"

"What?"

Thornhill threw his hand toward the truck. As if an invisible train hit the vehicle, the passenger side doors crumpled and the truck was thrown on its side. Time seemed to slow as Darren made out Kelly's silhouette in the truck. She appeared to be watching them, but as the truck flew back, she disappeared into a disaster of bent metal and broken glass. It smashed against the brick wall of the building behind the vehicle.

"No!" Darren cried out.

"Terrible thing. I'm sorry, boy," Thornhill said dispassionately.

Darren turned back to him, stepping forward and bringing the gun back up, pointed at Thornhill's chest.

"Back up!"

"You can't do it, boy. Just put it down."

The gun wavered, his hand trembling, as Darren thought of Kelly. Memories of Empyrean filled his mind, all the death of the Elites and the consumption events. Pinnacle had allowed it all to happen.

"Just put it down," Thornhill said softly as the gun inched lower, now aimed at the doctor's feet. "You can't stop this."

The visions of the faces of those consumed hung in Darren's mind, and he snapped back to the present moment.

"You cannot set the drug loose," he said and raised the gun. Thornhill raised his hand as Darren pulled the trigger. POP! POP! POP! POP! The muzzle flashed with each bullet.

Darren blinked and dropped his hand. He took in a deep breath as he watched Thornhill, expecting to see blood fill the three-piece suit before the man fell.

But he didn't fall.

The bullets were stopped in midair, inches from his raised hand.

"You can't stop it, because the drug is already in use," he said, then he flicked his wrist and the bullets shot back at Darren.

He flew backwards as the four slugs struck his chest, landing at the edge of the garage halfway in the rain and the parking garage. The stream of rain water tinged with red as the blood flowed from Darren's chest.

Thornhill straightened his vest and jacket as if shaking off dust, then went back to his car and drove away.

Darren gasped for air, blood filling his lungs and throat as his life faded away. The light faded. His eyes slowly closed.

Chapter 6

Kaden's eyes shot open. The cold, damp air pulled a shiver from his body as he gasped for breath. His hand shot to his chest, feeling for bullet holes that weren't there. He patted frantically, his fingers pressing into his torso, but found only intact skin beneath his tattered athletic clothes. No blood, no wounds. Yet the taste of blood lingered on his tongue and phantom pain radiated through his chest.

Darkness pressed in around him. He blinked rapidly, trying to force his eyes to adjust to the blackness. Gradually, faint outlines emerged – rough stone walls, a low ceiling, the shadowy shapes of support beams. The musty smell of earth filled his nostrils. He was underground, in the tunnels beneath Empyrean.

As his breath steadied, memories crashed over him like a tidal wave. The parking garage. Thornhill's cruel smile. The way he'd lifted his hand so casually, as if swatting away a fly, and invisibly sent the bullets firing back through the air. Kaden's stomach churned. Dr. Thomas Thornhill didn't need centuries to become Pinnacle–He already was.

A wave of nausea hit as he remembered Kelly in his truck. The sickening crunch of metal as the vehicle was tossed aside like a child's toy. He squeezed his eyes shut, trying to block out the image, but it was seared into his mind.

"Kelly..." he whispered into the darkness.

His eyes snapped open as realization struck. If Kelly had died, wouldn't Kira be awake here too? Unless... unless she died in both timelines at once. The thought sent ice through his veins. He tried to push himself up, to look around the small chamber, but his body felt like lead. Every muscle screamed in protest.

Alone in the darkness, Kaden let out a shuddering breath. The weight of failure pressed down on him like the tons of earth above. He'd tried to change things, to stop it all before it began. Instead, he'd only confirmed what he feared most – the monster who would become Pinnacle was already more powerful than any of them had imagined.

The silence of the tunnel pressed in around him, broken only by the occasional drip of water and his own ragged breathing. He prayed silently for others, to not be alone in the darkness. The Remnant. His friends. Anyone. But as his breath settled in this moment, the solitude felt fitting. He'd been rash but felt justified, however he failed them all – whether it was four hundred years ago in the time of Darren or this future world of Empyrean. He'd failed.

He stared up into the blackness, remembering Jericho's final moments. The way he'd stepped forward, almost eagerly, into Pinnacle's strike. He leaned in, embracing the fatal blow. What had he seen that the rest of them couldn't? What was the point of showing them the truth if they were powerless to change it? Kaden felt a fury that bubbled at Jericho's death, a fire only quenched by the fatigue throughout his body. He was too tired to form another grudge against the confusing savior the Remnant followed.

He sat up, groaning as he shifted the blanket off and felt the unyielding ground beneath. His eyes further adjusted to the darkness, and he saw three other bodies in the room. Although he felt a hope rise from not being alone after all, it halted before he could stand. Pausing, he sat studying the bodies of his closest friends. An eerie silence cut at him. There was no breath, no movement, no signs of life from Kira, Elba, or Enak.

A scraping sound echoed from somewhere nearby. The creak of hinges followed by soft footsteps.

"He's awake," a male voice came from the darkness.

"Impossible," a female whispered.

Light spilled into the chamber as they entered with a lantern. Kaden squinted against the sudden brightness, making out their faces etched with exhaustion and disbelief.

"We thought you were dead," Jace said. "All of you."

Jace and Aria entered the room, their eyebrows raised as they studied him.

“You weren’t wrong,” Kaden said.

"Only reason these two are down here is to help bury the bodies," Riggs's gruff voice sounded from the doorway. His large frame blocked most of the light from the tunnel.

"Beth-ell's power..." Aria trailed off, her eyes going to the still forms of Kira, Elba, and Enak. "It was more than an Agent has ever... The way she just..."

"We couldn't leave you there," Jace finished. "Not after what happened. Not after seeing Jericho... Well, you know."

"Convenient timing," Riggs growled. "Two Agents suddenly grow a conscience right when everything goes to hell."

"They made their choice in the face of overwhelming death," a cheerful voice called out. Alister stepped into view, his usual smile subdued yet ever present. "Just like you did once, old friend."

Riggs grunted but didn't argue.

"The others," Kaden said, his voice hoarse. "Why haven't they woken up?"

A heavy silence fell over the room. Alister moved to check on the still forms, his weathered hands gentle as he felt for pulses.

"There's no life in these bodies," he said finally. "But neither was there in yours." He looked at Kaden.

“I died, but woke up here. It’s usually reverse,” he said.

“What do you mean?” Jace leaned in, the group’s eyes on Kaden.

"I don’t quite know...” he said, then paused. “He's dead," Kaden cleared his dry throat. "Jericho’s dead."

"Wouldn’t be the first time." Alister's eyes sparkled in the lantern light.

“I saw it. We all saw it,” Kaden said in disbelief of the comment.

“I seem to recall prior stories of death in the desert, the battle of the lighthouse that The Tower won with great effect and fanfare.”

"This is different," Riggs interjected. "Pinnacle took his heart."

"And yet here he is," Alister said, motioning toward Kaden. "Alive when by all rights you should be dead. Tell us, how’d you die?”

“Thornhill, I mean Pinnacle, but back then before the world turned to, well, turned to what it is now and before Pinnacle was Pinnacle. I tried to kill him, but he sent the bullets back at me.”

“You tried to kill Pinnacle?” Riggs laughed. “Marks for courage, kid.”

“The bullets that killed you, where are their marks?" Alister asked.

Kaden's hand went unconsciously to his chest. The phantom pain was still there, but no wounds.

"Faith isn't about understanding everything," Alister continued. "It's about trusting even when we don't understand."

"Faith won't wake them up," Kaden said, looking at Kira's still form.

"No," Alister agreed. "But it might keep hope alive *until* they do."

"Speaking of hope," Jace said, his eyes darting to the tunnel entrance. "We need to move. The Tower will be searching the tunnels. We knew this was here, so do the rest of them."

"Already underway," Riggs confirmed. "First wave of Elites went through the eastern passages an hour ago."

Kaden's heart sank. "How many passages do they know about?"

"All of them," Aria said. "The maps we saw in class weren't partial layouts. The Tower has every tunnel mapped."

"If they know, yet haven't stopped us... They've been herding us," Kaden realized. "All this time, they've been forcing us deeper, exactly where they want us."

"I think Kira realized it before any of us," Riggs growled. "Like rats in a maze."

"Then why haven't they struck?" Kaden asked. "Why play this game?"

"Because they're looking for something," Alister said, his usual cheerfulness replaced by an unsettling certainty. "Or someone."

A groan from one of the bodies made them all jump. Kaden shot to his feet, ignoring the protest of his muscles as he moved to Kira's side. But she remained still, peaceful but cold.

In the silence, they heard a gasp for breath.

"Did he just..." Aria said, looking to Enak.

"Shhh!" Alister held up his hand. They all went silent, straining to hear. For a long moment, only the drip of water and their own breathing broke the quiet.

Then Enak's chest rose and fell – a deep, clear breath. Then, nothing, as if he slipped right back into his paralyzed state.

"Get them ready to move," Riggs commanded. "If one's waking up, the others might too. We need to be long gone when the Elites get in 'ere." He pulled out a collection of pipes and old clothes, the Remnant's version of a mobile cot that could carry the still bodies.

"And where exactly are we supposed to go?" Jace asked. "If they know all the tunnels..."

"Not all of them," Alister said with a familiar twinkle returning to his eye. "He left us a way out. Always has."

"You know another tunnel?" Kaden asked.

"Better." Alister smiled. "I know how to get to the lighthouse."

The words hung in the air like a physical presence. Kaden looked at Kira's still form, then back to Alister.

"Lead the way," he said.

Chapter 7

Entry #2

The changes in the trial subjects are deeply concerning. While my own transformation continues to amaze – healing, regeneration, enhanced perception – theirs follow a darker path. Their cellular structures are shifting in ways we never anticipated. It's as if their bodies are trying to match an impossible frequency, like a violin string being tightened until it's ready to snap.

Thomas dismisses my concerns. "Progress requires sacrifice," he says. But I see the hunger in his eyes when he reviews the data. He's not looking for healing anymore; he's looking for power.

Subject 17 exhibited the most troubling changes today. Her skin has begun hardening, taking on an almost stone-like quality. The transformation appears to be spreading from the injection site, consuming her epidermis cell by cell. When I tried to stop the trial, she begged me to continue. "I can feel it," she kept saying. "I can feel everything."

I understand what she means. Since my transformation began, I've experienced similar sensations – an awareness of the space around me, of the very fabric of reality. But where my changes brought clarity, these trial subjects seem to be losing themselves. They're being consumed by something I don't fully understand.

The board is pushing for expansion of the trials. They see the potential for "human advancement" but miss the cost to our humanity. Thomas leads their charge, speaking of evolution and necessity. He talks about saving humanity from itself, but his methods feel more like conquest than salvation.

I'm reminded of the story of the Tower of Babel – humanity reaching for godhood through its own strength. We never learn, do we? We're always trying to build our way to heaven, one corpse at a time.

Sarah found me in my study last night, lost in these thoughts. She placed her hand on my shoulder and asked, "What do you see when you close your eyes?"

"Light," I told her. "And it's surrounded by darkness."

The choice. That's what Thomas doesn't understand. True healing can't be forced. True change can't be mandated. Each soul must choose its own path.

I've started looking at properties up north, far north. Somewhere remote, where the sky touches the earth. A place to build something different. Not a tower reaching up, but a light reaching out. The visions I see when I sleep are taking more shape. If I pause and meditate on them, I can see them again, as if I'm there. It's the future and I'm preparing to build, yet building, yet have built all at once, a city for refugees. Time is melting together like ice becoming a river.

The changes in my blood could help so many. But not like this. Never like this.

The greatest gift we have isn't power, it's choice. And the hardest choice is often between what we *should* do and what we *will* do.

The darkness is growing. But so is the light.

Chapter 8

Kira

She rolled out of the truck in a daze. The world spun as her eyes fluttered open. Rain pelted her face through the shattered window, mixing with the warm blood trickling down her temple. The truck lay on its side, crushed against the building as if a giant hand had crumpled it like paper. Every breath sent waves of pain through her ribs.

Distant sirens wailed, the sound muffled as if she were underwater. Red and blue lights strobed through the rain, casting strange shadows across the wreckage. Her vision swam in and out of focus as she tried to make sense of the scene before her.

She couldn't remember the accident, only that she was sitting, trying to make out something... Darren came to her mind, but it was a haze. Another moment and she could see blurry outlines of Darren talking with someone. But who? And what hit the truck?

Across the street, a cluster of paramedics huddled over something on the ground. Through the haze of pain and confusion, a horrible thought struck her – it was Dr. Thornhill. And Darren was trying to kill him.

She'd remembered, and Darren succeeded. The body lay motionless and her stomach sank. She was an accessory to murder. How could she let him go through with this? Anything but this.

Darren was likely in custody or on the run. Did he make it out?

All thoughts echoed in her head as voices of paramedics around the crumpled truck leaned down, peering through the broken glass and calling to her. They could also touch her, mere feet away, but to her, they felt a world away.

Her eyes turned back to the body. They'd ask her what happened. How could she hold back the truth yet protect Darren? What did they know?

"Lord, anything but this," she said. Her mouth moved, but no sound came out.

The paramedics around the body shifted as they pulled out a body bag, and she caught a glimpse of familiar shaggy brown hair, stray pieces sticking out as if fighting to be matted down in the rain.

It wasn't Thornhill on the ground...

The world stopped.

Her thought of "Anything but this" ran through her mind. She lost control.

"No!" The scream started as a whisper, but then tore from her throat like a nuclear bomb ripping through a landscape. She scrambled up, screaming as the paramedics tried restraining her.

"Darren!"

Strong hands grabbed her shoulders, holding her back. Police officers materialized around her, their voices a jumble of questions she couldn't process. Her eyes remained fixed on the paramedics as they shook their heads and unfolded the black body bag.

"Ma'am, hold! Hold it. I'm sorry, he's gone," one officer said, his voice barely penetrating the fog in her mind.

“Darren!” she screamed again. Her voice reached decibels and pitches she never knew she had.

“Ma’am! Ma’am!” the men shouted around her, holding her tight as if she wore a straitjacket.

Her anguish turned to sadness as she sank to her knees in the rain, her body trembling. They draped a scratchy orange blanket over her shoulders as an EMT examined the gash on her temple. But she barely felt it. All she could see was the bag being zipped closed over Darren's face.

They guided her into an ambulance, still asking questions she hardly heard and couldn’t answer. Her mind kept replaying the blurry outlines of Darren and Thornhill. He’d raised his hand at the truck, so casual, so cruel. The impossible force that had crushed the truck. The vision of Pinnacle ripping out Jericho’s heart exploded in her mind. Darren, with a gun or not - if Thornhill was already Pinnacle - stood no chance.

"Ma'am? Do you know what happened here? Who hit you and what happened to him?" The officer’s echo finally broke through.

Kelly lifted her eyes from the body bag being loaded into another ambulance. In that moment, she saw the truth of both timelines stretching out before her – the past where Thornhill became Pinnacle, and the future where his power held the world hostage. With Jericho gone and now Darren dead, what next?

“His name is Darren McArthur and Dr. Thomas Thornhill killed him,” she said, and her limbs finally stopped trembling.

“Ma’am?” the officer questioned and looked at the paramedic examining her head. They exchanged a glance and the officer looked out the open door of the ambulance and up at the glowing letters of Pinnacle VC on the side of the building.

"Dr. Thomas Thornhill," she whispered, her voice breaking. "And there's nothing anyone can do about it."

The rain continued to fall as the ambulances pulled away, their sirens cutting through the night. Kelly closed her eyes, knowing that somewhere in the city, a monster who would become a god was smiling.

Chapter 9

Empyrean's Tunnels

The group moved silently through the tunnels, Alister leading the way with a flickering lantern. Three improvised stretchers carried their fallen comrades, the fabric straining under the weight of lifeless bodies. Kaden helped bear Kira's stretcher. With every step, he saw her head bob and he wished her eyes would open.

"We need to pause," Jace whispered, his arms trembling from the effort of carrying Enak. The group carefully lowered their burdens to the damp ground. Jace lifted his arms and stretched while Riggs eyed him impatiently, letting out an exaggerated breath as Elba lay below his feet.

Kaden knelt beside Kira, brushing a strand of black hair from her face. Her skin was pale but peaceful, as if she were merely sleeping.

"How much further?" Aria asked, rolling her shoulders as she rubbed her arms.

"The passage to the lighthouse isn't measured in distance," Alister replied, his usual cheer tempered by exhaustion. "It's measured in faith."

"We don't have time for riddles," Riggs growled. "The Elites are coming."

The sound of a rock tumbling somewhere distant in the tunnel made them all freeze. Kaden held his breath, counting the seconds until the sound faded.

"We're alright," Riggs assured.

"Let's keep moving," Kaden said.

As they lifted the stretchers again, Kaden noticed something odd about the tunnel walls. The rough-hewn stone seemed to shift in the lantern light, patterns emerging and dissolving like ripples in water.

"The walls," he whispered. "They're different here."

Alister nodded. "This section wasn't carved by human hands. He made these passages long ago, preparing the way."

"He? You mean Jericho?" Kaden asked.

Alister nodded.

Kaden remembered the gray eyes that saw through time itself, the gentle strength that masked immense power. He thought of Jericho's final moments, the way he'd stepped into Pinnacle's strike without resistance.

"I don't understand," Kaden said as they walked. "He could have fought back. Why did he let Pinnacle kill him?"

"Some victories only come through surrender," Alister replied.

"This is different; he's dead."

"Yet here you are," Alister said. "Death isn't always the end. Sometimes it's a doorway." Alister turned his head and stared into Kaden's eyes.

The pain from the bullet wounds and taste of blood bubbled up in his memory, the explosions and falling from the catwalk in the pastures, his first days as an Agent and taking a rock to the back of the head, and even his first trip to when Kaden was a boy when an Elite threw him down, cracking his skull. Every time he died in Empyrean, he woke up as Darren and then put back on the glasses. But now, he died as Darren and woke up as Kaden. The glasses were back in his world, somewhere four hundred years in the past and thousands of miles away. They could have been on Jupiter for all he could do to get them.

Then, the thought struck him: if Darren was dead, what happened if he died as Kaden?

The group trudged on through the damp tunnels, taking breaks periodically to switch positions and rest. Alister led the way. Riggs always stayed in the back, his eyes constantly trained on Jace and Aria.

"Keep it moving," Riggs urged from behind.

The words behind him barely registered as Kaden's mind raced. He remembered his first visit to Dr. Abrams's office, how the doctor had looked at him with those piercing gray eyes and said, "Once you see, you can't unsee." At the time, it had seemed like just another cryptic comment from an eccentric optometrist. Now those words haunted him.

He couldn't unsee Pinnacle ripping out Jericho's heart. The scene played over and over in his mind, but something wasn't adding up. Jericho had enough power to tear a hole in The Tower and save both him and Kira. He'd seem to shift through time, and carry Darren and Kelly forward as he held back Pinnacle's might long enough to get them to safety. But then... then he'd simply stopped, stepped forward and accepted a gruesome death.

"Why would he just give up?" Kaden muttered.

"What's that?" Alister asked, slowing his pace to walk beside him.

"Jericho. He had the power to fight Pinnacle. I saw him do it. He restrained Pinnacle as he pulled us out of The Tower. But after saving us, he just... surrendered."

"Perhaps saving you took everything he had," Alister suggested, but his tone suggested he didn't believe it.

He saw Kaden's eyes drop and guilt sink in.

“I didn’t mean it like that,” Alister said.

"No," Kaden said. "It's true. He's been saving me by sending me back and forth every time I die. But..." His face scrunched as he thought. "No, he was stronger than that. He chose his path. It was all on purpose. But why? And why..."

"Why what?" Alister asked.

"Why did he show me early conversations about the Hope Drug? The trials, the history. Why?"

"Have you read the book she found?" Alister said, nodding to Kira.

"No."

"You should. It gives good context to how the Hope Drug led to this fallen world," Alister said. "Regardless, I don't expect Pinnacle to do anything for three days."

"Three days?" Kaden asked.

Alister looked at Kaden curiously. "I forgot the things Kira told me. The little you may remember of this world. The Hope Drug evolved over the centuries. Everyone in the New Breed, including you and me, have it. If a person dies, sometimes they go black. You need to wait three days to find out."

"Black?"

"An Elite," Riggs hollered from behind.

"You mean they were dead?" Kaden asked.

"It's the Brown to Elite promotion ceremony. Not unlike ours when we got Blue, except you get killed..." Jace said. "If you wake up within three days, you're an Elite."

Aria's blank stare turned into a scowl and her eyes met Kaden's. He knew she already detested the promotion ceremonies that overly exposed the female Agents, a symbol for giving your whole body to The Tower, to Pinnacle.

"No way Jericho turns Elite. That's crazy," Kaden said.

“No telling what those demons are doing to his body. It’ll be to hell and back ‘fore three days, then that bast’r Pinnacle will either celebrate or have another high-powered Elite,” Riggs said.

"We're going the wrong direction," Kaden said, stopping abruptly.

"The only way to go back is to go forward," Alister replied. "Trust the path He laid out. We go to the lighthouse."

Kaden wanted to argue, but the memory of Jericho's willing sacrifice stopped him. If he'd learned anything about the man who was both doctor and legend, it was that nothing happened by accident.

"Only two days left," he whispered to himself as they pressed on into the darkness. "Two days to save a dead man."

All eyes in the group watched him.

“You can’t be serious,” Jace said.

“I’m going back to get his body out. That’s what we were doing when Beth-ell killed the four of us. Their deaths won’t be in vain. I need to get to Jericho’s body, to get it out of there and show the world he’s real.”

The tunnel was silent for a moment. Kaden turned around and faced Riggs. The large man was like a brick wall as he hunched to avoid the low tunnel ceiling. There was no going back except through him.

“I’m going back,” Kaden said.

Riggs’s mouth tightened, his eyes going from Kaden to Alister.

“I love a fight as good as any, but I can’t let ya get y’self killed,” Riggs said.

“I’m going back,” Kaden said again.

Riggs dug in, his posture leaning forward as he set Elba’s makeshift cot down.

They stared at each other, unmoving.

Then, Riggs started turning, his shoulder leaning away, creating a gap for Kaden.

“Thank you,” Kaden said, relieved.

Riggs's face turned to confusion. "I ain't lettin' anything!" The slow turn of Riggs's body accelerated, and in an instant, he was smashed against the wall, his body contorting unnaturally as he cringed in pain.

"Yes, you are going back, Kaden McCloud." Beth-ell walked into the light of their lanterns. Two oversized shadows, her Elites, hovered behind her..

"You're not taking him," Jace said, stepping forward. Aria moved to Jace's side.

"The two traitors." She shook her head as a wry smile creeped out. "The Tower will be looking for you, but for now, we all have a higher priority." Her eyes moved back to Kaden. "Come." She flicked her wrist and Kaden's body jolted forward.

"No!" Jace demanded.

Riggs grunted from his position against the wall, defying gravity. His face pushed against the hard rock.

"I didn't ask," Beth-ell said. As she moved away with Kaden, her two Elites stepped forward. They each threw up their arms and sent the group flying down the tunnel. Conscious and unconscious bodies rushed away like pebbles in a water pipe, the makeshift cots breaking apart as debris flew along with them.

"No!" Kaden called back, but with another invisible nudge, he shot forward again.

"Pinnacle would like to see you, and so would I," Beth-ell said.

Chapter 10

Kira

She stood outside Darren's apartment door, her hands trembling. The hospital had discharged her after treating the gash on her temple and the police taking her statement. The physical pain was nothing compared to the hollow ache in her chest. She'd watched them zip the body bag over Darren's face. The image was seared into her mind.

She usually knocked, giving a pause for those inside, but this time, she didn't enter after rapping on the door. Taking a deep breath, she stared down at the faded away doormat that at one time read: No Vampires Allowed. A joke from the trio's younger days on the mythical creatures never being able to enter unless invited in. Old episodes of *Buffy the Vampire Slayer* flashed in Kelly's mind, but the fond memories couldn't break her malaise.

The door swung open and Chris's face appeared, lighting up for a moment before registering her expression, the bandage on her head, and the haunted look in her eyes.

"What happened? Where's Darren?"

She opened her mouth, but no words came. Chris gently pulled her inside.

"Kirk!" Chris called out. "Get out here!"

Kirk emerged from his room, his usual smirk and bounce in his step fading as he saw Kelly's condition. "What's going on?"

Kelly sank into the couch, steps away from where the four of them discussed their time in Empyrean just hours earlier.

"He's dead," she finally managed, her voice barely above a whisper.

The brothers stood frozen, processing her words.

"What do you mean dead?" Kirk demanded. "He was just here!"

"Thornhill. Darren tried to kill him. To prevent Empyrean, but..." Kelly said. "He... he had powers. He threw the truck against a building so I couldn't see, but Darren was holding his gun—"

"He tried killing him?" Kirk shouted. Chris remained stone-faced as Kelly continued to speak.

"Darren tried to shoot him, but he..." She couldn't finish.

"He sent the bullets back. He's already powerful..." Chris said softly.

Kirk began pacing, his movements becoming more agitated with each step. "This is insane. We need to call the police!"

"And tell them what?" Chris asked. "That a venture capitalist used supernatural powers to kill our friend?"

"We tell them he murdered Darren! We were there, we saw—"

"We didn't see anything," Kelly interrupted. "I was in the truck, and you two were here. Besides, the police already know–I tried telling them. They took my statement and probably just threw it in the trash. They're probably calling Darren's parents right now."

"Good luck with that," Kirk sneered, and Chris shot a look at his brother.

Kelly looked to Kirk, then Chris.

"He never told you?" Kirk said.

"He never told anyone," Chris shot back.

"But he had to have told her," Kirk fired back.

"Told me what?" Kelly finally asked.

"You've never wondered about his parents, even after dating so long?" Chris asked.

"No, he never talked about them much. I figured I would soon, but I'm not going to push that."

"You didn't think that was weird. No pictures, no holidays at home?" Kirk remarked.

"No, I mean I'd love to but, wait, what is this about?"

"The only reason we know is because we were friends back then. He doesn't talk about it," Chris said.

Kelly just watched him, urging him with her eyes to continue.

"Darren had grandparents when it happened, but they passed away while he was still technically a minor. Our parents legally adopted him in high school so he could stay out of foster care," Chris said.

"But he still lived on his own most of the time, only selling the house to help pay for school and move out here," Kirk added.

"You've never met his parents because they disappeared when we were kids. Darren doesn't talk about it, and no one really knows what happened," Chris said.

"His dad probably kidnapped her, killed her, then committed suicide," Kirk said matter-of-factly.

"WHAT?" Kelly fell back.

"Bro, you can't," Chris said. "There's no evidence of that; not likely."

"You can say 'not likely' all you want. It's still the most logical and the most probable. Occam's Razor, bro," Kirk said, then he saw Chris and

Kelly staring at him. “What? His dad was PTSD out of his mind after Desert Storm, and those are Darren’s words, not mine.”

“Don’t you Occam’s Razor me, and his dad, he loved her. He wouldn’t have—”

“You remember when we were playing football? The semi drove by and blared its horn? His expression and how he dove for cover... I thought he was going to rip our heads off when he poked his head out and looked at us like the enemy. He was looney toons.”

“What I’ll take from this is that there were mental health concerns in his family, and Darren didn’t want to talk about it,” Kelly said.

Chris nodded sympathetically.

“To say the least,” Kirk retorted. “But whatever, what do we do now?”

Kelly and Chris were silent as Kirk stared at them.

“Let’s find that doctor who gave you the glasses,” Kirk said. “Let’s put them on again and see if we go back.”

“Again?” Kelly asked in disbelief.

“Yeah, we tried them on,” Kirk said.

Chris shrugged and confirmed. “We did.”

“Why would you...?” Kelly asked.

“This is a weird situation. When you two didn’t come back, we got curious,” Chris said.

“It didn’t work anyway,” Kirk said. “Even the purple ones. Thought they looked cute on you, bro.” He laughed.

Chris turned away and moved toward Kelly.

“Let’s wait and think about this. Maybe he went back to Empyrean. We don’t understand all of this,” Chris said.

“We can’t wait and do nothing?” Kirk said.

Chris stood up and moved toward his brother. “We have to stop and think.”

"Don't!" Kirk pushed him away. "This is exactly like Empyrean. We sit around doing nothing while they kill us one by one!"

"And what would Enak do?" Chris fired back. "Rush in anger and get himself killed too?"

The words hung in the air between them. Kelly watched the brothers, seeing echoes of Elba and Enak in their faces.

"At least Enak is trying," Kirk said, his voice dropping to a dangerous whisper. "What did Elba do? What did any of us do? We watched. We always just watch."

"And what about Darren?" Chris asked. "He tried to stop it and now he's dead. Is that what *you* want?"

Kirk's shoulders slumped. The fight seemed to drain out of him, replaced by a bone-deep weariness that aged him years in moments.

"I want my friend back. I want this madness to go away," he said.

Kelly felt tears rolling down her cheeks. "He wanted to stop it all before it began. Before The Tower, before the Elites. He thought..." She sniffed. "He thought he could save everyone."

Chris sat beside her, placing a gentle hand on her shoulder. "Like Jericho trying to save humanity from itself."

"And look what happened to him," Kirk muttered.

They sat in silence, the weight of two time lines' worth of grief pressing down on them. Outside, rain began to fall, pattering against the windows like nature itself was weeping.

"What do we do now?" Chris finally asked.

Kelly looked to the circular breakfast table where her purple glasses waited – her portal to Kira's world. They seemed to shimmer in the dim light.

"We keep fighting," she said. "Not with bullets or anger, but with hope. Like the Lighthouse Remnant."

"You're going back, aren't you?" Kirk asked incredulously.

She nodded. "Darren died trying to stop this future from happening. Maybe we're supposed to change it from within. We were going to get Jericho's body back before we ran into Beth-ell and her Elites. If we could sneak through, we could get into The Tower."

Chris studied her face. "You'll be alone this time."

"No," she said. "Maybe Darren's there already. Plus, Kira has the Remnant, at least what's left of it. And Jericho... something tells me we haven't seen the last of him."

Kirk turned away, but not before Kelly caught the glint of tears in his eyes. Chris squeezed her shoulder, a silent promise of support, as he nodded his head.

Kelly stood and moved to her glasses, knowing that somewhere in another time, another world, Kira was waiting.

"We'll go too," Chris said.

"And where's our glasses?" Kirk remarked.

"Last time, it was a dream; maybe we just go to sleep when she goes in?" Chris said.

"Not sure I can sleep, bro," Kirk said.

"Have a Pop-Tart and OJ, whatever you need to do, because once she goes, we'll be close behind," Chris said.

Outside, the rain continued to fall, washing away the blood from the streets where Darren had died, but unable to cleanse the memory from Kira's mind.

She looked out at the falling rain, then back at the glasses.

She put on the glasses and her body fell back on the couch as she traveled back to Kira.

Chapter 11

Kaden

Beth-ell led Kaden through the damp tunnels, the two Elites behind him. Their eyes fixed on him like predators stalking wounded prey. The charcoal creatures' presence sent waves of depression through the air, but something felt different – a hint of restraint in their usual overwhelming oppression.

Shards of light passed from ahead as the tunnels joined the sewers, spotlights from the world above that dotted their path forward. Beth-ell's disgruntled face was more intense than normal.

"What's the matter with you? You've won, he's dead," Kaden said.

"Who's dead?" she remarked sharply.

"Pinnacle's killed him and you know about all the tunnels. There's nothing left to stop you."

"Why are you back here?" she snapped.

"You and your demons didn't give me much choice."

"I don't mean these tunnels. I mean here." She held up her hands and looked to the city above. "I sent you *back there,* yet now you're back *here,* in Empyrean?"

Kaden remembered the cryptic message Beth-ell said when she killed him outside The Tower.

"I've been so caught up with coming back here... You did want me to kill Dr. Thornhill, didn't you?"

Beth-ell made no movement as she stared at him in the dim light of the sewers.

"I knew it." He shook his head. "But he was ready. I shot him, but... but the bullets just stopped, then came back at me."

He saw the whites of Beth-ell's faint grey eyes as they grew wide in surprise. She looked to her two Elites, who caught her stare, a silent exchange playing back and forth. The air around them crackled with an unseen emotion, as if lamenting through an invisible force.

"He had it that early..." she said, shaking her head and peering past Kaden as if looking through him. Her cold eyes settled back into her typical stare.

"Why do you care?" Kaden demanded. "You're his right hand. Unless..." He studied her face, seeing past the years etched into her features. "This is about power, isn't it? You want to take over?"

She scoffed, disappointment washing over her. Then her stern, wrinkled expression softened.

"Oh, Kaden. I wish you recognized me. It would have been a lot easier," she said, and the weathered muscles in her face seemed to relax for the first time.

His mouth hung open in confusion, unable to connect the dots of her comment.

“We've met before, you know. In a small office, over four centuries ago. You did all the paperwork, and got a cookie in return,” she said, a smile creaking from the corner of her mouth.

Kaden's mind raced back to Dr. Abrams's office – the clean and stylish waiting room, the dark hallway, the delicious cookies and... “Ms. Barbara?” he breathed in disbelief.

She nodded, a familiar warmth briefly replacing the hardness in her eyes. "I was one of the first to receive the Hope Drug. David – Jericho – was trying to help me. My cancer was spreading fast, almost as fast as his did before his treatments stopped it." She then gestured to her Elites. "These two were also early patients, with a connection to—” She stopped eyeing the Elites and then Kaden. “But where their bodies embraced the *transformation*, well, mine..." She held up her hand and the muscles tensed, and for a moment, Kaden saw patches of charcoal-like skin trying to form before fading away. "Mine rejected the darkness."

“Why do I still get the feeling that these two, especially this one, have been trying to consume me since day one?” Kaden pointed at the Elite who always showed up to sniff him out, to punish him.

“Let’s just say they know your scent. Jericho didn’t send you here without notice,” she said.

“You tried to kill me,” Kaden snapped at the Elite, who gave a wry smile in return.

“It’s not easy resisting the power they hold. It takes control no matter what the mind wants. Be glad you didn’t get consumed when they first smelled you,” she said.

“But wait, this means you've been working *against* The Tower? All this time?”

"Some of us saw what Thomas – Pinnacle – was becoming. When David left Empyrean to build the lighthouse, we formed a resistance within The

Tower itself. Who do you think has been helping the Remnant survive all these years? They always seem to find just enough food, just enough warning before the raids?"

The pieces clicked into place – the maps Ron-ell held of the tunnels, the way the Elites always seemed to arrive just after the Remnant escaped, Beth-ell's cryptic words before killing them.

"The cookies," Kaden said suddenly. "Did you really make a fortune from them?"

A ghost of a smile crossed her face. "Had to fund the earliest trials somehow, and couldn't use Thomas's funds *and* keep our identities a secret. I did enjoy serving them to patients." Her expression hardened. "But now Jericho is dead, and time may be running out."

"What do you mean?"

"You saw what the Hope Drug did to the Elites. Imagine that power in Jericho's body, corrupted and controlled by Pinnacle." She shuddered. "We have less than two days."

"You mean until the Hope Drug transforms him into something like an Elite?" he asked.

"Worse, considering his power," she said.

"Then help me get his body out," Kaden pleaded. "You have access, power like the Elites, like him."

"It's not that simple." Beth-ell started walking again, her pace quickening. "Pinnacle knows."

"What?" Kaden gasped.

"He's always known about us, playing his own game. Why do you think he wanted to see you?" She glanced back at him. "You're his bait, Kaden."

"Bait for what?"

"Think. Who would come for you? Who would risk everything to save you?"

Kaden's blood ran cold as realization struck. "Kira."

Beth-ell nodded grimly. "And through her, all of the Remnant. Through them..." She trailed off as The Tower loomed above them, its shadow stretching across the city like a blade.

"The Lighthouse," Kaden finished.

They walked in silence for a moment, the weight of centuries pressing down on them.

"Why tell me this now?" Kaden finally asked.

“We don’t know what will happen if the Hope Drug kicks in on Jericho. Even if nothing happens, the veil is torn, and life and death are commingled forever.”

“What does that mean?” he asked.

“If he doesn’t transform into an Elite, then Pinnacle will consume him. He’ll grow even stronger than he already is. Jericho could raise buildings from the ground. Who do you think built Empyrean? With that sort of power, Pinnacle wouldn’t need the Elites or Agents or anyone to uphold Empyrean.”

“We can’t let that happen,” Kaden said.

“If Pinnacle finds you, he’ll use you to wipe out the Remnant,” she said. “Or worse.”

Kaden’s shoulders rose and fell without a word.

“And if they don’t come, he’ll consume you and go find them. He’ll root them out, one-by-one, turning off the light of any opposition.”

“How do we stop him?” Kaden asked.

Chapter 12

Entry #3

The temporal episodes are becoming more frequent. Today, I watched a cup fall from my desk, but instead of shattering, it hung suspended. Time stretched around it like taffy, giving me seconds, minutes even, to simply reach out and catch it. The strangest part wasn't the suspension of time – it was how natural it felt, like finally remembering how to do something I'd known all along. Riding a bike.

The trials continue to yield disturbing results. Subject 17's epidermis has completely transformed. Her skin is obsidian black, cracked like dried earth, yet somehow still living. More concerning is that other subjects are beginning to show similar changes. It's as if the drug is rewriting their genetic code, turning human flesh to a deathly living stone.

But the physical transformation isn't what truly haunts me. It's their eyes. The light in them is dying, replaced by something hungry. They look at me the way a starving man looks at food. Thomas says it's a sign of evolution – the strong consuming the weak to become stronger. He doesn't see what I see: that their cells are consuming themselves from the inside out, and they'll need another source to feed on, and soon.

I tried explaining my concerns at today's board meeting. The words had barely left my mouth when every paper on the conference table began to float. The board members stared, mouths agape, but Thomas... Thomas smiled. That's when I realized – he's not interested in stopping these transformations. His interest is to accelerate them.

The changes in my own body continue to evolve in different ways. I can feel the fabric of space around me like a tangible thing. Sometimes when I focus, I can see through the walls of reality itself. This morning, I found myself standing in my office, but also in a place that doesn't exist yet – a city of towers and shadows, where stone-skinned creatures prowl the streets. Time has become fluid, like water flowing in multiple directions at once. I am learning to reel it back and forth like controlling a video that I can step into at any moment.

Sarah keeps asking me to come home earlier, to spend more time with the children. She's right, of course. But how do I explain that sometimes I'm already home, even as I sit in my office writing these words? How do I tell her that I can feel time wrapping around us like a spiral, showing me glimpses of what's coming? The horrible event ahead for our family.

I'm starting to understand why prophets in the Bible always seemed so troubled. Seeing what's coming doesn't necessarily mean you can change it. Sometimes witnessing is itself a kind of crucifixion.

The drug changed my blood, and it's nothing like what flows through the trial subjects. Mine brings life; theirs brings hunger. Mine reveals; theirs consumes. The question that keeps me awake isn't whether we should continue – it's whether I can, or should, stop what's already been set in motion.

I catch Thomas watching me sometimes, calculating. He thinks he's discovered a new force of nature to be harnessed. He doesn't understand he's playing with fire. Or maybe he does, and that's exactly what he wants – to watch the world burn so he can build his own kingdom from the ashes. His eyes are different. I see them throughout history.

My plans for the north continue to develop. Every day, it becomes more clear – a lighthouse standing against the coming storm. But I also see The Tower that will rise to challenge it, casting its shadow over what remains of humanity.

Time ripples around me as I write these words. I can feel reality bending, showing me paths that branch like lightning across the sky. In some, I fight. In others, I watch. But in all of them, I see The Tower rising, and I see what must be sacrificed to tear it down.

I pray this cup is taken from me. Nevertheless, not my will...

Chapter 13

Kaden

"The Elites weren't meant to be this way," Beth-ell said as they walked through the tunnels. "The first transformations were different."

Kaden watched the two charcoal demons that flanked them. Their usual oppressive aura felt muted, controlled. "What changed?"

"Power corrupts. The Hope Drug was meant to heal, but Thomas twisted it. Made it about control instead of healing." She stopped walking, turning to face him. "These two were some of the first. Before Thomas perfected his 'improvements,' and began the creation of the New Breed."

The Elite that had haunted Kaden since his first days in Empyrean. In the dim light, Kaden could see faint traces of human features beneath the stone-like exterior. The creature seemed more human, more familiar than before.

"The early patients retained more of themselves than the others," Beth-ell explained. "They can resist the hunger, but only to a degree. It eventually takes over."

"The hunger?" Kaden said, looking to his left and catching the other Elite's facial features in the light. Cracks on its charcoal skin appeared like deep canyons cut through a dry landscape. It turned to meet his eyes, and he saw sorrow in them. Yet, a fraction of a smile cracked on the edges as if a heart still beat somewhere underneath the hard, unforgiving surface.

"The New Breed is different, and part of its code is in us all. Elites have immense power, but it comes at a cost. You can see the most obvious cost." She motioned to the cracked, obsidian skin. "But the hunger might be even worse... An Elite's power comes from its cells. The cost of their power is the consumption. They must feed constantly. Without a proper intake, their cells starve from the inside out. They get fierce, animalistic."

"You talk like they have a conscience, a soul."

"They were once something different, some with noble intentions, but once they change..." She turned, looking at her Elite pair. "I've seen parents with hopeless health concerns seek out a Hope Drug transformation, thinking they would protect their families. But once transformed, the children didn't stand a chance. There wasn't a second thought."

"How could someone..." Kaden said in disbelief.

Beth-ell stopped and Kaden nearly ran into her. The cold stare she gave him seemed to push him back.

"You don't know *the hunger*. You don't know what it's like once it has you."

Her Elites stood stern behind her, eyes fixed on Kaden. The oppressive sensation they normally put out was completely gone now.

"And I hope you never do," she said coldly.

Kaden held his breath as her fierce stare stuck to him. He nodded and she turned back to leading the group. The two Elites watched him another moment, then turned to follow Beth-ell.

"But what about Jericho? He has the powers, but he doesn't consume. Does he?" Kaden asked.

"Dr. Abrams once said to me that man cannot live on bread alone. The original design was self-sustaining. A fasted state accelerated the flywheel of energy creation within the cells, giving him more energy than he'd ever need. Using an extreme amount sapped his physical appearance," she said.

"Like ripping a hole out of The Tower to save Kira and me?" Kaden asked.

She nodded. "But he always recovered and came back stronger, *without* consumption. However, he was the only one. Every other patient the Hope Drug affected had a yearning they couldn't control. As the catastrophes of the world stacked up, the Hope Drug was released."

"But you don't have the corrupted version, and if they were early patients, they don't have it."

"We all have it," she said coldly. "A drug doesn't need to be injected to get into a population. Thornhill ensured the entire globe had it. Once he contaminated the drinking water, everyone had it. It was dormant in some, those were the survivors, but in most, it healed in the short-term. It gave an incredible feeling of strength and vitality, but eventually, it ravaged them. Soon, the few children that were born had it inside them from the womb. And eventually..." She stepped toward the sewer exit and looked up. The Tower loomed, rising into the sky far above them. "Eventually, Pinnacle eliminated natural births. The world is sterile, Kaden. You were born in a test tube, a batch from The Tower meant to run the factories and shovel the crap, or worse, feed the Elites."

Kaden was silent, taking in the comment.

"The pastures aren't enough, are they? They can't feed all the Elites with livestock," Kaden soon said.

"They're enough," she replied, then saw Kaden's look of confusion.

"That might be the worst part when I look back. Encouraging the pastures was meant to curtail their hunger. But even with the livestock, most Elites choose humans." She saw Kaden's expression. "Pinnacle encourages it, and The Tower breeds for it," she said.

Chapter 14

Kira

Kira's eyes shot open. Her lungs expanded with a desperate gasp as if she'd been underwater for too long. The air tasted of damp earth and metal as it filled her chest. For a moment, she existed in a space between worlds – the phantom sensation of a wound on her temple, the memory of rain against her skin, and the crushing grief of watching Darren's body being zipped into a bag. But that wasn't her memory, it was Kelly's, and it danced further away as if a childhood dream from a lifetime ago.

She blinked, trying to orient herself in the darkness. Her fingers clutched at loose dirt beneath her. Voices murmured nearby, distant and muffled like they were coming through water. Pain radiated through her body – not the sharp agony of a fresh wound, but the dull ache of having been still for too long.

"She's awake!" a voice called out. A lantern approached, its light growing from a pinprick to a warm glow that illuminated concerned faces.

"Kira?" Alister's weathered face came into view, his usual cheerfulness subdued but present. Behind him stood Jace and Aria, their faces bearing the uncertainty of former Tower Agents amidst the Remnant.

"Where..." Her voice came out as a croak. She tried to sit up, but her muscles protested.

"Easy now," Alister said, placing a gentle hand on her shoulder. "You've been gone a while."

"Beth-ell," she whispered, the memory flooding back – the Brown Agent's cold eyes, the invisible force slamming into her body, darkness claiming her. "She killed us."

"I suppose not," Alister replied, helping her sit up. "Though not for lack of trying. Thank Jericho."

As her vision cleared, Kira saw they were in a cave-like chamber. The makeshift stretcher she'd been lying on was little more than pipes and cloth. Nearby, Elba and Enak were still unconscious on his own stretcher.

"Kaden," she said suddenly, looking around. "Where's Kaden?"

The silence that followed told her everything.

"They took him," Jace finally said. "Beth-ell and two Elites. We tried to stop them, but..." He gestured to a bruise blossoming on his jaw.

"How long?" Kira asked, her mind racing.

Before anyone could answer, Riggs shot in, "DID YOU KNOW?" He held a broken piece of plastic like a club and raised it at Jace.

"No." Jace shook his head, looking down at the club then back up at Riggs.

Riggs growled, his eyes shrinking to accusatory slits.

"This isn't helping, friend," Alister said through the tension.

"Ruttin' out a mole ain't *not* helpin', though," Riggs fired back, his eyes still not leaving Jace.

"Riggs, I saw him die. We went after Pinnacle before he was, well, before he was Pinnacle," Kira said.

Riggs and Jace both turned to Kira, "What?" they said in unison.

"There's more than what we see. And far more than I understand," Kira said, looking down and away.

"Tell me more," Alister moved in and crouched next to her.

"The memories fade, like a dream, but she's there. She's a part of me and I her."

"Who?"

"Kelly. She's me, but lives over four hundred years ago, before all this happened to the world," she said, looking up and around the tunnel.

"And Jericho sent her to you?" Alister asked.

"No, remember his journal? He described the cup falling and how he could stop it, rewind it as if he was stepping in and out of time, turning reality like a spinning record," Kira said.

Alister contemplated her statement.

"What's a record? You mean a wrecker truck, like a Twenty?" Riggs asked.

"No, I mean a spinning disc that produces music. It's a... Never mind. What I'm saying is Jericho can step in and out of time, and he's sending me and Darren here."

"And now who's Darren?" Riggs asked, frustration mounting.

"He's Kaden. Isn't he?" Alister asked Kira, a reassuring smile on his face.

Kira nodded.

"Jericho is moving us between different lives, different times. And when we die, we go back to the other," she said.

"That's how he survived the Outer Ring," Jace blurted out, turning to Aria.

"He didn't survive at all," Aria replied.

Kira shook her head.

"Jericho led me to him. I found him with his head split open, more blood around him than in him. But I stitched him up, and soon, he came back," she said.

Jace laughed and the others turned to him in confusion.

"And what's so funny, 'gent?" Riggs held back up the makeshift club. It appeared to be a broken leg of a table.

"Ron-ell was so furious when he came back." He laughed. "Three days in the Outer Ring for a new Agent; it's a death sentence."

"And you think it's funny?" Riggs moved in closer, coming within inches of Jace.

Jace leaned in to meet Riggs, his laughter subsiding.

"Let me remind you when we left The Tower, we became traitors to Pinnacle. We're marked for a death sentence and traitors don't die quick or clean deaths."

The two stood, eye-to-eye, both puffing up their chests and moving back their shoulders.

"What I'm hearing is that Jericho is keeping Kaden alive, and seems you as well." Alister disregarded the conflict as he spoke to Kira.

"I think so. Without Jericho, we'd be dead many times over," Kira said.

"There's two problems with all this," Aria stepped in. "They're still dead," she said, pointing down the tunnel to Elba's and Enak's bodies.

Kira's mind flickered back to Chris and Kirk.

"And what's the second?" Riggs asked, he and Jace finally separating to hear the conversation.

"Jericho is dead. Pinnacle ripped his heart out. How could he be moving you back and forth?" Aria said.

"I don't know..." Kira said softly. "But I know I'm here."

“And so are we,” Elba said as his previously lifeless body sat up. He coughed and winced as he moved.

“Well, I’ll be...” Riggs mouthed.

“Praise Jericho,” Alister said, a brilliant smile erupting.

“I have a headache,” Enak said as he sat up and rubbed his head.

Everyone’s confusion turned to joy to see the pair awaken, with laughter breaking out.

“It’s funny I have a headache?” Enak snapped.

“Oh, shut it,” Riggs said. He stepped forward and hugged both men in one gigantic motion.

“Did I catch tears in your eyes?” Elba said.

Riggs didn’t verbally answer but squeezed the pair tighter in response.

Elba’s eyes bulged and the group settled.

"You've been out for nearly a day now," Aria turned to Kira. "We thou ght... we weren't sure you'd wake up at all."

Kira closed her eyes, centering herself. The memory of Kelly putting on the glasses played in her mind. She'd felt the connection, the transfer of consciousness across time.

"They're taking him to The Tower," Riggs said, stepping into the light. His large frame seemed diminished somehow, bearing the weight of their setback. "To Pinnacle."

"We have to go after him, and Jericho," Kira said, pushing herself to her feet despite the protest of her muscles.

"And do what exactly?" Riggs scoffed. "Knock on The Tower's front door? Ask Pinnacle nicely to give him back?"

"We can't just abandon them," Kira insisted, her voice rising. "It’s not right to leave Jericho’s body there, and Kaden is the only other one to see both worlds. He knows more about what is going on than me. Jericho showed him more. We can’t let him suffer the same fate."

"Whatever they know, Pinnacle will know too," Jace said grimly.

"Consumption..." Riggs growled.

Jace nodded. "It's not a direct transfer of memories like The Tower wants you to think, but it's close. We were taught it's like knowing the other person's life in your dreams, like you know it all but can only grasp certain aspects. Holding sand."

"And those aspects were enough for them to wipe out most of our leadership during the food raid. Only Kira and we two made it out alive," Elba said.

"Or information was passed on," Enak said solemnly, his eyes dropping to the floor.

"We don't have traitors," Riggs said. Then his eyes turned to Jace and Aria. "But I'm not sure about former 'gents *claiming* to be on our side." His stare was as blunt as a falling rock smashing the ground.

"Let's focus on what we can control," Kira said.

"We can get to the Lighthouse, get out of Empyrean and regroup. Jericho would have wanted us safe. He took you and Kaden out of Pinnacle's grasp and sacrificed himself; we can't ignore that," Alister said.

"I'm in," Enak said in a hopeful tone. "Let's go." He took a step forward.

"Not so fast." Riggs held out an arm, blocking him. Enak rolled his eyes. "He saved Kira AND Kaden, and now that treacherous woman Beth-ell took Kaden back," Riggs said, clenching his fist.

"I'm not so sure fighting the Elites is the best path forward," Jace said. "They will all be recalled to The Tower after Jericho ripped a hole in it and dozens fell."

"Agreed; they'll be on high alert," Aria added.

"So says the 'gents," Riggs said in a demeaning tone. "But Kaden was right to go for the 'eart of the beast while wounded. You want to win a fight, you don't let the enemy back up. You pummel 'em down and keep 'em down for good."

"Beth-ell took all four of us out with a flick of her wrist," Enak pleaded.

Riggs looked Enak up and down, sizing him up, then flexed his massive chest. "I'll take my chances over yours."

"You can beat an Elite, eh, tough guy?" Enak snapped, pushing Riggs.

"You ungrateful little—" Riggs grabbed a fist of Enak's cloak and started raising him off the ground as the cloth tore.

"STOP!" Kira shouted. She forced out a frustrated exhale as the group turned to her. Enak scrambled to get free from Riggs, who held on longer than needed before shoving him away.

"Let's look at our options," she said. "We could go to the Lighthouse." Her eyes flashed to Alister. "We'd be safe there, and maybe other survivors are going there too."

"How many people know about the tunnel out of Empyrean?" Kira asked.

Alister winced and slowly shook his head no.

"So only a fraction of the Remnant is still alive," she thought aloud.

"That we know of," Elba said.

Kira nodded.

"We could go to the Lighthouse, we could stay in the tunnels of Empyrean—"

"A death sentence," Enak added. "The Elites know the tunnels."

"Or third option, we could turn and bring the fight to The Tower," she said.

"Get some," Riggs said with a steady nod and determined expression.

The members of the group looked between each other, each contemplating their ideas.

"Once, Jericho showed me the stars," Alister spoke up. "Do you know what he said? 'Like them, you are scattered light in darkness.' I thought it was just a pretty metaphor. But I think he was telling me something real – the Remnant is like those stars, scattered across Empyrean but still connected. We think there are only a few and I don't know of anyone else who knows the path, but I have faith that the Lighthouse isn't just a building; it's a beacon to call us together. There's more of us out there than we think."

"One vote for the Lighthouse," Kira said.

"Two," Elba said, stepping toward Alister. "We've heard since we were kids that Pinnacle and the Elites wiped out Jericho and the Lighthouse, but we know that's not true. There's more out there and we'll need everyone we can get." He grasped Alister's shoulder and stepped behind the older man.

"We can't leave Kaden to be consumed, and I know ways to get in The Tower," Jace said.

"You'd lead us back to our deaths," Riggs snarled.

"I've been in the consumption chambers, and I'm not going back," Enak said, stepping toward his brother and Alister.

"And neither am I," Aria spoke up. "But going to The Tower doesn't mean we go to the chambers. Something changed when Jericho sacrificed himself. If I'm going back to The Tower, I'm helping to bring it down. I'm in for the fight."

Riggs eyed her, a low, skeptical growl resonating from him.

"Well, big fella, it's three to two for the Lighthouse so far," Kira said to Riggs. "And I'm going to tie it up. We cannot leave Kaden. We cannot leave Jericho's body. I admire your faith to build back the Remnant." She nodded to Alister. "But I can't leave them."

"There ain't a world where two 'gents walk you back to The Tower without me," Riggs said. "I'm going."

"That settles it, then. Four to three," Kira said.

"It sure does," Alister said, nodding.

Kira began stepping away from Alister and the brothers, but Alister stayed motionless.

"It settles that you four are going back, and we're going out," Alister added. "You seem like a totally different person now than when we first met." He smiled. "I have faith that you have something inside now. Something more than you, or any of us, know."

With that, he turned and walked away.

Enak took a look at the group, catching Riggs's eye and giving a sheepish wave, then followed Alister.

Elba nodded, locking eyes with Kira. "See you soon," he said. Then he waved to the group and also left.

The darkness of the tunnel swallowed them, leaving the four silently looking into the abyss.

"Okay," Kira said, trying to sound determined and keep her voice from rising. She desperately hoped the others didn't know how much she was questioning herself.

The four stood in silence as Kira's mind raced. Moments ago, she was confident; now, she blanked on the next steps.

Riggs cut the silence. "If you two try to sell us to the Elites, I'll kill you myself." His face was stone cold as he held Jace's eyes and then Aria's.

"I'd like to see you try," Aria shot back confidently. Kira couldn't help but notice the edge of Riggs's mouth curl into a smile. She knew he didn't want to let on, but he must be enjoying this standoff.

"Elites may be already guarding all our ways in. Or have changed them entirely," Jace said.

Riggs growled at the comment, breaking his concentration on Aria.

"Jericho's body and now Kaden are in there. How are we getting in and then back out?" Kira asked.

"Well..." Jace turned to Aria. "All the exterior entrances are likely guarded. There are routes for maintenance and goods in and out, same as trash, but I'm thinking..."

"No. It's a mess down there... Don't say it," Aria said.

"Exactly," Jace replied.

"All the labs are dispersed and the lift is out of order," Aria said.

"You're a good climber." Jace smiled at her.

"Climbin'?" Riggs asked in disbelief. "I'm not climbin' on The Tower."

"No, neither am I," Jace said. "We're going to descend into the pastures and climb back up into the heart of The Tower. Have you heard of the pastures?" Jace asked.

Riggs looked at Kira, both of their eyebrows raised.

"I have," she replied.

"Looks like we're going up the belly of the beast," Riggs said.

Chapter 15

Kaden

Kaden followed Beth-ell through the dimly lit tunnels, the two Elites flanking him like silent sentinels. The charcoal-skinned creatures moved with an unnatural fluidity, their feet barely seeming to touch the ground. He could feel their presence at his back – not the usual oppressive aura that made breathing difficult, but something more controlled, focused. They were restraining themselves, and he wasn't sure whether to find that comforting or terrifying.

The tunnel gradually widened and brightened as they approached The Tower's entrance. Kaden's heart pounded against his ribs. The last time he'd been here, he was a Blue Agent being escorted out in disgrace. Now he was returning as a prisoner, a traitor to Pinnacle's regime.

"When we reach the entrance, say nothing," Beth-ell instructed, her voice barely above a whisper. "I talk, you shut up. Trust me."

"That's a lot to ask," he replied.

Beth-ell paused, turning to face him. The weathered lines of her face seemed deeper in the harsh light. "I could have let them consume you in the tunnels. I didn't. Remember that."

"I'm putting my life in your trust," Kaden said, now losing confidence, as the faded memory of Ms. Barbara was replaced with the sharp and cruel Beth-ell.

He glanced at the Elites, their oppressive nature still toned down. One time, they tried to consume him in the heat of battle, but now, he sensed a connection.

Ahead, the tunnel opened into a vast lobby. White-robed Agents stood at attention, flanking the entry points. Blue and Purple Agents moved with purpose across the polished floor. Kaden tensed, expecting alarms to sound, weapons to be drawn.

But as they approached, something strange happened – or rather, didn't happen. The Agents simply stepped aside, their eyes averted, shooting straight down as Beth-ell walked past. No one questioned why a Brown Agent was escorting a known traitor through The Tower's main entrance. No one dared to look directly at the Elites that accompanied them.

They entered the lobby unchallenged, and Kaden felt a chill creep up his spine. This wasn't just fear – this was power. Beth-ell's power.

"The central lift," she commanded, and the group moved toward the gleaming elevator doors at the center of the lobby.

As they crossed the vast space, Kaden noticed something unusual. The typically regimented atmosphere of The Tower seemed different. Agents huddled in small groups, their voices hushed. Others moved with unusual haste, as if rushing to complete tasks before some unknown deadline. The order that had defined The Tower was fraying at the edges.

"Something's changed," Kaden whispered.

"Everything's changed," Beth-ell replied without turning. "Jericho's death has shifted the balance. The Tower isn't just a building; it's a symbol, and he tore a hole in Pinnacle's perfect control. He revealed the illusion."

They reached the elevator, and the doors slid open silently. Inside, Beth-ell pressed her palm against a scanner, and the elevator began to rise. Not to the upper levels Kaden had seen as an Agent, but past them, to floors he hadn't known existed. Higher than the chamber where Pinnacle sought to consume him and Kira.

"Where are we going?" he asked.

"Inner Sanctum. Pinnacle's domain."

“The Tower up here is still... I mean, the hole from Jericho,” Kaden said.

“Jericho isn’t the only one strong enough to control buildings,” Beth-ell said, her eyes always staying forward, perfectly trained.

“He’s holding it together?” Kaden gasped.

“I’d say he can’t let it fall,” she replied.

The elevator was glass on one side, offering a view of The Tower's interior as they ascended. Kaden watched levels flash by – training facilities, living quarters, administrative sections. Color from various ranks of robes flickered by. Ants at work. But as they rose higher, the nature of the spaces changed. The walls became darker, the lighting more subdued. And the Elites – they were everywhere.

Unlike the Elites he had encountered in the Outer Ring or during sortings, these moved with greater purpose. They didn't patrol or hunt; they performed functions Kaden couldn't comprehend. In one chamber, a group stood in a circle, their hands extended toward a central point where the air itself seemed to bend and distort. In another, an Elite pressed its hands against the wall, and Kaden watched as the solid surface rippled like water.

"What are they doing?" he asked.

"Testing their powers," Beth-ell answered cryptically.

The elevator slowed, then stopped. The doors opened to reveal a corridor unlike any Kaden had seen before. The walls were nearly black, but with a strange luster that made them appear to shift and move in his peripheral vision. The air felt heavy, charged with an energy that made the hair on his arms stand on end.

As they stepped into the corridor, an Elite emerged from a side passage. The demon was larger than Beth-ell's companions, its skin so dark, it seemed to absorb the light around it. It turned toward Kaden, cracking black nostrils flaring. The oppressive feeling hit him like a physical blow – not the controlled aura of Beth-ell's Elites. It was an outward wave of hunger so intense that Kaden staggered backward.

The Elite moved with frightening speed, closing the distance between them in an instant. But before it could reach Kaden, Beth-ell's Elites intervened. They stepped between Kaden and the newcomer, their bodies tensing. A sound emerged from them – a growl mixed with a hiss, primal and threatening. The sound seemed to reverberate through the corridor, making the strange walls pulse in response.

The larger Elite paused, its opaque face somehow registering an angry surprise. Beth-ell stepped forward, her hand raised. The tension in the air thickened until Kaden could barely breathe.

"He belongs to your master, *not* you or me," Beth-ell said, her voice carrying an authority that belied her weathered appearance.

For a moment, the Elite seemed poised to challenge her. Then, with a sound like stones grinding together, it backed away and disappeared down another corridor.

Beth-ell's Elites backed down, but remained close to Kaden, their protective stance unmistakable. They weren't just guarding him – they were claiming him, like predators warning others away from their prey.

"What was that about?" Kaden whispered as they continued down the corridor.

"You have a particular scent," Beth-ell explained. "It scares them."

"That was it acting scared?"

"An animal backed into a corner."

"Understood," he said. "But your Elites?"

"They're... different. As I said, earlier versions, before Pinnacle perfected the corruption. They still have some choice left."

They turned a corner, and Kaden nearly collided with a group of Brown Agents hurrying in the opposite direction. The Agents scattered like startled birds, pressing themselves against the walls to allow Beth-ell's group to pass. Their eyes darted nervously to the Elites, then away, as if afraid that looking too long might invite attention.

"I suggest you go down a few floors," Beth-ell said, contempt filling her voice. The group offered no response, scurrying away.

As they moved deeper into the Inner Sanctum, the signs of disorder became more apparent. Doors stood half open, falling from broken frames. Various devices lay abandoned on surfaces. In one room, a shattered glass panel spread across the floor, the pieces untouched.

"The Tower is in chaos," Kaden observed.

"Not chaos," Beth-ell corrected. "Transformation. Pinnacle's grip is tightening, not weakening. He's squeezing The Tower as he holds it up."

They passed a chamber where three Elites stood with their hands pressed against a massive black sphere that hovered in the center of the room. Energy crackled around the sphere, and as Kaden watched, one of the Elites began to change. Its skin, already black, seemed to crack, revealing not flesh beneath but a pulsing light that hurt Kaden's eyes. The Elite's body contorted as the transformation took hold, its form elongating in ways that defied human anatomy.

Kaden looked away, bile rising in his throat. "What's happening to it?"

"Evolution, according to Pinnacle," Beth-ell said, her voice flat. "Consumption beyond physical bodies."

The sound like a gunshot rang out. Beth-ell and the Elites were unfazed, but Kaden flinched, side-stepping and looking back. The Elite that just contorted now rested on one knee, a sharp crack cutting from his shoulder down into its chest. The demon's arm lay dangling like a puppet whose string was ready to break.

“But the added power has risks,” Beth-ell said coldly.

They continued on, passing more scenes that challenged Kaden's understanding of reality. In one chamber, an Elite stood motionless as smaller, child-sized Elites circled it, reaching out with spindly limbs to touch its surface before darting away. In another, a Blue Agent knelt before an Elite, offering up a vial of dark liquid that seemed to move of its own accord.

Finally, they reached the end of the corridor, where massive doors of some unknown material stood closed. Symbols Kaden didn't recognize were etched into their surface, glowing with a faint internal light.

Beth-ell stopped, turning to face him. "Beyond these doors lies Pinnacle's private domain. I cannot go further."

"You're leaving me?" Kaden said.

"My Elites will accompany you. They answer to Pinnacle, but they will protect you as long as they can." She placed a weathered hand on his shoulder. "Remember what you've seen, Kaden. Remember who you are."

Kaden tried to force himself into confidence. The memory of bullets stopping before Dr. Thornhill entered his mind. The pain in his chest as he shot them back. The taste of his own blood as he choked on it.

“Do you want to know your scent, why the Elites react to you the way they do?”

Kaden nodded.

"You smell like him."

"Pinnacle?" Kaden gasped.

"No." She shook her head. "You smell like Jericho," she said, holding his eyes. "You have his scent because there's a part of him in you. Jericho lives, and it's in you, Kaden McCloud."

Before he could respond, the massive doors began to open, revealing a darkness deeper than any Kaden had encountered. Beth-ell stepped back, her face impassive, but Kaden thought he saw a flicker of something in her eyes – regret, perhaps. Or fear.

The Elites moved forward, guiding Kaden toward the open doors. As he stepped over the threshold, the air grew colder, heavy with a presence that pressed against his consciousness like a physical weight.

The doors closed behind him with a sound of finality. Ahead, in the dimness, something moved – a figure seated on a raised platform that resembled a throne. It leaned forward, and Kaden caught a glimpse of familiar features twisted into an unfamiliar smile.

"Welcome home, Agent McCloud," Pinnacle said.

Chapter 16

Entry #4

I stood on the northern cliffs today, watching storm clouds gather on the horizon. They're coming – the wars, the plagues, the final gasps of a world that chose power over healing. I see it all now, each domino falling in sequence. The Hope Drug will spread through the population, a cancer masquerading as cure, and the glowing embers of nuclear war will paint the sky the color of blood. Ninety-nine percent will fall. Tears of our elders will cry from eternity.

Of those who survive, another ninety-nine percent will perish in the aftermath. Eight billion down to less than ten thousand, and those that remain will be forever changed. The Hope Drug is already inside all the eventual survivors.

Thomas calls it evolution. Natural selection. The birth of his "New Breed." He cannot see that he's become the serpent in the garden, promising godhood through forbidden fruit. Or perhaps he does already see, and that's precisely why he pushes forward with such conviction. Before I came north, I saw his skin. It ripples with patches of obsidian black, like an evil crawling under his flesh. The others on the board pretend not to notice, too afraid to speak up. They don't realize they're watching their own extinction unfold before them.

I have shifted as time has shifted around me. David Abrams is a memory – a doctor passionate about healing the world through science. Thomas said my avoidance of 'necessary evolution' was a weakness, as if I was the walls of the doomed Jericho, waiting for the trumpets of God for me to fall. The irony of his comment is lost on him, the walls of his great city will fall on my command. I adopt his insult and turn the other cheek.

Now I stand as Jericho, a tear in my eye as I watch humanity tear itself apart, knowing I must let them choose their path. My heart weeps for their sorrow. The power in my blood could stop this. I could reach out across time and space, tear Thomas's empire down before it begins. But that would make me no different from him – another tyrant forcing his will upon the world.

Cold snow flurries around me as I excavate the earth to build. The foundations of Empyrean rise before me, built and yet to be built. A city of towers and shadows, the last refuge of a dying species. I see its greatness, and I see its fall. Like Eden, like Babel, like every city of man – it will corrupt from within. The Tower will rise at its center, reaching toward heaven but casting its shadow over all. I see the stone-skinned Elites prowling its halls, their hunger never satisfied. I see the Agents in their colored robes, believing they serve order while enabling chaos. I see the masses in the Outer Ring, crushed under the weight of control disguised as protection.

But that is why I will also build the Lighthouse.

Let them have their tower of iron and glass. Let them believe they've built a kingdom that reaches to Heaven. The Lighthouse will stand as a reminder that there is always another way. A beacon of hope visible on the horizon even from the depths of their darkness. While their tower seeks to pierce the heavens, my Lighthouse will guide people home. They venture into the desert of the unknown to overcome their greatest flaw.

I've begun construction already, though the end of the old world is still years away. The foundation must be strong to weather what's coming. Not just concrete and steel, but truth and hope set like cornerstones. The light at its top will burn with the same power that flows through my blood – not the corrupted version that transforms flesh to stone, but the pure light that heals and reveals.

Thomas believes the destruction of the old world is necessary for his new order. He doesn't understand that true order cannot be imposed – it must be chosen, just like love. So, after I build, I will give them a choice. The Tower or the Light. Control or freedom. Death or life. The survivors will need both – a place to shelter and a light to follow. Empyrean will be their refuge, but the Lighthouse will be their hope.

In the future, I see the faces of those who will look to the light. Their skin grows bright in contrast to the dark stone of their enemies. Generation after generation, seeking something more than The Tower's cold comfort. Some will make the journey across the wasteland, drawn by the beacon. Others will form the Remnant within Empyrean itself, keeping faith alive in the shadows of The Tower. I see their triumphs and their sacrifices, their moments of doubt and their unwavering hope.

I record these words knowing they will survive even after the city falls into shadow, and I see my own end in this story. My heart is in another's hands, but I also see what grows. The seeds of hope, planted in blood and watered with tears, will bloom even in The Tower's rubble.

Dr. Abrams and his family are gone, a past I can visit in my mind but no longer identify with. The horrible events of humanity's latest downfall rewrites history. Today, I am Jericho, watchman on the walls of a city yet to be built. Tomorrow, I will be legend, then myth, then hope reborn. The cycle continues, the light endures, and those who choose to see will find their way home.

Let those with ears to hear, hear.

Let those with eyes to see, see.

Chapter 17

Kaden

His form was both familiar and alien – the handsome features of Dr. Thomas Thornhill but evolved into this new ruler of Empyrean. He was still recognizable beneath moving patches of obsidian skin that spread across his face like a disease. His eyes, once dark and ambitious, now gleamed with an internal light that almost hurt to look at directly.

"Welcome home, Agent McCloud," Pinnacle said. “How’s your chest, Darren? Or is this an entirely new body?”

Kaden froze, his breath catching in his throat. Hearing his other name spoken aloud here, in this place, sent ice through his veins.

A thin smile stretched across Pinnacle’s face, revealing teeth that seemed too white, too perfect.

Pinnacle continued, rising from his throne with fluid grace. "Did you think I wouldn't recognize the boy who tried to put four bullets in my chest? Especially when he keeps appearing in my city, wearing a different name, different hair, but carrying the same... scent."

He descended the steps from his platform, each footfall soundless against the black floor as if never exactly touching the floor. As he moved, the patches of stone-like skin across his face and hands seemed to shift, sometimes expanding, sometimes receding, as if his very body was in constant flux.

He raised his hands and Beth-ell's two Elites slid back. Kaden heard them grunt, as if trying to fight, but Kaden knew the force on them; he'd felt it before Jericho saved him and Kira.

"Your scent is stronger now. I recognize who you are now," Pinnacle said, circling Kaden like a predator. "In My Tower, from white to blue, but all along a boy playing Jericho's game."

"I'm not a boy anymore," Kaden said. "I put away childish ideas, like your robes and ranks."

Pinnacle feigned surprise.

"And He's not playing games." Kaden found his voice, steadier than he expected.

"No?" Pinnacle laughed, the sound cracking through the air like thunder. "Then what would you call sending a child to do a man's work? What would you call hiding behind time itself for centuries instead of facing me directly? I'd say once he stopped playing, then his *heart wasn't in it anymore.*" He raised his eyebrows to add punctuation to his pun.

Kaden remained silent.

The chamber darkened further as Pinnacle spoke, as if shadows grew like vines up the walls. From the corner of his eye, Kaden saw Beth-ell's Elites tense, their rigid bodies somehow communicating alarm despite their expressionless faces.

"You speak of Jericho as if he's still alive," Kaden said, struggling to keep his voice steady. "We both watched him die."

"Did we?" He gestured to the shadows behind his throne. "Come. I have something to show you."

The shadows behind the throne parted like a curtain, revealing an Elite-like figure unlike any Kaden had ever seen. Where the Elites were solid, this being was fluid, its form constantly shifting like smoke caught in a breeze. Still tall and strong, but unlike their charcoal-stone skin, this creature seemed made of living darkness itself – a void given form. It moved with a terrible grace, wisps of shadow trailing behind it like ghostly fingers.

In its center, suspended in the darkness, pulsed an object that gleamed with red light. Jericho's heart – still beating, still alive.

"Beautiful, isn't it?" Pinnacle whispered, his voice almost reverent. "The heart of the only being who ever truly challenged me. The creator whose creation exceeded him."

Kaden couldn't tear his eyes from the grotesque sight. The heart beat with a steady rhythm, seemingly untethered to anybody, its light pulsing through the chamber like a beacon.

"What have you done?" Kaden breathed.

"I've kept it alive," Pinnacle said simply. "Just as I've kept you alive, or really allowed you to live. Did you think it was coincidence that you kept returning? That death can't seem to hold you?"

He moved closer to the shadow-Elite, running his hand through its darkness as one might caress a beloved pet. The creature shuddered, the wisps of its form weaving between his fingers.

"I created the Hope Drug to extend life, to evolve humanity beyond its limitations. Even in my earliest trials, I saw the possibilities." Pinnacle's voice took on a lecturing tone, as if he were still a doctor explaining a procedure. "Oh, how I love recalling those times, so long ago. But Jericho – David – he could never see the forest for the trees. Always worried about the 'side effects' of progress. I moved us forward."

The shadow-Elite shifted, moving closer to Kaden. He could feel its cold emanating like an open freezer, the air around it growing heavier as if it were freezing the very atmosphere.

"But then he lost it." He shrugged. "Changing the world isn't for everyone," he said before eyeing Kaden's confused expression and building on his speech.

"You know he killed his family, right? Then disappeared, running away to the Canadian wilderness as he fled authorities. Did he tell you that part? How he murdered his own family in the explosion at his house?"

"That's a lie," Kaden said immediately, though doubt flickered in his mind. The memory of driving to Dr. Abrams' residence, the house being destroyed, and Jericho hiding around the crime scene.

"Is it?" Pinnacle's eyes flashed with that painful light again. "He killed others too. It wasn't just his family. Our colleagues went to visit him, to handle business he'd been avoiding. No one left that house except him. He lost control. Why else do you think he hides, never surfacing for all this time? I would have loved to have him here at The Tower, working for me and a better world, but no... One of the brightest minds I've ever known... Such a waste." He shook his head.

"If that's true, why didn't you expose him? Turn him in to the authorities?" Kaden challenged.

Pinnacle laughed again, the sound echoing unnaturally. "Because by then, I had already seen what was coming. The wars, the plagues – the old world was on its path. Why waste time with human justice when the divine was at hand?"

He moved to a black surface near his throne. It shifted like liquid beneath his waving hand and a 3D image arising from the opaque surface – familiar landscapes rose then turned to wasteland, famous city skylines erected then reduced to rubble.

"The end came, just as we both foresaw. But while Jericho hid in his Lighthouse, pretending to save souls in his guilt, I built Empyrean. I gathered the strongest. I showed them how to survive in a world that was trying to kill them." Pride radiated from him like heat. "I saved humanity."

"You enslaved them," Kaden countered.

Pinnacle looked at him, a flash of anger showing as his eyes squinted, and Kaden felt his throat tighten. He gasped for breath and his throat released as Pinnacle's flicker of anger went to mild amusement.

"I built the New Breed," Pinnacle corrected. "I gave them purpose, direction. Some became Agents, maintaining day-to-day order. Others ensured all the necessary functions of a working world. While a few select..." He gestured to the Elites at Kaden's side. "Others became more. And we consistently evolve, a select few..." His gaze went to the shadow-Elite. "A precious few transcended far more than I could have first thought."

The creature seemed to preen under Pinnacle's attention, its darkness deepening, expanding.

"But Jericho," Pinnacle's face darkened, "Jericho could never accept the necessity of my methods. He kept interfering, sending his followers to sabotage my work, to 'rescue' people who were perfectly content in their roles."

His hand clenched, and the shadow-Elite visibly recoiled. The two were as one. "Worst of all, he found a way to move through time itself. To reach back and influence events, to plant seeds of rebellion even before Empyrean was built. Cockroaches... They never die."

Pinnacle's gaze fixed on Kaden with sudden intensity. "That's where you come in, Darren McArthur, Kaden McCloud. A vessel, carrying his influence across centuries. I knew you were different the moment you walked into this tower. Now all the dots are connected."

Kaden took an involuntary step back, but Beth-ell's Elites were held there, preventing retreat.

Pinnacle moved toward him so fast, it was like he teleported. He reached out, his fingers hovering inches from Kaden's face. "You carry his power within you. A fraction of it, yes, but enough. Enough to make you valuable. Enough to make you... delicious."

The word hung in the air like a line of drool off a dog's mouth.

Kaden realized the truth crashing down on him like a physical weight. He was brought back to be consumed.

Then a glimmer of hope popped into his mind. "You can't consume Jericho. You'd have all his power and memories already if you could," Kaden said.

"Which is too bad for you." Pinnacle seemed unfazed. "Our game of cat and mouse was nice, for a while. Tracking the Remnant here and there was like stomping out a bug that scurries along, but alas, now you're more useful in a different way."

He circled Kaden again, appraising him like merchandise. "When I consume you, I'll gain access to everything he's shown you. Every vision, every truth, every secret he's whispered across time. And then I'll go to the others close to you."

"Kira," Kaden whispered, horror dawning.

Pinnacle nodded. "Another vessel, another piece of the puzzle. Between you both, I'll unlock his magic tricks through time, how he continued to influence your life back and forth even after I ripped his heart from his chest."

Kaden stood motionless.

"Then after you two, I'll come back for the greater prize. With you in me, I'll consume his corpse, starting with the heart," he said, raising his hand back and forth like an orchestra conductor. The heart shifted in the hands of the shadowy figure, dancing as if on a puppet's strings.

"And once I have that power," Pinnacle continued, his voice dropping to a whisper, "The Tower will rise not just here, but everywhere, in every time."

The enormity of the threat stole Kaden's breath. This wasn't just about control of a single city, or even a single world. This was about the very fabric of reality itself.

"No," he managed.

"Fighting reality is no way to handle it," Pinnacle corrected, and his skin rippled with blackness and a haze of darkness rolled off him that blended with the shadow-Elite. The two were somehow one, the shadow an extension of him.

It moved forward, darkness extending toward Kaden like reaching hands. At the same time, Beth-ell's Elites slid back, their feet scraping the ground as Pinnacle pushed them away, their protection withdrawn.

"This is a great honor, your ascension. You will live forever in me," Pinnacle said, his chest puffing up like a bodybuilder preparing to flex.

The shadowy tendrils brushed Kaden's skin, colder than ice and burning like dry ice pressed to skin. He tried to pull away, but his body wouldn't respond, frozen in place by an unseen force. He felt his skin pull, the fabric of his being unnaturally stretched as the shadow prodded at him, tasting him.

"Your friend Jericho taught that the greatest love is to lay down one's life for one's friends," Pinnacle mocked. "Consider this your opportunity to show the ultimate love – giving your life to fuel the new creation."

The darkness of the Shadow Elite began to cover Kaden, creeping up his arms like a sun setting over a vibrant forest. Through the encroaching blackness, he could see the heart. It seemed to call to him with something deep within his cells. His body stretched in multiple directions as the darkness encased him, pulling at his soul.

Kaden's vision began to dim, the cold penetrating deeper, reaching for his core. He realized he was powerless at that moment. He could do nothing to stop this evil. With his last conscious thought on Jericho's heart, he reached out – not physically, but with something beyond the physical. A surrender to Jericho, a plea to be saved by the heart of a dead man.

The heart pulsed in response, its light intensifying instead by Pinnacle's manipulation.

And somewhere, in the depths of the tunnels beneath Empyrean, Kira's eyes snapped open as she felt a call she couldn't explain but instantly understood.

Chapter 18

Entry #5

The first refugees arrived today. A family of four, thin as rails and eyes hollow with hunger. They saw the Lighthouse beam cutting through the nuclear winter and walked for three weeks to reach us. The children's hair is falling out in clumps, but somehow their hope remains intact. The same hope that brought them here may be the only thing keeping them alive. Soon, they will die, but they leave breadcrumbs for others.

More will come. Streams of survivors flowing north like rivers in the wasteland. Each carries the Hope Drug in their blood, a poisoned salvation. Most don't understand what's happening to their bodies yet. As they feel renewed strength they believe they're blessed.

Thomas calls himself Pinnacle now. His broadcasts still reach us, even this far north. His voice crackles through the static, promising sanctuary in Empyrean. "Come to THE Tower," he says, "THE ONE place where order prevails and humanity evolves." What he doesn't tell them is the cost. I've seen his first "successes" – their skin black as coal, their hunger insatiable, and their power growing. They're already hunting the weak, consuming them to fuel their transformation. The energy and twisted pleasure from consuming livestock isn't enough for them. It never was.

The changes manifest differently in each survivor. Some, like those in Empyrean, turn to living stone. Others develop abilities they can't control – bursts of strength, moments of precognition, devastating waves of force. But a rare few, perhaps one in a thousand, show signs of true healing. Their flesh doesn't harden; their hunger doesn't grow. Instead, they begin to glow from within, like candles pushing back the dark. It is a mental state they have grown into that overcomes the fixed mindset that the stone survivors have become. The new minority are becoming increasingly unwelcome to those who grow to stone.

I'm building more than just the Lighthouse now. Underground chambers, hydroponics labs, medical facilities – everything needed to sustain life in this desolate world. The power in my blood lets me work faster than should be possible, bending space and time to accomplish in days what would take decades.

The hardest part is already knowing which ones will turn. I see it in their futures – which refugees will remain human and which will succumb to the hunger. Sometimes I catch them watching me with calculating eyes, their skin beginning to mottle and harden. They think I don't notice, their newfound strength building immense pride, but I see every step their transformation will take.

A group of thirty foreshadowed the coming storm of Empyrean. Their leader's eyes were already going black, the hunger beginning to show. He begged me to heal his group, yet before they arrived, half his group had been consumed by the other half. I heard their screams echo across the deserts. Being able to travel across time is a great power, but hearing the constant sounds of death scream from the past and future are the costs.

The survivors are learning to build, to farm, to heal. We're creating something sustainable here, a community based on giving rather than taking. But I see the shadow of The Tower in every success. For each person I teach to heal, Thomas creates ten who destroy. For every crop we grow or animal brought into the world, his Elites consume a hundred.

Tonight, as I write these words, I can hear children laughing in the underground chambers. New friendships forming, new bonds being forged in the crucible of survival. This is what Thomas doesn't understand – that true strength comes not from consuming others, but from lifting them up.

Soon I'll return to Empyrean, with souls of the past. The city needs to be built, the foundations laid for both salvation and trial. But here, in this moment, watching survivors become family and strangers become friends, I see the love of humanity, its potential. Not evolved through force, but transformed through choice.

Let the Tower rise. Let the Elites prowl their shadowed halls. Here in the north, where the light still burns, we remember what it means to be human.

This bitter cup awaits me. Still, not my will, but what must be done.

Chapter 19

Kira

"We need to move faster," Kira said, calling up to Jace ahead of her.

They clung to the side of a crumpled elevator shaft. The same lift that shielded Jace and Aria from the explosions Kira and team had laid in the labs before The Tower that overlooked the pastures. The same explosions that sent Kaden back to being Darren and left burn-scarring across some of the team.

"We can only climb so fast," Jace said back.

"Yeah, big boy back there is struggling as it is," Aria said from below Kira. "Come on, tough guy. It's all in the legs," Aria chided him.

Riggs grunted from his spot below. His forearms twitched as he gripped the damaged side of the shaft. He finally reached a narrow platform where he could put more weight on his feet and stretch his hands. His large upper body awkwardly angled to stay close to the wall.

"Easy for you to say. You're all skinny enough to stay close enough to use your feet," Riggs replied.

"I'm serious, Kaden is in trouble. We need to hurry," Kira insisted. She began climbing faster.

"I know, that's why we're here, to help out Kaden," Jace said.

"You don't understand." She climbed faster, now passing Jace. The sensation stuck with her, the urge to find him knowing he was in grave danger.

"We can't just jump out and say hi. Follow the plan, slow and strong," Jace said.

Kira didn't argue anymore, but kept on climbing faster. Her foot slipped once as she reached for a grip higher than she should have gone for, but through sheer determination, she moved up the shaft as if she were speed-walking.

Soon, a sliver of light poked through a crack in the unused doors above. Kira made it to them and began prying them open with her fingers.

Jace soon caught up. "Wait and listen; there could be anything on the other side of these," he whispered. He leaned his ear against the doors, but Kira didn't wait. Her fingers were wedged in enough for her to pop the doors. Once she overcame the initial friction, the doors slid open easily.

Jace held his breath as if the light from The Tower were a prison spotlight on an escaping inmate. Kira jumped out without a word or extra thought.

"Hey." Aria caught up. "Did she just?"

"Yup," Jace said. "Let's go."

The pair jumped out.

Meanwhile, below them, echoing up the shaft, Riggs grunted as he tried catching up.

Kira found herself in a dimly lit corridor. These weren't the sterile, white and steel hallways of The Tower's lower levels they had described to her. As she moved forward, unexpected changes appeared, darker materials on this level. The stainless steel walls grow opaque. They seemed to absorb light rather than reflect it, creating an atmosphere of perpetual twilight instead of the clean lab-like environment she first saw.

"Kira!" Jace hissed, scrambling after her with Aria close behind. "You can't just—"

"Shh!" She held up her hand, her head tilted as if listening to a distant sound no one else could hear. The pull was stronger now, an invisible tether drawing her forward. "This way."

She moved with purpose, no longer bothering to check corners or hide from security cameras. Something beyond conscious thought guided her steps, like an invisible tether.

Jace now noticed the walls and considered the implications. Aria ran up behind him and they locked eyes, expressions of concern washing over them as they eyed the black walls that were like deep space – devoid of light and life.

“We went too high,” Jace whispered, trying to call out to Kira.

“No, it’s changing. The Tower isn’t the same...” Aria said, leaning in close to examine the walls.

“Either way, she’s gone again,” Jace said as he darted away.

"Kira," Aria whispered, taking off to catch up. "This level isn’t for Blue Agents. We're in Brown territory now. Or worse..."

"But where is everyone?" Jace asked, his eyes darting to each shadowy corner they passed.

He was right. The hallways were eerily empty, devoid of the usual patrols that should have been present.

Far behind them came a muffled curse and the sound of metal groaning. Riggs hauled himself through the elevator doors, his large frame barely squeezing through the gap.

"Next time," he panted, "we find another way in."

"There shouldn't be a next time," Jace said as Riggs caught up. "Once Beth-ell realizes we're here—"

"She knows," Kira interrupted, her voice distant. "She's a part of this, somehow..."

The certainty in her tone gave them pause. Riggs exchanged a look with Jace, both men raising their eyebrows.

"It's getting worse," Kira continued, now starting to move ahead again. "Whatever Pinnacle's doing to him—" Her voice caught. "We have to hurry."

They moved deeper into The Tower's upper reaches. The hallways grew stranger, the architecture more unsettling. Angles that shouldn't be built or even possible, hallways that led to dead ends where doors should have been, and materials that seemed to shift when viewed from different perspectives. The Tower seemed alive itself.

"This isn't right," Aria muttered. "These corridors... they're all wrong."

"Pinnacle's work?" Jace theorized. "We've never been this high. Maybe the higher you go, the more his influence warps The Tower itself."

Riggs grunted in acknowledgment. "Feels like these walls have eyes. It's creepy."

A sound echoed from around the corner ahead – footsteps, multiple sets, approaching rapidly. Kira didn't slow down.

"Kira!" Jace lunged forward, grabbing her arm. "We need to hide."

Before she could protest, a group of Agents came around the corner. The groups of blue-robed Agents stopped, caught off guard and confused by this unexpected group.

Jace and Aria froze in surprise at who they saw.

Ryon stood at the front, his massive frame dwarfing the other Agents. Beside him was Vala, her face set in a cold mask of efficiency, the scar from the bull's horn a line on the side of her face. Four other Agents flanked them, their fingers touching the handle of their Spark Clubs like a gunslinger ready to draw.

For a moment, no one spoke or moved, a silent standoff as the opaque walls surrounded them. Then Ryon's face shifted to rage.

"Traitors!" he snarled, targeting Jace and Aria.

"So it's true. You left us for the Remnant," Vala said in disgust.

"You need to let us pass," Jace said, his voice steady despite the tension crackling through the air.

Ryon let out a bark of laughter. "That's not going to happen." He activated his Spark Club, the weapon humming to life with deadly energy. "No more sparring on the mats."

Vala and the other Agents followed suit, Spark Clubs casting an eerie electric glow across the dim hallway.

Ryon stared down Jace as Vala's eyes never left Aria's face.

"Last chance," Ryon said, his voice dropping to a menacing growl. "Surrender now, and maybe Pinnacle lets you live long enough to see tomorrow."

"We don't have time for this," Kira muttered, the pull toward Kaden growing more urgent with each passing second.

Riggs stepped forward, cracking his knuckles. "Then let's not waste any more."

The hallway erupted into chaos.

Ryon charged straight for Jace, Spark Club swinging in a deadly arc. Jace ducked beneath the blow, his training evident in his fluid movements as he countered with a strike to Ryon's midsection. Vala moved to Aria, their fight more measured as Aria went defensive to avoid the Spark Club.

Riggs met the remaining Agents head-on, his size and brute strength making up for his lack of a weapon. He grabbed one Agent's arm mid-swing and used the man's momentum to hurl him into a wall with bone-crushing force. As he swung the Agent, the other connected his Spark Club with Riggs's shoulder. He let out a growl, but more of annoyance than of pain as his left arm went limp, muscles twitching near the impact. His oversized hand shot forward and grabbed the Agent's wrist that held the Spark Club, shoving it back toward the man's chest.

Riggs's face tensed as he forced the man to electrocute himself. A crackling filled the air with the smell of burnt flesh. Finally, Riggs was able to let go. He shook his once limp arm, opening and closing his hand as if waking it from sleep.

Two more Agents stared at Riggs, now more measured in their approach.

Kira dodged past the fighting, intent on finding Kaden. One Agent broke away from Riggs to pursue her, Spark Club raised.

"Kira, look out!" Aria shouted as she dove away from Vala.

Time seemed to slow as Kira turned. The Agent's Spark Club descended toward her head in what should have been a killing blow. But instead of fear, something else welled up inside her.

She raised her hand to shield herself, but the contact never came.

A flicker of light emanated from her hand and the Spark Club deflected, narrowly missing her skull, and crashed down, cracking the floor next to her.

The Agent stumbled, the momentum of the miss carrying him off balance.

Everyone froze, noticing the bright flash of light in the dim hallway. They stopped their fight and stared at Kira.

"What was that?" Ryon's voice was barely above a whisper, his fight with Jace momentarily forgotten.

Kira looked down at her hands in confusion. They glowed with a pale light that pulsed in rhythm with her heartbeat. The sensation was familiar somehow, like remembering a dream she'd forgotten.

Before anyone could react, cracks erupted in the walls around them. The ceiling shifted and pieces fell. Aria dove, grabbing Vala, and pulling her out of the way as a chunk of black building smashed where they were once fighting. Vala pushed her off as the floor began cracking around the devastation.

Riggs moved and shielded Kira, while Ryon held up his Spark Club and knocked away a block from above him and Jace.

“Time to go,” Jace called out.

“Kaden is still up there!” Kira called out.

Amongst the shouting and chaos, the two groups scrambled together, Remnant and Agents standing side-by-side as The Tower broke around them.

Then it all stopped.

Like watching a movie in rewind, the cracks reversed and sealed themselves. The fallen pieces defied gravity and rose back to their place.

“What in the world...” Riggs growled.

“I want to leave even more now,” Jace insisted.

“It’s repaired, we move on,” Kira replied.

“No, this is worse,” Jace said. He looked to Aria and she nodded a quick agreement.

“Worse than crushed if it all collapsed?” Riggs interjected.

The Agents began to shift, standing together as they stood tall and confident.

"Elites." Jace's face went pale. "We need to move, now!"

“The Tower cannot fall,” Vala said. “He won’t allow it, and therefore, they won’t allow it.”

Jace took a step away but Ryon reached out and grabbed his shirt. "I can't let a traitor go," he forced out through gritted teeth.

"You're welcome with us. Get away from their control," Jace whispered to him.

Ryon squinted, pulling Jace in closer, their faces an inch apart.

"The Tower cannot fall," Ryon said back.

"It will. Jericho died for us, and for *you* too," Jace said.

The comment threw Ryon off, his anger dissipating into a flash of confusion, but quickly, he allowed the rage and desire for control to bubble back to the surface.

"You're not leaving," Ryon commanded, gripping him tighter as he began to unholster his Spark Club.

"Then I'm sorry, old friend," Jace said. In a flash, one hand reached and grabbed the back of Ryon's hand that held his shirt. He twisted it back, causing obvious pain. As Ryon winced, Jace's other hand shot down toward the Spark Club and ripped it away. The quick motion caught Ryon off guard, but he rescinded quickly, shooting a jab at Jace's temple with the hand that just lost the club.

Jace dropped low as he took the club, avoiding the brunt of the punch, but it caught the side of his head. His head bounced to the side from the impact, but he shook it off and moved like a boxer bobbing away, and still he held the club. Instead of turning it to the traditional position where he could ignite the deadly sparks, he held it backwards, his grip in the middle of the long rod that held the electrified ball. With Ryon's weight shifted forward, Jace rose back up and jabbed Ryon's side with the handle of his own club, striking his lowest rib. A cracking sound rang out and Ryon let out a shout of pain as he stumbled back, holding his side.

"Let's go!" Jace said, throwing the club down the hall and taking off. "The Elites are coming!"

"Restrain them!" Vala shouted.

The other Agents reached for their Spark Clubs and stepped around Ryon, but Riggs put his shoulder down and slammed into the Agent on the side. The much lighter man fell into the other Agent, who then slammed into Vala, the entire group falling over themselves.

"Kaden is still—" Kira tried to say, but Riggs scooped her up and sprinted after Jace and Aria.

They turned a corner, heading back to the center shaft, but the walls in this area were still falling apart. The entrance to the shaft was crumpled and filled with debris, impassable.

"Come on, this way," Aria called out and took off down another path.

"Aria..." Jace called out from behind as they followed.

"The vent system," she announced.

"Are you sure about that?" Jace replied, uncertain.

"Not at all," she said plainly.

The floors cracked and pieces of the ceiling fell as they darted through the halls. Behind them, the structure was fully restored.

"There!" Aria stopped at a large air intake. "Well, big guy, this is going to be uncomfortable." She looked at Riggs.

Riggs looked down at the small vent. "Ain't no way I'm fittin' in there."

Aria stomped on the side of the vent, breaking it open. With the wall crumbling around her, she ripped off the vent and tossed it aside.

"Either this or the Elites," she said, then without a thought, she jumped in, sliding away into the darkness.

"Ugh," Riggs said.

"Imagine you're smaller than you are, pull your arms in close," Jace said with a smirk, then he jumped in behind Aria.

"After you." Riggs turned to Kira.

"I can't leave Kaden. He called me here," she replied.

"You can't save him if you're dead. We'll find another way," Riggs said.

"Can you even fit?" Kira said.

"I don't... know..." Riggs put his legs in and wiggled his shoulders. "I hate these—"

A large crack around the vent began sealing and the small vent began constricting around him.

"Get in and go," Kira said. "They're close."

"Not without you—" Riggs started to say, but then his shoulders slipped through and his weight took him sliding down the vent like those before him.

Kira stood, looking back down the hallway behind her and then down at the vent below her waist. She cringed at the thought of leaving Kaden, but she knew that trying to take a pack of Elites head on wasn't the best way to save him.

She dropped down and slid her feet in the opening. Looking back, she saw dark figures come into view. At least five Elites were shooting toward her. They moved as if they flew over the ground instead of running. Leaning forward with their legs straight back, they hovered above the ground and shot forward toward her. Three of them focused on the walls around them, putting the damage back to their perfection, while the other two accelerated toward her.

She clenched her fists, furious at the idea of leaving Kaden.

"I'm coming back for you," she said, then dipped in and let herself slide down into the darkness.

She slid at an amazing speed, bouncing side-to-side as she shot straight down. Her straight black hair was flying up as she fell.

But then, she stopped mid-air. She winced in pain as her body jolted to a stop, as if hit by a car. Then she began to rise, being pulled up.

"No, no, no!" she said.

She looked up. At a distance above her, she saw a black figure in the faint light. Its cracked, charcoal fingers stretched toward her, pulling her up.

Chapter 20

Kaden

The shadow-Elite's darkness enveloped Kaden. He could feel its cold and hungry presence reaching through his skin toward his inner being. It wasn't just his body being consumed – he felt the creature probing for his memories, his thoughts, the very essence of who he was. Through the encroaching void, he could still see Jericho's heart, suspended in the center of the shadow creature like a beacon in a storm.

Pinnacle watched with delight, a thin smile stretching across his features where patches of obsidian skin shifted and swirled. Pieces of the shadow-Elite also warped around Pinnacle, as if the hazy black cloud were combining them.

The shadow's tendrils tightened around Kaden, squeezing the breath from his lungs as it pulled at the fabric of his being. His vision tunneled, darkness and intense cold creeping in from all sides. Every instinct screamed at him to fight, to pull away, but his limbs felt lifeless, unresponsive.

His eyes found Jericho’s heart once again as it sat beyond his grasp, a small red dot, a mere pin-prick of surrounding darkness, but still it was there. A thought came to his mind.

Once you see, you can't unsee.

The memory of Jericho's words cut through the darkness, clear as if the man were standing beside him. In that moment, Kaden saw – truly saw – the heart beating in the center of the shadow-Elite. It wasn't just an organ; it was a connection, a tether to something greater.

As consciousness began to slip away, Kaden reached out – not with his hands, but with something deeper, something that had always been there but never awakened. He reached for the heart with all his being, giving himself over to it, for Jericho, for the light, and not for himself.

The response was immediate. The heart pulsed once, twice, then began to beat in perfect synchrony with Kaden's own. Heat spread through his chest, pushing back against the cold of the shadow's embrace. Power surged through him – not the ravenous, hungry power of the Elites, but something cleaner, brighter, and with immense strength.

Light exploded from within Kaden, brilliant white radiance that burst from his skin like the sun breaking through storm clouds. The shadow-Elite recoiled with a sound like tearing fabric, its darkness fragmenting as the light pierced through it. For a moment, Jericho's heart glowed even brighter at the center of the creature, as if responding to Kaden's light.

Pinnacle's smile vanished, replaced by shock and then rage. "Impossible," he snarled, raising his hand toward Kaden.

The invisible force that had held Kaden tightened, but the light surrounding him seemed to act as a buffer, weakening Pinnacle's grip. Behind him, Beth-ell's Elites broke free of their restraint, moving with startling speed to flank Kaden.

"Consume him," Pinnacle commanded the shadow-Elite. The creature lurched forward again, but Kaden's light flared in response, pushing it back.

The room shuddered as the powers collided. Hairline fractures appeared in the dark walls, spreading like veins across the surface. The floor beneath their feet groaned as if under immense pressure.

Pinnacle's eyes widened as he looked around, momentary panic replacing the rage. "My Tower," he whispered, and for the first time, Kaden saw fear in those inhuman eyes.

Beth-ell's Elites seized the opportunity. They grabbed Kaden, one under each arm, and dragged him backward toward the massive doors. Dazed from the surge of power, Kaden stumbled between them, his body tingling with the aftermath of the light.

Pinnacle's attention was divided now. One hand remained stretched toward Kaden, invisible force tugging at him like a rope, while the other reached out to the fracturing wall. The shadow-Elite flowed to his side, its darkness spreading across the cracks as if trying to hold them together.

"I will have you," Pinnacle growled, an eerily confident smile crossing his face as his skin rippled with darkness.

The pull intensified, and Kaden felt himself sliding forward despite the Elites' grip. His feet scraped against the floor as Pinnacle's power dragged him back.

Then something shifted. Through the haze of pain and confusion, Kaden felt a call – distant but unmistakable. Kira. She was in The Tower, coming for him. The realization gave him strength, and the light within him pulsed once more.

The wave of energy that emanated from him wasn't as bright as before, but it was enough to momentarily break Pinnacle's concentration. His hold slipped, and Kaden lurched backward into the waiting arms of

Beth-ell's Elites as the cracks around the room intensified. Pieces of wall and ceiling began falling.

"Go!" Kaden gasped, finding his voice at last.

The doors swung open, and they half-carried, half-dragged him through. Behind them, Pinnacle's roar of fury was drowned out by the sound of cracking stone as The Tower violently shook.

The corridors outside were in chaos. Cracks spiderwebbed across the walls and ceiling, pieces falling away only to freeze mid-air and slowly return to their places while others shattered across the obsidian floor. Elites moved through the halls with purpose, their hands pressed against the fracturing surfaces, their bodies seeming to meld with The Tower itself as they poured their power into maintaining its structure.

Beth-ell's Elites didn't pause. They carried Kaden through the maelstrom, avoiding falling debris and rushing Agents who barely spared them a glance, too focused on their own desperate attempts to maintain order.

They reached the central elevator, its door warped from the stress on The Tower's structure. One Elite motioned to the doors and forced them open, metal groaning in protest. Once inside, the other pressed its stone-like hand against the scanner, but there was no response. The shifting structures rendered the lift useless. But without hesitation, both Elites shifted their hands and Kaden heard an intense scraping sound as the elevator shifted into life, beginning its descent. The glass side of the elevator cracked and shattered open, wind rushing into the chamber.

The levels of The Tower flashed by. Everywhere was the same scene of controlled panic – Agents rushing to stations, Elites merging with the structure, the very fabric of The Tower fighting to maintain its integrity. It was as if the entire structure were a living thing in the throes of a seizure, and every inhabitant a cell desperately trying to maintain function.

"Kira," Kaden managed to say, his voice hoarse. "She's here. In The Tower. We have to find her."

The Elites gave no response. Their focus remained on the descent, on escape. Whatever loyalty or protection they felt toward Kaden apparently didn't extend to rescue missions.

The elevator slowed, approaching the lobby level. The Elites opened the door and Kaden saw a figure waiting – tall, robed in purple, face set in cold concentration. Before anyone inside could respond, the Agent had him by the throat.

Kaden locked eyes with his former mentor.

Ron-ell.

"Traitor," he hissed, eyes blazing with fury.

The Elites stepped forward, ready to protect their passenger, but before they responded, the crack of electricity popped behind Ron-ell and his eyes rolled back in his head.

Beth-ell stood behind him, a Spark Club in her hand crackling. "It's time to go," she said.

Chapter 21

Kira

Kira slid through darkness, the sleek and cold metal shaft flying past her as she slid down. For a moment, she felt weightless, gravity pulling her down. Her body ricocheted from wall to wall, but then she stopped – not a gradual slowing, but an abrupt, impossible halt that wrenched her spine and knocked the breath from her lungs.

She hung suspended in the darkness, unable to move forward or back. The sensation wasn't physical restraint but something more fundamental, as if gravity itself had been twisted around her. Then, slowly, she began to rise.

"No, no, no!" she cried out, panic clawing at her throat.

Her body scraped against the metal walls as she was pulled upward, back toward the entrance. Looking up, she saw it – a sliver of light growing larger, and within it, the silhouette of an Elite. Its charcoal fingers stretched toward her, conducting her ascent like a puppet master pulling strings.

Kira thrashed wildly, her hands desperately clawing against the smooth metal walls. But there was nothing to grip, nothing to brace against. She was caught in the Elite's invisible hold.

"Kaden," she whispered, the connection to him still pulsing in her mind. She had failed him, left him behind, and now she couldn't even save herself.

She looked at her hands and remembered the brief flash of light that protected her from the Spark Club, but nothing came from them now. Shaking them, as if trying to force a miracle from thin air, she grew more frustrated. Nothing.

The light grew brighter as she neared the vent entrance. The Elite's face came into view – not the blank, featureless visage she expected, but something worse. Cracks split its obsidian skin, and from within those fissures gleamed an eerie, dark light, as if its very soul were burning inside the stone shell of its body. She could feel its hunger, like a ravenous lion on the prowl and she was in its sights.

A distant memory surfaced – Kelly sitting in Sunday school as a child, hearing the story of Daniel in the lions' den. "But God shut the lions' mouths," the teacher had said.

She shook her hands again, screaming at them for the power to deflect the enemy once again. But there was no response, no last-minute salvation. The Elite's outstretched hand reached for her, its fingers grasping air mere inches from her face.

Suddenly, The Tower shuddered. A tremor ran through the structure, metal groaning and concrete cracking. The vent around her buckled, the metal warping. The Elite's hold faltered for just a moment as it turned its attention to the failing structure.

Kira seized the opportunity. With all her strength, she pushed against the vent wall, propelling herself downward. For a heartbeat, she was free, sliding back into the darkness.

Then the Elite's power seized her again, more viciously this time. Her body jerked to a stop so violently that she felt something snap in her lower back. Pain exploded through her nervous system, setting every nerve ending on fire. Her legs fell limp, dangling below her waist.

Above her, the Elite's focus was divided. One hand stretched toward her, maintaining its hold, while the other pressed against the crumbling wall of The Tower. The creature's power was divided between capturing her and maintaining the structural integrity of its master's domain.

The vent around her began to collapse. Metal panels tore free from their moorings, the shaft itself warping as the forces acting on The Tower intensified. Pieces of the once smooth vent now peeled away, creating sharp edges that cut through the path above her. One jagged edge of torn metal hung just above her, trembling with each new shudder that ran through the building.

Kira felt herself being pulled upward again, inch by excruciating inch. The pain in her back made it impossible to struggle. All she could do was watch as the Elite's reach extended further into the vent, its stone fingers pulling her toward the sharp, broken metal and ultimately up to it.

Then The Tower convulsed again.

The tremor was different this time – not a shudder but more a violent spasm, as if the very heart of The Tower were skipping beats. The metal panel broke free, slicing downward like a spear shot down the shaft.

She didn't feel the impact. One moment, she was staring into the Elite's dead eyes; the next, darkness swept over her. Her lifeless body held in the shaft, but then the vent crumbled above her and the Elite lost its grip.

Her body fell, tumbling limp and broken through the ravaged vent system.

***

Kelly gasped awake on Darren's couch, her body shooting up as if shocked by a live wire. For a moment, she couldn't remember where she was or what had happened. Ghostly sensations lingered – the feeling of falling, of sharp pain, of a life slipping away. She touched her back, expecting to find it broken, but there was only the familiar curve of her spine, whole and uninjured.

The memories of Kira's final moments flashed through her mind like a nightmare from which she couldn't fully wake. She felt the hunger of the Elite, eager to consume.

She looked around the apartment, expecting to see Kirk and Chris, but the living room was empty. Peeking in their rooms, she saw each silently sleeping, seeming as peaceful as ever. The silence felt oppressive after the chaos of The Tower.

Her purple glasses lay on the couch next to her. They seemed so simple despite the portal they contained.

Kelly reached for her phone, checking the time. Only minutes had passed since she'd put on the glasses. It seemed impossible – a day in Empyrean that felt like a lifetime had passed in the space of a heartbeat.

Her hands still trembled as she unlocked her phone and opened a browser. She needed answers, needed to understand what was happening across these two intertwined lives. If she couldn't save Kaden in Empyrean, perhaps she could stop it all from happening here, in the past.

She typed "Dr. David Abrams cancer research" into the search bar. The results loaded, and her eyes widened as she scrolled through them. Medical journals, news articles about breakthrough treatments, photographs of a younger Dr. Abrams standing beside a tall blond man she recognized immediately: Dr. Thomas Thornhill.

She dug deeper, searching for connections between Abrams, Thornhill, and Darren. It seemed so crazy to her that Darren claimed to have an appointment one morning and then the office a ghost town only a few hours later. It wasn't possible. Something told her there had to be a link beyond the eye doctor visit that had started it all.

After twenty minutes of increasingly specific queries into search engines and generative AI platforms, her determination was rewarded. Her eyes grew wide when she saw it – a small local news article from fifteen years ago: "Experimental Cancer Treatment Claims Life of Local Mother."

Kelly's heart pounded as she read. The article mentioned a woman named Naomi McArthur, who had participated in early trials for a revolutionary cancer treatment developed by doctors at a research institute headed by Thomas Thornhill. The treatment had failed, and Naomi had died, leaving behind a husband, Jonah, a veteran of Operation Desert Storm, and their young son, Darren.

Six months later, the father disappeared on a solo hike in the Chattahoochee National Forest. Despite extensive searches, his body was never found. The article went on to say that Jonah McArthur had become increasingly unstable after his wife's death, insinuating that his pre-existing PTSD exacerbated by the loss of Naomi led to him taking his own life.

Putting together what she already knew, Darren, only ten years old at the time, had been raised by his maternal grandparents.

Kelly sat back, pieces falling into place. Darren had never talked about his parents – she had assumed they were simply estranged, not dead. And now she discovered something she suspected that Darren hadn't known, that early versions of the Hope Drug had played a direct role in the tragedy that had shaped his life.

She shook her head as she read through similar articles, repeatedly saying to herself, “It can't be a coincidence.”

Dr. Abrams must have known who Darren was when he came into his office. He had chosen Darren specifically, using the phoropter and later the glasses to connect him to Kaden, to show him the future Thornhill would create.

Kelly thought of Kira, of the light she had felt flash in her body that deflected the Spark Club as it crashed down. She thought of trying to bring the power back in the vent, but nothing. Yet, something was changing, evolving. The Hope Drug affected people differently – that much she had learned from her time in Empyrean. Some turned to stone, becoming Elites, but others... She leaned back and thought.

Her phone buzzed with an incoming call. Unknown number. Kelly hesitated, then answered.

"Hello?"

"Ms. Daye," the voice said. It was familiar – female, elderly, yet carrying an undertone of strength that belied its age.

"Who is this?" Kelly asked, though somehow she already knew.

"He asked me to call you, dear. To give you encouragement on your journey," the voice continued. "You understand what's at stake. The end and the beginning."

“Who is this?” she asked again.

"Time is more fluid than most realize, and he is not dead."

Kelly's mind recalled the bullets striking Darren’s chest. She saw him falling backward. "Darren is dead," she said. "Thornhill killed him."

"And yet Kaden lives," the woman replied. "But that’s not who I meant. He’s showing you that death is not the end."

Kelly looked at the purple glasses on the table. "I don't understand."

"You will," she promised. "Keep going, my dear."

The line went dead before Kelly could respond. She stared at her phone, then at the glasses.

Death is not the end. The words echoed in her mind, familiar somehow. A verse from Sunday school surfaced from the depths of memory: "I am the resurrection and the life. Whoever believes in me, though he dies, yet shall he live."

Kelly picked up the glasses, turning them over in her hands. The purple frames caught the light, glinting like a promise – or a warning.

“Death is not the end, huh?” she said aloud, staring at the glasses.

She slid them into her pocket and left the apartment.

Chapter 22

Kaden

Beth-ell moved with surprising agility for someone of her appearance. Her weathered face remained stern as she led Kaden away from Ron-ell's unconscious form. The two Elites flanked them, their charcoal bodies creating a barrier between Kaden and the chaos erupting throughout The Tower.

"This way," Beth-ell commanded, guiding them to a series of tunnels toward a service corridor. The walls around them shuddered, hairline fractures spiderwebbed like veins across the once pristine surfaces. Above them, distant sounds rumbled through the structure like rolling thunder.

Kaden stumbled, his legs weak beneath him. The surge of power that had protected him from the shadow-Elite had left him drained, as if his very lifeforce had been wrung out. One of the Elites caught him with surprising gentleness. Its cracked obsidian face remained impassive, but there was something deliberate in the way it steadied him, something almost... protective. Kaden began to notice slight differences between the two. Once, he saw them as carbon-copies of each other, but now, he noticed one was slightly bigger with broader shoulders.

"Stay on your feet," Beth-ell ordered, not looking back. "We've got a long way to go and little time."

They pushed through a maintenance door into a narrow passage that smelled of metal and dust. The sounds of The Tower's distress grew more distant, though Kaden still sensed tremors running through the floor beneath his feet.

"What's happening?" he gasped, struggling to keep pace.

"You tell me. What happened up there?" Beth-ell replied sharply.

Kaden couldn't find the words.

"Regardless," she said as she moved swiftly around a corner. "We need to be far from here when Pinnacle regains control."

The mention of Pinnacle sent a jolt of fear through Kaden's exhausted body. The memory of that hungry darkness reaching for him, of Jericho's heart pulsing like a captive star within the shadow-Elite's formless body – it all came rushing back.

"We have to go back," Kaden said suddenly, stopping in his tracks. "Kira's in there. I felt her. She came for me."

Beth-ell turned to face him, her gray eyes hard as flint. "If she's still in there, she's either dead or will be soon."

"You don't understand—"

"No, you don't understand," Beth-ell cut him off. "Whatever happened up there with Pinnacle has put The Tower into convulsions. Every Elite in Empyrean will be working to stabilize it, along with Pinnacle, and they'll consume anything that gets in their way." She stepped closer, her voice dropping. "What *exactly* happened up there?"

Kaden hesitated, looking from Beth-ell to the two Elites. The second one – slightly smaller with more fluid movements – tilted its head as if in curiosity or concern. Though its face was the same featureless black mask as all Elites, something in its posture conveyed a sorrowful patience, urging him to answer.

"He... Pinnacle... and the shadow... they tried to consume me," Kaden finally said. "But first, he showed me Jericho's heart."

Beth-ell moved in closer, her eyes like nocked arrows pointed at Kaden.

“It started beating, still alive somehow, inside this... thing. Not like a normal Elite. Like a shadow that was a part of but somehow separate from Pinnacle."

Beth-ell's eyes widened slightly at this – the first genuine emotion he'd seen on her face. "The heart beat, on its own?"

Kaden nodded. "And when the shadow tried to consume me, I... I don't know. Something happened. Light came out, from me, from the heart, I’m not sure. But it pushed Pinnacle and the shadow back, like it dazed them both."

The smaller Elite made a sound – not the usual oppressive, guttural force of words he’d heard before, but something softer, almost like a sigh. It looked at its companion, and though no words passed between them, Kaden sensed a communication, an understanding.

“What else?” Beth-ell asked.

"I tried to reach for the heart," Kaden continued. "Not with my hands, but with... something else. The light..."

Beth-ell studied him with a ferocious intensity, like a detective about to crack a murder suspect, but then a crack of smile came from the corner of the mouth. "He knew," she whispered. "And now we’re seeing it.”

“Seeing what?” Kaden asked.

“You're carrying a piece of him. He’s in you," she said so matter-of-factly, she could have been confirming gravity.

Kaden squinted, confused at what that meant, then another tremor shook the passage, more violent than before. Dust and small fragments of ceiling rained down on them.

"Must go," the larger Elite rumbled, its voice like stones grinding together.

Beth-ell nodded and resumed their hurried pace through the narrow corridor, which eventually opened into a larger maintenance tunnel. The harsh white lighting flickered intermittently, casting strange shadows across the walls and cross tunnels. In the distance, Kaden could hear shouting – commands being issued, panic barely controlled.

“They’re close,” Kaden said.

“No, they’re not,” Beth-ell replied confidently.

Another hundred yards down the corridor and she stopped, turning to the Elites with an unspoken command. They stepped to her side and raised their hands. The walls of the maintenance tunnel split as if an invisible drill were boring through. At first, it was only a pinprick, but quickly, it expanded to be a foot in diameter, then three feet, then six.

The tunnel arced upwards and light from the outside illuminated the far end. The smaller Elite went in and the walls of the tunnel smoothed around it as it went forward.

“Come on.” Beth-ell followed the Elite.

"Where are we going?" Kaden asked.

"Away," Beth-ell replied.

"I can't leave without Kira," Kaden insisted.

Beth-ell didn't slow her pace. "The light you summoned – can you do it again?"

Kaden clenched his fists, trying to recapture that moment of connection, the surge of power that had flowed through him. But there was nothing – only exhaustion and the dull ache of having been emptied.

"I can't," he admitted, frustration edging his voice. "I don't know how I did it the first time."

"Then going back is foolish," Beth-ell said bluntly from the other side of the tunnel. "For both of you."

The slightly larger Elite moved behind Kaden as if shepherding him to enter the newly created tunnel.

Kaden looked at the creature with new interest. There was something hauntingly familiar that he couldn't quite place.

"They won't keep it open all day," Beth-ell said, now exiting the tunnel.

Kaden moved in. The tunnel was cool and damp, soft below his feet. He rubbed his hands on the smooth walls. The fresh earth felt life-giving and he realized how absent fresh dirt was in Empyrean. It was always here, below The Tower and blocked away. The Elite moved forward, urging him on with its presence.

As they came out of the passage, Kaden felt a sudden sharp pain behind his eyes, followed by a flash of vision – Kira, sliding through darkness, then sudden terror as she was pulled upward. Metal tearing, a charcoal hand reaching, and then... nothing. The connection that had been pulsing at the edge of his consciousness went silent.

He stumbled, a cry escaping his lips. The smaller Elite caught him this time, its rough hands surprisingly gentle against his arm.

"Kira," he gasped, looking up at Beth-ell. "Something's happened to her. I can't feel her anymore."

Beth-ell's expression remained unchanged.

"What's the point?" Kaden demanded, anger flaring through his exhaustion. "If Jericho couldn't defeat him, if the Remnant keeps getting slaughtered, if everyone who stands against him dies – what's the point of any of this?"

The smaller Elite made that sighing sound again, and for a moment, Kaden thought he saw something glimmer in the cracks of its obsidian skin.

"The point," Beth-ell said quietly, "is that some victories don't look like victories. Not at first. Sometimes they look exactly like defeat."

"That makes no sense!" Kaden shouted in frustration.

Beth-ell's expression remained as consistent as ever. "Death isn't the end, Kaden. Of everyone who has eyes to see, you of all people should know that. Darren. Kaden. Death doesn't touch you because of *HIM*."

The comment stunned him. He'd been killed numerous times now, and each time, he awoke in the other's body and was able to return.

Behind him, the Elites closed the tunnel. In a few moments, cracked concrete was transformed and smoothed seamlessly over the area they crawled out of as if the tunnel never existed.

They continued in silence for long stretches, the only sounds of their footsteps. Sounds of The Tower faded away behind them and soon he smelled the acrid air of the Outer Ring seeping in.

Whenever debris came in their way, the Elites effortlessly cleared it as the group marched on.

"We're nearly there," Beth-ell announced.

"And then what?" Kaden asked bitterly. "Hide from Pinnacle forever? Watch more people die?"

"No," Beth-ell replied, her voice hard once more. "Then we learn how to awaken what's inside you."

Kaden looked at her in confusion. "What do you mean?"

"That light," she said, "it wasn't something external, and it wasn't something Jericho gave you like a tool to be used on command. It's something you've always had – something we all have, buried beneath layers of doubt and fear. The Hope Drug's corruption might be inside of all of us, but so is something else. The trouble is... making it accessible."

"If that's true, why can't I summon it again? Why can't I go back and save Kira?"

Kaden felt the gaze of the Elites on him – penetrating, knowing.

"Because," Beth-ell said, "power like that doesn't come through control. It comes through surrender."

"Surrender to what?" Kaden demanded.

"To the way, the truth, the light. In that moment, when you thought that shadow would devour you, you reached out with more than a plea. You put your life in Jericho's heart," she said.

"And it saved me?" Kaden said.

"The heart was working through you, like a partnership."

"Partnership... between me and a dead organ," Kaden said, letting out a breath of exhaustion.

"You still think Jericho's dead?" Beth-ell stopped and watched him. "Even after seeing his heart beat or after your life being saved?"

Kaden stood silent and soon Beth-ell's piercing stare left as the group continued on their path.

"Why didn't you tell me who you were before?" he finally asked. "Back at the eye doctor's office – Ms. Barbara. This is a lot to figure out."

A hint of a smile crossed Beth-ell's weathered face. "Would you have believed me – or him – if I'd told you that your eye doctor had unimaginable powers, that his secretary was his first disciple, that a global catastrophe was coming, and that you had a role to play in it all?"

"When you put it that way..." Kaden couldn't help but chuckle despite everything.

"Everyone learns in their own time," she said.

They moved through back streets and shadows, going further from The Tower and deeper into the Outer Ring. The foul air wasn't as awful as it typically smelled; now it tasted like freedom after the sterile confines of The Tower. Eventually, they reached a heavy metal door, rusted at the edges. The larger Elite moved his hand and the door slid open.

Looking back, he could see The Tower looming in the distance, its upper levels obscured by low-hanging storm clouds like a swirling mask in the darkness. Faint flashes of light pulsed within the darkness, the flickers of lightning in a storm cloud.

"What's happening up there?" Kaden whispered.

"By now, they've secured The Tower's structure," Beth-ell replied, following his gaze. "Soon, they'll begin hunting us down," she said.

"So, we're safe for now?"

"Not safe. *Never* safe. The days are evil, Kaden, and we must fight with every breath. But we have time to rest here." She turned to him, her gray eyes intense. "Kaden, what you did up there – the light you channeled – it's the one thing Pinnacle truly fears. Not because it can destroy him, but because it can free people from him."

"What do you mean?" he asked as they moved inside a large room.

The walls were spotted with rust just like the outer door as stale air hung. A few vents poked through the ceiling into the night sky and a mix of old boards and steel sheets made up the floor.

"The Hope Drug changed us all, but in different ways. Pinnacle's version corrupts, consumes, turns flesh to stone." She gestured to the two Elites who stood silently nearby. "But Jericho's blood – the original formula – it heals, transforms, restores what was lost. And somehow, a piece of that restoration is in you."

Kaden looked at his hands, remembering the light that had burst from them. "But I can't control it."

"You cannot command it, because it's not about control," Beth-ell said. "It's about trust. Faith. Surrender."

Kaden moved into the room and squatted down, staring at his hands as he leaned against the thin metal wall. His thoughts were interrupted as the Elites reached out their hands. Two of the square metal sheets that acted as flooring amongst the scattered dust and old boards rose up and began bending.

Kaden backed away and watched in amazement as the metal ripped apart, now four sheets floated before him. They turned and shaped like a crumpled paper ball, but soon something recognizable came into view, like staring at a beautiful piece of art and suddenly seeing the artist's intent. He couldn't help but smile as he realized what the Elites were doing.

"Chairs," he said with a laugh.

The metal pieces, now resembling large Adirondack chairs, gently lowered and rested on the ground. A faint memory of sitting in chairs like this as a young boy with his parents went through his mind. It was another life, young Darren's life, but he could feel the relaxation of the family event, a river peacefully flowing by during a long ago family vacation to his grandfather's cabin.

The Elites turned to Beth-ell and then Kaden, their cracked charcoal skin showing no sign of expression, but their eyes gave off a longing as if they knew what Kaden was thinking.

"My grandfather had a set of chairs like this. Well..." He stopped himself. "Darren's grandfather did."

"Thank you," Beth-ell said to the Elites as she took a seat.

Kaden followed, realizing that was the first time he'd heard Beth-ell use a polite word. It may have been the first time he'd heard someone speak to an Elite as if the creatures were human.

"Has it... have they... always been like this?" Kaden asked Beth-ell, nodding toward the Elites.

"No," she replied softly. "Only with you, and that's taken time for them to adjust to you." She paused and Kaden remembered nearly being consumed by them.

She continued.

"They were early subjects in the trials. Before Pinnacle understood what he was creating. They've certainly been impacted by the hunger, but..." She paused as if a heavy weight were on her shoulders. "They've retained more of themselves than most."

"They tried to kill or consume me every time," Kaden said, sitting down in the surprisingly comfortable chair.

"I wish I could say that was only for appearances. The hunger, and culture of this place..." She looked down. "Whether you're an Elite, or an Agent, it gets to you. Eventually, it gets everyone."

The look in Beth-ell's eyes told him there was more to her comment, much more. Kaden remembered being forced against a wall, his insides feeling they were being twisted out of place, and the fight in the Outer Ring. Now those same two Elites had helped free him and made chairs for his comfort. They stood next to him as he opposed Pinnacle.

"The days are evil, Kaden," she said, leaning her head toward him. "And the hunger is waiting for us all."

Chapter 23

Entry #6

I walked the perimeter of Empyrean today, watching the last sections of the Wall rise like a scar across the landscape. From here, it looks like a fortress – Thomas's pride, his monument to survival. But I see it for what it truly is: a prison, holding everyone inside.

The workers don't notice me as I pass. Their mind is elsewhere and my appearance continues to shift. My hair is completely gray and my eyes gleam with an inner light that unsettles those who look directly at them. The power flows through my veins like electricity, giving me the ability to bend perception and time. I can move unseen when necessary, but most people in Empyrean choose to not see me when I am right in front of them.

Every day, more survivors stagger toward The Tower's shadow. They come because Thomas broadcasts promises of safety, of order, of evolution beyond human frailty. What he doesn't tell them is the price of admission. I've seen them sorted – the strong separated from the weak, the "valuable" from the "dispensable." Those deemed worthy are given shelter in the Inner Ring, while the rest are relegated to the crumbling buildings of the

Outer Ring, where they serve a single purpose: to feed the growing hunger of Thomas's new creation. Soon, no more will come and Thomas will accelerate new life in his labs.

I desire to tear down these walls, to bring The Tower crashing down before it's even completed. The power is there, waiting to be unleashed. But it is not my will but something greater that must take hold. Ripping down these abominations would make no difference in their hearts – another tyrant forcing his vision upon the world. True freedom cannot be given; it must be chosen. True change cannot be imposed; it must grow from within.

So instead of tearing down, I build. Not just the Lighthouse in the north, but something less tangible, more resilient. A kingdom not made of stone and metal, but of hearts and minds. The Lighthouse Remnant grows daily, both within Empyrean's walls and beyond them. People who remember what it means to be human, who choose compassion over consumption, service over dominance.

They gather in shadows, in tunnels beneath the streets, sharing what little they have. I move among them, teaching, healing when I can, but mostly listening. Their stories are the true foundation of what's to come – tales of sacrifice for strangers, of mercy shown when cruelty would be easier, of hope maintained in the face of despair. Each story is a stone in the foundation of a different kind of kingdom.

My disciples – though they would never call themselves that – spread throughout Empyrean like seeds in fertile soil. There are those with inexplicable joy, and others who fiercely protect the vulnerable, and others whose names history may never record but whose actions will ripple through time like stones cast in still water.

Their numbers will rise and fall and will ever prepare for when the time is right.

The ranking system has begun as colored robes are donned by Thomas's "Agents," bringing "order" at the end of their electrified clubs. More Elites emerge from the bowels of The Tower, their skin blackened and hardened like cracked charcoal, their hunger a tangible force that precedes them. The people flee before them, not understanding what they're seeing – the physical manifestation of their internal corruption. These demons are a symptom of the disease that has taken root in Empyrean.

Thomas believes he is building a new Eden, with himself as both creator and god. Yet even among the Agents and Elites, hope is budding. Barbara survives and will journey through hell in the coming centuries to set a path. She goes forth.

The light shines in the darkness, and the darkness has not overcome it.

Today, I watched a mother share her last crust of bread with a stranger's child. I saw an old man stand between an Elite and a young woman, knowing it meant his consumption. I witnessed an Agent turn away from a hiding place rather than reveal the family concealed there. These are the seeds.

We build differently. We build with mercy, with sacrifice, with love that gives instead of takes. We build not by reaching up, but by reaching out. And when the light of day comes – as it surely will – when The Tower begins to crumble, when the walls that imprison humanity start to crack, we will be there to show another way.

I will offer no resistance when he takes what he believes is the source of my power. He will discover, too late, that my heart has never been mine to keep. It has always belonged to those who choose to see, and those who choose to hear.

Chapter 24

Kelly

"Please, I need to see him," Kelly stated firmly, her hands gripping the reception counter. The fluorescent lights of the county morgue cast harsh shadows across her face, emphasizing the dark circles under her eyes.

The receptionist – a middle-aged woman with carefully styled gray hair and sympathetic eyes – looked up from her computer. "I'm sorry, miss, but as I explained, only next of kin are permitted to view the deceased at this stage."

"Please." Kelly's voice cracked. "He doesn't have any living kin. *I was there,* when he... died..." The words echoed in her mind as she saw Darren's body falling to the ground.

"Are you family?" she asked.

"Girlfriend."

The woman's expression softened slightly, but her answer remained unchanged. "I understand, and I'm sorry, I really am, but the policy is clear. Without family authorization or police approval, I can't allow access."

Kelly closed her eyes to fight back tears, but she could no longer tell if the tears were from sorrow or from frustration. She'd spent the morning making calls – to hospitals, to the police, finally to the morgue – tracking Darren's body through the inefficient clinical system that somehow processed death with such impersonal efficiency. Each call, each transfer, each new voice asking the same questions that shielded the same "no" responses had worn her down.

"Is there someone I can call? Someone who could authorize it?" Kelly tried again.

The receptionist hesitated, then lowered her voice. "The medical examiner is here. An open-shut case for him for fatal gunshot wounds." She glanced toward a door marked 'Authorized Personnel Only.' "If he's still here..." She hesitated.

"Oh, if you could do anything," Kelly said hopefully.

"Let me see if he'll speak with you."

Kelly nodded gratefully and moved to the small waiting area. The plastic chair creaked as she sat, her fingers tracing the edges of the purple glasses in her pocket. *Death is not the end.* The woman's words from the phone call echoed in her mind. Darren's body was hidden somewhere in this building. She began wondering why in the world she was here. What'd she expect to find about life in a city morgue.

Five minutes stretched into fifteen. Finally, a door opened, and a tall man in scrubs and a lab coat approached. His face showed all the classic signs of exhaustion, but his eyes held kindness.

"Miss Daye? I'm Dr. Ruiz. Sylvia tells me you were present when Mr. McArthur died."

Kelly stood. "Yes. Please, I just need to see him. To say goodbye. He doesn't have anyone else."

The doctor studied her for a long moment, then nodded. "Follow me. Five minutes, that's all I can give you."

He led her through the door and down a sterile hallway that smelled of disinfectant and something Kelly didn't want to name. They passed several rooms before stopping at one with a small window in the door. Dr. Ruiz swiped his keycard.

"I should warn you," he said, pausing before opening the door, "seeing someone you love like this... it's never what people expect. Are you sure?"

Kelly swallowed hard. "I understand, and yes, I'm sure."

The room was cold. That was her first impression – a bone-deep chill that seemed to radiate from the walls themselves. The doctor moved toward a row of oversized drawers. Scanning the numbers, he pulled one out.

It slid with a smooth motion, revealing a black body bag that reflected the bright overhead lights. He put his hands to the zipper at the top, then stopped. He looked at her for approval, a sympathetic expression on his face.

Kelly nodded and the rhythmic sound of the zipper filled the room, bouncing off the stainless steel drawers. The bag fell slightly, then the doctor pulled it back fully.

There he was.

In the back of her mind, Kelly thought maybe it wouldn't be him. Maybe he wasn't really dead but just waiting for the next part of the plan with Dr. Abrams' guidance. But no, the lifeless body lay in front of her.

His face was pale, almost waxy. Rigor mortis had steeled his muscles, but his facial features seemed relaxed in a way they never were in life. She followed his face to his chin and down to his sternum, where discolored flesh curled up around his chest. She looked the area over, counting the bullet holes.

"I'll wait outside," Dr. Ruiz said quietly, stepping back into the hallway.

Kelly moved forward on legs that threatened to buckle. Her stomach seemed to collapse on itself as her insides felt empty. Yet, she forced herself to move in close. Coming to a stop beside the table, she reached out with trembling fingers to touch Darren's cheek. Cold. So cold.

"I'm sorry," she whispered. "I should have stopped you."

She continued to look upon his face, a tear rolling down her cheek, dropping onto the polished white terrazzo floor.

"Where is your mind now? The Tower? With Pinnacle?"

She pulled the purple glasses from her pocket and stared at them, thinking more about Empyrean. The weird connection had felt severed when she stopped being Kira and woke back up as Kelly.

"I don't understand what's happening," she said to him. "But I'm going to find out. I promise you that."

She leaned down and pressed her lips to his forehead.

She emerged from the room standing taller. The bags under her eyes seemed faded as a determined expression took hold.

Dr. Ruiz was waiting as promised.

"Thank you," she said. “I appreciate it more than you might know.”

He nodded. "Sorry for your loss."

She bent her head, silently acknowledging the condolences and then stepped away.

“You said you were there?” he called out before she left.

She stopped, turning back to him with a nod and curious look.

“I've seen all manner of deaths, and unfortunately, my share of gunshot wounds, but this one..." He trailed off, then continued more carefully. "The internal wounds, they’re not normal... It’s like the bullets rattled around inside. There’s evidence they entered from his back and chest.”

Kelly frowned. "What?"

"According to the police report, he was shot from the front, that he was facing his assailant."

"He was," Kelly insisted. "I saw it. Darren was facing Thornhill."

“Let’s avoid names,” Dr. Mahoney said, his expression remaining neutral, professional. "The physical evidence suggests otherwise. There are entry wounds on his back and front, as well as exit wounds on his back and front. There's no medical explanation, or from physics for that matter, for bullets traveling that way. That is *if* he was shot from *only* the front."

Kelly's mind reeled. She'd seen it happen – Thornhill stopping the bullets, then sending them back into Darren's chest.

“If he was in a crossfire, getting hit from both sides, that’d explain it, but that doesn’t match the police report, or what you witnessed. If I saw this body without those reports, I’d say someone wanted to make absolutely sure that your boyfriend was dead. This is more like gang violence to send a message.”

She nodded mechanically, her thoughts racing. No conventional explanation could account for what she'd witnessed. Thornhill had manipulated physical reality itself, and no autopsy report or police investigation would ever reveal the truth.

"Is there anything else I should know?" she asked.

“I was going to ask you the same thing. Is there anything else the police or I should know?” The doctor seemed to weigh his words carefully.

"Thank you for telling me." Kelly turned to leave, then paused. "Dr. Ruiz, do you believe in the impossible?"

A sad smile touched the corner of his mouth. "In this line of work, Miss Daye, I've learned that 'impossible' is often just a word we use when we don't yet understand."

“How about good and evil? I mean true, absolute good and true, absolute evil?”

He looked at her, his jaws tensing as he thought, as if he didn't want to answer the question.

***

The Haven Oaks Cemetery stretched before her, a seemingly endless expanse of granite markers and carefully manicured grass. The afternoon sun cast long shadows from the monuments, creating a pattern of light and dark like painted lines across the grounds. Kelly clutched the slip of paper with the plot number she'd obtained from the cemetery office.

Section L, Row 24, Plot 3.

After leaving the morgue, she'd driven straight to the public library to continue her research. There, she'd discovered more about the experimental cancer treatment that had claimed Naomi McArthur's life – a trial conducted by a research institute headed by none other than Thomas Thornhill. The more she dug, the more connections she found. Dr. David Abrams had been listed as co-researcher on the early papers, his name appearing alongside Thornhill's with increasing frequency until abruptly stopping fifteen years ago.

A cemetery database search had yielded Naomi's burial location at Haven Oaks, though there was no record for Jonah McArthur. With his body never recovered, Kelly assumed he might have a memorial marker beside his wife.

She walked slowly through the rows, counting markers until she reached Section L. The afternoon was quiet, with only the occasional chirp of birds and distant sound of traffic to break the silence. As she approached Row 24, her pace slowed. Something felt off, though she couldn't identify what.

Plot 24 came into view, marked by a modest gray headstone. Kelly stopped, staring at the name etched into the granite:

CORA MARCH

***1943**

–

2010*

Beloved Mother and Friend

Kelly checked the plot number again, confirming she was in the right place. This wasn't Naomi McArthur's grave. She looked around, wondering if she'd somehow misread the cemetery map, but the surrounding plots were clearly numbered 23 and 25. She checked the section and row again. All were accurate.

Pulling out her phone, she called the cemetery office.

"Haven Oaks Cemetery, how may I assist you?" a bored female voice answered.

"Hi, we spoke earlier. I'm the one looking for the grave of Naomi McArthur. Your records indicated Section L, Row 24, Plot 3, but there's a different name on the headstone."

"Oh, hello again!" the voice said, perking up. Kelly was thankful she was kind to the woman despite her frustration as she tracked down false lead after false lead.

"Hmmm, one moment, please." The sound of typing came through the line. "Yes, our records show Naomi McArthur was interred at that location in 2010."

"But the headstone says Cora March."

More typing. "Oh... Well, that's odd. You're at the right spot?" Kelly assured her she was. "Let me check our historical records." The pause stretched for nearly a minute and clicks from the keyboard dotted the line like sporadic elevator music. "I'm showing that Plot 3 was originally purchased in 2010, and ownership was transferred one month later. That's not uncommon while families sort out burial dates if trusts or the like are involved, or in the case of exhumation or relocation."

"Exhumation or relocation?"

"I'm afraid that information isn't in our system. You would need to speak with the family or obtain court records for that level of detail."

Kelly stood, looking at the gray gravestone, frustration and hopelessness bubbling up.

"I'm sorry, was Ms. McArthur a relative?"

"No," Kelly said distractedly, her mind racing yet coming up blank. "Is there any contact details, anything giving more information?"

"No..." Typing continued. "I can see the payment for services is tagged to an Empyrean Enterprises. Oh wait, that's personal details I cannot share. Forget I said that."

Kelly's blood ran cold as she held the phone.

"Ma'am, are you still there?" the friendly voice said on the other line.

Kelly hardly heard the question.

"Ma'am?"

"Thank you for your help," Kelly snapped back. "I couldn't even hear. The line must be breaking—" She ended the call and stood motionless before Cora March's grave, trying to process this new information. Bodies weren't typically exhumed without significant cause – criminal investigations, family requests for relocation, or court orders. Yet once again, all signs of confusion and death pointed back to Thomas Thornhill's organization.

The wind picked up, rustling through the cemetery trees and turning large, brown leaves into mini tumble weeds that bounced past the gravestones. Kelly shivered despite the pleasant afternoon. First Darren's body, and now his mother's missing remains. The caller's words from earlier in the day took on new meaning: *Death is not the end*. The woman had said she was giving encouragement... Kelly scoffed at the idea.

"Encouragement," she said aloud as the wind took on a chill. Her words floated away as if stolen in the air.

She stood shaking her head into the coming wind. Her fingers traced what was still in her pocket. She slid the purple glasses out and turned them over in her hand, watching the light reflect off the lenses. They seemed so plain, but just like the replaced gravestone in front of her, the story behind them was anything but plain.

Chapter 25

Kaden

The newly formed chairs scratched the concrete floor as Kaden shifted. He stared at his hands in the dim light that crept in through cracks in the rickety safehouse. Many hours had passed since their escape from The Tower, yet the memory of the light that had burst from within him remained vivid – a power that had saved him from Pinnacle's shadow-Elite but now seemed as distant as a forgotten dream.

Kaden closed his eyes, clenching his fists, trying to recapture that moment of connection. He pictured Jericho's heart pulsing in the darkness, reaching for that feeling of surrender that had preceded the light. Nothing came.

"Why won't you do it," he said to his hands, frustration edging his voice.

Beth-ell studied him with those piercing gray eyes. "What are you trying to do?"

"To bring back the light. To use it."

"That's your first mistake." Beth-ell rose from her chair with surprising grace for one who appeared so ancient. "You're trying to use it, to control it. Jericho's power within doesn't serve you; you serve it."

"That doesn't make any sense," Kaden said. "And if I can't control it, what good is it?"

Beth-ell moved to the center of the room, her gaze never leaving his face. She raised her hand toward a piece of metal in the corner of the room. Just like the Elites who had shaped the chairs earlier, she didn't touch it or even seem to strain, yet the metal began to ripple as if suddenly liquid, then rose slowly into the air.

"But only Elites can..." Kaden asked, his eyes wide as he watched the metal float. "You're not an Elite."

"Either I am or you need to change your definition of an Elite," Beth-ell replied. The metal sheet rotated slowly, catching the faint light. "I told you – I was one of the first to receive the Hope Drug, and from Dr. Abrams, not Thornhill's trials. My transformation was... different."

As she spoke and moved the metal, patches of her skin shifted, momentarily taking on the charcoal-like appearance of an Elite before returning to normal. Kaden had seen the same discoloration ripple across Pinnacle's face.

"The hunger is always there. It eats at you, demanding you bend to its will," she continued. She lowered the metal sheet back to the floor. "Always waiting. I feel it even now – the urge to consume, to take rather than give." She turned to him. "That's what Pinnacle's version of the Hope Drug does. It makes you hunger for power, for control. Pieces of this world get into you. The hunger is in us all."

"And Jericho's version?"

"It feeds you with something else." Beth-ell's expression softened almost imperceptibly. "Something that satisfies a *deeper need*, not a hunger."

"Why the darkness across your skin? I've seen it before, in Pinnacle."

"There have been many sacrifices for me to stay in The Tower," she said, looking away from him, then down.

Kaden didn't press the issue. A long silence followed and he began to pace the small room, his mind racing. "When I was in Pinnacle's chamber, and that shadow thing tried to consume me, I wasn't trying to fight it. I just... reached out."

"You reached out? To what?"

"For the heart. For *His* heart. It was like it was beating for me, but that doesn't make any sense."

"You surrendered," Beth-ell said. "Not to Pinnacle, but to something greater."

"But now I can't reach it anymore." He stopped pacing, turning to face her. "And Kira... I felt her in The Tower. I knew she was there, and could sense her presence. Then it just... vanished. Like a candle being snuffed out."

Beth-ell's face remained impassive, but something flickered in her eyes – knowledge, perhaps, or sorrow.

"What is it?" Kaden asked.

"Another series of pain. The trials we all face," she said.

"What does that mean? Is Kira in pain?"

She was silent for another long moment as she weighed something in her mind. Finally, she nodded. "The connection you feel with Kira exists across time itself. Just as Darren and Kaden are connected, Kira and Kelly, but that's not all. You two came here through the same power and are connected across time and space to your past selves, but so are you connected to each other. Your souls are blended together in ways most couldn't comprehend."

"But why did it cut out?"

Beth-ell shook her head. "I've found that when something is severed, we usually don't want the real reason. I imagine you can guess why it might have cut out." She turned away, moving toward the door.

"No, no, no," Kaden interjected. "She's here because of me. The doctor, Jericho, sent me here to do what, I don't know, but she followed. I can't let any—"

"Let?" Beth-ell interrupted. "You don't *let* anything happen; you either cause it or allow it. That's it."

"Cause, let, allow; what's the difference if she dies because of me?"

"Have you learned nothing from what *HE'S* done for you already?" she asked sharply.

Kaden shrugged off the comment and moved away, toward the door.

"Stop," she called to him, raising her hand as she did to move the metal sheet. "You need to learn. You're not ready to go back."

"I survived once, I'll do it again."

"I'll send my Elites," she said, looking at them. "They'll move quicker and more efficiently."

"I'm going too," Kaden insisted.

"No, you need to learn."

"Learn what?"

"To trust." Beth-ell stepped toward him. "Not in your own strength, but in a greater strength."

Kaden didn't respond, but she took his silence as a reluctant acceptance.

After talking with her Elites, Beth-ell returned to find Kaden standing in the middle of the room, eyes closed, breathing measured.

"Good," she said. "Quieting yourself from the outside can help. How quiet are you on the inside?"

“It’s an explosion of thoughts...” He shook his head as a forced exhale shot out of his nostrils. His eyes closed the entire time. “I keep thinking about that moment in Pinnacle's chamber, trying to recapture it.”

"You’re reaching for it, chasing it. Remember, you cannot command or run it down.”

“I don’t know what I’m doing,” he said, leaning backwards and sprawling out, looking up at the dilapidated ceiling.

“No one does,” she said, moving next to him and sitting. “It’s not you who figures out this power. We all have it inside, and Jericho made you aware. He gave it to you, and there’s nothing you can do to earn it or force it or whatever else. You simply embrace it. Through faith, you can let it lead you.”

Kaden nodded. Listening to her helped quiet his mind.

For the next several hours, Beth-ell guided him through exercises in stillness, in awareness, in surrender. She taught him to recognize the constant battle within himself – the need for control versus the freedom of trust. Things that Jericho had taught her.

"The Hope Drug altered us all, and Pinnacle capitalized on it," she explained. "Created a war inside us between consumption and compassion, between fear and faith. It magnifies existing human nature. Pinnacle chose his side long ago. Thomas Thornhill wanted to save mankind through control. Power without choice is tyranny."

"And Jericho?"

"He blazed the opposite path. Sacrifice instead of consumption. Service instead of dominance." She leaned forward. "That's the pattern you must follow, Kaden. Not seeking to wield the light like a weapon, but to become a vessel for it."

"How?" Kaden asked, frustration creeping back into his voice.

"By letting go."

Under Beth-ell's guidance, Kaden practiced. Sometimes, in moments of perfect stillness, he felt something stirring within him – not the blinding light that had erupted in The Tower, but small flickers, like embers waiting to be fanned into flame as he meditated and prayed.

"There," Beth-ell said during one such moment, as a faint glow emanated from Kaden's fingertips. "You see? When you stop striving, when you trust, it comes."

The glow vanished as Kaden tried to intensify it. "Ugh!" he exclaimed, slamming his fist against the floor.

Beth-ell watched him with a stern yet patient expression. "Faith isn't about instant results. It's about trusting even when you don't see immediate change. You can't *prove* faith, yet you have it or you don't."

"But what's the point if I can't use it when I need it?" Kaden demanded. "If Pinnacle finds us, if more Elites—"

"You're thinking like an Agent," Beth-ell interrupted. "Power isn't about domination. It's about transformation. Not forcing your will on reality, but aligning yourself with a greater will. The Word that created the universe is trying to show itself to you and you think it's just another Spark Club to smash your enemies."

Kaden opened his mouth to argue, then hesitated. A memory surfaced – Jericho, standing before Pinnacle, making no move to defend himself as his heart was torn from his chest. At the time, it had seemed like defeat, like surrender to a superior force. But what if it had been something else entirely? Not weakness, but a *different* kind of strength?

"When Jericho let Pinnacle take his heart," Kaden said slowly, "he wasn't giving up, was he?"

Beth-ell's eyes softened. "What do you think?"

"I think... he saw something we couldn't. A purpose in his sacrifice."

A ghost of a smile touched Beth-ell's lips.

“But he’s still dead,” Kaden added.

The faint smile faded away like smoke in the wind.

As evening approached, Kaden felt a change in the atmosphere – a subtle shift in pressure, in energy. Beth-ell sensed it too, her head lifting as if catching a scent on the wind.

"They're back," she said, moving toward the door.

Kaden followed, his heart suddenly racing.

The metal door slid open, revealing the two Elites. Behind them came three familiar figures – Jace, Aria, and Riggs. They looked battered, exhausted, covered in dust and blood. But it was what Riggs carried that made Kaden's breath catch in his throat.

Kira lay limp in Riggs's arms, her body caked in dried blood. Her head rested awkwardly in his elbow.

"No," he whispered, stumbling forward, and he saw why her head appeared differently. Her neck was bent to the side, broken.

Riggs's face was a mask of grief as he gently laid Kira's body on the floor. "We escaped through vents, she got caught..." he explained, his voice rough. "She... didn't make it."

Kaden fell to his knees beside her, taking her cold hand in his. The connection he'd felt – that invisible tether that had bound them across time and space – was silent, empty.

"She can't be dead," he said, voice cracking. "She can't."

Jace placed a hand on his shoulder. "I'm sorry, Kaden. We tried—”

"How?" Kaden demanded, looking up at them with burning eyes. "What happened?"

Aria stepped forward. "The vents collapsed during The Tower's convulsions. She eventually fell down the shaft and we found her, like this."

Kaden looked down at Kira's face, so still, so unlike the fierce, determined woman who had led the Remnant against impossible odds. Around them, the others stood in silence, heads bowed. Even the Elites seemed to radiate a kind of sorrow, their usual oppressive aura muted.

Beth-ell moved to stand beside him, her weathered hand coming to rest on his shoulder. When she spoke, her voice held a gentleness he hadn't heard in this place, but he knew it from his days as Darren.

"He once told me," she said, "death is not the end."

Kaden looked up at her, confusion mingling with grief.

“What we see is only part of the story. The rest is yet to be revealed,” she said.

Outside, night had fallen over Empyrean. In the distance, The Tower loomed against the sky, its upper levels still obscured by swirling clouds. Within those clouds, flashes of energy pulsed like a heartbeat – Pinnacle, rebuilding his domain, gathering his strength. Below the clouds, there were no more cracks or holes in the structure from when Jericho ripped a portion out.

The Tower was stronger than before.

Chapter 26

Entry #7

The walls grow higher, but not to protect, to imprison. The sorting ceremonies have become rituals of terror, dividing families, breaking spirits, and ending lives. The Inner Ring will drown in a facade of luxury while the Outer Ring starves. Children will be born not of love but of breeding programs, their futures decided before their first breath. Thomas's vision of "order" will become a machine that grinds humanity into submission, where obedience is valued above compassion, where control replaces connection.

His anger at me, his rage at the truth will be taken out on all of mankind.

The Elites' numbers increase daily as others seek power like Thomas, their transformation evolving. Their power grows in parallel to their insatiable hunger – a void that consumes but is never filled. I've watched them advance from Thomas's first subjects into something beyond human, their skin hardening like volcanic rock, their souls calcifying within. They no longer see people – only sustenance, only power to be absorbed. This hunger is their prison as much as their power. Even as they enforce control, they are slaves to their own appetites, believing themselves gods while truly being less than human. They have exchanged their birthright for a meal that will never satisfy.

The power flows through my veins like lightning, begging for release. But to do so would be to become what I oppose – another tyrant forcing my will upon creation, another Pinnacle believing that 'might makes right.'

Without choice, there is no love. Without the freedom to fall, there can be no true rising.

True transformation must come from within, a willing surrender rather than an imposed subjugation. Most will never choose the light. It breaks my heart, yet if I love them, then I must honor their freedom, even when that freedom leads to darkness.

The seed falls to the ground and seems to perish before new growth emerges. What looks like defeat will become victory. What appears as death will reveal itself as life. The seed in soil cannot be seen until its growth shoots up.

Let those who read these words remember: the darkest hour comes just before dawn, and what Thomas believes is my end is merely the beginning of what comes next.

Chapter 27

Kaden

Booming echoes of an Agent striking the dumpsters sounded all around him.

Kira was ahead of him, already running through the slim streets and alleyways in between a mix of patched brickwork and crumbling buildings. He followed, trying to keep up.

She bounced through shadowy pockets in between street lights, always steps ahead of him. Through the shadows, she flashed back and forth from hidden to visible like a ghost dancing in and out of reality. He ran after her, trying to catch her, but soon the echoing boom behind him became so overwhelming that he no longer ran *to* her but *from* the deafening noise. Fear pulsed in his veins pumped by his racing heart.

Kira pulled ahead further, but as he tried speeding up, he found his legs slowing. His body felt heavier. Heat pressed on him from behind and he stole a look back. A wall of fire, like a tidal wave rising from the horizon to overtake the sky, roared toward him. With every deafening boom, the wall pulsed and lunged closer to him.

Faster, faster. The beat picked up and the inferno sped at him. It ripped through buildings, destroying everything in its path as it crept closer to him.

He could feel the heat as he ran, still following Kira's path, but she stayed far ahead, out of reach.

Meanwhile, the fire behind him grew closer, larger. Inch by inch. He felt the heat on his back intensify. Soon, the back of his neck and legs felt like they might burst open, like his skin was sitting at two hundred and eleven degrees. One more degree and it'd boil.

The ghost-like Kira accelerated forward and out of view as it dashed behind a figure. The silhouette of a man stood at the top of the street. With the moonlight behind him, a man stood in a hooded jacket like a fortress that protected Kira. The wind whipped at the edges of the jacket, his body standing firm and confident against the elements, yet his expression gave a sense of relaxation. The contradiction of endless strength yet calm stood in stark contrast to Kaden's pounding fear of the fire wall at his heels.

But Kaden had been in this dream before. He'd seen it all play out already.

Still, the fire licked at his heels and Kaden sprinted at the man, following Kira's path. As he approached, the hooded figure held up his hand, stopping him mid-stride. As if frozen in time, one leg outstretched as the other pushed off the ground.

Jericho – The man in the hooded cloak.

Kaden thought of the fire overtaking him, his survival instinct screaming, urging him to move, but there was no fear in Jericho. The inferno could have been a tiny birthday candle to him. A split-second later, and the hooded-figure was nose-to-nose with Kaden. He came so fast, it was like a blink of light, a blip through space and time.

The overwhelming fear of the fire evaporated as he looked into Jericho's gray eyes.

Then, the fire caught them. But it didn't burn or consume them. It wrapped around them and Kaden knew he was only safe because of Jericho's protection. A strange power emanated from him, providing a bubble-like shield that held back the flames.

"The fire!" Kaden gasped as he felt the air being pulled out of his lungs by the hungry flames.

The man nodded, as if acknowledging the flames were real yet still locking eyes with Kaden.

"You're the fire," he said.

Kaden looked around, seeing the fire encasing them. He couldn't breathe, as the fire consumed all the oxygen. His lungs screamed as the air rushed out from him, stolen by the surrounding inferno.

Jericho's gray eyes closed and he leaned his head back, exposing his neck. The flames jumped at him like a hungry wolf on a wounded fawn, sinking its teeth into the soft neck tissue. Flames wrapped around his neck and tightened. Soon, the entire wall of fire was on him, his flesh catching flame as the cloak burned away. His skin turned a bright red, like iron in a furnace, then it went black, lifeless.

The ash held for a moment, like a charcoal statue. He could have been an Elite, just another man turned into a demon of Empyrean and forced to suffer the never-ending hunger.

But Kaden observed more this time. He'd been here before and seen this play out.

Inside the ash, there was a pulse. A glowing amber color beat slowly.

Jericho had absorbed the entire wall of fire and now stood as lifeless ash, but deep inside, Kaden still saw the tiny semblance of life.

He leaned in, trying to examine the pulse closer, conscious of the fresh air available to feed his lungs now that Jericho took the fire. But the wind picked up and the countless flakes of black particles floated away. The internal glow inside the ash was no longer visible.

As the burnt body left in the wind, the sun rose, bringing light to the night.

Kaden looked up, Kira stood ahead of him, and both turned their gaze to the heavens as the overcast clouds began to part.

He shot up from the cold ground, awake from the recurring dream. "You're the fire," sounded in his mind like a tolling church bell. It slowly faded as he panted, catching his breath as beads of sweat began rolling down his face.

The room was silent, everyone asleep.

He could hear Riggs's soft snoring and the wind blow past their safe house. Finally, he caught his breath and stood up. Beth-ell sat in one of the metal chairs, silently watching him. Her expression was cold and calculating, that of a determined researcher studying every move of her subject.

"Do you sleep?" he whispered.

"Not often," she replied.

"Dreams?" he asked.

She shook her head no. "Memories. Plagues of memories," she said, turning away.

"I am the fire," Kaden said.

"Is that right?" she mocked.

"Jericho is showing me something. I have a dream. The city burns down as I run through it. I'm trying to catch Kira, but I cannot. Jericho saves me; he takes the flames."

"He's saved everyone," she said.

"Yet we hide and rot," he said bitterly. "It's not over."

"And you're going to end it?" she said.

"Yes. I'm the fire."

When Beth-ell didn't respond, he continued.

"And I can't let it consume all of them," he said, motioning to the sleeping party scattered around them. "Pinnacle wants *me*. This is my fight, not theirs."

"You can't win that fight," she said plainly. "Not now. Not ever."

"I can learn to use the power, submit to it. I can do it, if it saves them."

"He gave you access to that power, but without submission, it's nothing."

"And that means do nothing?" Kaden worked hard to control his voice as his frustration rose.

"Rest is an asset," she said.

"I don't understand you. You hide in The Tower undercover, but when it comes time to strike back, you speak as cryptic as Jericho did. Now he's gone and you still wait."

Beth-ell looked away, her face showing a fatigue that only years of hardship could create.

Kaden moved to the door then stopped at the entrance and peered back. "You're not going to stop me?"

She shook her head.

Kaden turned and left the safe house.

Outside, he took one step and instantly found himself surrounded by her Elites. They were hidden in the shadows of the night, yet at this close distance, they felt like Roman centurions standing tall and strong, ready to defend the resting Caesar within.

He began walking, and to his surprise, they allowed him through. After a few steps, he turned back, whispering to the Elites, "You won't stop me either?"

Their black eyes moved to him, the silence stretching across the night, and Kaden could tell they were deliberating their response. Whatever thought process they held that could occasionally overcome their immense hunger, he'd learn to give them a beat to respond.

They moved forward, eerily gliding more than walking, and stood at his side, their dead eyes still looking down at him. He felt his heart pick up as fear bubbled. His fists clenched and he prayed to have the light in his hands if he needed to fight now.

But they didn't engage him. Their posture shifted and they moved to flank him just as they did when they escorted him into Pinnacle's chamber.

Kaden looked at them both, their black eyes now trained forward.

"Okay... Let's go," Kaden said as he moved forward.

Beth-ell's two Elites went with him.

Chapter 28

The Lighthouse

The desert stretched before them like an ocean of rust, endless waves of sand and stone under a sky that seemed too vast, too empty. Behind them, The Tower was a mere blimp on the map, like a raised finger off in the distance shrouded by storm clouds. Alister led the way, his weathered face serene despite the harsh conditions. Behind him, Elba and Enak trudged through the shifting dunes, their shoulders hunched against the flurries that carried biting sand.

They had emerged from the hidden tunnel three days ago, stepping from the damp darkness of Empyrean's underground into a world most believed was certain death. The Wall had always been the boundary of their known universe – the edge beyond which nothing survived. Yet here they were, walking under an open sky that stretched from horizon to horizon.

"How much further?" Enak called out, his voice rough from thirst.

Alister paused, turning back with that familiar, inexplicable smile. "Faith doesn't ask 'how much further,' brother. It embraces what is given.'"

Elba chuckled despite his cracked lips. "I think my brother's faith would appreciate a timeline."

"This is the way. The Lighthouse will be obvious soon enough," Alister replied, his eyes scanning the horizon. "Jericho prepared the way."

Enak kicked at the sand, sending a plume of dust into the air. "If there even is a Lighthouse. All my life, I've heard stories. Just stories."

"You saw Jericho with your own eyes," Elba reminded him.

"I saw a man die," Enak countered. "I saw Pinnacle rip his heart out while The Tower crumbled around us."

Alister's smile didn't falter, but something in his eyes deepened – not sadness exactly, but a knowing patience. "Once you see, you can't unsee," he said softly, echoing Jericho's words to himself just as much as to the brothers behind him.

They continued walking as the merciless sun beat down upon them. Their water supplies dwindled, their feet blistered and cracked. The land grew more desolate, scattered with the twisted remains of what once were great conifer trees, their stump-like forms frozen in time as if praying to the harsh environment for mercy that would never come.

As night fell on the third day, they made camp in a small inlet of a massive rock formation. The temperature plummeted with the setting sun, forcing them to huddle close around their small fire.

"We should have stayed with Kira," Enak muttered, his breath visible in the cold night air. "At least in Empyrean, we knew the enemy."

"We lived in a prison built on bones," Elba said.

"But we lived," Enak insisted. "Out here, you're waiting to die." He looked up at the night sky. “I used to think the stars in the sky were special.”

“Brother, they are, each created with a purpose, each unique as us,” Elba said.

“You sound like him.” Enak scoffed and turned to Alister.

Alister, who had been sitting silently across the fire, raised his head. His eyes reflected the dancing flames, giving them an otherworldly luminescence. "We're not waiting to die," he said. "We're walking toward life."

"Do you see any life out here?" Enak gestured to the barren landscape around them.

"That's because you're looking with the wrong eyes."

“Yeah...” Enak sounded, then shifted into a sleeping position, inching toward the fire and against his brother.

Elba gave a sympathetic smile to his elder and then shifted to sleep himself.

Alister looked at the fire, and then up to the stars, considering the vast universe around them and the tiny speck that Empyrean played in the distant landscape. The speck of Empyrean glowed, with a flash of electricity in the ever-present clouds that rolled over the isolated kingdom.

Soon, Alister lay down and his heavy eyes closed.

As he slept, a scene appeared in his dreams.

The bright daylight sky darkened as if a curtain had been drawn across the sun. The lush forest surrounding him withered, the bubbling streams ran dry. The Tower rose and then accelerated to the distance, holding a place on the horizon where the sun had set.

A mass of people gathered, looking toward The Tower, their faces contorted with fear from something unseen but felt.

From the horizon came shadows – dozens, then hundreds. The shadows grew to cover the horizon and approached like a rising black water. As it came closer, Alister could feel the fear welling up inside of the others, inside of himself.

They came within view.

An army of Elites.

The dead, hard skin of countless charcoal demons descended upon the valley like a plague.

"No!" Alister called out, but no one heard. He was locked in place, forced to watch as the Elites fell upon the crowd.

No one heard his calls. They stood like statues as the Elites smashed into the group, a sprinting war party against an unknowing group. The raging onslaught was like rush-hour traffic breaking through cones. The people crumpled, were thrown in the air, struck down, or consumed.

Some were spared, taken into groups and herded back toward The Tower, which had begun to change. Its spot on the horizon now grew higher, and came closer, stretching upward, becoming something more cruel and more domineering.

Alister felt the anger of The Tower in his soul, a vengeance that came from a deep sadness and grew stronger with the pain.

“We can’t stay here,” Elba called out, now on the other side of Alister. “Come on! Retreat!” he screamed to the crowd below him, but the words fell on deaf ears. The Elites continued to pillage the people too terrified to move.

Then, behind them, a light appeared. It brightened the dark sky and The Tower quit growing, holding its ominous position on the landscape.

Like a distant star growing brighter, it soon lit up the entire battlefield. The three of them turned, but the light was too bright to look upon. They shielded their eyes, turning away, and saw the Elites now rush to consume as many as they could as the light grew brighter in the valley below.

A figure walked out of the light; no, He was the light. His form was obscured by the radiance that surrounded him, but a clear silhouette emerged.

“It’s Him,” Alister whispered.

The light entered the valley. The Elites sensed it, turning as one toward the approaching figure. They moved to intercept, their forms rippling with darkness and a rage against the light that interrupted their feast.

What happened next was both beautiful and terrible. As the Elites reached the light, they simply… ceased. Not destroyed, not consumed, but unmade – as if they had never been. A thunderous sound echoed from the distance and The Tower trembled, sections crumbling away as the light grew brighter, until the entire valley was washed in radiance so intense that the trio could no longer shield their eyes.

Soon, the light dimmed, and when they could see again, the valley was empty. No people, no Elites, and The Tower was made into a stump. Sand blew in the wind as if no blood were ever spilled.

"He judged them," Alister's voice continued. "Those who had embraced the hunger, who had chosen consumption over compassion – they were *unmade*."

Alister didn't remember any further dreams when he awoke. He stood and saw the light of the sunrise to the east. Moments later, Elba and Enak woke, and they looked at each other as if having a secret to tell.

"There was a battle here," Elba said.

"You saw it too?" Alister asked.

Elba nodded.

They both turned to Enak, who was reluctant, but eventually shook his head yes.

"He's showing us what happened when the Elites stormed the Lighthouse. The Tower claims that's when Jericho died, when Pinnacle took full control," Alister said.

"Looks like he was the only one who survived," Elba said.

Enak remained quiet as if in deep thought.

The trio turned to see the sun peek over the horizon. Brilliant oranges and pinks moved higher into the sky as the bright daylight broke the distant mountains.

Something took shape next to the sunrise. They didn't see it the night before, too far to see in the darkness, but now they saw it and felt it as if something was waiting for them all along. Something that had once been abandoned but would soon be filled again.

As the sun rose higher, they began to see the shape more clearly.

A lighthouse emerged from the world, drowning in shadow.

Chapter 29

Kelly

Kelly stared at the purple glasses resting on the desk in front of her, their frames catching the fluorescent light of the public library. Her fingertips hovered over them, not quite touching. Each time she reached for them, the memory of Kira's death flashed through her mind – the sensation of falling through darkness, the Elite's cold grip, that final, terrible impact she felt in her neck before it all went black.

She pulled her hand back and returned to the computer screen.

For three hours, she'd been digging through financial records, SEC filings, and business journals. Her branch of the Atlanta Public Library's computer lab was nearly empty as the closing hour approached, just a few elderly patrons checking email, one of them typing replies with one finger as he searched for the right keys, and a college student dozing in the corner. The solitude suited her as she pieced together the puzzle of Empyrean Enterprises.

"It doesn't make sense," she whispered to herself, scrolling through another quarterly report. "Why would a pharmaceutical research company be selling off patents and shifting cash and assets?"

Artwork and crafts were her release, but Kelly had always had a talent for finding patterns in financial data. It was what made her successful as a corporate financial analyst. Where others saw disconnected numbers, she saw stories – narratives of ambition, fear, preparation, and strategy. And the story emerging from Empyrean Enterprises' financials was confusing considering their industry, which made it deeply disturbing. R&D should have taken the lion's share of reinvestment dollars when researching new drugs, but investment R&D was drying up.

She opened a new browser tab and typed in more search parameters, cross-referencing the subsidiaries she'd identified. Three years ago, Empyrean had undergone a significant restructuring, shifting billions in assets into a labyrinthine network of holding companies, trusts, and specialized corporate entities.

Kelly created a flowchart on her notepad, mapping the relationships between entities. It wasn't a typical corporate structure designed for tax advantages – this was something else entirely. The structure seemed designed to preserve assets through catastrophic events and position them for rapid deployment afterward. To an analyst, the strategy was pure madness for a pharmaceutical company, as if they were spreading billions into a complex network of commodity-like investments plus a web of speculative bets as a whole other layer.

"Perpetual trusts in South Dakota... distributed ownership across seventeen countries... resource rights acquisitions focused on water, precious metals, arable land, and rare minerals," she muttered as she wrote.

What caught her eye was a pattern of investments in what she mentally labeled "doomsday infrastructure" – self-contained production facilities, deep underground research complexes, seed vaults, and specialized medical repositories. All positioned in geographically advantageous locations – high elevations, regions with geothermal energy potential, areas with natural aquifer access.

Then there were the financial instruments – complex arrangements that would only make sense if one anticipated global economic collapse. Crisis-triggered options, contingent claims on infrastructure, and massive positions in commodities that would be essential in a post-industrial world.

"He's preparing for the end," she whispered.

Most disturbing were the "Phoenix corporations" – shell companies with minimal current activity but comprehensive plans and resources to expand rapidly into specific sectors after black swan-like events. These weren't publicly acknowledged, but Kelly recognized the pattern from a research project analyzing corporate raiders. These were positioned to swoop in and acquire critical assets at pennies on the dollar when markets collapsed.

A footnote in last year's annual report caught her attention:

"As part of our strategic refocusing on core pharmaceutical and healthcare initiatives, Empyrean Enterprises has divested all interest in Beacon Holdings LLC and its subsidiaries."

“But you’re *not* focusing on core pharmaceuticals...” she muttered.

Kelly's heart raced as she typed "Beacon Holdings LLC" into the search bar. The results were sparse – it was a privately held company with minimal public footprint. But one result made her breath catch: a small business listing for "Abrams Optical, a subsidiary of Beacon Holdings LLC."

Dr. Abrams's eye care office.

She dug deeper, searching for any connection between Beacon Holdings and Dr. David Abrams. Eventually, she found a medical journal article from fifteen years ago, crediting "research support from the Beacon Institute, founded by Dr. David Abrams."

Kelly sat back, pieces falling into place. Thornhill and Abrams had been partners, pioneers in the early Hope Drug development. But they'd had a fundamental disagreement – not just scientific, but moral, spiritual. They'd split, each forming their own corporate entities, each preparing for what they saw coming.

She remembered fragments from Jericho's journal that Kira had found in the tunnels beneath Empyrean. He'd written about the coming catastrophe, about nuclear war and environmental collapse. About the Hope Drug spreading through the population, corrupting and transforming.

But where Thornhill was positioning himself to emerge as the dominant power – to become Pinnacle – Abrams had Beacon Holdings for a different purpose. To preserve resources not for control but for hope.

“Is this how you built the Lighthouse?” she whispered as she read.

Kelly opened another quarterly report and noticed something she'd missed before. The timing of Empyrean's acquisitions and market positions didn't just suggest preparation for disaster – they suggested foreknowledge.

"He knows exactly what’s coming," she whispered.

Land purchases in specific regions just before previously unpredicted water shortages were announced. Short positions on European financial institutions days before a banking crisis.

These weren't lucky guesses. This was the financial footprint of someone who had foresight into very specific regional events.

“Correlation isn’t causation,” she reminded herself, but the dots were all connecting, and she knew that when something looked too good to be true on a balance sheet, it usually was. Yet with all the shifts in holdings over the past few years, the stock price was chugging along with consistent gains, but not extreme growth as to cause alarm. It was like a perfect index fund: gain two points, give back one, gain three, give back two.

Kelly glanced at the purple glasses again. The world was racing toward catastrophe. Thornhill was accelerating it, positioning himself to rise from the ashes as Pinnacle. And given what she'd seen of Empyrean's future, he would succeed. The Tower would rise and the current world was ignorant to it. Most of humanity would fall.

Unless...

"Death is not the end," she whispered, remembering the caller's words.

A profound realization washed over her. The end of the world as she knew it was inevitable. No amount of warning or intervention would prevent the catastrophes to come. But she had seen beyond that end – she had lived as Kira in the world that emerged from the ashes.

A bleak world, yes. A broken world. But a world where a resistance still fought. Where the Lighthouse Remnant still carried the torch of hope against The Tower's shadow.

She thought of Darren's body lying cold in the morgue. Of Kira's broken form in the rubble beneath The Tower. Of Dr. Abrams – Jericho – his heart torn from his chest by Pinnacle.

Death had claimed them all. But something continued. Kaden had returned multiple times. Something was persisting between worlds.

Kelly picked up the purple glasses, turning them over in her hands. The fear was still there, clutching at her insides – the memory of falling, of being hunted by the Elite. But now it was matched with a growing resolve.

Chapter 30

Kaden

The night seemed endless as Kaden followed the two Elites through the winding paths of the Outer Ring. The Tower's looming presence over all of Empyrean kept him focused as they moved forward. Shadows stretched across crumbling buildings, casting strange shapes that seemed to watch his every move. Each step took him further from Beth-ell's hideout, further from what remained of the Remnant, and closer to The Tower.

His mind kept returning to Kira's broken body, the way her neck had been bent at that impossible angle. The connection between them – that invisible tether that had guided him through The Tower – was gone, leaving a hollow emptiness that ached with each heartbeat. The idea of him returning to life as Darren after dying as Kaden loomed in his mind, but her neck, even if she could somehow come back, her body in no way could sustain life.

The Elites didn't speak; they rarely did. Their coal-black forms moved with unnatural grace, leading him deeper into the maze of streets. Occasionally, their heads would pivot in unison, scanning for threats, like a dog catching a scent, but they encountered no one. The Outer Ring was eerily deserted, its usual desperate inhabitants nowhere to be seen. Kaden was becoming used to feeling isolated as he went through the most impoverished outer parts of Empyrean.

Just as he let his thoughts steal his attention away, the Elites stopped. They perked up like bloodhounds picking up a scent. The old story of *Where the Red Fern Grows* flickered through Kaden's memory, a distant dream of Darren's mother reading him a chapter a night before bed.

The pair turned to each other, exchanging a knowing expression through the silence.

They shifted forward with a new swiftness as they turned down an alley. Their graceful forms flew through the alley and then slowed, now more reserved and cautious as they emerged into a small courtyard. Kaden ran behind and the courtyard opened up over their shoulders as it came into view. In its center stood a building unlike any Kaden had seen in Empyrean – not the gleaming perfection of The Tower, nor the decaying shambles of the Outer Ring. This structure was... preserved. Ancient. Yet, eerily familiar to Kaden.

A small stone chapel with a peaked roof and a rusted bell tower that appeared as if it hadn't rung in centuries. It was elegant albeit ancient, like a perfect little toy of a grand cathedral placed right in the middle of the otherwise despot Outer Ring.

The Elites stopped at the entrance, and looked back at Kaden, their charcoal-like bodies and matte skin seeming to absorb the moonlight. Their caution gave Kaden a distinct concern, yet one gestured toward the door, the cracked surface of its arm making a sound like grinding stones.

Though it had no visible eyes, Kaden felt the little chapel as if its gaze were boring into him. He felt watched and guided here, but eager to enter, like Hansel and Gretel first seeing the witch's house.

"He knows... He came to you," one of the Elites managed, the words emerging like air escaping a tomb.

Kaden's blood ran cold. "Who?"

“Pinn—” But the Elites were pushed back before they could say the name, like a forcefield keeping them away from the stone chapel. They stayed as close as they could, locking eyes on him and the chapel, but unable to follow him closer.

Every instinct screamed at him to run, to disappear into the maze of the Outer Ring. But the chapel called to him. And if it was Pinnacle inside, what would that accomplish? Pinnacle came out here to meet him, and he’d find him eventually.

Kaden took a deep breath, steadying himself as he walked toward it, and pushed open the ancient wooden door.

The chapel's interior was dim, illuminated only by moonlight filtering through high, narrow windows. The space was surprisingly intact – wooden pews lined up in rows, facing a simple stone altar. The musty scent of age hung in the air, undisturbed for decades until this moment.

And there, seated in the front pew, was Pinnacle.

He wore a black robe lined with bright white stitching, as if lines of light held the darkness of the material together. His appearance seemed calm, patient, as if he was in a state of peaceful meditation. The patches of obsidian that had rippled across his face in The Tower were gone. He seemed more Thomas Thornhill than the all-powerful Pinnacle that ruled Empyrean with an iron fist.

"Kaden McCloud," Pinnacle said, his voice echoing in the empty chapel. "Do you like this place?"

"I don't know this place."

"I make it when needed. A call back to the chapel I grew up in."

Kaden's eyebrows raised.

Pinnacle smiled. "You know more than most of our humble beginnings, back when the world was different. My parents passed when I was young, like you. And like you, my grandparents raised me. But for elderly children of the Depression, there was no place for a curious ten-year-old boy."

Pinnacle looked up at the stone altar as he spoke. Kaden moved down the center aisle, now close to the front pew.

"They sent me to a boarding school in New England. There I was, a southern kid used to playing in back streams and praying I could join my father deer hunting just one more time, sent off to live with all the trust-fund kids."

"It could be worse," Kaden said. "Some get abandoned."

"No, not for me. I was so mad when my parents died, and being shipped off just made it worse. I felt orphaned and out of control." He looked up at Kaden. "Please," he said, extending his hand to the pew across the center aisle. "Sit."

Kaden sat but did not take his eyes off of him.

"We had Chapel every Sunday, Wednesday, and Friday. In a place like this. *Exactly* like this."

"How did you know I'd come?" Kaden asked.

Pinnacle smiled, the expression never quite reaching his eyes. "I knew you'd find your way here, eventually."

"I grew up out here, but this place wasn't here. You built it for times like these?" Kaden guessed.

Pinnacle nodded in agreement.

"Why?"

"Sentiment, perhaps." Pinnacle ran his hand along the weathered wood of the pew. "Or perhaps to remember what we left behind. Faith. Superstition. The belief that something greater than ourselves was watching over us." He turned back to Kaden, his eyes gleaming with an unnatural light. "We are those greater beings now, Kaden. We've become what humanity once prayed to."

Kaden leaned in, drawn to the conversation despite inner warnings to run. "Is that why you brought me here? To gloat at how you're in control?"

"No. I include you in that definition now. You've come a long way from the boy sitting in David's office."

Kaden's jaw clenched at the memory.

"I brought you here because this is neutral ground," Pinnacle replied. "Neither Tower nor Remnant. A place reminiscent of our past where we can speak honestly."

"What do you want?" Kaden asked.

"To offer you a choice," Pinnacle said simply.

"You're having me sort myself now?" Kaden scoffed. "As you decide who lives and who gets consumed by your Elites, or by you?"

"No." Pinnacle's voice remained steady in his simple answer, undisturbed by Kaden's hostility. "A true choice. For the first time since you arrived in Empyrean."

"I've made my choice when I left The Tower."

"Have you?" Pinnacle turned to face him fully. "Or has Jericho made them for you? Sending you back and forth through time, manipulating your life and your very identity. Darren McArthur. Kaden McCloud. Two lives, yet neither fully your own."

The words struck Kaden like a physical blow. He'd never considered his situation that way before.

"He gave me sight," Kaden replied.

"He gave you a burden," Pinnacle countered. "Made you a pawn in a game you don't understand." He leaned closer, his voice dropping to a confessional whisper. "I could free you from that burden. Cut the puppeteer's strings and give you a real purpose."

"I've seen your purpose." Kaden's hands clenched into fists. "Control. Consumption. Fear."

"You've seen what Jericho wanted you to see," Pinnacle replied. "The Tower as a prison rather than the sanctuary it was meant to be. The Elites as monsters rather than evolved beings." He gestured to the chapel around them. "But there's so much more to the story."

"Like what?"

"Like the fact that I saved humanity when no one else could," Pinnacle said, his voice rising with passion. "When the wars came and the old world burned – I finished what he couldn't, what he wouldn't. I preserved what could be preserved. I sorted the strong from the weak so that we might survive. I suppose the saying is right: 'you either die a hero, or you live long enough to see yourself become the villain.'"

"At what cost?" Kaden demanded. "Ninety-nine percent dead?"

"They were already dead," Pinnacle shot back. "Annihilation was inevitable, whether from health causes or a nuclear winter. I gave them the Hope Drug. It was their only chance in the face of insurmountable odds. Is it my fault that not all bodies could adapt to it in time? But I gave them a chance, and those who survived—" He spread his hands. "We became something more. Something that could endure what was coming."

Kaden shook his head. "You're talking about the apocalypse like it was inevitable."

"No one questions Noah after the flood because he died a hero," Pinnacle insisted. "I saw it coming and I lived through it. Jericho saw it too. The difference between us was that I acted while he philosophized." His face hardened. "He could have joined me. We could have saved more, transformed more. He was brilliant in his time, but he chose his lighthouse over reason–His precious morality and small band of believers."

"And you chose The Tower," Kaden said.

"I chose survival," Pinnacle countered. "I chose reality."

A silence fell between them, broken only by the distant sound of wind whistling above the chapel.

"Why are you telling me this?" Kaden finally asked.

Pinnacle remained silent for a long moment, taking in breaths and releasing them as if in deep thought. "Because you're different, Kaden. There's something in you – something Jericho placed there. A spark I haven't seen in anyone else since... Well, not since him."

"The light," Kaden said.

"Yes." Pinnacle nodded. "You may call it light. I've called it by other names throughout the centuries. Quantum resonance. Cellular transcendence. Neural acceleration. But yes, sure, light." His eyes gleamed with that unnatural brightness. "And I want you to join me in spreading that light."

Kaden laughed, the sound hollow in the empty chapel. "Yesterday, you tried to consume me; now you want me to join you? Forgive me if I can't tell the difference. You want me to forget all you've done and don a purple robe this time, or better yet, become an Elite?"

"No," Pinnacle said, leaning forward. "I want you to stand at my side. Not as an Agent, not as an Elite, but as a partner. Together, we could transform Empyrean into what it was always meant to be."

"And what's that?"

"A new Eden," Pinnacle replied, his voice dropping to a reverent whisper. "Not just the last city, but the first of many. We could reclaim the wasteland, expand beyond The Wall. With your light and what I've built as a foundation, we could heal the world, Kaden."

He waved his hand and the stone altar before them rose and shifted. Every rock seemed to disintegrate and reform, creating a mosaic of Empyrean. The Tower in the center and gorgeous, pristine buildings that stretched out into lush forests instead of being held in by the immense wall surrounded by deserts.

“All of this would be yours,” he said.

Despite himself, Kaden felt a flicker of interest. "How could you heal it?"

"The Hope Drug was never meant to create monsters," Pinnacle explained. "It was meant to save lives. To cure disease. To extend human potential beyond its natural limits. The result wasn’t exactly what David might have foreseen, but we achieved the outcome of survival, there’s no doubting that. But what if... What if we could perfect it? Find the balance Jericho and I sought before our paths diverged? What if we could return to humanity?"

"You mean before you corrupted it," Kaden said.

Pinnacle let out a breath and shook his head. "You’ll have to understand that circumstances force adaptations. Go back to Darwin," he corrected smoothly. "But with you – with what you carry – we could find a new way forward. Yours is a gift that we cannot spoil."

Kaden's mind raced, weighing the possibilities. "Why would you want a partnership now? Why offer me this position when you are *so powerful*?"

Pinnacle leaned back, studying Kaden with those unsettling eyes. "Because I'm tired, Kaden. I've carried Empyrean alone for centuries. Built it, maintained it, protected it from inside and out. The Hunter of Hunters, the Chooser from the Chosen." He gestured to his face, where the black veins pulsed beneath his skin. "It takes a toll, even on me."

"So you need help," Kaden said, unable to keep the skepticism from his voice.

"I need balance," Pinnacle corrected. "Just as the old world needed both light and darkness, both order and chaos, so does Empyrean need both Pinnacle and..." He paused, smiling slightly. "What would you call yourself, I wonder?"

The question caught Kaden off guard. What would he call himself? He'd never thought beyond survival, beyond resistance, to a life of abundance.

Pinnacle noticed the pause. "It's natural to want purpose. It's a hallmark of a builder, and if you're not a builder, you're a destroyer," he said.

"The Remnant has purpose," Kaden replied, but the words sounded hollow even to him, more of a question than a statement. With Kira gone, with Jericho dead, what was left of that purpose? He felt like he was right back in front of Ron-ell, eager to find his purpose by becoming an Agent.

"They're dying, Kaden," Pinnacle said gently. "This isn't the first time resistance has risen and then fallen. It's sad to see the waste. One by one, they fall. I'm sorry to tell you, but you saw it. Jericho is dead. So is Kira." He shook his head. "It's a shame. How many more will you lose before you accept that their narrow road leads only to extinction?"

"They died fighting for freedom," Kaden insisted.

"And what fruit did it bear? Their actions are admirable, sure, but what changed? They died in vain," Pinnacle countered. "But *you* could ensure their sacrifices had meaning. Join me, help me reform Empyrean from within. Make it a place worthy of their memory and then expand to the world."

Kaden stood, needing to move, to think. He paced the length of the chapel. Pinnacle didn't turn back, yet Kaden still felt watched. The offer swirled in his mind, tempting in ways he hadn't expected. Not the power, but the purpose. Not merely trying to survive in tunnels, but being part of creation.

"And what about the sorting?" Kaden asked, turning back to Pinnacle. "The consumption? The Elites feeding on the weak?"

Pinnacle spread his hands. "Necessary evils, in a world of scarcity. But with your help, with your light, perhaps we could find alternatives. You've seen the pastures. There can be more humane methods of maintaining balance."

"You're lying," Kaden said, but doubt crept into his voice.

"Am I?" Pinnacle stood, his tall frame casting a long shadow in the moonlight. "Or am I offering you the one thing Jericho never did – a *real* choice?"

The words hit Kaden like a physical blow. Did Jericho ever truly give him a choice? Or had he simply been moved like a piece on a game board, sent back and forth through time to serve a purpose he barely understood?

"I've seen what you are," Kaden said, struggling to hold on to his convictions. "In The Tower. That shadow-Elite with Jericho's heart. The way you tried to consume me."

"You threatened me," Pinnacle replied. "You came to kill me, both in the past and in Empyrean. What would you have done in my position?" He stepped closer, his eyebrows slightly raised and his palms up. "But now I'm stepping back and offering peace. A new beginning."

Part of him wanted to believe Pinnacle, to accept the olive branch. It was tiring to think of a never-ending fight. To have purpose beyond resistance, beyond mere survival. To build something new from the ashes of the old.

"And what about the others?" Kaden asked. "Beth-ell. Riggs. Jace. Aria."

Pinnacle's response came out smooth as silk. "Three traitors and a lifelong fighter of The Tower?" He shook his head. "Yet... Those who are willing to put aside old grievances for the greater good would be welcome in the new Empyrean."

"And those who aren't?" Kaden asked.

Pinnacle's expression hardened slightly. "There will always be those who cling to the past, who cannot embrace change. They must be handled appropriately."

"Consumed," Kaden translated.

"It wouldn't be necessary for all." The underside of his eyelids grew tighter as focused on Kaden more sharply. "You understand that utopias are fiction, right? That's not the real world of hard decisions. Compromises must be made. If you join me and want your friends to come too, that'll be a hard sell to the Elites. You'd need to show that you are aligned to the mission. You'd need to make a commitment." He smiled again sympathetically, yet the expression never quite reached his eyes.

"What kind of *commitment*?"

"From what I've seen, you could rise as far as you want. My right hand man. You'd be Joseph saving Egypt from famine. The Pharaoh gave Joseph his ring to signify his power, and all of the world knew Joseph's authority. Then he used it to save his family."

"And your *ring*?"

"You could take the test, become an Elite to show the world your authority. Think of what you could do across the centuries!"

Kaden felt his face go pale at the thought of becoming an Elite.

"I already have allies among the Remnant, Kaden. People who see the futility of resistance, who are ready for a new path. Lead them with me. Point them in the right direction."

Kaden felt a cold knot form in his stomach. "What do you mean 'allies'?"

"The Remnant has always harbored those who waver in their faith, who question Jericho's path. Aren't we all seeking the same outcome? But living like cockroaches isn't the way to do it." He paused briefly and tilted his head as he leaned into the conversation.

"How do you think I've always known where to find you? How the Elites always seem to arrive just as you're escaping? Coincidence?" He shook his head. "I have eyes everywhere, Kaden, including in the Remnant, and that's a great thing! There are many who recognize that and embrace it, more than you'd think."

Faces flashed through Kaden's mind – Riggs with his perpetual suspicion, Jace and Aria with their ties to The Tower, Enak with his bitter complaints about Kira's leadership. Any of them could be a traitor.

Kaden heard a sound like rock scraping rock from outside. Pinnacle's fingers flickered and the sound disappeared.

"You're turning us against each other," he said.

"I'm showing you reality," Pinnacle countered. "The reality Jericho tried to shield you from – that humans are not perfect and never will be. That means they're weak. That they break under pressure. They'll betray when it serves them." He stepped closer, his voice dropping to a confidential whisper. "But we could be something more, Kaden. Something beyond human weakness. That's what I'm building here, and something *we* could build together."

To have purpose, to have power, to be more than a pawn in someone else's game. To build rather than merely survive. Kaden saw himself standing at the top of The Tower, a lush landscape below him that entwined a thriving metropolis. The Garden of Eden on a massive scale that would flourish for all time, and he'd be the one making it happen.

The temptation was overwhelming.

But as he thought, and Pinnacle spoke, something stirred in Kaden's memory. The desert surrounding them, the death he'd seen. This world was bearing no fruit.

Then Jericho's words came to mind, echoing across time: "Once you see, you can't unsee."

He had seen The Tower for what it was – not a sanctuary but a prison. He had seen the Elites for what they were – not evolved beings but souls trapped in endless hunger. He had seen Pinnacle for what he was – not a savior but a tyrant clutching at godhood.

And he had seen something else too – Jericho standing before Pinnacle, making no move to defend himself as his heart was torn from his chest. Not a weakness, but a strength. Kaden was only beginning to understand. He saw Jericho's heart, and it beat. The heart was still beating.

"No," Kaden said, the word barely audible.

Pinnacle paused. "What was that?"

"I said no." Kaden's voice grew stronger, more certain. "I *won't* join you."

Disappointment flickered across Pinnacle's face, quickly replaced by calm. "Think carefully, Kaden. What is the wise thing to do here? Given what you've seen and what is to come, what is the wise thing to do here?"

Kaden remained silent. The scratching sound came in again from outside, and once again, Pinnacle's hand flicked and the sound disappeared, but now a subtle wave of black rolled across his face as it flashed a millisecond of frustration.

"You have one chance to save them. I'm afraid I can't offer this again," Pinnacle said.

"Good," Kaden replied. "Because my answer won't change." He braced himself for Pinnacle to erupt, but to his surprise, Pinnacle sat back down where he'd been when Kaden first entered.

"Why?" Pinnacle said aloud, as if to himself. "I'm offering everything – power, purpose, a chance to rebuild the world!" he said, shaking his head.

"Because I see you for what you are – the serpent in the garden," Kaden replied.

At this, Pinnacle erupted in laughter. At first, a small chuckle, then it boomed as if rolling thunder coming across the plains to flatten everything in its path. The small chapel shook as his laughter grew.

"Youth is," he laughed further, "wasted on the young." Then, abruptly, his laughter stopped. He stood, turning to Kaden and looking down at him, his chiseled jawline clenched and his eyes set with fury. "You cling to Jericho's fairy tales. Myths that poison your soul," he said, and the air around him trembled.

"Not myths," Kaden replied. "Truth. Once you see, you can't unsee."

"And you've seen?" Pinnacle sneered.

"That true power comes through surrender, not control," Kaden said, remembering Beth-ell's lessons. "That real strength is found in sacrifice, not consumption."

"How much has surrender and sacrifice accomplished for the Remnant? Jericho is dead. Kira is dead. Your precious resistance crumbles while The Tower stands strong."

"He saw what you can't – that some victories look exactly like defeat, at first."

"The comments of a hopeless loser. I held his heart in my hand."

"Yet, it still beats," Kaden said with conviction.

Pinnacle's lip curled and the chapel around them shook. The walls bowed with tension like a coiled spring.

"You couldn't consume me because it still beats in your shadow-pet. And HIS light flows through me. Through all of us who choose to see."

The world seemed to stop as Kaden's words left his lips. In less than a second, a quick succession of events happened nearly instantaneously.

The scratching noise from outside the door came again, more forcefully and sharper than before. It came as Pinnacle's skin rippled with the rolling darkness, rage erupting and manifesting in the air around him. The stones that built the walls of the small chapel broke free from the mortar. All of the beautiful little chapel's building materials came free and shot at Kaden. The structural artwork of Pinnacle's creation turned into countless deadly weapons that collapsed onto Kaden as if he were in the center of a blackhole.

The barrier made by the chapel's doors and walls was now down. The scratching noise previously at the door revealed itself. Beth-ell's Elites shot forward at nearly the speed of light. Two blacks blurs from behind Kaden, they shot ahead faster than the collapsing building could reach him. They wrapped around him and one shielded him as the other went low, digging out a tunnel in the ground like a meteor striking the earth. The cacophony of stone crashing into the Elite shielding Kaden was like an explosion to his eardrum. All perception of sound left him, as if a concussion grenade went off.

A moment later, they shot out of the ground into a nearby building of the Outer Ring, but they didn't stop. The Elite leading the escape raised its hand and smashed through walls, then brought them back into the ground, throwing away dirt like blowing aside dust. Behind them, the building collapsed just as the chapel did before, more building materials shooting toward them. They weaved through the earth, coming up and out, but the rage behind them kept striking as it devoured their path. They stayed a half step ahead of the destruction, but as Kaden's senses came back to him, he could see the Elite as his back was fading. It had taken the brunt of the chapel's force and its charcoal exterior was cracked. They barreled through the Outer Ring, now more buildings around them coming apart and shooting toward them.

Their lead on the destruction diminished, the wounded Elite now being hit by the growing cloud of debris. With each seemingly random movement they made to stay away from Pinnacle's wrath, the destruction got closer. Like a rabbit trying to outrun a wolf, with each agile shift, the wolf closed in. Inch by inch, the Elite protecting Kaden was being wounded.

Kaden looked down and saw its black eyes. They met, and for the first time, there was a spark in them. One star in a cloudy night sky whose light barely flickered, yet visible.

Cradled in the protection of their supernatural escape, Kaden leaned back and put himself in the path of the chasing death. The Elite shifted, trying to not let him, but it was too weak to stop him.

The first piece that hit him was a dull thud that knocked out the feeling in his right arm. The next struck the middle of his back and he felt as if multiple ribs were broken. Another struck his left elbow with such force, the joint hyperextended. The pain radiated through Kaden as he was being crushed to death by the never-ending onslaught of bricks and buildings. The wounded Elite shifted, trying to move back to his protective position, but Kaden wrapped his arms around the creature. It was too weak to resist as the Elite at their front charged forward and pulled them behind.

Another piece struck Kaden near his wrist and he felt his hand erupt in searing pain as pieces of bone cut through skin.

The Elite in the lead glanced back to see Kaden's shifted position in protection of the other Elite. Its pace slowed only a fraction of an inch, but it was enough for Pinnacle's wrath to catch them. A flicker of light emanated from Kaden's skin, but it was soon blotted out as the city block of debris crashed down on the trio.

As if a gigantic snake had slithered through the Outer Ring, a trail of destroyed buildings and unlucky inhabitants' bodies in its wake. At the head of the trail of destruction was a mountain of debris.

Kaden and Elites, crushed underneath.

Chapter 31

Kira

A thunderous roar of crashing material tore through the night, shaking the floors of Beth-ell's hideout and jolting the Remnant group from their fitful sleep. The sound didn't stop but built like an avalanche picking up momentum.

Riggs was on his feet in an instant, muscles tensed and ready for battle. Jace and Aria moved like trained soldiers in practiced unison toward the small window at the front of the shelter, their Agent training evident in their fluid, coordinated movements.

"What was that?" Jace whispered, peering through the grimy glass from side angles.

In the distance, a massive cloud of dust billowed upward, obscuring entire blocks of the Outer Ring. Even from here, they could see buildings ripped apart and entering the cloud as if they were a part of a violent chain reaction – like a massive serpent was writhing on a dusty surface, kicking up individual buildings in a plume of dust that rose and crashed back down.

“Where’s Kaden?” Aria said.

"He's gone to him," Beth-ell said, her voice cutting through the darkness. She hadn't been sleeping like the others; she sat in the same metal chair as before, her weathered face illuminated by the faint light filtering through the window.

Riggs turned to her, his massive frame casting a long shadow. "You knew?"

She nodded, her eyes looking past them to the destruction in the distance. "He chose his path."

"And you let him walk to his death?" Riggs growled, taking a menacing step toward her.

Beth-ell remained unmoved. "His journey can’t prevent suffering, but if we’re lucky, he’ll find what he needs within it."

"Your cryptic nonsense helps no one," Riggs spat.

Another tremor shook the building, stronger than the first. Dust rained down from the ceiling as hairline cracks appeared in the walls. The devastation was spreading, and inching closer to them.

"We should go," Jace urged, grabbing a pack of their meager supplies. "Now."

Aria nodded in agreement, but then her eyes focused on the cot behind them. "Wait... Riggs, can you get her..." She motioned for Riggs to pick up Kira’s body but trailed off as she stepped toward the body. Something seemed different.

In the dim light, Kira's body lay on the makeshift stretcher where they had placed her hours earlier. Her neck had been bent at that horrific angle, her skin pale and lifeless. But now – a subtle change. A faint coloring returned to her cheeks, and her chest – imperceptibly at first, then unmistakably – began to rise and fall.

"That's not possible," Aria whispered.

From across the room, Beth-ell watched with no trace of surprise in her ancient eyes. "Death is not the end," she murmured.

Then the first subtle crack of bone resonated in the large, dingy room as Kira's vertebrae began to realign.

***

Darkness.

Then pain – excruciating, overwhelming pain radiating from the center of her being. She couldn't breathe, couldn't move, couldn't scream. It was as if every cell in her body was on fire.

Memories of Kelly and of Kira flickered like dying embers and swirled together.

Putting on the purple glasses back at Darren's apartment. The sensation of falling, sliding through the metal shaft. The Elite pulling her upward. Pain in her back. The snap of her neck.

I died, she realized with startling clarity. *Kira died*.

Yet consciousness remained, Kira's consciousness now returning. Trapped in a broken vessel, aware but unable to move. The darkness seemed infinite, crushing.

Then came the heat. Not the searing pain of injury, but something else – a warmth that began deep within her chest and radiated outward. It pulsed with her heartbeat – a heart that shouldn't be beating.

Lub-dub.

She felt the spark of life.

With each pulse, the warmth spread further. She felt it reach the shattered vertebrae in her neck, and the pain intensified as broken bone fragments began to move. The sensation was like glass shards shifting inside her flesh, her bones breaking, yet guided by some invisible force.

Lub-dub.

Her lungs expanded suddenly, drawing in a ragged breath that felt like the first she'd ever taken. Oxygen rushed through her, feeding the warmth and the healing as a fullness swelled from within.

Lub-dub.

Her heart beat.

The bones in her neck continued their unnatural movement, realigning themselves like a macabre puzzle finding its proper form. She felt each fragment settle into place with a tiny click that resounded through her being. Tissue reconnected, blood vessels repaired themselves, severed nerves sparked back to life.

Lub-dub.

The pain began to recede, replaced by an odd tingling sensation, like a million pinpricks, that spread from her neck down her spine and into her limbs. It was as if thousands of tiny repair agents were crawling beneath her skin, rebuilding her from the inside out.

Lub-dub.

Her fingers twitched. A small movement, but monumental. Sensation returned to her arms, her chest, her legs. The horrifying numbness of death gave way to the sweet ache of life returning.

Lub-dub.

Lub-dub.

Behind her closed eyelids, light began to filter through – not from outside, but from within. It pulsed with each heartbeat, growing stronger, pushing back the darkness.

Lub-dub.

Lub-dub.

Lub-dub.

The final vertebra slipped into place with a dull crack, and Kira's eyes shot open. A gasp tore from her throat – half pain, half wonder – as her body arched upward.

She was alive. She was Kira again.

Her blurred vision slowly focused on the faces staring down at her – Riggs, Jace, Aria – their expressions frozen in disbelief. Behind them sat Beth-ell, watching with the slightest of smiles, and eyes that held neither surprise nor confusion, but something deeper. Recognition.

Kira tried to speak, but her newly healed vocal cords produced only a rasp. She swallowed, wincing at the dry tenderness in her throat, and tried again.

"Kaden," she managed to whisper. "I can feel him. He's in trouble."

Riggs dropped to his knees beside her, his weathered face struggling between joy and terror. "You were dead," he said hoarsely. "Your neck was – I held you—"

Another tremor rocked the building, stronger than before. Dust and small chunks of ceiling rained down on them.

The destruction crept closer.

"Help me up," Kira asked, her voice growing stronger with each word. She extended her hand, and after a moment's hesitation, Riggs took it, pulling her gently to her feet.

Her body felt strange – familiar yet different, as if it had been taken apart and rebuilt with subtle changes. Each movement brought new sensations, nerves reawakening to their purpose – the feeling of being alive felt and not taken for granted. Beneath the physical disorientation lay a certainty, a knowledge that pulsed through her veins alongside her restored blood.

"I know where he is," she said, turning toward the window and the billowing dust cloud beyond.

Beth-ell moved to her side, studying her with those ancient eyes. "You've seen," she stated simply.

Kira nodded. "I've seen."

Another violent tremor shook the building, and large fissures emerged, sending fist-sized pieces of the ceiling falling around them. The wall nearest the window developed a large crack that spread upward like lightning.

"We have to go," Jace insisted, more urgently now.

"Yes," Kira agreed, but her eyes remained fixed on the destruction in the distance. "We're going straight at it."

A light flickered around her fingertips. It didn't die away but continued to glow, casting soft shadows on the walls of the crumbling shelter.

"Why is it always straight at the fight?" Jace said, turning to Aria, but Riggs's eyes saw what Kira's fingers were doing.

Riggs looked at her hand, then at her face. "What happened to you?"

Kira met his gaze, and in her eyes was a certainty that hadn't been there before – a purpose that transcended fear, transcended even survival.

"Death is not the end," she said, echoing Beth-ell's words. "It's a doorway."

And with that, she stepped toward the exit, toward the chaos, toward Kaden – her body moving with newfound strength – a strength reborn.

Chapter 32

The Lighthouse

The Lighthouse rose from the desert floor like a defiant finger pointing skyward. As dawn broke fully over the horizon, its weathered stone facade caught the sunlight, transforming from a shadowy silhouette into a structure of surprising grace. Against the barren landscape, it seemed both out of place and perfectly positioned – a beacon in a wasteland that had once been a thriving world.

Alister stopped several hundred yards from the base, his weathered face tilted upward as he took in the full height of the structure. His eyes gleamed with an emotion that neither Elba nor Enak could name – something beyond reverence, a vindication of a lifelong belief.

"This is it," he said simply. "The Lighthouse."

Elba stepped forward, squinting against the harsh morning light. The structure was both smaller and larger than he'd imagined – perhaps a hundred feet tall, cylindrical, with a glass-encased apex that reflected the sunlight in prismatic patterns across the desert floor. Its stone walls were a pale sand color, almost blending with the surrounding terrain, yet standing in stark contrast to the chaotic, jagged structures of Empyrean.

"It's real," Elba breathed, awe evident in his voice. "All these years... I still thought it might just be a story."

"All stories begin somewhere," Alister replied, his usual cheerfulness tempered by something deeper. "And some are truer than others." He winked toward the brothers with uncontainable delight.

Enak hung back, his face unreadable. Since waking from their shared vision in the night, he had been quieter than usual, his typical complaints and outbursts subdued by something that seemed to be churning within him.

"We should check for Elites," Enak said finally, his eyes scanning the horizon. "If it's real, they've been here before."

Alister shook his head. "No... No Elite has set foot near here since the battle. They can't."

"Can't?" Elba asked.

"Won't," Alister corrected himself. "This place isn't what they think it is."

He began walking again, his pace measured but deliberate. The brothers exchanged a glance before following, their feet dragging through sand that seemed to resist each step, but now they felt stronger.

As they drew closer, details emerged that weren't visible from a distance. The stonework of the Lighthouse was intricate, patterns carved into its surface in a script none of them recognized. Most striking was the door – a simple arch of weathered wood, unassuming yet somehow inviting, the work of a master carpenter.

Alister moved toward the door.

“I hope it’s unlocked,” Enak muttered.

"He's left it open for us," Alister said. His weathered hand touched the wood and a subtle vibration ran through the structure – not a tremor or quake, but a response, as if the building itself had sighed in a friendly recognition.

The massive, yet perfectly balanced door swung open without a sound.

Inside, cool air rushed to meet them – a blessed relief from the desert heat. They moved into a circular chamber, its walls lined with shelves that reached toward a spiral staircase at the center. The staircase went both up toward the apex and down into chambers below the ground. Daylight filtered through the high, narrow windows, casting slanted beams across floors of polished stone.

But it was the silence that struck them first. After the whistling winds of the desert, the interior of the Lighthouse seemed to exist in a different dimension – a pocket of sacred stillness.

"It's empty?" Enak said, his voice echoing slightly. The shelves contained no books, the tables no instruments.

"I don't see it as empty," Alister corrected gently. "It's been resting."

"Still empty," Enak said under his breath, and Elba flashed a dismissive look his way.

Alister moved to a stone table near the center of the room, running his fingers along its smooth surface. "This is where he worked. Where he planned."

"Planned what?" Elba asked.

"Everything. The resistance. The Remnant." Alister's eyes took on a distant look up toward the windows. "The future."

Enak wandered to the bookshelves, his fingers tracing the empty spaces. "If this was so important, why leave nothing behind? No weapons, no supplies, nothing to help us?"

"You still think in terms of The Tower," Alister replied. "Of physical power. Jericho left something far more valuable."

He closed his eyes, breathing deeply, as if inhaling memories. "When it happened – when the Elites came – they expected to find armies, weapons, and resources. Instead, they found one man waiting for them. Just him, standing alone."

The room remained silent as they circled the walls and took in the Lighthouse.

“We all saw what Jericho wanted us to see in our shared vision last night,” Alister said, catching Elba’s and Enak’s eyes. “The Tower and its Elite have been slaughtering the population, Jericho stood up to it.”

"Then what?" Elba prompted.

"Light," the older man said simply. "Light... like nothing the world has ever seen before or since. Not just brightness, but... clarity. Truth. As if everything false was burned away, leaving only The Truth." He opened his eyes, focusing on the brothers. "I had always wondered why it would still be standing. Think about it, if you’re Pinnacle and your Elites won, you beat Jericho out here in the Lighthouse and killed him. Why wouldn’t you destroy this place?”

The brothers looked at each other and shrugged.

“Maybe not worth the effort?” Elba said.

Alister shook his head. “No, I don’t think that’s the case. Empyrean is fed the myth that Jericho died long ago, but we’ve seen him. I think no Elites ever returned. I think as soon as they left the walls of Empyrean, the judgment was set. They all burned away in Jericho’s light.”

Enak scoffed quietly. "But what good did that do? The Tower still stands. Pinnacle still rules. People still get consumed."

"The light persists," Alister said firmly. "In you, in me, in everyone who chooses to see."

"I'm tired of stories," Enak said, his voice rising. "I'm tired of symbols and metaphors when people are dying. We came out all this way to find an abandoned silo. There's no power here to fight Pinnacle; it's as hollow as Jericho's chest after Pinnacle ripped his heart out."

"Hey!" Elba shouted.

"It's true," Enak retorted sharply. "Tell me I'm wrong." He raised his hands and looked around at the emptiness around them.

Alister studied him with compassion. "What did you see in your vision last night, Enak? I saw a battle and Jericho's light overwhelming the Elites."

The younger man flinched, his eyes darting away. "Nothing."

"What did you see?" Alister repeated gently.

Enak's jaw tightened, tension visible in the cords of his neck. "I saw something similar... yet more... possibilities."

"What kind of *possibilities*?" Elba asked, a note of concern in his voice.

"Stop," Enak snapped. "Just... enough talking. Let's see what else is here."

He turned abruptly and moved toward the spiral staircase, disappearing down its winding path. Elba made to follow, but Alister placed a restraining hand on his arm.

"Let him," the older man said.

Elba hesitated, watching the empty staircase. "He's not himself. Even before the vision, something's wrong."

"I believe the light reveals what's already there," Alister said. "In all of us."

Elba's troubled expression didn't fade, but he nodded and turned his attention back to the chamber. "So what are we looking for here? What's something he left behind—"

"Not something," Alister corrected. "Someone."

Chapter 33

Kira

The devastation spread before them like a scar on the Outer Ring. Where there had once been homes, buildings, and narrow streets, there was now only rubble – a wasteland of broken stone, twisted metal, and settling dust that choked the air. The destruction cut a jagged path through the sector, as if some gigantic beast had thrashed its way through the fragile structures, leaving nothing but ruin in its wake. Sparks flew and streams of water and sewage flowed through various sections like blood trickling out of a wound on the Outer Ring. The leaking utilities this far from The Tower were like the last molecules of air in a deflated balloon.

Kira led the way, her stride purposeful after her recent resurrection. Behind her followed Riggs, Jace, and Aria, their faces grim with determination and awe – both at the destruction before them and at the woman who walked ahead, somehow restored from death itself.

Beth-ell brought up the rear, her weathered face constant as always. Her watchful eyes missed nothing.

"There," Kira said, pointing toward a massive heap of debris that rose like a small mountain amidst the devastation. "He's there. The connection I felt before, it's faint, but it's there."

Riggs squinted through the dust. "That's a lot of rock," he said as they approached the heap cautiously.

What had once been several buildings was now compressed into a chaotic jumble of concrete, rebar, and shattered glass. It seemed impossible that anything living could survive beneath such weight.

“It's pure devastation,” Aria said as she peered to the side of the gigantic pile of rubble and saw the collateral damage – bodies of the unfortunate that were caught in the melee.

"Even if he is under there," Jace said quietly, "how do we... It's like an earthquake–"

Before he could finish, Beth-ell stepped forward, her expression like someone interrogating a solvable puzzle.

“This isn't from nature. It's what a child's tantrum looks like when it has nearly unimaginable power.”

She raised both hands, and the group watched as patches of her skin briefly darkened to a charcoal hue before returning to normal. The rubble before them shuddered, then began to shift – not randomly, but with purpose, as smaller pieces rose and larger sections pivoted to create a narrow passage. Like a sand castle pulled away from a rising tide, the destruction pulled away and a path to the center formed.

"Whoa," Aria breathed, instinctively stepping back.

Beth-ell's face tightened with concentration, the charcoal patches appearing more frequently across her skin. Sweat beaded on her forehead despite the cool morning air. She didn't speak as she strained and focused, the group looking between her and the shifting mass.

As a path formed, Kira took off into it without hesitation. She ducked into the passage Beth-ell had created, moving with surprising agility through the precarious tunnel of debris. Riggs followed close behind, his large frame barely squeezing through the narrower sections. He turned his shoulders, weaving behind her as he kept up.

"Kaden!" Kira called out, her voice echoing oddly in the confined space. "Kaden, can you hear me?"

The tunnel moved deeper into the heart of the destruction. Dust filled their lungs, and the weight of the rubble around them created an oppressive presence that seemed to press down on their very souls. Occasionally, they would hear the groan of shifting debris or the breaking of falling glass, reminders that this passage existed only through Beth-ell's continuous effort.

Behind them, they could hear Jace and Aria's encouragement from the edge of the pile.

Kira pressed on, drawn by a faint pulse of a connection she felt. The connection that had been severed in death was humming back to life, gradually beating stronger now, guiding her through the destruction. She rounded a corner in the makeshift tunnel and stopped abruptly, Riggs nearly colliding with her back.

"What is it?" he asked, peering over her shoulder.

Ahead, the tunnel ended in a wall of densely packed rubble. But there was something different about this barrier – a faint luminescence seeped through the cracks, casting soft blue-white light that danced across the dust particles in the air.

"It's him," Kira whispered in astonishment. She pressed her hand against the barrier, and the light seemed to respond, pulsing in time with her touch. "Kaden!"

"You need to hurry up in there!" Jace called as Beth-ell began to twitch, beads of sweat across her forehead. The dark patches that flowed over her skin grew in size and became blacker, an obsidian-like lack of color as if draining her life.

From the other side of the barrier, they heard a muffled sound – not quite a voice, but something alive.

Riggs didn't wait. He stepped forward, his massive shoulders bracing against the confined space, and began tearing at the debris with his bare hands. Blood soon streaked his fingers as sharp edges cut into his skin, but he didn't slow his effort.

Kira joined him, pulling away chunks of concrete and twisted metal. The light grew stronger with each piece they removed, until it was almost blinding.

"Come on now," Riggs grunted, heaving aside a large section of wall as if he fought the debris itself. "Get outta the way!"

With a final effort, they cleared enough debris to create an opening. The light flooded out, momentarily blinding them. When their vision cleared, they found themselves looking into a spherical chamber within the heart of the destruction – a perfect bubble of space where the crushing weight of the collapsed buildings somehow couldn't reach.

In the center of the tiny, impossible sanctuary lay Kaden, his body bloodied and broken, yet somehow still breathing. The light emanated from him in pulsing waves, creating the protective sphere that held the compacted rubble at bay. On either side of him, the two Elites lay motionless, their obsidian bodies cracked and flaking away like dying embers.

Kira didn't think twice as she moved into the barrier, passing through it as she crawled through the opening, rushing to Kaden's side. His face was covered in blood, one arm bent at an unnatural angle. But his chest rose and fell with shallow breaths.

"He's alive," she called back to the others, relief flooding her voice. She slid her hands under him and tried turning him over but felt the wetness of blood. His back was shredded as if countless lashing from iron spikes had torn all the skin away.

“Help me get him up,” she said, and Riggs tentatively slid through the light barrier and pulled Kaden up.

“My God...” Riggs muttered upon seeing Kaden’s condition, his eyes wide as he took in the perfect sphere of protection amidst the chaos. "How is this possible?"

"The light," Kira said simply, cradling Kaden's head gently. "It’s in him."

“He doesn’t look alive,” Riggs muttered, then jumped back as one of the Elites stirred, its cracked obsidian form shifting slightly.

A sound like grinding stones emerged from its core as it tried to move toward Kaden. Its efforts only caused more cracks to spread across its surface, like a crack in glass expanding.

Riggs set a fighting stance then instinctively stepped forward and raised his boot, about to crush their charcoal skulls.

“No!” Kira called out. "They’re together," Kira realized, looking at the two broken Elites. "Kaden is protecting them too. The three of them are in this together."

“You need to move now!” Jace and Aria began calling into the tunnel. Beth-ell’s muscles twitched as larger pieces of debris shifted, sending dust raining down where gravity craved to pull the opening closed.

“She can’t hold it forever!” Aria shouted as Beth-ell dropped to one knee, her skin mostly charcoal now.

“I’ll get him, you get them!” Kira shouted. She began moving with Kaden on her back.

“What? I’m not carrying them!” Riggs said. The walls of compacted debris shook around him and Kira was gone.

"They *helped* him," she called back.

The further away she moved, the more the light dimmed and the rubble around them creaked. Dust and smaller pebble-like pieces fell like the first drops of rain before the skies opened up.

He looked down at the pair of Elites. "I can't carry... You demon..." he muttered and shook his fists in frustration.

"Ahhh," he called out in anger then bent down, moving to pick one up and felt like it was the weight of ten men. "You *heavy* demon..." He managed to get one on his shoulder and then the other, his massive frame struggling under the incredible weight.

He stood, holding them both, his balance wavering. Pieces of jagged rock and rebar began to fall around them.

"Oh no, no, no!" he grunted and started forward.

Like a freight train, slow moving at first as it chugged into gear, and then picking up a head of steam, he ran through the tunnel as it crumbled around him. He didn't bother weaving in and out of objects that stuck out, but rather plowed through, using the Elites' hard skin like a shield as he rushed out – a bull in a destroyed china shop trying like mad to escape. A violent tremor shook the passage, and larger chunks as big as cars and small houses crashing down behind him.

He burst out of the deadly heap into the open air, falling forward as the Elites crashed to the ground. A sound like grinding gears rose up and they skidded forward. Riggs gulped for fresh air and turned to see the passage crumble.

Beth-ell, now on one knee, with her back arched awkwardly like a struggling weightlifter, had finally released her hold on the mountain of destruction. Her face, a mask of pain and charcoal patches, now began to relax as her body folded over. She inched forward to her Elites, placing her hands on them as if searching for a sign of life.

Behind them, the mountain of rubble settled in a series of thunderous shifts, sending clouds of dust billowing into the brightening sky.

Kira sat next to Kaden. His breathing was shallow, his broken body somehow seeming smaller, more vulnerable. His eyes stayed open as his breathing settled.

Beth-ell turned toward Kaden. "You saved them," she said, then turned to Riggs. "And you as well."

"They saved me first," Kaden said.

Riggs merely scoffed, still noticeably uncomfortable with two Elites lying before him.

"Will they..." Kira began to ask.

"They'll live, but they need energy to heal," Beth-ell said.

"There's the catch," Riggs muttered, shaking his head.

"It doesn't have to be," Aria said, coming into the conversation.

"The pastures. Livestock," Jace added.

"Yes," Beth-ell replied softly, her skin gradually returning to its prior color. But she appeared older than before, more wrinkles that seemed to hang from her bones. She always appeared elderly to Kaden, but also somehow extremely fit. Now he saw the price of her power as the firmness of her toned muscles was deflated in her exhaustion. It reminded Kaden of the first time he saw Jericho in Empyrean, in his role as a humble mechanic. He appeared weaker than at other times, as if a battery needed to be recharged.

"Your ability is like theirs," Kaden asked. "You need to replenish it as well?"

Beth-ell nodded.

"How?"

"Time. And prayer," she replied.

"Is that how Jericho's power worked too?" he asked.

"No," she replied. "When he was weaker, he chose it. He became like us, to show us."

"Show us what?" he asked.

The group stood quiet, drawn in as they waited for her response. Behind them, the sun broke through a thinner patch of the overcast clouds, washing the broken landscape in brief golden light.

"That we don't need to consume to be strong," she said. The silence hung in the air.

Kaden eventually stood on wobbly legs. He winced in pain as he tested himself. Bruising was already taking hold and one arm where his elbow was hyperextended was noticeably weaker. Yet, he extended a hand to help Kira up.

"Come on," he said to the group. "Let's go."

Chapter 34

Entry #8

The skies over Empyrean darkened today with more than the usual poison clouds. Pinnacle's Elites have doubled their patrols in the Outer Ring, and three Remnant safe houses were discovered and emptied. Their inhabitants now feed the hunger of The Tower. I feel each consumption like a knife between my ribs.

The Remnant grows restless. They look to me to fight back directly, to use my strength and advantages we've quietly accumulated, to strike at The Tower's foundations and overthrow Thomas. They mistake my refusal as pacifism, my restraint as fear. They cannot yet understand that what appears to be weakness is in fact our greatest strength.

Thomas sent a message today, delivered by a Brown Agent with trembling hands. The message was simple: surrender the Lighthouse and those who harbor there, and I alone may live in "peace under his oversight." His arrogance blinds him to the truth – I do not avoid confrontation because I fear defeat. I avoid it because victory through force would only replace one tyrant with another.

Throughout history, the greatest warriors understood when to lower their swords. The king who gives up power rather than unleash civil war. I often think of the American President who, even as his nation tore itself apart in bloody conflict, spoke of "malice toward none, with charity for all" toward his enemies – not from weakness, but from the profound understanding that only reconciliation, not retribution, could truly heal his fractured land. I think of the German theologian who stood against a monstrous regime, knowing it would cost his life, writing from his prison cell that "the ultimate test of a moral society is the kind of world it leaves to its children." The greatest warrior who ever lived laid down his arms at the moment of apparent triumph, allowing enemies to nail him to wood, knowing that this defeat would ultimately transform the world more powerfully than any conquest. I follow in those footsteps.

I, too, have seen what must come, and must bear my cross. In visions that cut across time like lightning across the night sky, I see Thomas's triumph and my defeat. I have seen my own heart torn from my chest, still beating in his grasp as my body crumples. I have felt the cold stone beneath my back, the weight of The Tower pressing down, the light extinguished.

But I see beyond that moment.

My death is not the end but a doorway through which light will flood Empyrean. The seeds will bloom in the aftermath. The power that flows through my veins will not die with me but multiply through others. What appears to be Thomas's greatest victory will become the fracture through which his entire empire begins to crumble.

I have told my closest followers what is coming, but they cannot hear it yet. Their love for me blinds them to the necessity of my sacrifice. When I speak of my death, they protest. When I explain that Pinnacle must win so that he might ultimately lose, they suggest alternative plans, escape routes, preemptive strikes. They mean well, but they cannot yet see beyond the patterns of power that have shaped this fallen world.

Even now, I can see the faces of those who will betray me. If Thomas knew the ultimate results, he would not proceed.

The true battle is not between The Tower and the Lighthouse, between Thomas and myself. It is between two visions of what humanity might become and the battlefield is in the mind of every man and woman. He believes power comes through consumption – through taking, controlling, dominating. I know that true power flows from sacrifice – from giving, releasing, transforming. His path leads to perfected chains. Mine leads to freedom, though the cost is high.

The walls of corruption fall not through force but through truth revealed. The Tower could be physically destroyed tomorrow, and another would rise to take its place unless hearts are changed. This is what Thomas has never understood about power. He builds his throne on fear, but fear melts away like morning frost when touched by genuine love.

The Elites will soon come to the Lighthouse. I gathered the Remnant and told them this story:

***

There once lived two brothers who each built a kingdom in the valley. The elder brother built his kingdom on a mountain. He constructed high walls of stone, and from his tower, he could see all who approached. His soldiers were the strongest, his weapons the sharpest. He built great storehouses and filled them with grain taken from the surrounding lands. "Safety comes through strength," he told his people. "Survival requires taking what we need."

The younger brother built his kingdom beside a river. Instead of walls, he planted orchards. Instead of a tower, he built a lighthouse whose beam guided travelers at night. His people kept watch and shared their harvests. "Safety comes through community," he told them. "Survival requires giving what others need."

When drought came to the valley, the elder brother sealed his gates and doubled his guards. From his tower, he watched the suffering in the lands below but felt nothing. "They should have prepared," he said, "as I prepared."

The younger brother's kingdom suffered too. Their crops withered, and the river ran low. But they continued to welcome strangers, to share what little they had.

One night, the elder brother woke to find his storehouses empty. In rage, he called his strongest warriors and marched on his brother's kingdom to take their supplies by force. But when they arrived, they found no walls to breach, no army to fight – only tables set with modest meals, and people who offered them seats.

"Where are your storehouses?" demanded the elder brother.

"We have none," said the younger.

"Then how have you survived?"

The younger brother pointed to the countless people from all directions sharing what little they had. "The more we gave, the more that came to us. We are the storehouse."

The elder brother raised his sword, but found he could not strike. One by one, his warriors laid down their weapons and sat at the tables. Some wept, tasting kindness they had forgotten.

"Your kingdom will fall," said the elder brother. "By my hand or another."

"My kingdom is the only one that will stand in the end. It is evitable," the younger brother replied.

***

When my time comes – and it approaches rapidly – I will not resist. Not because I lack the strength to fight, but because my surrender is the strongest action I can take. When my heart is torn from my chest, it will beat more powerfully than ever before.

In the end, Thomas will discover too late that in taking my heart, he has not eliminated a threat. He has unleashed one.

Chapter 35

Dawn broke over Empyrean, spilling pale light across the devastation of the Outer Ring. The makeshift shelter Beth-ell had led them to stood nestled between two half-collapsed buildings, hidden from view. Her skin and energy not returning to their prior state, she was showing many signs of tiredness that no one in the group had ever seen before, yet she insisted on this particular location with her usual determination.

Pinnacle's recent destruction sat only a block away with plenty of rubble crowded around the safe house as if car-sized pieces of building were street art scattered on every corner. Inside, Kaden lay on a thin mat, his body still recovering from injuries that should have killed him. Kira sat beside him, her fingers gently tracing the healing wounds on his arm.

"You should rest too," Kaden said softly.

Kira shook her head. "I don't need it." She looked down at her own hands, marveling. "Whatever happened when I... came back... it changed something."

Across the room, Riggs paced like a caged animal, his massive frame seeming too large for the confined space. Jace and Aria sat quietly in a corner, their expressions intense as they discussed various ins and outs of The Tower and the patrols.

Beth-ell entered, her feet shuffling and her weathered face showing exhaustion, yet even in her exhausted state, she carried on. Behind her came the two Elites, moving with a stiffness that hadn't been there before. All three had borne significant injuries and fatigue from the event, but the Elites' obsidian bodies bore new fractures that oddly elicited hope when the group looked upon them – not the damage of battle, but something different. In the dim light, the faintest glow emanated from within these cracks, like magma beneath a cooling stone.

"They need to feed," Riggs said bluntly, eyeing the Elites with suspicion.

"Plenty of meat on you." She hadn't lost her sharp wit. Riggs shrugged off the comment as Beth-ell continued. "There's something you all need to see."

She moved to one wall of the shelter and pressed her palm against a seemingly random spot. A section of the floor slid away, revealing a narrow staircase descending into darkness.

"I've maintained dozens of these safe houses throughout Empyrean for centuries," she explained. "This one leads to something that few know," she said, her eyes moving to Kira, who perked up in curiosity.

One by one, they followed her down the stairs. Kaden leaned on Kira, still unsteady, while the Elites remained above, closing the path behind them. The staircase led to a series of tunnels lit with a running row of lights on the ceiling that led to a small chamber, its walls lined with metal shelving.

"This place..." Kira whispered as if asking herself a question. A memory replayed in her mind.

Beth-ell approached and held up her hand. The earth shifted at her command and they entered another hidden chamber. Kaden felt as if they were entering a series of Russian nesting dolls as the hidden layers of rooms unfolded. Finally, the next shift didn't open a doorway but a small, compartment-like space set in the wall. She carefully removed an aged leather journal, its cover worn smooth by time and handling.

"I've been here before," Kira said with confidence.

"The only way you've been here is if He brought you here," Beth-ell said. Her tiredness seemed to blossom into a renewed strength at the thought of Jericho.

"It's a journal, HIS journal, isn't it," Kira said, looking at the book in Beth-ell's hands.

Beth-ell nodded.

"When they found me and brought me to The Tower, before Jericho pulled Kaden and me out, I thought it was lost," Kira said.

"It can never be lost," Beth-ell said.

"How?" Riggs interjected.

"Because every time I lose it or it's taken or burned or destroyed, it shows back up. I've stopped questioning it after all these years and have simply come to realize that Jericho's words cannot die. The book shows up every time," Beth-ell said, her message as plain as if describing the sun rising in the east.

"I've read it, and so did Alister. He gave it to Barb," Beth-ell said and then turned to Kaden. "You remember Barb, your former work leader at the EMR."

"She's a leader in the Remnant. You must know her well," Kira said.

"Yes," Beth-ell said, her head bowing down as she rubbed her fingers on Jericho's journal. "But long before this version of the Remnant."

"Is she like you?" Kaden asked. "From our time, centuries ago?"

"She is old, but not *that* old." Beth-ell smirked. She looked up from the book and caught Kaden's eyes. "She's my daughter, named after me from my past life." She released the statement as if it were a trapped prisoner.

"Your daughter? From when, with who?" Kira inquired, her curiosity taking over.

"Alister gave this book to Barb, and then Barb gave you to The Tower," Beth-ell said.

"What?" Kira leaned back.

"Pinnacle can find you, if he chooses, when he wants. But his mind was focused elsewhere, on Jericho for the longest time. Now it's locking onto someone else." She looked at Kaden. "There are traitors in the Remnant. Not everyone has a light inside that remains bright in the face of temptation. All of us would fall if not for Jericho, yet most fall despite him here to save them."

"Kaden survived," Riggs snapped. "And Jericho is gone. Kira and Kaden are making that light to save themselves."

"Did *they* make it?" Beth-ell said. Her head tilted as she glanced at Riggs and then back to Kaden and Kira.

"Who sent you here? How many times have you died, yet come back? Even in Jericho's apparent absence, you two only grow stronger. Why is that?" Beth-ell questioned.

Kaden and Kira had no response.

"He's still working through you, whether you all believe it or not. Your faith helps, but," she scoffed, "I know from my own doubts and drifting, HIS work will go on whether you care or not. And usually, it'll work on you in the process. He is in the flow of time yet somehow timeless. Jericho is inevitable."

The group remained quiet as she looked back down at the book. "His writings," she said, her voice taking on a reverence that transformed her typically stern demeanor. "There are many copies hidden throughout Empyrean, but this one..." She paused, handling the journal with careful hands. "This one he brought me to when I was lost. It's the foundation for how I survived undercover in The Tower, witnessing terrible things, for all these years. Being a part of horrible things in order to protect the Remnant."

She opened the journal to a page marked with a thin strip of fabric. The handwriting was precise yet flowing, the faded ink like a work of art.

"Entry Number Nine," she read aloud.

Chapter 36

Entry #9

They come for me now. I sit up all night, in such deep prayer and concentration that my sweat seems to be turning into blood. The Tower prepares for their victory over the Lighthouse through my death. It will come soon. I wish this burden to pass off me, yet it must be done.

Thomas sees only what he wishes to see – my defeat, my temporal end. He cannot comprehend an alternative.

When my heart is taken, it will continue to beat. Not merely as muscle and sinew, but as the Word of life beats within the Remnant. For three days, it will resist him, fighting his attempts to consume and corrupt what it contains. On the third day, the window opens – not just over flesh, but over time itself. The veil will be torn when they strike this temple down. On the third day, I will rebuild it.

***

Beth-ell looked up from the page. "He wrote this decades ago. Long before Pinnacle tore his heart out."

"That's impossible," Jace said, shaking his head. "Unless..."

"Unless he could see the future," Aria finished quietly.

"You all should see what they have seen, lives from hundreds of years ago." Beth-ell nodded toward Kaden and Kira. "Jericho could see more than the future; he walks across time."

Beth-ell continued reading:

***

Through them, the light will spread, not as conquest but as invitation. Even those most corrupted by hunger can be transformed if they choose to see.

***

Kaden and Kira exchanged glances. There was no denying what they had both felt since their resurrections – that pull, that rhythmic pulse like a distant beacon calling to them.

"There's more," Beth-ell said, turning the page.

***

The third day is critical. The Hope Drug is in everyone's blood, and once death takes hold, it changes. The skin hardens. The hunger takes over, awakening its host.

Elites are born from death. Shadows that walk the earth, a physical form of the hatred and pride within the person before death.

***

Beth-ell closed the journal gently.

"Tomorrow is the third day," she said simply. “We need to be there for Him.”

The silence that followed was heavy with implication. Riggs broke it first.

"So we're supposed to walk into The Tower, grab a corpse, and just stroll out?" He laughed, a sharp, bitter sound. "Suicide."

“And what do we do with it once we have it?” Jace asked. “What if he turns to an Elite?”

"It’s not just any corpse," Kira said quietly. "It’s Jericho's body."

"And we won't be walking in blind," Kaden added, his voice growing stronger. "We can feel it... his heart. It's like it's calling to us."

"Calling to you," Riggs corrected. "The rest of us don't have your... whatever this is." He gestured vaguely at Kaden and Kira. “We ain’t got your nine lives.”

"That's not entirely true," Beth-ell said. She looked toward the staircase. "Come up. There's something you need to see."

Back in the main room, the Elites had moved to a corner, their massive forms hunched as if in pain and they were charging up their internal batteries. As Kaden and Kira approached, they straightened, turning toward the pair as flowers might turn to the sun.

"Watch," Beth-ell instructed.

Kaden stepped closer to the Elites. The cracks in their obsidian skin widened slightly, the light within growing stronger – not blinding, but clear and steady.

"What's happening to them?" Aria asked, her voice hushed.

"Transformation," Beth-ell replied. "I've never seen it before, but Jericho spoke of it. Being near Kaden and Kira is accelerating the process."

The smaller of the two Elites moved forward, its movements still stiff but deliberate. The grinding sound of stone-on-stone filled the room.

"This is what Jericho meant," Beth-ell explained. "The light doesn't just protect – it transforms. Even those who seem most lost to the hunger."

"Are you saying these things can be... saved?" Riggs asked incredulously.

"These *'things'* were human once," Beth-ell reminded him sharply. "Before the Hope Drug corrupted them. Before the hunger took hold."

The Elite struggled to speak, the effort clearly taxing. "Others... changi ng..."

Kaden stepped closer, ignoring Riggs's warning. "What do you mean, 'changing'?"

The Elite raised a charcoal hand toward its chest, where the faint light seeped through the cracks. "Since... *His* heart taken."

"It's happening throughout The Tower," Beth-ell said. "Jericho's heart – even removed, even in Pinnacle's possession – is having an effect. The purest form of the Hope Drug is calling out to its corrupted versions. Changing them. I dare say, healing."

"But it won't be enough," Kira said, a new understanding dawning on her face. "Not unless we bring His body to strengthen the effect."

Beth-ell nodded. "The journal alludes to this. The heart resists for three days. After that..."

"Pinnacle breaks through," Jace finished grimly, "and gains whatever power he's been trying to access. If he consumes Jericho's heart and body, he'll be able to walk through time," he said looking at Kaden. "That's why you come back. Jericho sends you back and forth."

Kaden nodded.

Kaden placed his hand on the Elite's arm – a gesture that would have been unthinkable days ago. The creature's cracked stone skin flinched, more light spilling from the cracks in its skin.

"These were early test subjects," Beth-ell explained. "Cancer patients before Pinnacle evolved the drug to new iterations. They've retained more of themselves than most. But even the later Elites can be reached. Jericho believed that completely."

"So we're supposed to risk our lives based on a belief that Elites can be saved?" Riggs asked, his agitation growing with every word. "Do any of you remember the raid on the pastures? It wasn't that long ago they consumed most of the Remnant, only Kira's group came out. They consumed us, my friends! Elites are eating us alive. They absorb our very soul and even speak in our tongues just to torment the rest of us on their dinner plate. Ain't no way in this hell or the next I'm going in there to save more of 'em bastards!" He slammed his fist against the wall to his side. The entire safe house shook and dust fell from above.

"Look around you," Kira countered, her voice gaining strength. "I died. My neck was broken. Kaden was crushed beneath half the Outer Ring. Yet here we stand."

"And now you want to walk back into the lion's den," Riggs said, shaking his head. "These 'gents are probably just waiting to lead us into the spider's web," he said, pointing a finger uncomfortably close to Jace's face.

"Maybe you should go back to The Tower, see how long you survive," Jace snapped back.

"You'd like that, wouldn't you!" Riggs fired back.

"Stop it," Aria said, moving to break them apart.

"You're right there with 'im, aren't ya?" Riggs raised his arm, pulling it away from Aria.

"Stop it!" Kira shouted into the argument.

Beth-ell stood watching as the chaos erupted. Kaden looked at her, and the Elites. The light glowing from their cracks was fading.

"Then don't come with us," Kaden said softly. The group hardly noticed, but Riggs caught his comment.

"Excuse me?" Riggs asked, an angry defensiveness in his voice.

"Don't come with us," Kaden said again, slower and with more calmness.

"I ain't scared of that place, but I ain't fighting for—"

"It's okay," Kaden interrupted with a raised hand. "I don't expect you to fight for Elites. Before today, I wouldn't have. These two saved me, and somehow by Jericho's light in me, I saved them. I'm not going to *just* save some Elites or even Agents. I expect very few, if any, we'll even be able to save."

"What do you mean?" Kira asked.

"Jericho could have wiped out Pinnacle. He stopped him from consuming us and ripped open a hole in The Tower," Kaden said.

"You have mentioned he seemed weaker after using lots of his power," Kira said.

"Yes, but He wasn't weaker, not that time. I look at you and see the change in you since you've discovered his journal. Kira, you're different. You're a leader who inspires me to fight for the right cause. Without you, I'd be an Agent right now, likely trying to kill all of you – whether I knew what I was doing or not. And without Jericho's sacrifice, you two," he motioned to Jace and Aria, "would still be in The Tower as well. How do you think Ryon and Vala are doing? I'd guess pretty miserable, but feeling quite powerful. They made their choice."

"Choice," Riggs scoffed.

"I think I'm finally getting what he was trying to tell me," Kaden continued. "I was so mad at him. The last time I saw him, I blamed him for all the pain in this world over all the years and generations because *HE* alone could have stopped it, but he gave us, he gave everyone, a choice. We're making ours right now, and those in The Tower are making theirs."

He pointed toward the entrance of their safe house. The looming tower hovered above them like a big brother watching their every move through the cracks in the doorway.

"Jericho's power has saved me from my errors so many times that I'm losing count. And now it's saving her, the woman I love. I don't know what will happen with Jericho's body once we get it free, but I know his heart is calling to us, so I'm going to get it, and his body, out of The Tower before Pinnacle can consume it. If that inspires others to change their choice, or helps spread the light," he looked to the Elites, "then that's all I need. Pinnacle has tried to kill me over and over. He's won this world, but not my soul. Jericho won't let him. I'm going to use the life granted to me for good."

He took a deep breath and looked around the room, holding each person's eyes for a moment.

"I'm going to help get His Body and His Heart out of hell."

Chapter 37

The Lighthouse

The light of early afternoon filtered through the high, narrow windows of the Lighthouse, casting elongated shapes across the stone floor. Alister moved about the circular chamber, his weathered hands tracing the empty shelves as if they held invisible treasures. Elba watched him from the central table, where he had spread out what meager supplies they'd managed to bring from Empyrean.

"I thought there would be others," Elba said, as if speaking to himself more than to Alister. "Do you think anyone else will come?"

Alister paused, his eyes lifting to the windows. "Faith doesn't ask 'if,'" he replied with that perpetual smile. "Only 'when.'"

Enak scoffed from his position by the doorway. Since their arrival at the Lighthouse, his mood had grown increasingly dark. He paced like a caged animal, venturing outside periodically to scan the horizon before returning with reports of nothing but endless desert that nobody asked for.

"I've been through this whole place, which is way more massive than it looks. By the way, there's nothing," he said as he shrugged toward Alister.

Enak gave him a stare that only an older brother could.

“Fine... I'll check again," Enak muttered, disappearing through the downward staircase.

Elba watched his brother go, concern etched on his face. "He's not handling this well."

"The desert has a way of bringing what's inside to the surface," Alister said. He moved to the spiral staircase and peered upward toward the apex of the Lighthouse. "I'm going to check the light mechanism again. I might be able to get it working. Think of what The Tower would do if this light started burning bright across the landscape?" he said, smirking.

Elba smiled.

As Alister's footsteps echoed up the stairwell, Elba rummaged through their dwindling food supplies. They had enough for perhaps two more days – three if they rationed carefully. After that... He stood staring at the rations, as if somehow the food would multiply on its own. If there were no supplies out here, they had barely enough to get back to Empyrean. They'd have to make a choice, and soon.

Then a sound caught his attention.

Footsteps.

“Hello?” he hollered toward the door, moving toward it.

A few more steps on the stone floor outside the gigantic wooden door. Then it stopped.

He stood watching the door, silence hanging in the air as the wind whipped the sand outside.

Then the heavy wooden door swung open with a creak that echoed through the chamber. Elba watched and expected to see Enak's scowling face as if his brother had found a way outside through the rooms below. Instead, a figure he never thought he'd see again stood silhouetted against the harsh desert light.

"Barb?" he breathed, disbelief coloring his voice. "Barb!"

The stocky woman stepped into the Lighthouse, her familiar stern features softening slightly as she took in the circular room. Her Tower-issued work clothes were torn and dusty, but her eyes were alert and calculating as ever.

"You made it," she said in mild surprise, her gruff voice filling the space. "All those days in the EMR when I shuffled him back to work. Telling him this place was a dream." She laughed under her breath. "Alister actually found it."

Elba rushed forward, taking her calloused hands in his. "How did you get out? The Tower had locked down so much after Jericho... well, you know. The EMR is so close to The Tower."

Barb shook her head and pulled away her hands, dismissing his comments. "Oh, come on, I'm more resourceful than to let a few demons lock me down. You think so low of me?"

"No, I just, never mind. I'm happy you're here, Barb," Elba said.

Footsteps echoed from the stairwell as Alister's shouts echoed down ahead of him. "Hey, Elba, there's something out—" His face appeared and lit up at the sight of Barb. "No way? The old windows up there, the wind and the sand, I couldn't quite see but thought I saw someone. Thank Jericho, Barb!" he said, rushing forward to embrace her. She accepted the hug stiffly, her arms remaining at her sides. "Praise Jericho! I *knew* others would find the way!"

Barb stepped back from Alister's enthusiastic welcome. "The way wasn't hard to find once you know what to look for," she said, her eyes scanning the chamber. "So this is it? The Great Lighthouse?"

There was something in her tone – a note of disappointment, perhaps disdain.

"It's been abandoned for centuries," Alister explained, not noticing her tone, but he did catch Elba giving him a concerned look. He dismissed it. "But it's a shelter, a beginning. I thought I saw more outside. Who else came? Kaden and Kira?"

Barb walked around the perimeter of the room, her hand trailing along the empty shelves. "No."

From out of the descending stairs, Enak popped out. His eyes widened at the sight of Barb, then narrowed with a strange intensity.

"Barb?" he said, then perked up as if forcing a smile. "You made it."

She nodded twice to him, a silent exchange that carried weight Elba couldn't decipher. Enak moved to stand beside her, his posture changing subtly – straighter, more confident.

"I knew there would be more of the Remnant out here. Jericho always said there is more for us than against us," Alister said.

"We do have help," Barb said, but her tone once again caught Elba. A chill ran up his spine.

"What kind of *help*?" Elba asked.

Before Barb could answer, a sound reached them from outside – not the whistle of desert wind, but something else. Something organized. Rhythmic. Footsteps. Many footsteps coming off the sand and onto the platform leading up to the immense wooden door.

Alister's face brightened. "The others! You brought them!" He moved toward the door, but Barb made no effort to follow. Neither did Enak. "I thought I saw a group, but from that height and the dirty windows, it was all shadows. I thought my eyes were playing tricks on me."

"Alister, stop," Elba demanded, the warning in his mind now screaming for attention. "What's going on here?"

Alister ignored the warning and stepped outside, his back in the doorway. “Oh...” he said in shock, then his shoulders dropped and any excitement in his voice was lost. “I see.”

Elba rushed to the doorway, dread propelling him forward. What he saw froze the blood in his veins. Before him stretched rows of Elites – not one or two, but dozens. Their charcoal skin gleamed in the harsh sunlight.

"No," Elba whispered. He turned and dashed at Enak. “Brother?” he shouted in confusion and anger.

But Enak didn’t speak or defend himself; instead, he aggressively stepped into Elba as if a caged animal finally freed. He thrust a hidden dagger into his brother. He thrust again and again, digging the blade up, destroying vital organs as if to pierce the heart from under the ribs.

“No!” Alister called back, but a force from the Elites behind him held in place.

"It’s time I step out of your shadow, brother," Enak's voice whispered close to his ear, a terrible sincerity in his tone. "It's time..."

Pain exploded through Elba’s midsection, stealing his breath, his thoughts, his strength. He tried to look up, to see his brother's face one last time, but his body wouldn't obey. Enak bent down as he still held the dagger in his brother and met his eyes. He watched the life fade from Elba’s eyes before letting his drop on the polished stone floor.

Barb walked passively by Elba and to Alister.

"It's an abandoned building," she called out to the raiding party. "Nothing more."

The first Elite moved with unnatural speed to the doorway, lifting Alister by his throat and hurling him through the circular room, smashing him against the stone wall of the Lighthouse. The impact made a sound like branches breaking, and Alister crumpled to the ground.

Elba reached up, toward Alister, instinctively trying to help, but his hand hardly rose before falling back to the ground. Through dimming vision, he tilted his head and watched as Enak stepped over him and moved toward the door.

"Why?" Elba mouthed a silent question.

Enak paused, looking back at his dying brother. For a moment, something flickered in his eyes – regret, perhaps even grief. Then his face hardened.

"Time we stopped living in tunnels or waiting for a dead man to save us."

"Jericho... lives," Elba gasped, a whisper of voice.

"His heart was torn out!" Enak spat. “I've spent my whole life hiding, running, fighting for scraps, all for what? For fairy tales about light and hope? Pinnacle offered me something real.” He motioned to Barb. “We have a seat at the table now, brother, not beneath it, fighting for crumbs.”

He moved to the doorway, where Barb and the Elites waited.

“Destroy it,” the lead Elite's voice said, as if stones were grinding together as it spoke.

"Nothing worth your time," Enak confirmed. "It’s as empty as an old man's promises."

Barb's eyes swept over the Lighthouse one last time, lingering on Elba's fallen form and Alister's crumpled body. Then she turned away.

"Let's go," she said. “This place will crumble on its own.”

The lead Elite threw his arm across his body and a gigantic crack erupted through the center of the lighthouse. The cracks spiderwebbed as the weight of stone creaked. Content with the damage, the demon turned and led the Elites away. They moved off in formation, Barb and Enak walking at their center. Their footsteps receded into the desert, leaving only silence behind.

Elba's vision darkened at the edges. He tried to move, to drag himself toward Alister, but his body refused. Blood pooled beneath him on the ancient stone floor. He grew cold and his limbs began shaking, an uncontrollable twitch stopping his movement forward.

The wooden floor creaked as Alister shifted. Searing pain shot through his body. One leg bent back, clearly broken, and a pool of blood now stained his clothes where a broken rib punctured out of his skin. He tried dragging himself to Elba. His face a mask of pain, yet determined, one arm hanging uselessly at his side. He pulled himself across the floor with one working arm and leg, one excruciating inch at a time until he reached Elba.

"Hold on," Alister whispered, his voice thick with pain. "Just... hold on." His head lowered, resting on Elba's shoulder as if he were preparing for a nap.

“Enak... Don't hate him," Elba whispered.

"He betrayed you," Alister said, disbelief coloring his fading voice.

"He's afraid," Elba replied. "Always... afraid."

Alister's good hand found Elba's, squeezing weakly and nodding in agreement.

They lay together on the stone floor, two broken vessels leaking life. Around them, the empty lighthouse that was once so promising rested like a crumbling headstone. A hope of living things emerging from the desert was now long gone. Outside, the desert wind began to rise, whistling through the cracks in the ancient structure.

Alister picked up his head and watched as the light faded from Elba's eyes, and felt the final tremor pass through the younger man's hand.

He wasn’t far behind; his own body was failing as blood filled his lungs with each labored breath. The pain had receded to a dull roar, his consciousness floating above it like debris on a rising tide.

Life left Elba. His body went limp.

"Not like this," Alister whispered to the empty chamber. "It can't... end like this." His head fell back on Elba's shoulder and his eyes closed.

The pair lay motionless.

Alister's face didn't flinch, at least not at first, when a light from outside the Lighthouse shone like a sun rising from every angle around them. The light intensified, transforming from a gentle glow to a radiance that filled every corner of the chamber. With a last ounce of unconscious strength, Alister squinted. It was unlike anything he'd ever seen – not the harsh glare of The Tower's artificial illumination, but something alive.

As consciousness slipped away, Alister found himself enveloped in the light, cradled by it.

Chapter 38

The embers of the fire in the center of the safe house faded away. The smell of ash filled the room and gradually escaped through the cracks in the dilapidated building.

"You ready for this?" Kira whispered to Kaden. He was already alert, having woken up hours ago, and mentally played out the day in his mind countless times. He examined all the ways it could go wrong, and the one way it went right.

"Born ready," he replied, forcing confidence.

The group woke and solemnly prepared themselves. Determined faces. Focus. Readiness.

The parting groups hugged as they split up.

Kaden, Jace, Beth-ell, and the Elites moving toward The Tower.

Kira, Riggs, and Aria moving away.

"I'll see you in there," Aria said, forcing a smile as she hugged Jace.

"Keep him in line, will ya?" Jace said, nodding toward Riggs. The swipe of humor caught Riggs off guard and cut the tension. The group chuckled at the large man's confused expression.

"He's just a big ol' teddy bear," Aria said, giving Riggs an elbow. All of Riggs's confusion melted away as he looked at Aria, their growing affection for each other slowly breaking down Riggs's skepticism of the former Agents.

"We'll need the strength of a bear from him, and all of us, today," Kaden said.

The group nodded, but Beth-ell stepped forward, disappointed with the comment. "Physical strength..." She shook her head. "You have something more. Spiritual strength from Jericho." She looked around the group, catching each of their eyes. The jovialness shifted back to determination and she pointed to Kaden and Kira. "Jericho's power shows in you now. You lead the way. Yet, you're only an example of what everyone in Empyrean has before them. The light is in you *all*, and one-by-one, you'll choose how this ends. In light of salvation, or in the endless hollows of death."

As if on cue, the pair of Elites came in from outside as if a warning of what they knew was ahead. They exhaled a breath that growled from within and stood firm, like living statues of immense strength that flickered a light of concern, a crack of weakness in their stone-like skin that somehow gave them a new appearance of strength through their care of the mortals they stood over.

"You could still go back," Kaden said to Beth-ell. His voice was low and direct but with a sense of feeling. "You have enough influence to get back into The Tower's ranks. You could still work from the inside out."

Beth-ell shook her head, and without a word, she showed her resolve. She'd been with them only two days, yet she seemed to age decades. The transformation from an early version of the Hope Drug had given her unbelievably long life, which she used to infiltrate the darkest areas of humanity. Now that she was on the outside, her body seemed to fade away – her skin looser, the underlying muscles no longer as tense and strong. Only her eyes showed a flicker of change to the positive – a peacefulness escaped like a twinkle from a star in the night sky. The kind of star you see when camping far from civilization that allows the beholder to appreciate the wonder of creation and yet be thankful for the work put on their own shoulders to be a part of it.

As Kaden held her eye, the determination he saw in her four-hundred-year-old eyes was unflappable.

"We'll be ready when you set it off. Get them out and charging," Kaden said, his eyes on Kira.

"And chaos ensues," she replied with an ironic smile creeping up on the side of her mouth.

"This is going to be fun." Riggs nudged Aria then cracked his knuckles.

"You be ready on your side. You won't have the numbers or the space to move like we will," Kira said to Kaden.

"Once we're in, there's no more running," he said. He gave Kira a hug, feeling her squeeze him tight in return, and moved out of the safe house. The two groups went on their way, their eyes catching as they each said a silent good-bye.

They understood the risks as they crafted and refined their plans through the night before, the high probability that they'd never see each other alive again.

***

"You know this is madness, right?" Riggs said.

"Scared you're too slow?" Aria prodded.

"If you can get Spark Clubs, we need 'em to fight, not wrangle cattle," Riggs replied.

"These concerns would have been more helpful when we were making the plan," Kira added. "And yeah, he's scared he's too slow," he said quietly to Aria.

"I heard that," Riggs muttered, his face a picture of uncertainty as he looked over the herd in front of him.

"Good, because I said that," Kira called back. "You ready?"

"No," he called back as he inched toward a large steer grazing, his massive size dwarfed next to the animal. "But let's do it," he finally added.

Kira and Aria caught eyes and then began jogging away from each other, getting into position.

"Okay there, guy," Riggs spoke to the bull. Its horns stretched four feet on either side, set atop of hulking mass of muscle. It picked up its head, centering its attention on Riggs as it snorted in dismissal of him.

"Let's not make it harder than it has to be," he spoke to the beast. As he stepped closer, the beast threw its head up and down and snorted louder. "No, no, I just want you to run. Do you want to stay down here and wait for the slaughter? Neither do I. We're on the same team here."

Louder snorting as it lowered its head.

"We can be friends. I bet they don't even name you here. I'll name ya," he said with a quick pause. "Billy. Yeah, that's a good name. Billy the Bull. How do you do, friend?"

Its front hoof scraped at the ground like a revving engine.

"Oh, don't you do that toward me," Riggs spoke to the beast like a parent to a child.

It grunted a final warning. "Jericho, be with me..." Riggs whispered. Then his posture tightened and his feet dug in the ground with a wide stance, a front-line warrior bracing for the enemy's charge. He snarled back at the beast and his fists wrapped around the Spark Club.

"Okay, Billy. It's time."

Billy stared, the beast on guard in the midst of the standoff.

"Come on, ya sow!" Riggs bellowed through the pastures like the starting gun to kick off a race, the veins in his neck bulging as his muscles flared.

The bull took the challenge and stepped forward, but before it could finish its first step, Riggs snapped the Spark Club out from a holster and gripped on its electric field. The pop startled the beast and it reared back.

"Don't let your balls drop on me now, Billy!" he screamed as he charged at the herd holding the Spark Club ahead. The cows behind it took notice, the herd's attention fully on Riggs as mini lightning bolts rose and fell off the mace, crackling in the air and sending the bull in a panic. Like a giant plasma ball without the glass cover, the Spark Club sent electrons into the air with an unnatural intensity.

The stampede had begun.

Kira and Aria now came forward from either side in a coordinated pincer attack, pushing the herd into a tighter ball. They funneled toward the staircase leading up to the Outer Ring. As the beasts plowed into each other, they were a dozen wide.

"We need to slow them down," Kira shouted. "Circle them so they go in single file!"

"We can't slow them down!" Riggs screamed back incredulously.

"They'll rip the staircase apart!" Kira screamed.

She tried charging to the front, but it only shifted the head of the pack away from her. She called back to Riggs, but the thundering hooves drowned out her call.

"No, no, no!" Kira called out as she was losing control of the herd.

Then she saw the front of the pack. Aria had jumped in the direct line, at threat of being trampled, but she'd seen the same thing Kira had.

Aria snapped her Spark Club and directed the pack into a circular motion. She ran with the bulls, feeling more free than she'd ever felt. A smile wrapped around her face as she ran alongside the animals. Riggs came into view and they met eyes from a distance. His confusion and concern melted away at seeing her genuine smile.

"Fine..." Riggs said to himself, his concern now drifting into eagerness at the challenge in the face of uncontrollable danger that stampeded at him.

"Billy! We need you in a line, Billy!" Riggs shouted to the massive pack of steers.

As Kira and Aria shepherded the herd into a circle, the pack naturally thinned into more of a line. The largest bull now led the way with the pack growing behind it, other huge beasts flanking Billy. They slammed into each other's sides but bounced off and kept running.

"Riggs, you need to lead them!" Kira shouted over the roar of the failing stampede.

"These women can't be serious," Riggs said as he watched Billy and the stampede charge at him.

"You can do it, Riggs!" Aria shouted.

"Okay..." he said under his breath as the thundering roar of the herd charged toward him. He felt like a one-man army, trying to hold the line as the enemy's front line advanced.

"Hold," he called out to himself as if he led an entire battalion.

"HOLD!" he said again, his smile growing even as fear ripped at the back of his mind.

"HOOOOOLLLLDDD!"

The stampede was only yards away.

"You heard 'em, BILLY! LET'S DO THIS!" Riggs screamed and put away his Spark Club. He ran ahead of the pack, guided their melee toward the open doors of the stairwell. Quicker and more agile than he thought he could be, Riggs stayed ahead of the pack, Billy right on his tail. The stairwell was in sight, and Billy was gaining on him, charging behind.

Only a hundred yards away, Riggs realized Billy's horns wouldn't make it through.

"The doorway is too small!" he called out.

Kira and Aria paused a moment, not able to hear over the stampede, but Riggs pointed ahead as he sprinted. They looked at the doorway.

"It's too small," Kira said. "IT'S TOO SMALL!" she yelled to Aria.

They dashed to the doorway and pulled their clubs out. Swinging with all their might, they smashed the door frame and bent back the metal structure of the walls.

"It's not wide enough," Aria called out.

"It's too la—" Kira began, but they jumped aside as Riggs blew past them.

He shot up the stairwell, screaming like a charging madman. Billy the Bull followed, his horn catching the doorframe and ripping it out like flicking toothpicks. The bull followed Riggs up the stairs, but then its right horn caught the center rail of the spiral staircase. It bounced to the left like a boxer taking a hard cross, but his hooves found the steel mesh staircase and it kept going. The center rail acted as a guide to help the beast stay on the circular stairs, its horn touching and spinning up the rail as it charged up.

Behind them, Kira and Aria slowed their rush and gradually shepherded the herd through the doorway. Soon, the entire herd was charging up the staircase.

Riggs felt the staircase shake below his feet. Tons more weight than the steel was ever designed to carry raced up the structure.

"Come on, Billy my boy!" Riggs screamed as he lowered his shoulder at the top and blasted the doorway open. Billy followed only steps behind, his massive horns exploding the door frame. Chunks of stucco, wood, and metal shot out like fireworks as the herd now rushed into the Outer Ring.

"This way, Biiiiiiilllllllllyyyyyy!" Riggs kept running and Billy kept following.

They ran straight at The Tower.

***

"There's a lot of people inside," Jace said, uncertainty filling his voice.

Kaden's head bobbed up and down. "You're right," he said, lighting the torch. He held it up and Beth-ell's Elites lifted their hands. Subtle winds blew through them, their hair blowing in the breeze and the fire from Kaden's torch jumping in the wind to light the others.

"We're bringing the fight to The Tower, we are the flame," Kaden said, five blazing torches in their circle.

Without another word, they each scattered, sneaking through the nearby shadows and putting the flame to the base of The Tower. They reunited and together ran to another spot at the base of The Tower.

As the sun rose and their flames grew brighter, people moving through the Inner Ring took notice. The groups of people walked mindlessly, just as Kaden had done to the EMR every morning, but now some stopped. At first pausing in confusion, the people watched the five tiny flames dart along one side of the massive base. Behind them, flames grew, climbing the walls.

But shouts of confusion and help never went up. The working class walked along, on their way to their destination, ignoring the flames. A lifetime of keeping their head down culminating into no additional action, they simply kept their head down.

The lack of involvement gave Kaden and the others more time, setting more fires at the base of The Tower. Soon, a blue-robed Agent screamed out for the group to halt.

"H—" he started to shout, but hardly a syllable escaped as Beth-ell's Elites flickered their hands in unison and his vocal cords were cut off. Their joint movement magnified the force on the Agent and threw him back and into the air. He went up like a leaf in the breeze and came down like a brick.

They moved halfway around the base of The Tower, igniting small fires that grew larger and larger, reaching up the side of the first few floors. Agents acting as guards and sentries were each thrown aside or crushed by the weight of the Elites' powers.

"Last light," Kaden said. "Next entrance is ours."

The group sprinted forward, but Beth-ell stopped, her Elites slowing and looking back.

"Keep going!" she called ahead. Her head turned behind them as if sensing something nearby.

Kaden and Jace threw their torches at the base of The Tower and moved to a door.

"No, bring them in!" Beth-ell shouted to them.

"It's a distraction. We can't burn it while we're inside," Kaden called back.

"You must flush out the evil from the inside out, use everything you have and never give up! These matchsticks won't change the heart of Empyrean!" she demanded. She waved her hand and the pair of torches flew from the ground back to Kaden's and Jace's hands.

"She really is far more powerful than a Brown Agent," Jace said in astonishment.

Kaden looked back at Beth-ell, uncertainty in his mind as their plan shifted.

"Get them in," Beth-ell called to her Elites. The pair turned to The Tower and raised their hands. They could have ripped any door off its hinges or made one in a wall if they chose.

Kaden looked to Beth-ell as the Elites moved to create an opening. In her focus on them, she took attention from what she and her Elites had sensed.

The Spark Club swung at her, but she sensed it too late. As she turned and shifted her weight,, the club swung low, catching her knee. The heavy mace crackled with electricity and the sound of her knee shattering overtook the electrical pop. The weapon's momentum caved in her knee from the side and threw her sideways in the air.

As she spun in the air, Kaden caught a glimpse of her attacker. He wore a purple robe with an unmistakable scowl of disdain.

Ron-ell.

His strong and swift swing now reared back as he took the follow-through from the blow and spun the club back around, now coming from above like an executioner's final blow on Beth-ell just as she struck the stone ground.

Her Elites reached out, deflecting his blow with an invisible force, but Ron-ell had his own pair of charcoal monsters. The demons darted forward as if shot from a cannon from the shadows behind Ron-ell. Larger than Beth-ell's pair and with a running start, their ominous glide was like a bullet train levitating over tracks at hundreds of miles per hour. Beth-ell's Elites put up their hands but were steamrolled, smashing into the ground like meteors making a crater. A spiderweb of cracks shot out from under them across the polished stone that surrounded The Tower.

Kaden shouted to Beth-ell as Ron-ell once again reared back his Spark Club and lunged it down in a murderous blow upon her. She raised her hand in the split second before it crushed her chest, pushing him back and sliding herself away at the same moment. The club smashed the stone an inch from her head, making its own crater and sending pieces of rock soaring above them as Ron-ell sought to regain his balance.

Beth-ell pushed against the ground, and like a bird taking flight, she flew up and back, landing on one leg. Like a graceful crane, she stood with her damaged leg held back behind her.

"Get inside!" she called out to Kaden as she reached toward The Tower. She clenched her fist as if grabbing an invisible rope, yanking it away. A chunk of wall erupted like it had been loaded with dynamite. "Go!" she demanded.

As much as she was pushing the issue, she wouldn't use her power to force him in.

Kaden hesitated as he looked back at her and saw her move her attention to her Elites. The attacking pair was now above them, but Beth-ell flicked her wrist and pushed them from behind, using their momentum against them. They stumbled past Beth-ell's pair, the subtle touch just enough to give her Elites time to respond. They rose up and took a stand as the attacking pair regained their composure.

But Beth-ell's extra movement toward the Elites gave Ron-ell enough time to recover and send another deadly blow her way. He went with quickness, jabbing the club at her midsection. Beth-ell shifted, but she wasn't fast enough; he caught her hip. She winced but kept her balance as she slid back, as if on air, yet Kaden saw her favor her hip.

"Go!" She sent her last command to Kaden, flicking her wrist and moving him and Jace a step toward the opening that hung open like a wound in The Tower's wall.

"Come on," Jace said, pushing Kaden's side as they ran in.

Behind them, Beth-ell turned her attention to Ron-ell. Kaden heard the crackle of the Spark Club and sound of stone smashing as the fight between the two trios waged on.

Kaden and Jace, torches in hand, sprinted deeper into the opening and into the belly of The Tower.

***

As the bellowing of the stampede echoed through the narrow streets of the Outer Ring, Kira and Aria rushed out of the stairwell, watching as the last of the cattle rushed to catch up with the herd. Dust billowed in their wake.

"That'll get their attention," Aria said, a tight smile on her face.

"Now comes the hard part," Kira replied, her eyes scanning the area. Already, people were emerging from their homes, drawn by the commotion. Confusion painted their gaunt faces as they watched the cattle storm through their streets – an unprecedented sight in the tightly controlled confines of Empyrean. Many stayed at the edge of their doorways, not taking a step outside.

A woman clutching a small child approached them. "What's happening?" Fear trembled in her voice.

Kira stepped forward. "The Tower is weakened," she said, her voice carrying farther than it should have. "Today is the day we stop hiding."

The woman stepped back, her eyes widening. "But... but they'll kill us."

“Death is not the end,” Kira said.

The woman stared at her in confusion. Kira recognized it, the same look she had on her face when she first heard the words.

Kira raised her voice, addressing the growing crowd. "People of the Outer Ring! The Tower has fed on your fear for too long. Today, Jericho's light returns! We are His Light to carry on!"

As if in response, sounds of destruction came from The Tower's direction. Rubble from an old weakening building fell to the streets as the herd plowed through. Kira could see the roof of an abandoned complex fall like a sinkhole. Then bright lights of rising fires came up from various points along The Tower's perimeter. Sounds of astonishment and comments grew as the sounds of the thundering herd rattled off in the distance.

"That's our cue," Aria said, nodding toward a building with access to the water distribution system. "I'll head that way, redirect the flow as planned."

Kira clasped her arm. "Slow, steady, strong."

"You know it." Aria's eyes flicked to the distant tower, where smoke had begun to rise. "We can't let the boys have all the fun."

As Aria slipped away toward the water controls, Kira turned back to the still growing crowd. Faces peered from windows and doorways, while others cautiously approached.

"What is this madness?" An old man stepped forward, his face creased with years of hardship. "You'll bring the Elites down on us all!"

Murmurs of agreement rippled through the crowd.

"The Elites are already coming," Kira replied calmly. "They've been consuming you for generations. Breeding children for you to raise and grow to love, only to rip them away for sorting. They use fear to control us." She lifted her hand as if in defiance, and a soft light emanated from her palm – not blinding, but clear and steady as her passion grew. "But there are things stronger than fear."

The crowd fell silent, transfixed by the light.

"Love. Sacrifice."

People looked amongst each other, then back to Kira.

"I died," Kira continued, her voice carrying to every corner of the gathering. "I felt my neck break. I felt the darkness take me. But the light brought me back." The glow intensified, spreading up her arm. "Jericho's body might be gone, but His spirit lives on. He brought me back. I was aimless out here, following the world as we all knew it, but He showed me the light and gave me new life. The light in me now is the same light that's in all of you, but only if you choose to see it."

A depressive sensation like a blanket of humidity entered their air. It struck so fast and hard, it could have been a tremor shaking the ground beneath their feet – the first signs of The Tower's response. Elites were zeroing in on their area. They'd all felt the life draining feeling of an Elite. In the distance, figures in white and blue robes appeared, moving in formation toward the commotion. The wave of The Tower's counterattack.

"They're coming," someone in the crowd warned.

"Let them," Kira replied, her voice strong and firm. "Today, we stop running."

A man in tattered clothes pushed through the crowd. "My daughter was taken in the last sorting," he said, his voice breaking. "They said she was needed for the greater good of Empyrean."

"They lied," Kira said softly. "There is no greater good in consumption."

She raised her voice again, addressing the entire gathering. "The Tower teaches that strength comes from taking, from consuming those who are weaker. But true strength comes from standing together! From helping your fellow man and woman." The light spread further, illuminating her entire body now. "I'm not asking you to die today. I'm asking you to truly *live* for the first time!"

Electric crackles filled the air as the approaching Agents activated their Spark Clubs.

"What can we do against their weapons?" a woman called out.

Kira smiled, encouraged by the question. Before she responded, Riggs appeared. He rounded a nearby corner at full sprint. Behind him thundered Billy the Bull, followed by several other cattle helping to lead the herd. They were being chased by a squad of White Agents, their robes billowing as they ran.

"WWWWOOOOOOOOOWWWWWWWWEEEEEE!" Riggs bellowed with a smile.

The crowd scattered instinctively, pressing against buildings to avoid the charging animals. Riggs, however, directed the bull straight toward the wave of approaching Agents. The massive beast lowered its horns and plowed into their formation, sending white-robed figures flying.

Riggs skidded to a halt beside Kira, breathing hard.

"Ha HAAA!" he gasped. "But more are coming... Blues and Purples. And... Elites," he said as he caught his breath.

Kira nodded, unsurprised. "We need to split them up, draw them away from The Tower." She turned back to the crowd, which had regrouped at a safer distance. "For generations, The Tower has taught you that you're nothing without them. That you need their protection, their order." Her voice strengthened. "They're wrong. You are the heart of Empyrean, not its scraps!"

As if in response to her words, the old man who had questioned her earlier stepped forward. He straightened his hunched back as much as age would allow. "My grandson was an Agent," he said. "He believed in The Tower's promises of a better life. We never saw him again after he put on that white robe."

Others began calling out similar stories – loved ones lost to The Tower's hierarchy, promising children who disappeared into its depths.

"If we fight, we die," the old man continued. "But we've been dying every day anyway." He turned to the crowd. "How many more generations will we sacrifice to their hunger? I say if we die, we go down fighting!"

A rumble of agreement spread through the gathering. Kira watched as something changed in their expressions – fear giving way to a different emotion. Resolve.

The ground shook. Kira turned to see a black-robed Elite gliding down the street toward them; behind him, a bull flattened against a building, smashed unnaturally. The demon was flanked by a pack of Blue Agents with Spark Clubs at the ready. Behind this first wave came others – more Agents, more Elites.

Kira stepped forward to meet them, the light within her pulsing stronger. Riggs moved to her side, his massive frame tensed for battle.

"This is your moment," Kira called to the crowd without taking her eyes off the approaching force. "Not just to fight, but to choose life over death. Because once you see, you cannot unsee."

The old man picked up a length of pipe from the rubble. Others followed suit, arming themselves with whatever they could find – tools, bent rebar, pieces of crumbling buildings.

"For my grandson," the old man said, stepping up beside Kira.

"For my daughter," said another.

One by one, others joined them, forming a line that stretched across the narrow street. The light from Kira seemed to touch each of them, not visibly, but in a way that straightened spines and lifted chins. They held confidence and strength.

The Elite stopped several yards away. Its black skin seemed to absorb the light around it. The air around them vibrated with that familiar oppressive force – the hunger that had kept the Outer Ring cowering for generations.

But this time, the people didn't shrink back. Their numbers grew, now in multiples of the Agents and the oncoming Elites.

"Disperse," commanded one of the Blue Agents. "Return to your dwellings immediately."

"We are home," the old man replied, his voice steady despite the tremor in his hands. "It's you who don't belong here."

The Elite made a terrible grinding sound – a horrid version of laughter. It raised a charcoal hand and the nearest Blue Agent stepped forward, his Spark Club crackling. The other Agents all gripped their Spark Clubs and the crowd immediately realized their pipes and makeshift weapons were up against sophisticated weapons of death.

Kira felt the fear and moved forward anyway. She stopped to intercept the first Agent, but before she could reach him, something the Agents never expected happened. From a side street, a torrent of water suddenly erupted, shooting perfectly toward the oncoming Agents. The flood knocked the lead Agent off his feet and sent him sliding across the cobblestones. His Spark Club hit the water and shocked him before the weapon shorted out. Unelectrified, it was as effective as all the other pipes, stones, and discarded pieces of rebar.

Aria spoke up from a nearby corner, her hand on a valve wheel. "The pressure's been building up for years," she called. "Thought it was time for The Tower to share!"

The crowd roared in approval as more water gushed forth, turning the street into a rushing river that disrupted the Agents' formation. As Agents of various colors struggled to hang on in the flooding streets, some were electrocuted by their own Spark Clubs while others were aware enough to turn them off and holster them. The closest Elite, however, remained unmoved, its feet somehow anchored against the current and water flowing around it like iron filings avoiding a magnet.

"Kira!" Riggs shouted above the commotion. "You need to go!"

“I can’t leave now!” she shot back, nodding to the crowd.

“If you don’t go now, you never will,” Riggs fired back.

She nodded, understanding. "I'll meet you inside."

"Nope, my place is here. In this fight,” he said.

“You can’t stay—”

"He'll have company," Aria shouted. "Someone has to keep him in line."

"Are you... sure?" Kira said, seeing the smile on her face matching Riggs's expression. She wanted to push harder, to bring them both inside The Tower as planned, but seeing them together now... How could she pull them apart? They seemed at home, in the fight for the Outer Ring, and together.

"Born sure," Riggs said with a smile, and then he held up a massive pipe, thrusting it into the air like a warrior raising his sword. He roared like a lion defending his pride and the people rallied around him. His roar was taken up by the growing dozens, now over a hundred as more and more people came out of hiding.

The people of the Outer Ring charged The Tower's forces. What they lacked in training, they made up for in numbers and desperate courage. Aria opened another flow of water that erupted toward a flank of the Agents. The electricity in their weapons shorted out in the deluge. Soon she was running to catch Riggs and screaming with him as they led the crowd forward. A raging charge running through the watery streets and smashing through the first line of Agents like a medieval war with the first lines of each army clashing.

Kira took off down a side street, passing a group of bulls that were rounding a corner and charging back into the madness behind her, Riggs's war cry calling them.

Chapter 39

Kaden

The interior of The Tower was a shock of pristine order compared to the chaos erupting outside. Polished obsidian floors and smooth steel walls reflected the dancing flames of their torches as Kaden and Jace sprinted through the opening Beth-ell had created. Behind them, the sounds of her battle with Ron-ell faded – the crack of Spark Clubs giving way to the ever-present hum of The Tower.

"We need to find an elevator," Jace said, his voice low.

“Yeah, and not a vertical lift,” Kaden said.

Jace paused, catching the humor and letting out a breath like he’d just come up from a prolonged time under water. They began forward.

"Pinnacle's chambers are near the top, but Jericho's body won't be kept there. They'd have a special containment area – probably a higher-level research lab."

“I think I saw it, when Beth-ell’s Elites brought me to Kaden. The highest level of the labs, one under Pinnacle’s chamber.”

They moved deeper into The Tower's labyrinthine structure, their torches leaving trails of smoke along the ceiling. Occasionally, White Agents rushed past a cross-corridor toward the commotion outside, too focused and confused on the external threat to notice, or care, about the infiltrators. The fires spreading outside and Riggs's cattle stampede were doing their job.

"This way," Jace whispered, leading them down a narrower corridor.

As they approached the end of the corridor, the floor beneath them trembled. Kaden glanced back to see a patch of darkness spreading across the wall behind them – not smoke or shadow, but something living. The obsidian surfaces seemed to ripple like water disturbed by a stone.

"Tower's responding," Jace muttered. "Pinnacle knows we're here."

“We’re setting the place on fire; I sure hope he knows,” Kaden said.

They reached a set of metal doors with thin windows – simple compared to the elegant design of the rest of The Tower. Jace punched the button, the light flashed, and the doors slid open to reveal a wide, service-style elevator.

They stepped inside, and Jace pressed the floor button to rise up.

The elevator hummed to life, beginning its ascent through the heart of The Tower. Through the small window in the door, Kaden watched as floor after floor slipped past – glimpses of laboratories, training rooms, and dormitories where Agents lived in controlled comfort.

"Feels like old times," Jace said, breaking the tense silence. "Except last time I rode one of these, I wasn't planning to burn the place down."

Kaden managed a small smile, remembering his first trip up The Tower's main elevator as a new Agent recruit. "Remember when Ryon said these things were just 'fancy boxes pulled by ropes'?"

"And Vala corrected him that they used magnetic fields, not ropes." Jace chuckled.

“She would know that, with exacting detail,” Kaden said.

The moment of levity was short-lived. The elevator shuddered violently, then jerked to a halt between floors. The lights flickered, plunging them into darkness save for the orange glow of their torches.

“It would be bad if we were trapped in here,” Kaden said, looking at their torches as the elevator filled up with smoke.

"Power’s out," Jace said, immediately moving to the control panel. "We're still five floors short, maybe more."

Kaden raised his torch higher, examining the ceiling of the broad elevator. "Can we get through there?"

Before Jace could answer, the elevator doors were wrenched open from the outside with a screech of protesting metal. Harsh white light flooded the small space as they found themselves staring at a wall of Agents in blue and purple robes.

At their center stood Ryon, his massive frame filling the doorway, a Spark Club crackling in his hand. His eyes widened briefly in recognition before narrowing with hatred.

“Traitors. Both of you,” he sneered.

Behind him stood Vala and a squadron of at least a dozen Blue Agents. At the rear of the group, two Elites loomed, their charcoal skin like black holes absorbing the light around them.

"Ryon," Jace said, his voice carefully neutral. "We're not here to fight you."

"I don’t think it would be much of a fight," Ryon replied. “And odd, not wanting a fight yet committing arson?"

Kaden stepped forward, torch raised. "Last chance to step aside, Ryon."

The bigger man feigned surprise. "Or what? You'll wave your sticks at us? You’re trapped and outnumbered."

"Better odds than I thought we'd get," Kaden replied. “You know, there is something about fire. It multiplies.” He looked at Ryon, who appeared to be impatient already. “I had a dream once that I was chased by a fire that kept growing. It consumed everything. It doesn’t care who you are or what you do; it just consumes. Kind of like Truth; it doesn’t care if you believe in it, it just is. Someone way smarter than me tried showing me that, but I didn’t get it. But now I am starting to. Maybe at the end of this, you’ll be the one consumed, either by fire or the truth, or worse.”

Ryon looked back at the pair of Elites behind the group. The Agents parted and the Elites stepped forward with their eerie glide of a walk.

“Disagree,” Ryon said. His confidence was rising, like a little brother whose older, and much larger, brother was now joining the fight on his behalf.

“Ryon, we’re not trapped here with you,” Kaden said, Ryon and the pack of Agents behind him watching with the Spark Clubs at the ready. “You’re trapped here with us.”

At the moment the words left his lips, he thrust the torch forward, knocking Ryon back and catching his robe on fire.

Jace moved with practiced efficiency, driving his shoulder into Ryon's side while the big man was momentarily off balance. Despite his size advantage, Ryon flew backward into the agents behind him, creating a momentary opening.

"Let’s go!" Jace shouted.

They burst out of the lift and into the corridor, immediately splitting in opposite directions to divide their pursuers. Kaden sprinted left, torch still blazing, while Jace went right. As expected, Ryon bellowed commands, sending half his forces after each fugitive. The Elites shoved the Agents off of them and raised a hand to stop the invaders, but Kaden and Jace each turned a corner, out of their grasp just in time.

Kaden ran, his mind racing to remember the Tower's layout from his brief time as an Agent. It was a maze of laboratories and containment chambers, each more secure than the last. He needed to find the stairs to get up to the highest level.

Behind him, footsteps pounded on the obsidian floor. He risked a glance back to see Vala leading three Blue Agents and one of the Elites in pursuit. The Elite moved with that unnatural gliding motion, gaining on him with each second. He must stay far enough ahead and out of direct sight or be stopped by their gravity-like force.

Kaden rounded a corner and found himself facing a sealed security door. No time to bypass it. Instead, he pressed his back against the adjacent wall and waited. As Vala and the first two Agents rounded the corner, he swung his torch like a bat, and the flames erupted like fireworks, catching the Agent's robes in a growing blaze and creating a barrier of flames between them.

The Agent screamed in pain and the other two stumbled back, but Vala pressed forward, her face set in grim determination. She activated her Spark Club, the electrical field crackling as she jumped through the flames.

"I always knew you'd bring destruction, McCloud," she said. "From the moment you showed up late on day one."

"You don't understand what's happening, Vala," Kaden replied, backing away as she approached. "Pinnacle is lying to all of you. The Tower isn't salvation – it's a prison."

One of the screaming Agents flew down the hall, the flames blown out by the push. The Elite was closer.

"And the Remnant is freedom?" she scoffed. "Living in tunnels like rats? Stealing from The Tower that provides and protects what's left of humanity?" She gestured around them with her free hand. "Look at what you're doing – bringing fire into the last safe place on Earth."

"Safe for who?" Kaden demanded, still retreating. "For the Elites who consume people at the sortings? For Pinnacle, who tears out hearts with his bare hands? I saw your face at our promotion, when every Agent let eyes on you. What have they done to you so you could *earn* your place, so you could have *safety*?"

"No!" she screamed and swung the club. Kaden shifted back, avoiding it as it smashed into the stainless steel wall, leaving a massive dent like a meteor strike.

The Elite behind Vala moved forward, its obsidian form rippling with impatience. Vala held up a hand to restrain it, her eyes never leaving Kaden's.

"You've been misled," she said. "You and Jace and all the others who ran. Jericho wasn't a savior. He was a terrorist, and was executed for his crimes."

"I've seen both sides, Vala," he replied. "I've worn the robe like you, and I've lived in the tunnels. I've seen what The Tower really is. You don't know what you're following."

The Elite made that horrible grinding sound – an insistence for aggression. Vala stepped aside for the creature.

"You're coming with us, or going inside it." Vala stepped aside, her Spark Club at the ready, as the Elite stepped forward.

It raised its hand and pushed Kaden's torch close to his skin. He tried leaning away, but the Elite toyed with him, getting the fire just close enough for pain.

Kaden's back hit the wall. He was running out of corridor, out of options.

The Elite swung its hand and the torch flew off, smashing against the wall.

"Have you seen Pinnacle's Shadow?" Kaden asked, his eyes turning to Vala and ignoring the Elite.

She ignored him and the Elite jammed its hand toward Kaden's neck, but it stopped before making contact. The demon was surprised. Then it struck again, but its hand deflected away as a shimmer of light came off of Kaden.

The harder the demon pushed at him, the more it deflected away. The Elite was growing furious, like a boxer trying to pummel its pinned-down opponent in the corner, yet the opponent slipped every punch.

Kaden leaned off the wall, his skin radiating.

"What...?" Vala looked on in surprise.

"The Shadow Elite that Pinnacle holds on the highest floors. I've seen them, but they couldn't hold me," Kaden said, a faint light illuminating off of him. "Seems neither can you."

"No," she said, a rasp in her tone of true anger, hatred.

"I'm here to help you, Vala. And you too." Kaden looked at the Elite, the light shining into the cracks of the dead, stone skin.

The charcoal face of the Elite tensed in anger, as if each word taunted it.

"Whatever you've figured out, it won't last." Vala stepped forward, swinging her club.

But the club never landed, as the Elite and Vala were thrown aside. Kaden looked back down the corridor to see Beth-ell's Elites moving toward him, clearing a path through Agents and Elites alike.

As the pair came closer, Kaden could see obvious signs of damage. Chunks of their black skin were cut away, creating canyon-like ravines across their surface.

"You made it! How's Beth-ell?" Kaden asked.

The pair looked at each other, then back to Kaden and gave a nod signaling she'd survived.

"Thanks for the help." He nodded to the Elite and Vala, now far down the corridor. "We need to go up. He's higher. I can feel it."

The trio took off, finding the next lift and taking it up to the highest level of the labs. They came out and found Jace and Ryon facing off.

Ryon's Spark Club lay on the ground, its handle broken in two. A last wisp of electricity sputtered off it as it died.

"Jace!" Kaden called out, running toward them.

Jace turned to Kaden, and Ryon pounced on the chance, shooting forward and taking Jace down. Jace countered and the pair wrestled for a dominant position.

As Kaden and the Elites ran to them, an eerie darkness overtook the hall. Kaden felt the red eyes before he saw them. Instantly, all three of them were thrown back and pinned against a wall. Kaden's skin flickered with a brilliant glow, but still the cloudy darkness pressed him back. Just as they were thrown back by the Shadow Elite, Ryon was empowered by it. He overtook Jace and slammed his shoulders to the hard ground, sitting on his chest in a mounted-like position. Jace tried pulling him back down in a Jiu Jitsu style defense, but Ryon was too strong with positional advantage. The darkness swirled around Ryon and rolled the broken Spark Club to his side.

Ryon knew what to do with it.

"Ryon, don't let it force you!" Kaden yelled as Jace squirmed under the bigger man.

"It's not doing anything. I am," he said, picking up the club. He turned it around, showing the sharp point of the busted steel handle to Jace.

"No, no, no, no, no." Jace reached up and resisted as Ryon pressed down. Slowly, the sharp point descended toward Jace's heart, Ryon's weight and strength inching it down as Jace futilely tried pushing back.

"Ryon, don't do this!" Kaden screamed. He tried to focus, to bring out the light.

His skin lit up and pushed back the darkness, the three of them falling off the wall.

The Elites quickly shot out a hand to control Ryon, but the darkness of the Shadow Elite swirled away from Ryon and focused all its attention on the trio. They resisted but couldn't overpower it.

Kaden screamed from their stalemate as he watched Ryon slowly push the sharp handle into Jace's chest. It went deep, piercing his ribs, then his heart.

Jace convulsed as Ryon forced it deeper. Blood poured up; like a bubbling spring, it rose from Jace's chest and soaked his clothes and skin. Ryon kept pushing until he hit the floor underneath them. The two men locked eyes as one killed the other.

Jace's eyes began to roll back as life left his body.

"NNNNOOOOOO!" Kaden screamed and light erupted from deep inside. The Shadow Elite and Ryon were thrown back.

CHAPTER 40

Riggs and Aria

Livestock stampeded through the Agents, even knocking down an Elite. The unruly mob began to overwhelm the Agents. They capitalized on the mayhem and took their pipes and bricks to the fallen Elite. The charcoal skin was a pile of dead rock as dozens took turns getting their shot in. But their eagerness gave the other Elite room when they might have overtaken it.

Carnage erupted as the remaining demon took vengeance after its slain partner. It ripped attackers in two with a quick movement of its hands. Others, it flicked its wrists up and threw them careening high in the air as if flicking a bug. The victims plummeted back down to smash against the hard stone. Motionless bodies stacked up as the Elite moved through, attempting to clear a way for overwhelmed Agents to get back into the fight.

Riggs squared off with a blue-robed Agent on the side of the main fight, picking up a broken piece of rebar from a nearby shattered concrete wall to combat the Spark Club.

The electricity was out from the water spill, but the Agent still used the mace as a blunt weapon. The Agent was fast and Riggs's massive frame struggled to avoid and defend against the repeated blows. After a barrage of successive jabs, Riggs stumbled back, losing his footing in the debris and wetness, the Agent took an overhead swing. Riggs held up the rebar and blocked the blow, but the iron rod bent, each using all their strength as their weapons locked. Then, the electricity of the Spark Club popped back on with a jolt. The shock sent the two flying apart.

The Agent recovered first, moving to end the fight as Riggs lay on the ground, his arms twitching as he briefly lost control on his muscles from the shock. Riggs looked up as the Agent brought up the Spark Club, the deathly crackle of electricity snapping out like a lightning storm as the Agent brought down the club toward Riggs's skull.

Riggs kept his eyes open and expected the end. If this Agent ended his life, he'd see it happen and struggle to see, to live, at least one more moment until his demise.

But in the chaos of the fight and the leftover water rolling over the streets, Riggs hadn't heard the galloping sound of hooves on the broken cobblestone. He did see a flash of color above him and heard the thump of horns against the Agent's chest. Air flew out of the Agent as if his lungs exploded. The tail end of Billy the Bull flashed next to Riggs as the beast ran through the Agent and carried him forward.

"Billy!" Riggs screamed with joy.

The bull had lowered its head, catching the Agent square in the mid-section with one of its horns, then flipped his horns up and sent the man flying in the air.

He lost control of his club while in the air, and as he came back down, Riggs heard the crunch of his spine breaking as his back landed on the unforgiving metal ball end of the club. The Agent's blank eyes stared upward as blood trickled out below him from an unseen rupture.

Riggs turned to see Billy plow through the crowd, throwing Outer Ring fighters and Agents alike. Through the melee, he saw Aria deftly fighting another Agent. He caught himself watching her graceful motions as she swept the man's legs from under him and pounced on the Spark Club as the crowd took over, overwhelming the Agent.

Aria stood up, hoisting the stolen club in the air like a captured enemy flag. The crowd roared in excitement.

Riggs moved to get close to Aria, but the crowd swelled, moving him back and further away. They caught eyes for a moment before she turned to see the next wave of the fight. Before her, two Elites came from around a corner. They mowed through the Outer Ring fighters like hot metal through butter.

He saw that she was directly in their path.

"Aria!" Riggs called out, muscling through the crowd.

A blue-robed Agent stepped in Riggs's way, but he instinctively grabbed his arm and twisted it back with a crack as the Agent screamed in pain. He threw him away with a kick to the back, sending the man face first to the hard stone ground and into the belly of the furious mob.

Riggs, Aria, and small pockets of Outer Ring fighters struck an admirable blow to The Tower's forces, but their numbers slowly dwindled, no longer supported with additions from the fed-up people of the Outer Ring. Gradually, the Agents and Elites pushed them back. Each Elite did countless damage, like a modern fighter holding a machine gun going against farmers with pitchforks and axes. If the Outer Ring fighters got close enough and with enough numbers, they could overwhelm their enemies, but two more Elites that were heading toward Aria turned the tide and magnified the impact of every Agent as they thinned out the freedom fighters.

More and more Outer Ring fighters fell.

The stampeding livestock were dispersing.

The spraying water main lost pressure.

The Agents and Elites surged forward.

Riggs focused on Aria, but so did the Elites – they knew to target the leaders and let the followers fall into chaos.

He began shoving those on his side to reach her sooner.

Aria moved forward, using the gained Spark Club and her prior training. She was a deadly fighter. Two Agents came after her and she pivoted gracefully, swinging the club like a piece of her body, knocking out the legs with a bone-crunching snap to the first Agent's left knee. With a quick turn and squat, she avoided the next Agent's club and sent the butt end of her club into his jaw with a catastrophic uppercut, sending him flying backward, unconscious as he struck the ground.

Her movement with the club cleared the space around her, but it only gave room for the Elites to move toward her. One Elite flew like a bullet train on magnetic rails at her. She shifted to her side, a millisecond ahead of the demon, and swung the club catching its arm. Pieces of black shot off like charcoal exploding, and the creature crashed down and rolled like an airplane that lost an wing. Aria jumped to the fallen Elite, ready to bring the club down on its head as she gracefully leapt.

The second Elite was now close enough to extend its invisible force on her. This one was methodical, pressing its unmatched advantage over rashness. It reached out its dead, black hand and Aria froze in mid-air, the Spark Club above her head cocked and ready to come down on the impulsive Elite who rushed her, but now the club froze along with her body. Her muscles twitched as she struggled to free herself.

"Aria!!!" Riggs called out as he fought through the crowd, but her focus was on the Elite in front of her. With an arm limp at its side, the other hand raised; it moved to her, coming nose-to-nose. It sneered with fury and the Spark Club in her hand popped like a lightning bolt from the heavens. Aria's face trembled in concentration as she resisted the force.

The demon invisibly forced her wrist to bend unnaturally as it guided the club, turning her grip. The weapon crackled with deadly electricity, and moved closer to her head.

Sweat dripped from her bright red face, her teeth clenched as her wrist broke. She let out a scream as if she was holding the weight of the world and refusing to let it fall.

"NNNOOOO!!!" Riggs called out, too far away to help.

She screamed in pain as she resisted, unwilling to relent, but the force was too much.

The club inched closer and soon touched her temple as it exploded with a burst of power. Her body convulsed and her eyes rolled back in her head. The demon kept it there, electrifying her more than needed. A line of smoke rose from the contact point as the skin around her temple bubbled from the heat and her body twitched uncontrollably.

"NO!" Riggs screamed as he shot forward.

Aria's body fell. The club cracked the stone as it crashed next to her limp body. Smoke rose from her body like mist rising off a lake.

Riggs kept moving and reached the distracted Elite who killed Aria. He jumped on its back, wrapping his arm around its neck and wrenching it back. A grinding sound erupted, a deathly howl of pain from the creature. The powerful motion was too quick for the Elite to respond. Riggs put his knee to the demon's back and turned his arms, ripping its head off its charcoal body.

Its body fell with a thud next to Aria. Riggs held its head as a black ooze of altered blood streamed out of its head.

The crowd cheered for Riggs and the death of an Elite, but Riggs didn't notice. His eyes went to Aria, dead before him, but he knew the fight wasn't over. His rage moved him to the other Elite. He ran at it, throwing the severed head of its partner at it. It struck the Elite and caught its attention, distracting it from the death it dealt to other Outer Ring fighters.

The creature moved both hands; one held back Riggs as if it grabbed him by the neck and the other ripped a chunk of the stone ground out and sent it flying at him. The deadly rock caught his shoulder and crushed bone. Searing pain ignited his upper body and his arm went limp, shoulder broken.

The Elite ripped out three more chunks of the pavement, raising them to be at eye level. It eyed Riggs like a patient sniper dialing in the perfect kill shot.

The rocks shot like a bullet out of a gun, but a split second after, the Elite was pummeled by a flying pipe from the crowd. Before it could recover, another wave of bulls reentered the fight. They trampled the stone creature, sending pieces of charcoal-like skin.

"Billy!!!" Riggs screamed as the bull saved his life a second time. "Billy my boy!"

The flying stones meant to kill Riggs fell to the ground without their master's control, and rolled past Riggs as the hold on him was released.

The wounded Elite began to rise, but like a trained fighter trying to end the fight when the opponent stumbled, Riggs pounced on it before it could gather itself, using his one good arm to send a barrage of fists down on its head. Tears rolled down his face as he screamed and ended the demon, caving its charcoal head in as pieces of debris flew in the air. The creature went limp, lying flat on the ground, but Riggs continued.

His hand bleeding from the downward fists, he stood and stomped on its neck and head, smashing the being further until he stumbled back.

He kept stepping back, his body wavering from exhaustion and lost blood. He came to Aria's body and fell next to it. One arm limp, hanging at his side, as gashes and battle fed the blood that covered him. He looked up at the fight they felt The Tower started generations before and they were trying to end, but the battle continued. So many dead bodies lay around him. The death toll seemed ten to one as the people of the Outer Ring once again fell to The Tower's might. And now he looked back down at the woman he'd grown to love lying dead next to him.

Across the fight, he saw four more Elites coming toward the battle.

His head fell. Exhausted. Feeling hopeless.

"Jericho..." he said aloud. It was but a whisper in the cacophony of the violence around him. He took Aria's hand and said a prayer to Jericho, asking for strength.

When he looked up, the four Elites were already in the fight, cutting through the few remaining fighters. Soon enough, they'd bring the battle to a close and add more to the seemingly endless body count.

One of the Elites broke off and caught his eye. It was moving toward him, and quickly.

"Okay..." he said to himself, squeezing Aria's hand one last time. "Come get some!" he said as he slowly stood.

The Elites shot toward him, covering what felt like a hundred yards in one blink. It stood nose-to-nose with him.

He was so close to it, he could see the cracks in its dead, charcoal skin. The thing took all the heat from around it and Riggs felt a chilling cold.

Through his wounds and tired muscles, he hardly felt the blow that killed him. This demon was more experienced and knew not to give its enemy a chance. It held Riggs as it shot at him, holding the weapon and ensuring it found its mark.

Riggs looked down and saw the rebar through his chest. The Elite didn't move close to him to jeer or snarl; it ensured the more ferocious enemy was dead, with a piece of rusted iron through his heart.

Riggs fell back and looked up at the sky as life left his body. He could still see the Elite above him. The creature looked forward, to the next victim in the fight, but its usual menacing expression weakened, and it even appeared afraid.

The demon's black skin reflected a bright light off its charcoal skin.

An incredibly bright, glowing light.

CHAPTER 41

Kaden

Kaden knelt beside Jace's body, unable to tear his eyes from the horrific wound in his friend's chest. Blood pooled beneath them both, soaking into Kaden's pants as it spread across the obsidian floor, giving the floor an even more unnatural feel as if it were liquified. The handle of the broken Spark Club still protruded from between Jace's ribs, its tip buried deep in his heart.

Ryon was gone, retreating to surely regroup and bring more Agents and Elites after being thrown back by Kaden's explosive burst of light. The Shadow Elite that had pinned them to the wall was also blown back, no doubt back with Pinnacle now. But the victory felt hollow as Kaden gazed at Jace's still face.

"I'm sorry," he whispered. He tried to say more, feeling like there was an endless debt owed that he could never repay. His jaw moved up and down as he searched for unfindable words.

He wiped his eyes and reached out with trembling fingers to close Jace's eyes. Beth-ell's two Elites stood silently behind him like soldiers in formation awaiting orders, their cracked bodies motionless in respect for the fallen.

"It'll never stop, will it?" he said, and it echoed in the long hallway. How many more would die? Beth-ell could be dead or captured after fighting Ron-ell outside. Riggs, Aria, and Kira were somewhere in the chaos of the Outer Ring, their success a low probability. And now Jace. Everyone *could* be dead, but seeing one of his friends dead, killed in the battle next to him, made it more real than any planning could.

"Keep going," Kaden said aloud, though he made no move to stand. The words felt like a betrayal, leaving Jace here in this cold corridor. "We need to keep going. Jericho's body is close. I can feel it." Still, he remained kneeling, one hand on Jace's shoulder.

A sound echoed from down the corridor – footsteps approaching rapidly. Kaden tensed, the light flickering beneath his skin again. The Elites shifted, positioning themselves in defense of whatever approached.

"Ryon," Kaden growled, rising to his feet. His hands clenched into fists as the footsteps grew louder.

The footsteps broke into a run. Kaden braced himself, the light swelling within him, ready to erupt again. The Elites raised their hands, preparing to engage.

A figure rounded the corner, skidding to a halt at the sight of them.

"Kaden!"

Her voice struck him like a fresh breath of life empowering him. Kira stood before him, her clothes torn and bloodied but her face alight with determination. Her eyes widened at the sight of Jace's body, then moved back to Kaden's face.

"Kira," he breathed, the tension draining from his body. "You're here. You're alive."

She moved toward him quickly, stepping carefully around Jace's body to embrace Kaden. For a moment, they clung to each other, each an anchor for the other.

"I felt you," she said. "Like before, but stronger. I knew where to find you."

Kaden nodded, his heart warmer with her by his side. "Ryon did this, and the Shadow Elite," Kaden said, his voice hollow as they separated.

Kira looked down at their fallen friend, her expression hardening. "I saw what's happening outside. The Outer Ring is fighting back, but they won't last long against the Elites." She raised her eyes to meet his. "We need to get to *Him*."

Kaden nodded, resolve replacing grief. "His body is close, maybe one or two floors up. I can feel it calling."

"Then let's get him and get out," Kira said. She looked to the Elites, staring into each one's eyes. She evaded countless Elites in her days, never close enough or daring enough to look any of them in the eye. But these two were different, yet she couldn't tell exactly why.

“Let's go,” he said.

They moved down the corridor together, Kaden leading the way with the Elites flanking them. The Tower shuddered around them, the walls occasionally cracking and repairing as the structure responded to the attack both inside and out.

“I don't like that,” Kira said. “The Tower was shuddering before. It's like a living thing.”

“If Pinnacle is going to keep this place upright, he's going to need to focus all his attention on it. All we need is enough time to get in and out with Jericho.”

They turned a corner and found the main vertical lift. The door was open, as if inviting them in, but there was no elevator, only an empty tunnel into a black, bottomless pit.

"Think we can climb it?" Kaden asked as he stuck his head in the shaft. “Better yet, you two guide us up?” he said to the Elites.

The pair of charcoal creatures looked at each and then stepped forward, a curious expression on their faces. One lifted a hand and the ceiling above them ripped apart. Another motioned as if pulling their hand down and debris from the obsidian structure formed a staircase. The material flickered, as if fighting back and not wanting to conform to their power, but with both Elites fully focused on it, they bent the material to their will. It relented.

“Brilliant!” Kira said.

“Let’s go,” Kaden moved forward. But before he could take the first step up, The Tower shuddered. The Elites were thrown back and the hole closed. Like a protective dog whose toy was ripped from its mouth, the stair snapped away from Kaden and pulled back, rejoining the ceiling. The hole now fully reformed as a subtle tremor moved through their area, the ceiling rippling.

“It was worth a shot,” Kaden said to the Elites as they tried pulling again at the ceiling, to no avail. The greater power, Pinnacle, was preventing them from altering his creation.

"We need to find the stairs. The existing stairs," Kira said.

She peered down one of the corridors. "This way. I came up some," she said, pointing ahead.

They moved forward, but as they approached the door, the floor beneath them trembled. The door burst open before they could reach it, and a flood of blue- and purple-robed Agents poured out, led by at least a dozen Elites. They packed the corridor full.

Kaden and Kira froze, instinctively backing up. The Elites formed a wall of charcoal-like flesh, their dead eyes fixed on the intruders.

Behind them, another door popped open and dozens of Agents spread out, Spark Clubs at the ready. Soon, a group of Elites walked forward through the crowd to take the front row.

Ryon stepped forward, his head overlooking two Elites as he taunted Kaden.

“You’re not running away this time,” Ryon said in a menacing, almost teasing-like tone. He was relishing being the victor. “You’re his. All his.”

"There's too many," Kira whispered.

But as the mass of The Tower forces spread out, Kaden caught sight of two non-Tower figures in their midst – not being dragged as prisoners or in robes. They walked freely among the Elites.

"Barb?" he said, recognition dawning. "And... Enak?"

Enak stood beside her, Empyrean's former EMR supervisor, both moving with purpose through the ranks of Elites. They showed no fear of the creatures, no signs of being captives.

"They got to the lighthouse. Alister and Elba must be captured, or worse..." Kira said with sadness in her voice.

"Wait." Kaden tried to grab her arm, but she was already pushing past him.

The light erupted from Kira's skin as she charged forward, a blinding radiance that pushed back the nearest Elites. Kaden had no choice but to follow, his own light flaring to life as he joined her.

Together, they carved a path through The Tower's forces, their combined light creating a corridor of safety through the mass of enemies. The Elites nearest to them recoiled, the cracks in their obsidian skin widening as the light poured into them.

"Barb! Enak!" Kira called out. "This way!"

They reached the center of the group, their light holding back the pressing forces on all sides. The Elites pivoted, allowing them through as Kaden extended his hand toward Enak, who stared at him with an expression Kaden couldn't read.

"Come on," Kaden urged.

A slow smile spread across Enak's face, not of relief or gratitude, but something colder. More calculated.

"Kaden McCloud," he said, his voice carrying an edge Kaden had never heard before. "Always rushing in to save the day."

Beside him, Barb's stern face showed not a flicker of recognition or appreciation. Her eyes were hard as she surveyed Kaden and Kira.

"You didn't need to make it so easy," she said.

The realization hit Kaden like ice water. He looked back and saw Beth-ell's Elites were restrained by dozens of other charcoal demons.

"No," he said. "You're the traitors Pinnacle mentioned?"

Enak shrugged with a 'you guessed it' expression.

The light around Kaden and Kira pulsed as their shock registered. "The Remnant," Kira said. "What did you do?"

"Nothing the remnant hasn't already done to us," Barb answered. "Given us away, piece by piece. It's how the raids found us, isn't it?"

Enak gave a sympathetic look as if looking down on Kaden. "Pinnacle has had you from the beginning," he said, his voice carrying a note of satisfaction. "You've never had a chance. He controls all this and you think he hasn't had eyes everywhere? He's been seeing through my eyes, hearing through my ears."

"Your brother," Kaden said, a sickening realization dawning. "Elba—"

"Learned his final lesson," Enak cut him off, his face hardening. "The ol' timer Alister too."

"Why?" Kira demanded, her light flaring with her anger. "After everything The Tower has done – the sortings, the consumption?"

"Pinnacle offers a seat *at* the table," Barb said simply. "Not *beneath* it fighting for crumbs."

As they spoke, Kaden noticed something changing in the corridor around them. The walls rippled, the obsidian surface flowing like black water. The ceiling above them shifted, lowering in some places, rising in others.

"The Tower... Like it's alive," Kira whispered.

"It's not alive," Enak corrected. "It's obedient."

The floor beneath them began to move, rising slowly like a rising platform while walls formed around them, separating Kaden and Kira from the mass of Agents and Elites. Beth-ell's Elites shot forward, joining Kaden and Kira while everyone else, including Barb and Enak, were on the other side of seamless obsidian barriers that rose from the floor. They were caged.

"He's had you this whole time," Enak's voice called through the closing gap. "The *world* is his, the air itself bends to him, not only The Tower."

The ceiling parted and the platform continued to rise, carrying Kaden, Kira, and the two Elites upward through the heart of The Tower.

"I don't like this," Kira said, her back pressed against Kaden's as they watched the walls. The walls didn't move, but they felt the upward motion, like being held in a box that lifted off the ground. With a smooth halt, the motion stopped.

“We'll find a way. We can't be trapped forever,” Kaden said.

The walls began to lower. They were on a new floor, in Pinnacle's chambers.

"You've always been trapped," a familiar voice said matter-of-factly from the shadows.

A figure emerged limping from the darkness – Beth-ell, her weathered face bearing new wounds, her posture still proud despite her obvious injuries. One leg was severely damaged, dragging behind her as she moved closer.

Her Elites moved toward her, but she raised a hand and they stopped, stepping back to Kaden's side.

"What are you..." Kaden said, the light in his hands intensifying.

Beth-ell's expression didn't change. "Open your eyes and discern," she said, her voice carrying that same cryptic quality that had frustrated Kaden from the beginning. "Judge each by the fruit they bear."

"What fruit?" Kaden demanded. "We trusted you!"

"Not everything is as it appears," Beth-ell replied, her eyes flicking to the Elites that flanked Kaden and Kira. "Some trees bear good fruit. Others, poison. Even in death, there can be good." Her eyes locked onto her Elites.

Kira stepped closer to the Elites, studying them with new intensity. The cracks in their obsidian skin had widened during the battles, and through these fissures, faint light glowed – not the sickly luminescence of the Shadow Elites, but something cleaner. Warmer.

"Kaden," she said slowly. "I recognize them."

The Elites stood motionless, their cracked faces expressionless as always. But there was something in their stance, something protective, as they positioned themselves slightly ahead of Kaden and Kira.

"They've been protecting you. Have you wondered why?" Beth-ell said.

"Why?" Kaden asked, his voice barely above a whisper.

"Because they know you," Beth-ell replied. "They've known you since your beginning."

Kira moved closer to one of the Elites, peering into the cracks in its face. There, in the depths of the fissures, human features were faintly visible – like a person trapped within stone.

Kaden felt a drawing to them, like they were a distant memory, long-forgotten.

“I researched something when I was back,” Kira said, visions of pictures from a newspaper entering her memory. “You killed us to send us back,” she said, turning to Beth-ell.

“Death is not the end,” she said without another word.

“They were early test subjects,” Kira said. “Their skin is the same, but that’s why they’re different. They were early test subjects, like you.”

She gasped and stepped back as a revelation dawned on her. “Kaden,” she said softly.

Still Kaden looked closely at the Elites, examining their faces as if mentally unlocking a puzzle.

"Kaden..." Kira breathed, turning to him. "They're your parents."

The words hit Kaden like a physical blow. He staggered back, staring at the Elites with new eyes. "That's not possible," he whispered. "My parents died when I was a child."

"They were early subjects in the Hope Drug trials," Beth-ell explained. "Your mother’s diagnosis started it. Your father next, when her loss and his PTSD from Desert Storm became too much to bear. It took time after their hearts stopped beating, but the drug worked, and when they awoke, it transformed them. But soon, the hunger controlled them. You have brought something out in them, though. Something lost to the centuries."

"All this time," Kaden said, his voice breaking. "All this time, they've be en..." He couldn't finish the sentence, couldn't form the words to describe what they'd become.

"They've been watching over you," Beth-ell said. "With me, and through Jericho. They maintained enough of themselves to remember you. That's the miracle, Kaden. That's the light at work."

Kaden moved toward the Elites – toward his parents – reaching out a trembling hand. One of them – his mother? – raised a charcoal hand in response. Their fingers were inches apart when the room plunged into darkness.

A cold wind swept through the chamber, extinguishing all light save the faint glow from the cracks in the Elites' skin. Beth-ell's face tightened as she looked past Kaden and Kira.

"He's coming," she warned.

The darkness coalesced at the far end of the chamber, swirling like a storm cloud before taking shape. Pinnacle emerged from the shadows, his tall form radiating power. Behind him floated his Shadow Elite, Jericho's heart still pulsing at its center like a captured star.

"I'm already here," Pinnacle said, his voice carrying that familiar blend of charm and menace. His skin rippled with patches of obsidian that appeared and disappeared like waves on a dark sea.

"Welcome home," he said to the group, then he turned to Beth-ell. "Well done," he said to her.

Kaden's and Kira's eyes shot to her; they knew she acted as a double-agent but now weren't sure to which side.

"You act surprised?" Pinnacle said. "This world is mine, yet being double-crossed by someone who has served me for centuries surprises you? I thought you grew up, boy."

He walked as if gliding on the black stone floor of the expansive, domed chamber, coming to stand at Beth-ell's side as the two looked over the group.

"I can't blame you too much, though; you're mere pawns used to help forge a stronger unit. Dissent is required every few decades to pluck the weeds and invigorate the core."

He studied Kaden, Kira, and the two Elites as if reading the label on a test tube. Then, slowly, his head turned to Beth-ell.

"I wonder if you'll be surprised."

Kaden noticed her face flickered with concern, but it quickly steeled itself.

"After about two hundred years of serving me loyally, you had me going. I questioned it from day one, but all those sortings and all those consumptions? I'm not sure how you can live with yourself, claiming to be a true follower of Jericho and a double agent in The Tower, yet how many have died under your watch?"

She met his gaze, and without a word, stepped back in a defensive posture.

"I know every hair on your head. I can feel and control every molecule of air you breathe. You act as if I wouldn't know your double-crossing thoughts from all these years of actions," he said, shaking his head gently as if reasoning with a child. "You served your purpose when the right time came. And speaking of *time*, boy." He turned to Kaden. "You'll help me unlock the last piece of the puzzle. The one thing I have yet to control."

Beth-ell raised her hand, but he was infinitely quicker. He pulled his hand with a flick of his wrist and she was lifted off the ground as if lassoed by a never-ending rope that wrapped her entire body. Her eyes bulged as her fingers and feet twitched from the pressure.

Her two Elites stepped forward, but with a flick of his wrist, Pinnacle had the Shadow Elite on them. He didn't change his gaze as it moved like a lightning bolt, pinning them to the ground and sending a painful grinding and cracking noise in the air as the shadow forced their hard skin against the stone.

"I knew I'd always have tabs on *him* if I kept you close," Pinnacle said to him. "Now with his body about to turn and these two joining my being, I'll cut our relationship off here." He squeezed and Beth-ell's mouth opened as if an invisible anaconda were constricting the life from her body. Her face grew red, then gradually into a purple hue as all the air left her lungs.

"Stop!" Kaden called out, but Pinnacle paid him no mind. He watched Beth-ell as a trickle of blood ran from the corner of her mouth, then from her nose. Her face was now a solid purple and veins popped as life left her. Her hands flailed at her sides but to no avail.

"NO!" Kaden said again and ran toward Pinnacle. After two steps, his body froze, Pinnacle holding him in place as he drank in Beth-ell's agonizing death.

"Don't worry, she'll be back in a few days. An improved version that won't have the silly thoughts of serving Jericho any longer," he said, pulling tighter, and Beth-ell's body jolted. She fell lifelessly, hitting the ground with a hard thud.

Only then did Pinnacle turn to Kaden.

"You two, however, will be joined with me. We'll finish what your friend so rudely interrupted when he damaged my tower." Pinnacle flicked his wrists and Kaden and Kira were lifted off the ground, held as if an invisible hand lifted them off the ground by their throat as Beth-ell was, brought within a few feet of Pinnacle. "You're the last remaining light of Jericho. Hmmm, the word *last* has a nice ring to it. Your last is my next step."

"You're wrong," Kaden said through gritted teeth as his body clenched.

"There once was a time when I took comments like that personally, but now it's like you're speaking a different language. You can say the color red is actually blue, but no one will argue with you, they'll know you're a fool. And leave a fool to his own folly."

"You'll never put out *His* light," Kaden said.

"Never," Kira added.

"I am tempted to let you live to see the next iteration of Jericho, when he bows to me and leads my army across time. But alas, the key is in you for my own walk through days."

"Why would someone so powerful rely on an army? It shows weakness," Kaden said.

The invisible bonds around him tightened and his face bulged.

"You think that Empyrean is the whole world? I do have to give my old friend credit. When he left this place and focused on the lighthouse, he found stragglers. All the lost and wandering souls that came to him grew strong. That's why I needed to eliminate the lighthouse and protect Empyrean. The New Breed has been honed over many generations." He looked at Kira and then back to Kaden. "You two are as much brother and sisters as two petri dishes. You think you're special and blessed by Jericho?" He laughed. "He may have planted something in you, but I grew you both. This tower was your womb, the Outer Ring your nursery. The weak die and the strongest survive, evolution at its finest, your comrades being the latest example as they died in their futile uprising."

"Wh..." Kaden's mouth hung open, unable to say the words.

"A handful of rebels fighting a system entrenched and honed for hundreds of years. You really thought releasing some livestock and starting a riot would do it?" Pinnacle said.

"It helped us get in here, didn't it?" Kira replied.

"I wanted you here!" Pinnacle snapped and the invisible bonds around them shook. "And I also wanted everyone else around you dead," he said as his eyes moved to Beth-ell's motionless body.

"They're not gone forever," Kaden replied.

Pinnacle held up his hand. "The traitors, Jace and Aria, both dead," he said, counting two fingers. "Her." He nodded to Beth-ell and counted a third finger. "The big man—"

"Riggs. He has a name," Kaden snapped back.

Pinnacle counted a fourth finger as he flashed a scowl and Kaden's bindings tightened again. His breaths were growing shorter and shorter.

"Maybe we'll look at the other party, the three out who went to the lighthouse? The old man, dead, Elba, dead, and Enak's still alive because he made the right decision. The escape tunnels are monitored. All the interior tunnels are monitored. You scurry around like rats under the floorboards and yet are oblivious to pest control. You're not burrowing to freedom; you're mice in my maze."

"There will always be survivors," Kaden said, yet he sensed his heart dropping. His instinct told him Pinnacle wasn't lying and doubt crept in. Who was he to try and overthrow this structure?

"Yes, and like we've honed, the survivors feed the Elites, making them stronger yet. The flywheel keeps spinning. You're the result of scientific progress built on the shoulders of a giant: The Hope Drug! Now even the weakest in the Outer Ring, when they die, they'll gradually turn. The next generation won't die off but be Elites, and Jericho's power in me will fuel it further. I'll control an undying army and walk across time itself. All eternity is my oyster!"

"You've forgotten one thing about the light," Kaden said, the grip on him almost unbearable.

Pinnacle's eyes rolled. He stepped to Kaden, coming within inches. His demeanor shifted from annoyed to a devilish grin, that of the wolf before it sought to devour Little Red Riding Hood.

"Say your last words and then be honored by your consumption," he sneered.

"The light shines in the darkness, and the darkness has *not* overcome it," Kaden said, and he erupted with an explosion of light.

Pinnacle and the Shadow Elite flew backwards.

The heart held by the Shadow Elite ignited as if on the same fuse. Like a grenade inside the shadow, the heart exploded and a massive hole ripped through the cloudy demon. It screeched an unnatural cry of pain as it was thrown back, the room now as bright as a desert sun.

"Come on, we're getting to that body," Kaden said as he grabbed Kira by the hand and moved to the Elites, his parents. He looked them in the eyes again. Above them, the bright light from the heart dimmed and disappeared, faded away after the explosion.

They helped up the Elites and scrambled forward. The Elites turned back to Beth-ell, resisting the urge to leave her.

"Come on!" Kira called, and they all turned away from Beth-ell's body and dashed out of the chamber.

Kaden followed a path that he only knew. Like a magnet, he was drawn forward, knowing exactly where to go.

"Wait." Kira stopped abruptly. "The heart. That *thing* still has Jericho's heart. We have to get it back."

"It exploded. It wasn't there anymore," Kaden replied.

"But we came for the heart and the bo—" The walls around her shifted, like an earthquake shook them.

An groan came from their Elites, urging them to keep moving.

"He won't be down forever; we need to move. We find the body, we can get it out," Kaden said. "Even Pinnacle can't overcome the light!"

Again they took off down the hall. Kaden led them forward and turned down a corridor with glass windows surrounding them. Ahead of them, a door to a laboratory sat at the end of the hall.

Kaden stopped, staring at the door. "That's it. He's in there."

All the pressure of the situation seemed to stop as he took in a breath and slowly let it out. With Kira and the Elites behind him, he stepped forward and extended his hand. He took the handle and turned.

But before the latch clicked, the hallway around him shook more violently than before. The Tower was like a dog shaking off water as the walls rippled with an intensity that threw Kaden back and knocked all of them off their feet.

"We MUST get inside!" Kaden shouted. He scrambled to his feet and despite the chaos of the structure all around, he felt a sensation inside himself, a calming strength beating from his heart that guided his steps, as if his blood pumped with a renewed strength. He didn't notice his skin glow as he moved forward through the hallway. With every step, the structure around him changed, shifting away from him, but the light coming off him quelled the trembling floors and walls.

Again he reached the handle and turned, but a scream from behind froze him. Turning, he saw Pinnacle, standing above Kira.

"Go!" she shouted.

"Yes," Pinnacle said, as calm and confident as ever. "Go, and I'll kill her, rip these two limb from limb, and then come after you. I'll consume all of you. One by one, you can live inside the depths of what I have felt for centuries."

"You can't stop the light," Kaden said.

"I don't want to stop it. I want to gain it. Abrams abandoned me and I'll show him and the entire new world what I can build WITHOUT HIM!" he shouted and the earth shook at his rage.

The newfound strength inside him helped him stay calm in the chaos of the storm. Kaden ignored the threats and turned his head back to the door.

He twisted the handle.

"So be it," Pinnacle said. A shadow grew from him and one piece of the black, cloudy haze sharpened to a point. The shadow took the shape of an immense sword only a giant could hold. It thrust down and ran through Kira's midsection.

She gasped, the air unable to leave her throat as it fled her body through the hole ripped in her lungs. The demon sword kept moving, cutting through her heart as her body convulsed.

"No…" Kaden mouthed as he looked back, but he held himself in place at the door. His jaws tensed and he held on.

The black demon emanating from Pinnacle then took hold of the Elites, Kaden's parents. Through Kaden's watering eyes, he caught their stare. There was no apology in their eyes but a satisfaction, as if they were happy with their decision, content to run their race after pivoting so late in life to help their long lost son, even after years filled with death and destruction.

The shadow encased them, grabbing hold of each limb, and their neck like an octopus curling around a crab. The shadow tentacles tightened and a horrible grinding noise filled the air. It reverberated in Kaden's mind like a dentist's drill down to his bone. A final crunch echoed through the hall as his parents' bodies were torn to pieces.

"Are you still so sure that *your* light shines here?" Pinnacle said. He stood in between Kira's motionless body and what remained of his parents in a heap of charcoal-like body parts and torsos.

Kaden's head sank. His insides felt empty like his heart was torn apart, yet he never took his hand off the door handle. After a pause as his purpose came back to the front of his mind, his head rose and he looked back at Pinnacle.

He was here for one reason – Jericho.

"It was never *my* light," he said as he pushed on the handle and threw the door open.

Kaden looked on into the room. He was filled with amazement, but not a joyful kind; this was confusion. He was bewildered.

The lab he was inextricably drawn toward was empty.

Jericho's body was gone.

Chapter 42

Entry #10

The hour approaches when the shadow and the light will meet. I have my cup to bear and these words are the last I will write in this format, though not the last testament from those who bear the light. The stories of my disciples will carry on.

My heart has known from the beginning what my mind long resisted – that the seed must fall to the ground, be buried, and die before new life can spring forth. The Tower rises ever higher, casting its shadow across what remains of humanity, consuming flesh and spirit alike because of their choices. Thomas believes that in taking life, he gains power. He does not understand that true power comes only through surrendering it.

To readers of these words: Do not mourn what appears to be defeat.

Be strong and courageous.

The darkness swallows light, only to find itself transformed from within. When Thomas takes my heart – as he surely will – he believes he will consume my power. Instead, he invites transformation into his very core. He invites in his own demise.

Three days. The Hope Drug that corrupts the flesh will be modified by deceit and will require three days after death to claim its host. And three days after my heart stops beating, a window opens – not just between life and death, but between all moments of time. What seems final is merely threshold as the veil is torn.

Those in the Remnant, you are scattered like stars in the night sky: You carry the light through tunnels of darkness, through sortings and consumptions, through betrayal and doubt. You will live a hard life where the world is against you. Now I ask you to carry it through my perceived absence. When the Tower seems strongest, when the light seems most distant, remember that what appears to be extinction is often merely transformation. The seed in the soil.

Do not seek to destroy The Tower through force. Violence merely feeds the hunger that Thomas has unleashed upon the world. Instead, be vessels of the light. Where there is hatred, sow love; where there is injury, healing; where there is doubt, faith; where there is despair, hope; where there is darkness, light. Loving each other will let the world know you are my followers. Portraying the fruits of a well-lived life shows you accept the gift given.

My blood carries the original Hope – not the corrupted drug version that turns flesh to stone and hearts to hunger, but the pure essence that heals rather than consumes. This essence now lives in you, in all who choose to see. When the moment comes – and it will come – let it flow freely. Let it transform rather than destroy.

The Lighthouse was never merely a building of stone. It was, and is, a beacon carried within each heart that chooses light over darkness, sacrifice over consumption, love over fear. Even as the physical structure falls, its purpose remains – to guide the lost home.

I have seen beyond the veil of time, beyond the moment of my apparent defeat. I have seen The Tower tremble. I have seen light pour through the cracks in stone walls. I have seen the charcoal skin of the consumed break open to reveal the humanity still beating within. I have seen you – all of you – stand in places you cannot yet imagine, bearing light you do not yet comprehend.

The path ahead is narrow and treacherous. Some will fall. Some will betray. But do not lose heart, be strong and courageous. Remember that victory does not always wear the face we expect. Sometimes it comes disguised as defeat, as surrender, as sacrifice. Then, like a Trojan horse, we realize our victory as transformation around us takes hold.

When my heart stops beating in my chest, it will begin beating in yours. When my light seems extinguished, it will ignite within you. When my voice falls silent, yours will rise.

The Tower seems impenetrable, yet Thomas's greatest fear is not that you will tear it down, but that you will transform it from within. He fears not your hatred, but your love. Not your resistance, but your surrender to something greater than yourself.

I go not in fear but in perfect understanding of what must be. The seed falls to the ground. The heart stops beating. The light seems swallowed by darkness.

But the light shines in the darkness, and the darkness has not overcome it.

When the third day comes, the veil between two worlds will be torn.

Chapter 43

Kaden

He looked at the empty lab and felt more than a pit in his stomach. It was like his entire insides fell through and he was hollowed out. His jaw hung open in disbelief. All of those close to him who had risked and lost their lives. The weight of everyone in the Outer and Inner Rings who they fought for. Even the misguided Agents rushing to uphold order.

Everyone.

He'd failed everyone.

Behind him, rubble from his parents' bodies lay strewn about. They turned, they changed, helping him after four hundred years of living death from being poisoned by the Hope Drug.

It was all for naught.

Pinnacle won anyway.

Kaden felt the ruler of this dystopian world step behind him. He felt like an empty vessel, a cold piece of wasted life, dead emotion in a human body floating in this foreign world. The empty lab in front of him reflected the emptiness of all he came to believe. There was nothing there.

Gone.

All gone.

His fate rested behind him. He felt like an ant under a giant's boot. Pinnacle had been closing in on him since the beginning, gradually pulling him closer like a celestial body with a stronger gravity.

Death was inevitable.

Kaden had told him the light would shine in the darkness, but a thought flashed in his mind – a black hole absorbs light. It *consumes* the light, never to light up the universe again.

"It's not possible..." Kaden whispered. "It can't..." His shoulders sank.

Then he was jolted by the roar from behind him.

"NO!" Pinnacle shouted in rage. "It can't... He can't..."

Kaden's entire belief system was shattered in front of him – the lab was empty, Jericho's body was gone. Pinnacle fought Kaden to keep him away from this spot while Kaden was drawn to it, but now, nothing.

Yet, Pinnacle didn't like this outcome either... He, in fact, hated it.

"No..." Pinnacle growled, and The Tower shook. "You will not. YOU WILL NOT!" The passion in his voice was more than anger. It was pure rage, unfiltered and raw that shook the air around them like an earthquake riding airwaves. Cracks ripped through the walls next to Kaden. Pieces of the obsidian stone at The Tower's core broke apart as dust fell around them.

Kaden turned to look at Pinnacle. As much as Kaden looked on the empty lab with confusion, disappointment, and heartbreak, Pinnacle looked on it in a maddening rage. He was Bruce Banner ready to transform into the Hulk, the black ripples that periodically rolled across Pinnacle's skin intensifying as if he was boiling from the inside out. He could not have cared less about Kaden as he looked past him into the empty lab. A moment ago, he focused all his power on controlling The Tower to stop him, but now it was as if Kaden didn't exist.

A thunder-like sound erupted behind Pinnacle and deeper cracks ripped through The Tower and the outer wall of Empyrean. Stone fell away from the wall behind Pinnacle as tremors swept around them and a gaping hole emerged in the side of The Tower silhouetting the monster.

Wind rushed in and flooded the corridor, pushing pieces of Kaden's parents around, and Kira's hair whipped up in the air.

"You abandoned me, so I took the company from you. I took the drug from you. I took Empyrean from you. I took your heart. I TOOK YOUR LIFE! AND I'LL TAKE YOUR MEMORY FROM THIS WORLD!" Pinnacle raged. The blackness under his skin grew. The Shadow Elite pulled away from hovering over Kaden's parents and moved to Pinnacle. It surrounded him and pulsed like a giant black heart. It swelled and contracted as he raged, still with eyes glued to the empty lab as wind ripped through the corridor like an airplane at ten thousand feet after the door blew out.

"I CONQUERED YOU AND YOU WILL *NOT* CONQUER DEATH!"

The shadow exploded, throwing Kaden back into the lab as The Tower around him cracked further.

"I will kill every single one of them. I won't allow them to be consumed by others. I! I, the ruler of this world, will rip out the heart of every single soul you love and watch them die. All of them will burn in my fire and suffer because of YOU!"

Kaden watched Pinnacle, his emotional fury carried outside of himself, as if invisibly ejecting off his skin and smashing into the once polished floors and walls. Endless cracks like spiderwebs surrounded Pinnacle and like a crack in glass, they each spread. Pieces of the ceiling fell into the floor, pieces of the floor broke apart and opened gaps up, and chunks of walls collapsed.

"And I'll start with this one. He'll be the last to be honored with a consumption," Pinnacle said, his eyes finally shifting down from the empty lab and focusing on Kaden.

Pieces of the ceiling fell around him as the wide, hungry eyes of Pinnacle looked down on Kaden. He drifted forward, levitating over areas of missing floor. Kaden saw the whites of his eyes, but soon a black cloud rippled over Pinnacle's skin and filled his eyes. The whites of his eyes disappeared, as if pulled in by a black hole and only empty, black space remained. His skin and eyes now like that of an Elite, a dead, cracking charcoal-like surface.

Kaden felt a pull and tried resisting. His skin glowed bright as he tried channeling his power, but still his body inched toward Pinnacle.

The shadow now flowed in and out of Pinnacle's skin as if they were one being. It swelled, filling the space of the corridor and blocking out the hole in the side of The Tower.

Kaden felt his skin stretch. The memory of seeing a consumption flashed in his mind. The poor souls' faces covered in agony as they stretched like Silly Putty. Now, he was resisting and losing to the same fate.

How many times had Jericho brought him back to life? Dr. Abrams sent him to this horrible future world, and as Jericho, he wouldn't let Kaden die. His head had been bashed in. He'd fallen from the catwalk in the pastures to his death. He died numerous times and easily could have killed so many more. Each time, Jericho's power protected him or jumped him back to the other reality, only to soon return with new breath in his lungs and a healed body.

But being consumed... There was no return. Jericho led him here, to this gruesome final fate, and now there was no return.

His body cried out in agony as his skin stretched, muscles tore, and bones bent and snapped to Pinnacle's power.

He tried resisting. He tried calling on the light that had pushed Pinnacle back before. Yet in his mind, he felt this inevitable; it was all over. He wouldn't wake up as Kaden or Darren. This was death. It was all over.

But even if this was his fate, he wouldn't go easy.

He resisted.

Chapter 44

Alister, The Lighthouse

Alister didn't feel himself die as he lay next to Elba. His senses faded and drained away his awareness of the world. He had felt the cold, hard stone under his body. He had felt Elba's body, now motionless and losing warmth. The harsh air of the desert around him dried his throat and nostrils. And he had felt the brightness of a strange light. But the extreme blood loss ended his senses. The light faded away as darkness took over. There was only nothingness left. An extreme unbearable nothingness. Yet, there was no anger or frustration at the nothingness, only an awareness. It was what it was and Alister was simply aware. Yet, as time went by, he became more aware of the lack of feeling. No anger or frustration, yet no joy or happiness. It was a nothingness without fear but also without love.

He was a part of the nothingness, and felt nothing. Yet, he sensed. He knew what the nothingness lacked. All the horrible things and all the wonderful things.

His awareness extended to being aware of the nothingness around him, yet there was something. Something that did not lack everything.

From outside his being, he felt a longing from somewhere else. Something that not only realized that this nothingness lacked all feeling and sensation, but a *something* that craved to have *something with him*.

The feeling grew closer, stronger. Alister's being, which was entangled and part of the nothingness, could now sense the *something* growing. It came to him and it brought an urging.

It yearned for *something*, and it locked onto him. Alister could not see or feel, but he sensed and somehow knew that this *something* was here for him.

The *something* joined him.

A warm feeling overtook Alister and everything changed.

The awareness without emotion now took on emotion. He now felt pain again, yet he was held tight, wrapped in love.

Love.

His awareness grasped it like it was life itself, holding on to it with all his might. The *something* around him seemed happy. His new yearning to be a part of the *something* overtook the nothingness. Pain, memory of death, loved ones dying and friends murdered; they all flooded back into Alister's awareness and filled him with pain. Such sorrow seemed to bend his reality, as if a hammer beating on his soul. Yet, the new sensations of love, joy, peace, and happiness rose, mixing with but ultimately flooding out the horrible sensations. He could focus on the awful or give in to the uplifting joy.

Everything around him lit up.

The black nothingness slipped away, and the world was wrapped in brilliant light.

Alister opened his eyes. The pain from his body was gone. He felt strong, alive.

Next to him, Elba was standing. His friend glowed as if every cell in his body was its own lighthouse, calling out to the world to show it the joy of life itself, but somehow the pain they traversed made his light more real, as if once you know the pain of the nothingness, your light can shine brighter for those still in the dark.

Alister blinked and looked past Elba. There were others. From his vantage point, he saw all the legs first. They were like a forest of glowing trees, each person's skin glowing with a natural radiance as if they were a physical representation of the sun itself.

Alister could feel the strength in his body grow. His muscles yearned to move. He knew he must get up and go forth, his awareness as sharp as ever in this rebirth. He knew he must go do good works in the world.

He looked up as his muscles shifted his body, bringing him onto his feet. His jaw dropped as he saw the one above him.

Before him, there He was.

Chapter 45

Riggs, The Outer Ring

He felt the strange sensation in his chest like a deep exhale outside of his control when the Elite flew at him. It quickly turned into intense pain as his body realized the Elite pushed a broken piece of rebar through his chest, piercing one lung and his heart as it ripped through his midsection. He tried to breathe, maybe say a word, but the air didn't come through.

His muscles lost blood and his body crumpled. From his back, he saw the Elite above him. The demon looked down on him, only for a moment, and the pain in his chest burned, extending to his whole body. Riggs's sight focused on the Elite, tunnel vision on his upper body and cracked charcoal face. Above him, the creature looked away, looking forward as it moved on to its next victim in the battle.

The pain faded as Riggs's wound wasn't burning anymore. It turned cold. His whole body went frigid. Above him, the Elite didn't move forward to attack the next combatant. It looked on as if in confusion or in awe. One of his last thoughts was intrigue, wondering what the Elite was doing, then his mind slipped away from reality as the freezing cold and fatigue took him over. He could have sworn the Elite lit up as if a spotlight turned on and ignited the demon like a Broadway actor at centerstage.

His consciousness faded away from his senses. His sight no longer took in the Elite as the demon flew backwards like a leaf in the wind. His senses in the traditional sense were gone. All he felt was an awareness, an awareness of the nothingness around him. The whole world, the whole universe, everything was gone. He thought it a blackness, but it wasn't black, it was empty. The nothingness surrounded him and went through him. It was him and he was the nothingness.

There was no more pain, no cold or no fatigue from the wound. No sorrow from the loss of Aria and no feeling of failure that he felt when he realized he was dying and looking up at his killer. The worst feelings he'd ever felt were compacted into the final moments of his life, but now they were gone. The feeling of love he felt for his friends, for their cause, and the memory of the woman who raised him were gone too. The romantic love he felt for Aria was also gone. When he was alive, he secretly questioned how their romance might work in a world like this. He told himself to avoid the thoughts of the future, to carry on with the cause and keep fighting for his friends. So he did. That was what he always did. He felt the love of his friends and it fueled his conviction. But now, that conviction, the feeling... it was all gone. The only thing that remained was the nothingness.

The pain. The love. The sorrow. The hope.

Gone.

He didn't feel any more pain or sorrow or joy with it all being gone. It simply was what it was. The nothingness didn't care. He didn't care because he could not care. The nothingness was just that, nothing, and now he was in and a part of the nothingness.

No emotion. No feeling.

Then a light came into the nothingness. No, it wasn't a light, it was a warmth, or rather a sensation that crept into his awareness. Riggs didn't really know what it was, but it was something. Inside this nothingness, there was now somehow a something, and he knew everything changed. It could no longer be nothing if there was something.

Riggs felt something, and he knew he was no longer a part of the nothingness. The nothingness had to go; it moved on like water flowing downhill. Gravity didn't have to command the water to flow; the water just flowed in a natural obedience. And now the nothingness obeyed the something, it just faded away.

The sorrow returned. The pain of lost love and failing friends returned. But a loving warmth returned as well. With love, there was hope, and with hope, there was joy.

Riggs opened his eyes and saw the clouds above him moving. The always overcast skies were quickly moving, being blown away as blue skies poked through. The blue couldn't be held back anymore and the gray gave way, just as water obeys gravity and just as the nothing gave way to something.

Riggs rolled onto his side and blinked. His vision took a minute to focus. He didn't believe it at first, but there she was, draped in a glow as if her skin were light itself.

Aria.

Behind her were others, each glowing like her. Each was as if their own sun and they walked forward together. There were no Elites standing with them, only rubble of charcoal skin scattered across the ground.

Aria looked at him and met his eyes. Her eyes made his heart leapt.

In the group behind her, he recognized more. Elba. Alister. They were all together, each with skin as bright as the sun, yet the blaze was gentle on the eyes.

Riggs didn't feel any pain in his chest as he sat up. His eyes were so focused on his approaching friends that he didn't see the one right in front of him.

When the man reached down to help him up, Riggs's world shifted. His friends walking toward him was one thing, but now standing above him... This was another.

This was Him.

Riggs took his hand and joined.

Chapter 46

Kaden

Darkness gradually engulfed Kaden as Pinnacle and the surrounding Shadow Elite consumed him. The shadow grew as if it were a tidal wave above him as his vision blurred. His consciousness, body, and mind pulled into the darkness. As his body deformed and entered Pinnacle, he felt an immense pain. At first, it was all physical as his bones and muscles deformed, buckling under the awesome force of Pinnacle's power. As the darkness overtook him, the pain switched from external to internal. He no longer felt his torso being compressed or limbs bending. They were gone. His consciousness was all that was left, and all it could feel was hate, pain, and abandonment.

An intense anger overtook him, drowning out all memories whether from Darren or Kaden. The lives of both didn't flash before his eyes – they didn't need to – because he knew his two lives were stolen away by the one who abandoned him. He gave his life to following the promise of Jericho, a promise of a better future and a better world. The hope to help others and the hope of a savior. Now he saw it like Pinnacle saw it. They were all lies.

His consciousness swirled in the darkness and could sense other sources of anger, endless amounts of other bodiless beings who stewed in their bitter rage and abandonment.

How could Jericho lead him to his death? How could he be such a fool to trust such a simple liar? A snake oil salesman promising more than he ever could deliver. Kaden fell for it. Darren fell for it the moment he sat in the optometrist's chair. Magic tricks of hypnotism or whatever his lying game was. The false prophet took Darren for a fool and hypnotized him into hope by showing him Kaden, Kira, and seeds of hope in the future world. Then he stole it all away.

Kaden boiled in his rage. It festered and grew in the blackness of an endless abyss. The other raging sensations around him didn't change; they didn't welcome him or try to kick him away. No, there was plenty of room for everyone in the darkness and hate. It became easy to hate, to loathe everything he knew. Kelly and Kira. Chris and Elba. Kirk and Enak. Ms. Barbara and Beth-ell. His bosses at one time in both worlds: John and Ron-ell. Jace. Aria. Ryon. Vala. Barb. All of them were fools wasting their lives. It was useless. In the end, they'd all end up here in the darkness with him, with the others. Kaden hated those that were still living and he hated those that were dead.

He swirled in the endless hate.

But then, something different.

Then there came a different feeling. It wasn't hate or contempt but like a warm glow of a street light guiding him home. Far in the distance, it called to him. The light wasn't exactly a light because he had no eyes to see it, but it was different, like a sensation of warmth when you're in a bitter cold. It was a light in otherwise hate-filled darkness.

The new sensation didn't belong. It confused the other feelings of hate. The endless beings that raged next to Kaden and were a part of the darkness did not like the different sensation. They screeched at it and ran. They ran and hid, or at least tried their best to escape. There was endless space to go and yet nowhere to go. Still, the other feelings of endless hate swirled and screeched as if in agonizing pain. Kaden felt them vibrate in the void like glass hit with a high frequency.

Amongst all the chaos and feelings of rage, Kaden didn't run from the new sensation. He hated it, of course, because he hated everything, yet as the new sensation grew, he realized that he hated himself more than anything. His consciousness was changing as the glow of this new sensation entered this void. He knew he was angry, but he also knew he was sad.

Sorrow.

He wasn't abandoned; he felt like he failed. He felt sorrow. He felt ashamed. He felt unworthy of the glowing sensation off in the distance.

Kaden was also confused. The glow seemed to be calling to him. Why would this new sensation come into all this hate and darkness and call to him? There were countless others hating and raging, yet they ran away from the new, strange sensation. They were screaming and raging, unable to hear the glowing sensations call. Kaden had stayed and felt the sensation calling to him.

It grew closer.

Larger.

All around him.

As it grew, Kaden's hate dwindled. His feelings of sorrow compounded with a feeling of being unworthy. Yet, even in his wretched state, this thing... this sensation kept coming to him. Kaden felt its pull but not a pull as Pinnacle and the shadow pulled on it. It was an invitation. The sensation yearned for him. Everything else ran from it as if it were a poison, yet as it approached and Kaden sensed it, he wished it came closer. He wanted to fulfill the invitation.

If his consciousness could have cried, it would have. He was so ashamed, so hopeless, and so aware of his failure that he couldn't stand up to the new sensation, YET IT CAME CLOSER. Kaden couldn't believe it. Why? Why in the world would it long for him as if it loved him and it would sacrifice itself by reaching itself into this abyss of pure hatred and violence to save a wretched fool like him –

It hit him like a ton of bricks.

Everything changed.

When it dawned on him, he accepted it, and instantly, the glowing sensation ignited and engulfed the darkness like a supernova.

Kaden woke up.

He was on the ground, as if spit out back to the spot where he was before being consumed. Above him, Pinnacle and his Shadow Elite were pinned to a cracking wall.

Outside, through a massive hole in the side of The Tower, Jericho floated in and stood before them. His skin was as bright as the sun yet gentle on the eyes.

Jericho stood before Pinnacle and the shadow as they were pinned to the wall. Kaden couldn't tell if Jericho held them there or if they were like magnets in repulsion, unable to stand in the glory of the glowing Jericho.

Jericho looked at them and then his eyes drifted down.

He looked at Kaden, and he smiled. It was a warm smile, yielding a sensation in the midst of chaos that gave Kaden peace.

In that smile, Kaden knew everything would be okay.

Chapter 47

Kaden lay on the ground, his body aching, but he was whole again, and feeling better every second as he stared up at the impossible scene before him. Pinnacle and his Shadow Elite were pinned against the cracked wall of The Tower. Their shadows writhed and contorted, as if trying to escape the blinding light that filled the chamber. Kaden realized they were struggling the same way as the other beings of hate when he was in darkness. He had been consumed and saw the inside of Pinnacle, his true nature. Where sorrow seemed to once reign but led to only feelings of hate.

Through the massive hole in The Tower's wall, Jericho floated in, his form radiant with light that should have been painful to behold, yet somehow was gentle enough for mortal eyes. His body was whole, yet scarred – a significant wound over his chest. But the heart that Pinnacle had torn from his chest now was no longer held by the Shadow Elite. It was in Jericho, pulsing with a rhythm that seemed to make the very air vibrate with life.

Behind him came others, each clothed in the same brilliant yet gentle radiance. Kaden's breath caught as he recognized faces – Jace, whose body had lain broken in the corridor; Beth-ell, strangled by Pinnacle; Riggs, whose tenacious spirit had been extinguished in the Outer Ring; Aria, who had fallen before Riggs; and most incredibly, Kira, walking forward with a serene smile, her body whole and unharmed. Kaden had seen them all die or had known it. Just as he knew what lab to run to, he knew in his heart as his friends were killed. Yet, here they were...

"Impossible," Kaden whispered, yet it wasn't a question but more of an elated astonishment. At this moment, nothing seemed beyond belief. He stated the impossible was indeed right before him, with the scars to prove it.

"Nothing is impossible," Jericho said, confirming Kaden's speech. His voice carried the gentle authority it had always held, yet now amplified with power that made The Tower's walls tremble. "Death is not the end. It never was," he said.

As Jericho landed and walked forward, two more figures rose and stood behind him, their forms no longer the obsidian black of Elites but restored to a human appearance. They glowed with the same inner light as the others who chose Jericho's side. As they drew closer, Kaden recognized them from a life away. The last time he'd seen them, he was a young boy in a different body, over four hundred years ago.

"Mom? Dad?" he whispered, his eyes watering.

They smiled at him, their eyes filled with a love that transcended the centuries of corruption and hunger that had twisted them into monsters.

They were restored by Jericho, made whole.

Pinnacle struggled against his invisible bonds, his face contorted with rage. "This is MY world!" he rasped as spittle flew from his mouth. His voice took on an inhuman tone, a low bass as if the entire tower spoke in rage. "You had your chance! I AM ITS GOD NOW!"

The Shadow Elite surrounding him pulsed and swelled, darkness flowing from every crack in The Tower to join with his form. The temperature in the room plummeted as the Shadow absorbed everything it could reach, growing larger, more menacing.

"You are not a god, Thomas," Jericho said quietly, using the name Pinnacle had abandoned centuries ago. "You have forgotten what it means to be *human*."

"I am MORE than human," Pinnacle snarled and writhed like a vampire at sunrise. "I evolved beyond weakness, beyond mortality. I conquered death itself!"

"No," Jericho replied, his voice sorrowful rather than angry. "You delayed it by stealing the lives of others. And in doing so, you embraced a darker death – the death of love, of compassion, of everything that makes us truly alive. Your insistence to act for yourself in the present, instead of in sacrifice for others' future, has sealed your fate."

Jericho stepped forward, his radiance intensifying. The beings of light behind him – Kaden could no longer think of them as merely human – fanned out in a semicircle, their combined light pushing back the darkness that swirled around Pinnacle.

"And what now, *David*?" Pinnacle sneered, his once handsome looks now a flood of darkness flowing under his skin, rippling like black lava that rolled across his body. The shadow still pulsed behind him, growing larger. "Would you kill me? Tear out my heart or consume me as I would you?"

"No," Jericho said.

"That's why you'll always be weaker," Pinnacle spat out as if the words were a poison.

"I will offer you what I have always offered – a choice."

He extended his hand toward Pinnacle, and for a moment, the Shadow Elite seemed to falter, withdrawing slightly from its host as if zooming out to better see the offer before it. In that brief window, Kaden caught a glimpse of Thomas Thornhill as he was and as he might have been – brilliant, passionate, driven by genuine desire to heal and save. His skin and features were the same as the day when Thomas met Darren in Dr. Abrams's office.

"It's not too late," Jericho said softly. "Let go of the hunger. Let go of the need to control. Choose life instead of this half-existence you've created."

For one breathless moment, something flickered in Pinnacle's eyes – doubt, perhaps, or the faintest spark of remembrance or regret. But only for a brief moment. Then his face hardened and the obsidian patches spread, covering every inch of his skin, more Pinnacle in this moment than any before.

A sorrowful expression passed over Jericho.

Pinnacle began to open his mouth as the shadow behind him swelled like a tidal wave. Kaden knew he should have feared it, or at least would have feared it in his prior life – the life before Jericho. But now with Jericho standing near him, there was absolutely no fear. Pinnacle was a defanged viper, hissing away without any bite.

"Then you have made your choice," Jericho said.

He lowered his hand, and the Shadow Elite rushed back to envelop Pinnacle completely, melding with him until there was no distinction between the man and the darkness. The mass roiled and expanded as they were still pinned high on the cracking facade of the corridor in The Tower.

"What you have chosen cannot remain here," Jericho said, his voice carrying a finality that made the air itself hang in obedience. "Shadow cannot exist where there is light."

Then the air around them moved like a raging wind. It swirled through the chamber, growing stronger with each passing second. The light emanated from Jericho and the transformed beings intensified like a dimming switch being turned up to full power. The shadow around Pinnacle shrieked in pain and fear, trying to expand, to escape, but the light held it, compressed it.

"No!" A voice sounded from the shadow that was no longer recognizable as Pinnacle's – it was older, deeper, a chorus of countless hungers speaking as one. Kaden recognized them from his time in the darkness. All the voices from the abyss were now scared for their existence. "You cannot! I am eternal! I am—"

"You are a shadow," Jericho interrupted in a calm, simple voice, "and shadows cannot exist where light fills every corner."

The wind reached a fever pitch, and with it came the roar of the air blowing past Kaden's ears, but the roar wasn't of a common wind. Inside the wind were voices – thousands upon thousands, generations sang a harmony that seemed to resonate with the very fabric of reality. The Tower shook, more pieces crumbling away, as the combined light and sound pressed in on the writhing darkness.

Kaden felt a hand on his shoulder and looked up to see his mother, her face gentle yet sorrowful as she watched the scene unfold.

"Not all chose the light," she said softly.

As the shadow compressed, other pieces of darkness crept out from the growing cracks in The Tower. They rushed into the larger shadow like ghosts seeking their home tomb, yet the Shadow didn't expand. It became more dense.

Within the compressed shadow, Kaden caught glimpses of familiar faces – Ryon, Vala, countless Agents and Elites who had enforced Pinnacle's will. But most devastating of all, he saw Enak, his face twisted with rage as the darkness claimed him completely.

"My punishment is too great to bear!" a cacophony of tortured voices shouted from the shadow, Enak's image at the forefront of the sounding voices. Yet, in all their screeching, they could not overcome the wonderful harmony that resonated from the winds.

In a closing gesture, Jericho lowered his hands, and the dense cloud of shadows imploded, compressed to a single point of absolute darkness, then shot away from the light like a shotgun shell erupting from the muzzle. It blasted through The Tower, further crumbling the shaking walls and vanishing into the storm clouds that had perpetually hungover Empyrean. The clouds rolled away, now far in the distance at the edge of the horizon.

The wind that carried the sounds of the overarching beautiful harmony of voices faded away into a gentle hum and then was gone. The Tower continued to crumble around them, but more slowly now, as if the structure itself was exhaling after centuries of holding its breath, a muscle finally relaxing after countless hours of tension.

Kaden looked around as gigantic pieces of the obsidian structure fell away. None of the forces of light seemed to notice or care. Where the floor fell out from under some, they didn't falter. They were as solid as if still standing on a foundation of rock as they hovered in the air.

A piece fell from under Kaden, and he reacted, trying to move but was too late. However, gravity didn't take him. He realized he was floating like the others.

As he looked down, he caught a glimpse of his hands. For the first time, he realized he was glowing like the others. He stood on the invisible base supporting him and a growing number of the others. The once intimidating Tower crumbled, falling away around them, yet the group stood together. Kira came to Kaden and they embraced. They moved to meet Kaden's parents, embracing them and soon the others. They all glowed in the skeleton of The Tower as the brilliant light of Jericho wrapped them.

Outside the embracing group, Jericho stood patiently. Most of The Tower around them had fallen away and the group hovered in the sky where the peak of the structure used to be.

Kaden turned to Jericho.

“Where did you send them?” Kaden asked.

“Away,” Jericho said. “They are banished, not destroyed. Their judgment will come in the final days."

Jericho extended his hand and Kaden took it. Jericho pulled him into an embrace. The feeling was warm, solid – not the ghostly sensation he might have expected from one who had died and returned. It felt like the most real thing he’d ever experienced as if he were wrapped up safely in the fabric of reality itself.

"What happens now?" Kaden asked, looking around at the transformed beings who had once been his friends, his parents, his enemies.

"Now," Jericho said, a smile spreading across his face, "we rebuild.”

He gestured toward the distant horizon, where the perpetual overcast skies and storm clouds were breaking apart, allowing rays of true sunlight to reach Empyrean for the first time in centuries.

"The wall has been broken," Jericho continued. "The light reaches far beyond Empyrean, to others who have survived in the wilderness, to places most thought lost forever."

“Survivors?” Kaden asked.

“There are so many more of us than there are of them,” Alister added, stepping forward from the group. “Come, see for yourself.” He motioned toward an opening in the side of The Tower, down to the streets below. An army of glowing soldiers were in concentric rings around The Tower. Pockets of light emanated from areas in the Inner and Outer Rings.

“Amazing,” Kaden whispered.

Kira stepped forward, taking Kaden's hand. “It really is,” she said.

“Where did they come from?” he asked.

“From all over, yet also from within. Those living in the deserts and those living in others,” Jericho said.

“The consumed? They’re free?” Kaden asked.

"If they choose to be. You made that choice when you escaped Pinnacle, but not all did," Jericho said.

The Tower continued to crumble around them, now more gone than still supported. As simply as if he were walking down a few steps, Jericho walked to the edge and stepped out of The Tower. The group floated behind, protected as if wrapped in an invisible bubble. They moved to the base of The Tower, yet the thought of THE Tower changed in Kaden's mind. It was a mere skeleton of itself and teetering like a stray tall weed swaying in the wind. *THE* Tower became simply: a tower.

Jericho walked forward from the base of the structure and into the countless bright beings around them. With every step away from the structure, it was as if life fell away from the tower. It fell on itself, imploding into a plume of smoke that rose into the atmosphere. Kaden and Kira looked back, watching the dust take the shape of a mushroom cloud that dissipated into the winds. It floated out to the desert and reminded Kaden of a slow-motion reenactment of how Jericho banished Pinnacle.

"Where shall we rebuild first?" Kaden called out to Jericho.

"We'll start right here," Jericho said, then he turned back to him. "But not you two."

Kaden and Kira looked at each other and then back at Jericho.

"Now that your vision is corrected, you'll rebuild in the past," he said with a gentle smile.

Kaden's face shifted with confusion. His eyes moved from Jericho to his parents. They stayed close to him as the group descended from the tower, and now his father put a hand on Kaden's shoulder.

"We'll be here, son. We'll be ready for you," his father said.

"But, Dad... I can't leave now. You and Mom. All this," he said, motioning. "I can't leave this, them, you two."

Kaden squeezed Kira's hands and she squeezed his back.

"Whatever we build in the past is going to fall anyway, leading to this," Kaden said.

"There's more in the past than you think," Jericho said, walking to Kaden and Kira. "You'll see them again. I promise." His smile gave Kaden all the confidence and warmth he could ever feel, yet a piece of himself was still confused. This whole world seemed at peace and a part of Jericho, yet there he stood, hand in hand with Kira, feeling like there was a secret that only the two of them didn't know.

"What's in the past that we need to go back for?" Kaden asked.

Jericho looked at him and then at Kira and back to Kaden.

"The next generation," he said.

The End

Continued in Jericho Book 3 – Jericho's Legacy.

***

Enjoy a Preview of Book 3 – Jericho's Legacy

Chapter 1

Gabriel McCloud pressed his back against the granite kitchen counter, the cool stone a stark contrast to the heat building in his chest. The afternoon sun streamed through the bay window, illuminating the dust motes that danced above the hardwood floors his mother had insisted on when they'd moved into this house when Gabriel was a toddler. Everything about their home screamed stability—the crown molding, the stainless steel appliances, the family photos arranged just so on the mantle in the adjoining living room. A perfect suburban sanctuary, and he was poisoning it with his lies.

His parents stood before him like judges at a tribunal, and Gabriel felt seventeen years old in the worst possible way—caught between childhood and adulthood, too young to be taken seriously but old enough to face real consequences. His father, Darren, leaned against the kitchen island, arms crossed, wearing the patient expression that meant he was trying very hard not to lose his temper. His mother Kelly occupied her favorite purple chair by the window, the one she'd insisted stay within view near the orange sofa that added a carefully coordinated color pop to the crisp black and white interior design.

"So let me get this straight," Darren said, his voice carrying that dangerous tone that preceded most questions leading to Gabriel's groundings.

He ran a hand through his shaggy brown hair that sparkled with grays. He turned his head and Gabriel caught sight of the thin scar on the back of his father's head—a pale, raised line that Gabriel never noticed before. He felt even more disconnected from his parents not remembering such a noticeable scar as they prepared their cross examination.

"Tyler's parents are going to be there the whole time, eh?" Darren asked.

Gabriel's inner dialogue raced and his stomach performed an elaborate gymnastics routine.

He knows.

No he doesn't know.

He's leading me.

Stick to the story.

The kitchen suddenly felt smaller, the walls pressing in as his carefully constructed story went under the microscope. He forced himself to nod with what he hoped looked like earnest sincerity.

"Yeah." *Lie.*

The word tasted like ash in his mouth. Tyler's parents were in Cabo. Well, at least his dad was with someone Tyler didn't say, but he'd let slip to Gabriel that his mom was visiting her sister in Tennessee. The planned trip for their twentieth anniversary, that led to an escalated argument they hadn't yet recovered. Tyler announced the trip to their closest friends, which meant the entire junior class and most of the school knew there would be an open house party, an unsupervised free-for-all – exactly the kind of event Gabriel's parents had spent years warning him against.

But Gabriel wanted to go so badly it physically hurt. Not because he particularly enjoyed parties—most of the time he felt awkward and out of place, watching other people have fun while he nursed a Coke in the corner. He didn't even particularly like Coke. No, he wanted to go because Lisa Morrison had been texting him all week, and her eye contact before and after class seemed to grow more consistent each day. Or maybe that was because Gabriel was looking at her more everyday. Lisa Morrison, with her perfect blonde hair and her way of biting her lower lip when she concentrated in chemistry class. Lisa Morrison, the perfect ten who was also in all the Honors classes who had somehow noticed Gabriel existed and seemed interested in spending time with him.

His mother, Kelly, shifted in the purple chair, the old springs creaking in a way that usually comforted him. Today the sound felt ominous. Her auburn hair caught the afternoon light streaming through the bay window, highlighting the natural waves that she'd passed down to Gabriel along with her hazel eyes and her unfortunate tendency to never let a mystery go unsolved.

"And there won't be any drinking?" Kelly pressed, her voice carrying that maternal radar that seemed to detect lies like a shark detected a drop of blood.

This was the moment. The crucial junction where Gabriel could come clean, admit that yes, there would definitely be drinking, that Tyler's older brother had already promised to use his fake ID at the store on the edge of town that never questioned cheap fakes. A keg had been mentioned more than once already. He could confess that he planned to drink—not because he enjoyed it, but because it might give him the courage to actually talk to Lisa without stuttering. He could acknowledge that the whole evening was designed around poor decisions and teenage stupidity.

But being a seventeen-year-old who makes poor decisions driven by the stupidity of adolescence, he didn't think twice.

Instead, he doubled down on the deception.

"Mom, come on. Tyler's not like that." *Tyler was exactly like that.* The lie expanded in his chest like a balloon, pushing against his ribs until it hurt to breathe. "Besides, you know me. I don't like to drink."

That part was *technically* true. Gabriel had tried beer exactly once, at his cousin's graduation party, and decided it tasted like someone had dissolved pennies in dish water. But his parents didn't need to know about the marijuana or gummies that would definitely be circulating, or about texting Lisa and dancing around the subject of breaking away to a private room. They also didn't need to know that Gabriel had spent chunks of time every night for the past week asking AI about how to be cool, how to flirt, how to be the kind of person a girl like Lisa Morrison might actually want to spend time with. He'd never had a girlfriend before, only a 'will you hold my hand on the bus and then too scared to ever have a conversation again' sort of relationship in middle school. How did he balance his crazy eagerness while still being cool?

"I just want to know you're being smart. What would you be concerned about if you were in our shoes?" Kelly said, but as the words left her mouth, something impossible happened.

Her face flickered.

The literal outline and features of her face. The crows feet from a lifetime of laughing with her husband Darren, the slight elevens in between her eyebrows that she was fighting off with periodic botox injections, and highlighted auburn hair – they all changed for a brief instant. It was like watching a television with bad reception, the image dissolving for a fraction of a second, lines not matching up, before snapping back into focus. But in that brief moment, Gabriel saw someone else entirely—a younger woman with straight black hair instead of auburn waves, younger than his mother by at least twenty years, but she held the same auburn eyes that matched her natural hair color.

Gabriel blinked hard, his heart hammering against his ribs and forgetting the conversation. The afternoon sun continued streaming through the window. The hardwood floors still gleamed. The family photos on the mantle still showed their carefully curated life—vacation shots from Disney World, Gabriel's middle school graduation, last Christmas morning with everyone in matching flannel pajamas that Kelly had insisted on buying. Gabriel hated them but his dad's goofy farmer jokes were so bad that they made the entire day, and pajamas, so good.

Everything else looked normal. Everything except the growing certainty that something was terribly, impossibly wrong. He looked to his dad to see if he'd noticed, but that didn't help.

"Gabriel?" His father's voice sounded strange, like it was coming from a different person. It was similar, but not the same. "You hearing us?"

Gabriel forced himself to look harder, and the bottom dropped out of his world.

His father's face flickered too. One moment he appeared normal—mid-forties, the comfortable softness that came with suburban life, the slight wrinkles around his eyes from years of squinting at computer screens in his home office and never wearing sunglasses. The next moment he looked twenty-five, lean and hard-muscled, wearing clothes Gabriel had never seen before—light blue pants and a white shirt, like scrubs from off-duty medical personnel. His brown hair that sparkled throughout with gray turned into short black, with no gray.

Then he flickered back to older, much older, with deep lines etched into his face and gray streaking his temples. Then young again, but different young, like he'd lived a dozen different lives and Gabriel was seeing them all at once.

"What..." Gabriel's voice cracked like it hadn't done since eighth grade. "What's happening?"

"Gabe... You okay?" his father asked. He turned to look at Kelly and Gabriel saw the line of thick scar across the back of his father's head, surrounded by black hair. That scar had never been there before. Or had it? Gabriel questioned reality before him. The line disappeared as the hair shifted back to brown with gray – back to “normal”.

The panic started as a flutter in his chest, then spread outward like spilled ink. His vision tunneled. His hands began to shake. This had to be a breakdown of some kind—stress from exams, being right for Lisa, from constantly lying to his parents, from the pressure of trying to be someone he wasn't. People had psychotic episodes, right? They saw things that weren't there, experienced hallucinations so vivid they seemed real. Well, now he was one of them.

But everything felt real, not a hallucination. The granite counter was still cool beneath his palms. He could smell his mother's burning vanilla candle in the living room, could hear the neighbor's dog barking three houses over. All his senses insisted that this was happening, that his parents were somehow becoming other people right in front of him.

"Are you lying to us?" The question came from the woman in the purple chair, but it wasn't his mother's voice anymore. This voice was younger, more urgent, threaded with pain.

Gabriel looked at her and his knees nearly buckled. The woman sitting where his mother should be was beautiful in a fierce, been-through-danger sort of way—maybe twenty-five years old, with straight black hair that framed his mother’s same eyes. She wore a white shirt Gabriel had never seen before, and her posture suggested someone accustomed to fighting, to running, to surviving things Gabriel couldn't imagine.

"Because we need to know the truth, Gael," she continued.

“What...” he whispered. When she said the other name, it resonated in Gabriel's chest like a struck bell.

"Who's Gael?" he said, but even as he thought, some part of him already knew the answer. She was talking to him, or at least some version of himself. The certainty was irrational and absolute, and it dawned on him – was he flickering as well? Was he changing into someone else too?

He needed a mirror, but the woman who wasn't his mother stood up from the purple chair. She moved like someone in serious pain, one hand pressed to her side. When she lifted her hand to gesture toward him, Gabriel saw blood seeping through the white fabric—bright red, spreading like spilled wine.

"Mom?" The word escaped him as barely a breath. He wanted to run to her, to help somehow, but his feet felt rooted to the kitchen floor.

She stumbled and his father grabbed her.

"We need to get to the hospital," the man who wasn't quite his father said, his voice carrying the authority of someone used to making life-and-death decisions. This version of Darren looked harder, rougher, like he'd seen combat and was one of the few who survived it. "Kira's hurt. She's hurt bad, and we don't have much time until they take more of her."

Kira? Another name that resonated in Gabriel's bones, like an ancient word that lived deep below the earth and was now being excavated.

Ancient.. He thought. I've heard that name before.

"I don't understand what's happening," Gabriel said, hating how young his voice sounded, how scared. He needed to be stronger. He needed to be more like his dad, or at least like the man his dad appeared to be – steady, in control, a survivor who came out better after the perilous journey. The panic was building now, making it hard to think clearly. His perfect suburban kitchen felt like it was tilting, reality sliding sideways like a house built on sand. All he wanted to do was go to his friend's party.

"It'll be a choice," his mother said in her normal voice, but her voice was weaker as the blood stain spread, now over a quarter of her shirt. "You have to choose, Gabriel." Her voice changed again, now sounding twenty years younger. "Gael, it's lies or reality. Don't come find us. They want that."

Her body slipped again and his father held her tight.

"It's time to go, son," he said. His eyes were still the same as they always were but his hair and other facial features altered back and forth like two radio stations crossing paths. One moment his brown and gray hair and smooth-shaven face, the next split second it was short black hair and black beard stubble.

His voice was harder. Gabriel wanted to help this altered half-dad version of the man in front of him.

"I'll get the keys," Gabriel said, but he still didn't move. His mind locked onto the altering version of his parents.

His father carried her now. His mother's cozy house slippers were now gone as her dirt-covered bare feet floated over the surface of the hardwood floors. Where did her feet get dirty?

"Gabriel, move," Darren said with such conviction it finally shattered the invisible force that held Gabriel in place. But he only moved a few steps before the altered version of his father spoke again and his son refroze.

"You can't touch her."

"..." Gabriel opened his mouth but the question stayed in his throat like a scared dog hiding in the bed from a thunderstorm.

"Not her. Not me. Do *NOT* touch us. Do you understand?" His eyes locked on Gabriel.

"Why not–"

"We need to move. Now," he said in a commanding voice. Gabriel's posture snapped up straight. "She's lost a lot of blood," he said softly as he leaned in to examine her. Concern and heart break now mixing into his face.

"But, Dad–"

"Get the keys," he said, picking her up. His mother went limp just as his dad scooped her up. When they touched, the flickered shot through

Darren. His whole body rippled and turned into another, much younger man who wore similar clothes to the younger woman his mother turned into. A white shirt and blue pants with an elastic waist band.

The man that was his father, now carrying the woman who was his mother, stared at him. “Let’s go,” he said.

Chapter 2

The emergency room smelled like cleaning materials and felt like embodied anxiety.

Gabriel sat in the plastic chair, bouncing his legs. Nurses moved around in scrubs, squeaking across the floor. The fluorescent lights hummed overhead with the subtle flicker that made you think you could be at the start of a horror film. Everyone waiting looked sick.

His dad paced near the front desk. His hair, features, and body were now back to the parental version that Gabriel grew up with. He'd been more solid ever since handing off Kelly to the paramedics at the entrance. His hair was brown with gray highlights that overtook the areas behind his temple and above his ears. Gabriel had been watching him, waiting for the scar on the back of his head to return or his hair to change black, or the face to shift into the young man that could have been Gabriel's brother. A brother raised in a harder world, hardened through survival. Gabriel had stopped trying to make sense of it. His father's and mother's eyes were always the same, even as their bodies had changed around them. The eyes were always the same. The window to the soul.

Every part of his brain screamed this was impossible.

But his own eyes wouldn't lie. He knew he saw what he saw.

The waiting room walls were that boring hospital beige that looked pinkish in the right light. A TV played some news show with low sound and so many commercials it seemed the news interrupted the ads. The vending machine buzzed in the corner.

It didn't feel designed to make you wait and worry, but they certainly weren't designing for peace and comfort. The flickering overhead lights and incessant beeping echoed through the hallway when a nurse opened the door, making it seem like entering the bowels of the hospital were like Frodo, Ring of Power in hand, venturing into that dark cave where the giant spider lived.

"McCloud?"

A nurse appeared out of the forbidden hallway. Young, maybe mid-twenties, with dark hair in a ponytail and Jennifer on her nametag. Bags under her eyes showing that she was losing the battle with the doomed hallway beyond.

"Come on back," she said in a pleasant voice as she motioned to Darren and Gabriel.

Gabriel's stomach dropped. He'd been dreading this moment since they'd carried her out of the house. The woman who might be his mother, bleeding through that white shirt. His Dad stood, unafraid, while Gabriel felt more like Samwise Gamgee, wanting to pull on his dad's arm.

“Please, Mr. Frodo,” he imagined himself saying. “Please, Dad. Don't go ahead without me. There's danger in that cave. There's danger in following Gollum.”

He remained seated, looking up at his dad. Darren looked back, his face, body, and voice were all still his father's at the moment. His eyes told Gabriel everything. The eyes never lied. Father and son exchanged a glance, as if the father said “I know it's dangerous, but we have to get the Ring to Mordor, to Mount Doom – we have to get your mother.”

Gabriel's motivation wavered. How long until his father's shirt was soaked in blood and he stopped being his dad? "I can't let you go forward," Gabriel said with eyes.

He didn't have to say it, his father knew what his son felt because his father felt this before.

"It's time to go forward, son."

His dad stepped forward, moving past the nurse like he'd been here before and knew exactly where to go.

Gabriel stood. Hours ago the night started with dinner, the three of them enjoying themselves, then he began asking about the party. Correction, he began lying about the party and thinking of how he'd look cool to Tyler, his friends, and most importantly, find time alone with Lisa.

His father turned the corner ahead of him, moving out of sight, as Gabriel approached the nurse. Darren never wavered, like his was the undeniable truth – the anchor of the situation. He was a modern 6'2" Frodo who stood up straight with his shoulders back, no one would stop him from getting to his wife just as nothing would stop Frodo from getting the One Ring to Mount Doom.

"Is she..." Gabriel started asking the nurse, then realized he didn't know what to ask.

"She's stable," Jennifer said. Which wasn't really an answer. "But she's been asking for you. She keeps saying a name that starts with G. I saw Darren and Gabriel on the charts." She smiled at him pleasantly. "You can't separate a mother's love," she said, and Gabriel wondered if she was being sincere or Gollum luring them into *her* lair.

He wanted to see his mother, but what if she was saying Gael. Was she even his mother anymore?

The thought hit his chest like a punch.

Gabriel stood on shaky legs and followed Jennifer down endless hallways. White-ish pink walls, numbered doors, beeping machines that seemed to grow louder and louder with every step. The smell got stronger as they walked. Not just bleach now, but something underneath that made his brain want to run.

They stopped at room 316.

Through the little window, Gabriel could see someone in the bed. Tubes and wires everywhere. Monitors showing wavy lines that looked important and scary.

"Try to keep it short, five minutes?" Jennifer said, then she tilted her head sympathetically. "Sorry, she needs rest, but she was pretty insistent about seeing you."

Gabriel's hand shook as he reached for the door handle. Cold metal against his palm.

For a second, he wanted to turn around. Walk out. Go home and pretend this never happened. Later he'd go to Tyler's party, drink some beer, wake up with nothing worse than a hangover and his parents would be fine. But that world was now dead, he was Samwise looking over the cliffs. All alone, separated, his father ahead of him and being led into the same danger as his mother. He could ignore it. If he made it back to the Shire, the party, the friends, the girls, but lost his family... Well, then it wouldn't be the Shire anymore, and it wouldn't be worth going back. The cave of the spider was Samwise's worst fear, and now opening that door to discover a dying mother was Gabriel's.

Leaving wasn't an option.

His parents were right here, changed into people he didn't know. The only way out was through this door. He needed to enter the cave. His greatest fear held what he sought most.

He pushed the door open.

The woman in the bed looked tiny against the white sheets. Hospital gowns and beds and all the various wires and beeps made everyone look fragile, but this was different. Her younger, fiercer frame of this new woman was fading away with whatever blood she'd lost.

The nurse or the EMTs that took her in mentioned nothing about the conflict of how this woman, seemingly in her twenties, was Darren's wife and Gabriel's mother. They accepted it as if their eyes saw her before the change.

Her face was pale. Straight black hair spread across the pillow like spilled ink. One look at her Driver's License would show her hair color was drastically different.

But when her eyes opened at his footsteps, they were definitely his mother's eyes. Brown with gold flecks, a perfect blend that seemed auburn from far away and grew more intricate as the viewer grew closer. Eyes that his father fell in love with. Eyes that had helped him with homework and worried when he stayed out late. Eyes that held locked on to him when he lied to her about where he was going.

"Gabriel," she whispered. Her voice was weak but real.

"Mom?" He moved toward the bed slowly. Like she might disappear. "Are you okay?"

She tried to smile. It looked more like a grimace. "I've been better."

Her eyes searched his face. Like she was looking for something specific.

"You're scared."

Not a question. Gabriel nodded.

"I need you to understand something," she said, her voice getting stronger. "What you saw at home, what's happening to us—it's real. I know it doesn't make sense. But it's real."

Gabriel felt his eyes watering. "I don't understand. What's happening to you? To Dad? Why do you keep changing into different people?"

He reached out his hand, toward her.

"DON'T!" His father's voice snapped from the corner of the room.

Gabriel jumped back like a spooked deer dashing away. He hadn't noticed his father in his fixation on his mother's frail frame.

"It's just..." Darren paused, his body in the shadows, in between soft lights of the city flowing in through the window and a shadow cast by the bright lights of the room.

"Dad?" Gabriel said, hearing something in his father's voice.

His dad stepped forward out of the shadows. He wasn't his father anymore.

"Dad..."

"You can't touch her, or me son. We're not all here anymore. We're in both, we are both," Darren said.

His mother's hand moved on the blanket. Just a few inches, but Gabriel could see how much it cost her.

"Time isn't as straight as we think. Past, present, future—sometimes they get mixed up. Especially when there are powers involved that don't follow normal rules."

"Powers?"

"Spiritual powers, Gabriel. Light and darkness. Good and evil. The kind of thing most people never have to think about." She breathed hard. "Your father and I got pulled into something twenty years ago. We thought we escaped. But it found us again."

"We were *shown* something, Gabriel. It changed how we saw the world. The sacrifice we witnessed in the face of such hate... It's hard to comprehend, son," Darren said.

"But why us? We're nobody. Dad is an entrepreneur. You're his CFO. We're just normal."

A sad smile crossed her face. "Sometimes…" she trailed off looking to her husband to finish her thought.

"Sometimes normal people get picked for big things. Sometimes ordinary families become the key to fights they never asked for. God doesn't call the qualified, he qualifies the called," he said. She nodded in agreement.

Gabriel wanted to ask more, but his mother's hand moved again. Reaching toward him as if to point.

"We need you to make a choice, Gabriel. Right now," she said.

"Choice?"

"Something in Empyrean is coming for us," Darren said. The words sounded crazy as Gabriel listened, then he realized he was speaking to two totally different people – twenty years younger than his parents with different faces, hair, and bodies with scars and muscles not found in his parents.

"We need you to go home," she said.

"What?" Gabriel said in dismay.

"You can walk away. Leave this hospital. Go home and pretend this never happened. Live your normal life. College, marriage, kids. Be safe and ordinary," Darren said.

"But Dad?"

"We were dead before meeting Jericho," his mother whispered.

"We'll be fine, son. He'll save us, but we can't let you…"

"That sounds good," Gabriel said, but the words felt empty. His heart pulled towards his parents but his mind took the escape hatch. They were giving him the freedom he craved. He'd be the master of his fate, governing what was wrong and right instead of being shielded by curfew and social expectations.

"But what if I don't leave?" The words left him as surprised as his parents.

They turned and looked deep into each other's eyes, a thousand conversations happening in the silence of the exchange. Gabriel saw the pain in his mother's eyes and a subtle shake of her head. His father's eyes held a sorrow but his expression became resolute and his posture straightened. Kelly's eyes dropped, then raised back up, her head bobbed just once, reluctantly.

"Then you step into a bigger story." Her eyes locked on his.

"Gabriel, if you choose that, nothing will ever be the same. There's no going back," his father said.

Gabriel stared at his mother's hand. It looked normal—his mother's hand, with the scar on her thumb from when she cut herself opening a can. The little mole near her wrist that looked like a heart.

But he remembered his dad's warning. Don't touch her. Don't touch me.

"What happens if I touch you?"

The room went quiet except for the machines. Gabriel thought about Tyler's party. About the lies he'd told. About his ordinary teenage problems that had seemed so important this morning and were now so far away they could have been from another life.

His concerns felt like toys now, like toys you find in an attic or basement trunk that take you back decades with a soft smile and memory but deep down you know you could never play with them the same way again.

He looked at his mother, wounded and changing, hooked up to machines. He thought about his father, no longer flickering but standing as this younger man.

The choice was already made. Probably the moment he saw them change in the kitchen.

He couldn't walk away, he couldn't pretend this wasn't happening, even as fear welled up in his chest making it hard to breathe, like a giant hand wrapping around his lung.

"I understand if you're scared," Darren said. "I was too."

Gabriel looked at his father and remembered the man he looked up to as a kid. The idea of his father being scared of anything was almost as foreign as seeing his parents in different bodies.

Kelly flickered in bed, like static from an out of place antennae. She went back to being Gabriel's mother, then back to the younger woman.

"Kira!" his father lunged toward her and grabbed her hand. As soon as he touched her he flickered as well, and his face contorted from intense pain, one second Darren the next the other man.

He dropped down to one knee, still holding her hand at the bedside. Gabriel shot forward but his father held up his palm.

"No, if you... they want *you*," he said, his voice sputtering in two different tones.

"Dad! I'm scared," Gabriel said, coming closer without touching him.

"You should be."

"I don't understand," Gabriel said.

"They want what we have, and they want *you*."

"What do we have?"

"Peace."

As the word left his father's lips his mother quit flickering and went unconscious. His dad then lost a grip on his body, falling limp to the peach-colored tile floor. Gabriel watched his father's hand slowly slide off his mother's and down the bedside, falling at his dad's side.

He shot out of the room, sprinting toward the nurse's station. "Help! Nurse!"

Jennifer was talking with two older nurses. She leaned over the counter laughing with them as they sat. All three turned to Gabriel and followed him to the room, where his father and mother lay unconscious.

"Get some help," Jennifer ordered one of the older nurses as she shot past Gabriel. "Back up kid."

He moved in to help but the nurse again told him to back off, he felt in between being an observer and accused of causing the situation. His timidness of touching his parents played into their protocol and soon Gabriel stood watching as the room soon filled with men and women, not being able to help if he wanted. Before he knew it, his father was in a bed and hooked up to all the same monitoring equipment as his mother. All their questions seemed a blur, he went through the motions, saying everything he could say. No one seemed to notice or care when we mentioned the flickering. He said they looked different, they spoke different, and *something unknown*, likely spiritual or other-worldly, was affecting them. In response, they assured him that sudden health changes could be hard to take. They were going to do all the tests to determine the severity of the strokes his parents had suffered.

"I'm sorry, son," one doctor said. "You know, I lost my parents when I was about your age."

Lost? Lost! Gabriel wanted to smack the clip board out of the old man's hand. His parents weren't lost, they were right in front of him! The heart rate monitors and breathing sensors all said their bodies were alive. Why else would they tolerate all the insufferable beeping of the machines if the bodies they monitored were now corpses?

He felt like a child lost in a giant store. Unable to find his parents and all the workers telling him to go upfront to the cashiers, so they could call his parents. "Lost child at register four. Could his parents come and make him feel safe again because he's too young and immature to do anything about his situation." Gabriel fumed.

An hour later he was back in the waiting room, his anger subsiding as the toll of the day and night sat heavy on his eye lids. Finally, he let his eyes close. He imagined when he awoke, he'd no longer be in this strange dream. His parents would be back to normal and they'd leave this place, or better yet, he'd wake up at home. In his cozy, warm bed. He'd smell his parents' fresh coffee and bacon in the oven. Pancakes would be soon after, with butter melting off the sides.

He drifted off to sleep.

***

It was dark.

Not a soft gentle darkness like camping away from the city where the stars were nature's nightlights. It was an aggressive darkness that poured into him through every sense. Darkness with weight that moved and breathed, it held a pressure to it as if it wanted things, intangible things only held inside of him. His heart. His soul.

Gabriel felt himself falling through space with no up or down. He tried to scream, but no sound came out.

Just falling through black space, alone and terrified.

Then in the distance. Two specks of lights peeking through the darkness like two stars overcast clouds couldn't block.

They grew. The stars went from a distant twinkle to taking a shape, a symmetrical almond-like shape.

Eyes.

Gray eyes with bright silver flecks. They watched him from across the void. They weren't cold or scary. The opposite. There was warmth in them, and patience, and something that felt like love — the opposite of the hungry and oppressive darkness that wrapped around him.

As Gabriel stared, he saw tiny points of light in each pupil. Like stars being born in a dark and void galaxy.

The eyes seemed to get closer. The darkness around him changed, becoming less like a trap and more like a summer night sky. The falling sensation turned into floating, being carried toward those steady gray eyes. The fear of being in the darkness subsided in the light of the gray eyes.

"Gabriel," a voice said.

***

His body jumped and he fell out of his chair. It took him a moment to remember he was in the waiting room connected to the Emergency Room. It was still dark outside, the dawn coming soon yet the lights of the ER dominated the black top roundabout outside the waiting room windows.

Standing up, he saw Jennifer the nurse was still there. Her bloodshot eyes above dark bags. The end of a twelve-hour shift. She didn't ask if he was okay or make a quip about his startled awakening – her energy and personality running on E.

“Want to see them?” she asked.

He nodded and followed her back. She brought him to the door, waving a hand and then walking off. Gabriel slowly opened the door.

Before stepping in, the room already seemed different. There were no deafening sounds from the machines blaring in his ears. The lights from all the LED readouts were gone.

It was black and silent.

He stepped in and felt like he was back in his dream, surrounded by darkness. As his eyes focused, he could see two tiny twinkles of light, he walked toward them. They grew as he approached and focused on them. They took an almond-like shape and soon he was directly over them. The light called to him, urging him to reach out and join it.

He opened his palms and put his hands over each gray light, then fear ripped at him. If he followed the light... He didn't know. Behind him, he *did* know: his friends, his school, his seventeen year old self and his seventeen year old problems, but ahead of him, in this light... He didn't know.

As the fear raced through his body, he stopped thinking and followed his heart, dropping his hands to grab hold of each light.

He couldn't see how the outside street lights reflected off his parents' patient bracelets, giving the same impression of gray eyes he saw in his dreams. He also didn't dwell on his father's warning to not touch him or his mother. All Gabriel knew was he was in darkness and the light was reaching out to him. So he took it, and the world around him disappeared.

Thank You!

I hope you enjoyed the preview.

- Find it at **https://store.jamesbonk.com/** and enjoy a 15% discount with the code BESTSELLER when you buy directly from the author.

- You can stay in touch by signing up for my newsletter and getting special offers:

https://hello.jamesbonk.com/signup/

The Author

James Bonk writes Christian Fiction to develop his own faith and to share with others. He lives in the North Georgia area with his wife, two daughters, and fluffy Chartreux cat, Porkchop. When he's not writing, he's usually swimming or building forts with his girls!

His Light of the Ark book was the #1 New Release in its category upon release, with multiple five star reviews from adults and young adults alike.

Besides writing, parenting, and being a husband, James Bonk is a supply chain leader and business intelligence professional. He has a BS in Mechanical Engineering, MS in Industrial Engineering, and an MBA. He previously held his Professional Engineering license in Industrial Engineering.

Find out more at and get access to all his books at:

https://store.jamesbonk.com/

You can also find James by searching James Bonk Author on your favorite platform or following the below links:

- Goodreads (https://www.goodreads.com/author/list/21997660.James_Bonk)

- Facebook (search '*James Bonk Author*' or go here: https://www.facebook.com/people/James-Bonk-Author/100092204034685/)

- BookBub (https://www.bookbub.com/profile/james-bonk)

The Author - James Bonk

www.ingramcontent.com/pod-product-compliance
Lightning Source LLC
LaVergne TN
LVHW010638110826
845149LV00014B/2870